Walking the fine line of being
unknown to all sides...

On board the Sea Wolf, alarms were sounding as well. That's when JD sent word to Isaiah that his time of rest was over. Jumping to his feet and heading for the control room, Isaiah was briefed on his way there by an excited young ensign who gave him a blow-by-blow of the last twenty minutes in a few quick comments. As he entered the control room, JD was making ready to get under way.

"I'm afraid we may have to sink one of our own in a few minutes if they keep it up," said JD.

"I've got an idea, if what the good ensign here told me is correct," said Isaiah. "He actually gave me the idea when he described how they were dropping sonobouys from several hundred feet up."

"What do you mean?" asked JD.

Truth and Honor

Paperback
ISBN: 978-1-935188-21-6

Ebook
ISBN: 978-1-935188-22-3

Library of Congress Control Number: 2011924611

Edited by Janet Elaine Smith
Cover and interior by Star Publish LLC

A Star Publish LLC Publication
www.starpublishllc.com
Published in 2011
Printed in the United States of America

Truth and Honor

D. Benfer

A Star Publish Book

Dedicated to

Andrew, Melissa, Fresia, Isaiah

And

To the Grandchildren to come who are Angels with
"Poppy" until God's timing brings them to their earthly
Parents

To

Harold and Margaret

Thank you for your support and contribution to this
novel. You will always have a special place in my heart
and are deeply loved

Chapter 1

Travel Away from Danger

Jerusalem, Friday, October 6th, 1307 AD

The life of a Knight of the Templar realm had always been his pride. He believed deeply in the rites and rituals of the Temple, and had sworn his life to protect the belief in Christ and to uphold and bring that light to the rest of the world...beginning with the eastern Islamic horde. For two hundred years, his brothers had paved the way for the English and French knights to take and hold the holy city of Jerusalem.

The Templars had been the key to the Crusades, creating a flow of new knights to the front lines and bringing the wounded back to the homelands, but the writing was on the wall. Being in the inner circle of Templar knights, Sir Tristan could easily see that the time of the Templars was quickly coming to an end. He reached up and fondled the gold charm that hung around his neck—a shield with two words upon its crest: Truth and Honor. He'd sent his own son to his ancestral home of Lorraine three years earlier, with his own shield around his neck.

Sir Tristan knew instinctively that the time of betrayal by the King of France (Edward I) and the Pope (he instinctively spat as he thought about him) were nigh at hand. For that reason, the Templars had been secretly moving their masses of treasure they had found beneath the Temple mount and the gold and silver they had earned from their securing the passage of knights to the Crusades to a new place of solitude and secret. Seventeen ships had left LaRochelle a week ago and would be here tonight, ready to load, at night of course.

Rumors had begun just a few weeks before about the impending order of arrest for all Templar knights. In just seven more days, Friday the thirteenth, rumor had it that King Edward would make an arrest decree. For Tristan, he knew he must disappear. He knew it. He was much too well known in the Templar world. Even so, he had plans to try and make his escape.

Absently, he again reached up and rubbed his shield. It felt wrong to be running. Truth and Honor. The "truth" he knew, but the King had shown no honor, and that left him in the position of having to disappear.

Planning... It all had to go perfectly. If it did, the greedy King of France and his pitiful but powerful ally the Pope would be left holding an empty bag, just the trappings of the Templar properties around the known world. The real treasure of the Templars would never find its way into the dishonest hands of those men if Tristan had any say in the matter...and he did.

He would rather have the treasure never again see the light of day than end up furthering the kingdoms of money-grubbing kings who had squandered the fortunes of their own people and then set about looking for someone else's money to steal...and a pope who was no longer worried about Christianity, but money instead. It was sacrilegious. Yet here he was, the one being called a devil-worshipper.

The treasures he had seen with his own two eyes were enough to verify the stories of Solomon's Temple. If ever there was a believer in the Christian story, it was Tristan. If there had ever been a supporter of the Church and their Holy Crusade, it had been Tristan. He saw this as a holy war, one that he was afraid would never end. He had seen for himself the Ark of the Covenant, and had been in places so holy he thought that he himself might die just by being there. Seven more days! He knelt and prayed for guidance from God above.

Friday, October 13th, 1307 AD

Friday the thirteenth arrived, and with it a new ship entered port bringing word from the king, just as expected. All Templar knights were to be arrested and all Templar possessions were to become property of the king and the Church. Any who resisted were to be put to the sword. But in the harbor, something was amiss. Twenty-four ships. The entire Templar fleet was gone. No one had heard a word or seen a thing. No rumors, no loose tongues wagging the day before, just an empty harbor that had been full the night before. It was as if God had reached down and plucked them from the sea and hidden them from the rest of the world.

Inside the Templar castles a similar theme was being played out. While the king's own guard entered the inner sanctum of the Templar holdings, all appeared normal, except that there were no people, and no treasure. The huge treasure rooms were as empty as a grain bin after a 7-year famine. To say the least, King Edward was furious. All across Europe, anyone known to have been involved with the Templars was picked up and arrested. While a few Templar knights were found, an order of thirty thousand knights seemed to also have vanished overnight.

For those accused of having been associated with the Templars, it was indeed a terrible day, a day which would be forever remembered as a day of bad luck—Friday the thirteenth.

On a ship bound west across the stormy Mediterranean sea, Tristan rubbed the shield around his neck and smiled inwardly as his flotilla of ships sailed the calm waters, knowing that only God could stop him now, and he had great faith that God was on his side.

Friday, July 13th, 2007 AD

Juan David Lightfoot Gilhooley III. His name was a paradox, so he just went by JD. Named for his each of his grandfather's grandfathers, it spoke much about his multi-national birthright: Spanish, Jewish, American Indian and Irish. At twenty-four years old, his weathered face would have been more at home on someone ten years older, right down to a streak of premature grey just behind his left ear. His 6'2" frame was solid, without a trace of fat so prevalent among his heavy drinking college peers.

While others his age had been spending celebratory years away from Mom and Dad, enjoying the times of their lives, crashing sorority houses and spending weekends drinking beer and cheering on the old alma mater, JD had been working grueling hours on a research boat, the LeiLani, off San Diego Harbor, earning both a Bachelor's and a Master's Degree in Marine Biology at the prestigious Scripps Institute of Oceanography. Long hours spent tracing the origin of marine creatures and the effect of the Pacific currents on the marine biology had left his American Indian skin even darker than usual and his dark auburn wavy hair three shades lighter from the constant attack by the sun. Along with his piercing blue eyes, the overall effect was mesmerizing and unusual, to say the least.

He held his hand up and whistled loudly as he motioned the helmsman, Isaiah, to circle the LeiLani for another pass over the object that was lighting up the magnetometer display.

Isaiah Diego was not just the helmsman; he was also JD's friend. For two years, JD and Diego had worked together aboard the LeiLani, each working toward a different goal. JD's goal was to attain his degree, and Isaiah's to pay off the mortgage on his pride and joy, the LeiLani. The shirtless Isaiah was shorter by three inches than JD, but he was still tall compared to the average Hispanic male. Another thing that distinguished him from the typical Hispanic was his green eyes. He also was twenty-four years old and in great physical shape, as anyone could see by his ripped abdomen and chiseled biceps.

While he lived aboard the LeiLani, his Latin charm, easy way and dark good looks gave him the opportunity to spend quite a bit of his spare time sleeping wherever he wanted, should he choose to. He could have been the consummate Latin Lover, but he was raised not to play that game. His mother had taught him to respect the fairer sex. For that reason, people often described him as "serious." The truth was, he was focused on his dreams, which didn't include falling in love or chasing women who would steal away the precious time and money that he needed in order to achieve those dreams. He often kidded his mother that she was his only true love, followed closely by the LeiLani. He and JD had become as close as brothers over the previous two years and JD often ate with Isaiah and his mother.

The picture painted by the magnetometer made it out to definitely be something manmade down there, but it would take several more passes before it could be positively identified as to what. It could be anything from a stove or dishwasher to a chest of iron, but whatever it was, it didn't belong there. The real question at this point was, what was it doing here? Just outside of San Diego Harbor, northwest of Point Loma where the sea floor rose up to 100 meters, all the known wrecks and junk had been plotted, and this anomaly just didn't belong.

JD fingered the gold chain and charm around his neck. Was this the uncovered piece of an old hull? Or was it just trash that had been heaved overboard by a trawler? Had they stumbled onto a new find in just under 150 ft. of clear blue water? It just didn't make sense. There hadn't been any unusual weather to speak of inside of a month, and suddenly they were faced with a new plot in a location away from the regular channels. What he didn't realize was that even as he pondered the oddity, his boat was also being monitored, and as he had Isaiah turn the boat for another look, a torpedo was being targeted on them and would be fired if any wrong move was made.

It took two more passes before JD could definitely see that what was under twenty-five fathoms of water was larger than a stove, but its shape still eluded him; it was large, but impossible to get a good look at. Sonar had been no help at all; the reflection seemed to just disappear on the sea floor. It was as if there was a hole on the sea floor, roughly the shape of a small ship. Suddenly it occurred to him; that's exactly what it was. A submarine was often described as "a hole in the ocean." Now he had found a hole on the sea floor. Obviously, a submarine was lying on the ocean floor under 150 ft. of clear blue water. By the looks of it, it was a fairly new design, but something was not quite standard about it. Of course he would need a closer look to know for sure, and that's just what he decided he'd do. But for now, the less others knew about his discovery, the better.

"Shall we make another pass, JD?" yelled Isaiah above the roar of the engines. JD shook his head "no" and motioned for Isaiah to return to the original heading. He marked the spot on his GPS and continued on his predetermined path, picking up right where he'd left off. As they continued on their original path, the silent watcher continued to monitor the small boat, keeping its entire elint—Electronic Intelligence—package fully on the LeiLani as she swept back and forth, mowing a pattern in the ocean. If they attempted to send a radio message, the message would be jammed and the boat sunk.

Isaiah finished the picket lines just as they had been plotted before taking off this morning and didn't notice JD delete the four lines of data from the memory of the magnetometer, but he didn't fail to notice the far away look in JD's eyes as they finished out the day's work. It was pushing 7:00 PM before Isaiah, JD and the LeiLani pulled into the slip and were tied off.

As he unloaded the equipment from the boat, visions of salvaging a lost submarine, no matter what the nationality, swam through JD's mind. A find like this could be worth a mint to both of them, he told himself, but why was there no search and rescue mission going on? Where were the headlines about a missing submarine? Why hadn't he seen US navy ships pounding the area with sonar? Then he recalled that the entire US Navy fleet stationed there in San Diego harbor had charged out two weeks ago, only to return en-force last week without much warning...just a local headline saying they were playing their ASW games offshore again. Maybe they had sunk a real one after all. All these questions added up to an answer that sent chills down his spine. This was a foreign sub inside of US waters that the US Navy had sunk or had tried to sink. The other question that continued to trouble his mind was, why was she dead and lying on the bottom of the ocean floor with nobody chasing the LeiLani away from her?

Isaiah pushed JD playfully as they headed for the Jeep, trying to rouse him from his reverie.

"Want to stop off for a cold one before I drop you back at school, man?"

"No thanks, Isaiah," came JD's reply. "I've got too much data to go over tonight."

"Has it got anything to do with the sub we went back and forth over this afternoon?"

JD's hand went instinctively to the gold shield at his throat as he replied, "Yeah, but I think we'd better keep it just between us for now, man. I haven't seen or heard anything about a wrecked sub out here, have you?"

"No, JD, I haven't, and I can imagine if it were known everyone would want to dive on it."

"That's kind of what I was thinking too Isaiah. If it's not known about, maybe, just maybe, we can dive on it and maybe even salvage it. What you think?"

Suddenly, Isaiah's mind flashed over all the same thoughts JD had had earlier. "Yeah, but there are a lot of unanswered questions on this one. I think maybe we should do some real research first before we dive."

"I agree, Isaiah," replied JD. Isaiah's mind was calculating the value of a salvaged submarine, and the fleet of boats he could buy with his share.

"I think this just might be our lucky day," he said, turning toward JD.

JD's mind was five miles away and 150 feet down as he replied, "Maybe so, Isaiah. Maybe so."

"You know, JD," said Isaiah, "why don't you come home with me tonight? You know you love my mom's cooking."

Snapped from his reverie by the thought of home cooking, JD's head swiveled in Isaiah's direction. "You're on!"

April 1st, 2004 AD Tehran, Iran

Osama Bin Laden gave thanks to Allah for the scientist that the Iranian President Ahmadinejad had the foresight to have trained at America's Johns Hopkins University. Macmoud Mohammed Al Hossein—yes, that was his name. He again praised Allah. It had taken three years and nearly a million British pounds to accomplish, but the water-borne biological agent was ready for testing. Ten subjects had been chosen for the first test—from the rebellious Sunni's of Iraq of course—and were secluded in the 3rd floor of Tehran's national hospital. These were called "Group A."

The first test was by a single cup of water, which had been treated by the hospitals normal water treatment and with chlorine added, just like it was done in America. The Group A subjects were wary of the smell. They were not used to the chlorination process, and four of them refused to drink the foul smelling water...until given a choice of drink or die. One still refused and had to be replaced, but after an eventful first day, all ten had received the cup of tainted water, along with a normal diet of healthy food. As an added bonus, the subjects' food was laced with extra vitamins and nutrients that were supposed to be what most Americans took in their vitamin pills.

Ten new subjects, "Group B," were placed in close proximity to the original ten after the third day. By the fourth day, they were all praising Allah for the wonderful food and accommodations they were receiving.

April 8, 2004

By the end of day 7, nine of the original ten members of Group A were showing the first signs of a slight fever. Macmoud was very pleased with the results. He checked the temperature readings from the nurses a second time. Yes, all nine were running with at least a full degree of temperature higher than normal. Only Subject Number 6 showed no sign of infection. He immediately prescribed a full spectrum of antibiotics for all ten of the subjects. The nurses, who had up to this point been wearing masks while on the floor, decided that they would like to have the full face masks—"moon suits" they called them—with self contained oxygen from now on.

April 12, 2004

Subject Number 6 still showed no sign of infection; however, the other nine subjects continued to show increased signs that the infection was spreading quickly, and as a bonus, two of the subjects from Group B were displaying elevated temperatures. It was time to put all twenty on full spectrum antibiotics.

Macmoud scratched his head and reread the data on Subject Number 6. What was different about him? Other than being the oldest of the group by a scant two and a half years, nothing else seemed to stand out. The diet was exactly the same, his intake of vitamins and minerals was closely watched, and all of his bodily functions were being watched and analyzed to the smallest detail, yet he still displayed perfect health. Something was different, but Macmoud couldn't yet figure out what it was. What was more troubling, though, was a near rebellion on the nursing floor. He was having trouble getting any of the nurses to don the plastic moon suit and check the subjects.

April 15, 2004

Three of the original Group A subjects failed to make it through the previous night and it was most probable that at least three more would fail to make it through the day— 60 percent in two weeks. Macmoud was forced to take the subjects' daily morning readings himself. Three of his nurses had failed to show up for work, and the other two flatly refused to enter the ward.

It was then that Macmoud had to show them that the plastic suits with the self-contained breathing pack would allow them invulnerability. He cursed their superstitious nature, and contemplated having their families eliminated for their failure to perform their needed work. He decided to make an example of the three who failed to report in to work... Later that day they and their families would be taken to the prison. The women would be shot, their husbands sent to prison, and the children, who could be placed with family members, would be watched for signs of maladjusted behavior, and those without family would be shot. It didn't pay to fail in your work when so many important people were watching, and Doctor Hossein knew it well.

Along with the deaths of six of the original group, now six of Group B were displaying signs of infection. Still, Subject Number 6 continued to remain in good health, and still Macmoud was scratching his head in consternation as to why.

April 16, 2004

The three remaining Group A subjects, except for Subject Number 6. died shortly after dawn—90 percent in 15 days. The first six dead subjects had been cremated the previous evening, and the three new nurses wasted no time in suiting up and removing the three newly dead subjects and preparing them for cremation. The first two subjects of Group B were getting worse, but the other four who were just coming down with the fever didn't seem to be getting any worse. One more was showing signs of elevated temperature leaving only Subject Number 6 from Group A, and Subject Numbers 1, 4, and 8 from Group B with no symptoms. Macmoud was still at a loss as to why Subject Number 6 continued to defy the odds. Now Subject Number 6 wasn't even the older of the two groups; Subject Number 3 from Group B was older.

What was unknown to Macmoud was that as a child, Subject Number 6 had been given the vaccine for small pox at such a young age he didn't remember it and had failed to reveal it during the pre-test interview. Since this was a virus that used small pox as a carrier for the Ebola strain, it had a hard time getting past his immunity to the carrier.

April 21, 2004

Only Subject Number 6 from Group A continued to show no signs of infection. Four of Group B had already died, and the other six were well on their way. It was obvious that it was just a matter of time until they also would die. No regimen of antibiotics had been found to even remotely slow down the virus. It was nearly perfect, except for Subject Number 6. Macmoud was unhappy with his inability to locate the reason for Subject Number 6's continued good health, but he decided that 95 percent was good enough so he had the test concluded. All the remaining subjects were executed, including Subject Number 6, thus ending his consternation.

His results were published and a meeting was arranged so he could explain it to Bin Laden himself. Macmoud was ecstatic and felt as if he were a key member of Osama's inner circle. Osama Bin Laden made sure that this was how it remained for this somewhat frumpy little bio-chemist. He wanted to make sure that this Macmoud would remain a dedicated Martyr of Islam, if necessary.

May 1, 2004

The Japanese ship building company known as Nakatani Shipbuilding Co. LTD. was approached by two South Korean businessmen with a rather odd request. The oddest part of the request was the secrecy involved, but the money was good, and the timing seemed to be acceptable and their new management, whom most of the Japanese engineers despised, was supportive, so a deal was agreed upon.

Nakatani had never built a submarine before, but like many things the Japanese prided themselves on, they believed they could do anything better than anyone else, if given detailed enough plans. And they were given good enough plans, plans, in fact, that had been stolen by a disgruntled US Naval captain that had been passed over for his own boat for the third and final time. Upon retiring, he decided that he had been mistreated by the Navy and wanted to get even, so when the opportunity to sell the plans to a Norwegian gentleman arose, he jumped at the chance for the bargain price of only one million dollars. What he didn't know was that the Norwegian gentleman had been born in Tehran and was, in fact, an Iranian, and not a Norwegian at all. What Nakatani didn't know was that the two South Korean businessmen were on the payroll of the Iranian government.

As the parts and plans started to come together, the Iranian Navy was well on its way to becoming a member of the Nuclear Naval club. What they were beginning to find out was that it took patience, cunning, and a whole lot of money to join that club. Fortunately for Iran, they had plenty of all three.

Nakatani had both the problem and the blessing of having never built a submarine before, so they began playing with the design of the ship, adding some new touches that they thought would make the ship faster, more efficient, and quieter. They added features not found on other submarines, like a pair of deep submergence vehicles that could be dropped from her like she was giving birth.

The two "South Korean" gentlemen had no more knowledge than Nakatani, so they were amicable to most of the changes to the design. Nakatani, in fact, made some radical changes to the hull shape and propeller design. They designed in double and triple redundancy on not just most of the components, but all of the components. They changed the specifications to non-magnetic steel everywhere there was steel, and reinforced the hull's titanium with better grades and stronger alloys that were new to the market.

All in all, Nakatani took great pride in making what they believed to be the first of many submarines into the finest submersible ship ever to be assembled anywhere.

The finishing touch was a pair of completely self-contained nuclear power plants that produced enough energy to drive its two electric motors to push the boat through the water at better than 60 knots. This ship was going to cruise in almost complete silence at 50 knots, at a depth of 1200 feet, without even breaking a sweat, thanks to the new 13 pronged propellers. What was even more impressive was the software necessary to run the super-sub made it so easy to manipulate that while there was room for 65 crew members and 6 officers, the sub could literally be maneuvered with a crew of 3, as long as you trusted the computer to be your automated crew.

Automated loading and unloading of torpedoes in both the fore and aft torpedo rooms, automated decoys and self-defense systems, self-contained power, and electrical systems, as well as self-contained water and air systems provided the sub with the ability to literally be run from the control room. Funny, the one thing not totally automated was the galley. One of the three crew you really needed was a cook. They had re-written the book on submarines, adding things not thought of before, and improving things that they found outdated. The engineers at Nakatani were ecstatic, even if they could never reveal it.

May 1, 2007

Nakatani was on schedule, right down to the day. They turned over the new submarine ship to their good friends from "South Korea" and received a sizable bonus for building the boat in three years. The larder was filled with enough food stores to last a full crew for a three-month cruise. All the charts were electronic, and almost magical.

The current system was all in Kanji, but could be changed to any of two dozen languages with a few mouse clicks. Guidance was as simple as plotting the course on the plotting table and putting in a starting and ending time. The sub would literally do all the calculations necessary for running at the best possible speed to arrive at the destination without being seen or heard by any other traffic. Its guidance system was gravitational first, but used all data available to itself to constantly check its location in the ocean.

The systems were all linked together. The computer could literally run the whole trip, but could be switched to manual operation at any moment. The computer listened for traffic all around itself, and would dive to an appropriate depth to get beneath thermal layers as necessary to remain undetected. It was also cognizant of the most detailed topographic maps found anywhere, and was self-learning. It updated the input data it had with any real world data that it discovered along its path. It literally could learn as it swept the ocean floor with its sonar and grav-arrays.

As it moved through the seas, a three-dimensional video display put the data in spatial proportion, giving those in the control room a view outside as if you were looking through a window at a well lit space surrounding the submarine for a distance of up to 5 miles in all directions. Not only that view, but with the click of a mouse you could "fly" along behind and above the submarine, viewing it as if you were following behind and watching her sail. With a few more clicks, you could also see any and all contacts within a 100-mile radius. All that remained for the new owners to do was to load any weapons they might want on board.

The ship was launched in the Sea of Japan at midnight on May 2nd, 2007, and christened the "Sea Wolf." Not a single reporter covered the launching, nor was the press invited. The team from Nakatani was surprised that only a skeleton crew of five individuals took possession of the ship and immediately removed the Nakatani group without the slightest interaction between them. Even so, Nakatani prided itself on their documentation and ease of use for everything they had designed into the sub, and the 1.6 billion dollar price tag with 5 percent on time bonus went a long way toward silencing their questions. Still, it was strange.

May 15, 2007

Captain X of the Iranian Navy and his crew from the ancient diesel submarine, Khomeini, took possession of this brand new submarine, a weapon that truly Allah had blessed him with. With this shining example of western technology, he would be able to use their own technology against them, just as his martyred brother had on September 11th of 2001. It was almost enough to make him cry out in sheer pleasure. He rubbed his hand across the anodized rubber-coated titanium triple hull, knowing that no more would his position be given away by the tell-tale echo off of his hull. No more would the sound of his ancient engines give away his every movement. No more would he fear the speedy torpedoes of his enemies. Now he could outrun almost any torpedo made. Now he could fire on his enemies and escape before they knew they were under attack. Oh, praise Allah for the Japanese and their stupidity in allowing him to acquire this weapon! He'd make sure to sink one of their fat car carriers headed for America, just for the fun of it. He praised Allah again and again for this gift.

Before he could go out and have his fun, he had a mission to perform—the mission this weapon was built for—to deliver a single cruise missile to the shores of the great Satan. His name would live throughout time as the warrior who brought the great Satan to its knees. He would be the man who was able to defy her magnificent aircraft carriers and sleek new cruisers and destroyers, who slipped past her stealthy submarines and dropped a devastating payload into the drinking waters and killed millions of the American infidels. This would finally get their attention. Accept Allah as God or die. It was quite simple.

His first act as captain of the Sea Wolf was to change her name. From this point forward his ship would be known as "The Sword of Allah." He chose twenty of his best sailors and five dependable officers from his old "pig boat." He immediately set about training his young sailors to run the ship.

Changing the language to Farsi, the captain saw that Japanese didn't translate well into Farsi, and there were several things that were a little confusing if you weren't well trained; he'd have to make sure that his crew was. The young sailors had been chosen for service on submarines because they had been raised on the seaports of Southern Iran. In truth, most were fearful of service on the submarine fleet that Iran owned. It was well known that many accidents had occurred sealing the fate of seven of Iran's twelve submarines. The captain boasted to his young crew about the capabilities of their new sub. He hoped to allay their fears and boost the morale among the young crew.

While he had chosen the best twenty-five men he could find, the software and computers used to run this modern marvel were like magic to them and most preferred running the ship in manual mode. Most of them had never run a computer before, much less one interfaced with a GUI supplied by the Japanese. The men struggled with the capabilities of the sub, and stuck to the most minimal procedures needed to accomplish their individual tasks. Two twelve-hour shifts of ten crewmen and three officers were settled on to run the ship. After two weeks of intensive training off the Eastern coast of Madagascar, the crew was proclaimed ready by the eager captain of The Sword of Allah.

Secret Submarine Base just North of Oman in Iran, May 16, 2007

In the dead of night, beneath a sheltered submarine dock, the Sword of Allah made slow turns until the hull gently bumped against the rubber bumpers. She was quickly tied in place by her crew, most of whom were anxious to leave the confines of the ship. Even so, the crew had to admit that there was much more space aboard their new ship than on their previous assignment.

No leave would be granted to the crew as they expected. Instead, a single small, rather frumpy looking scientist came aboard their craft. He had cold black eyes behind thick circular rimmed glasses that reminded the crew of a shark's eyes peering through a porthole. As time went by, that became Dr. Hossein's nickname "The Shark." Dr. Hossein brought with him the sealed orders for Captain X.

Captain X invited Dr. Hossein into his spacious quarters for the opening of the orders. Reaching the cabin, he placed his right hand on the doctor's back as he ushered him into his cabin and pointed to a comfortable chair, one of six surrounding an oval walnut table. He was proud of the beautiful office, and loved showing off his own obvious importance, but somehow the scientist did not seem impressed. It was hard to place, but for a small man he seemed to be unmoved by the obvious importance of the captain. To say the least, the captain was put off by the superior attitude the man exuded, not to mention the other feeling that the scientist seemed to put off as well. The captain couldn't quite put it into words, but there would be time for introspection later. For now, his orders awaited.

While he was not surprised by the general orders—the mission had been rumored for over a year—but the destination came as a shock to him. He was sure that they were bound for America's east coast— Washington, or New York, or even Baltimore—but instead, they headed to Las Vegas, Nevada. His surprise was evident on his face, and Dr. Hossein took this as his queue to flaunt his superior knowledge and relationship with the "inner circle."

"You see captain," Macmoud said as he settled into his lecture voice and began speaking as if he were speaking to a lowly freshman, "We have decided on Las Vegas because of the remote location and size of its water supply; while affecting the local residents, it is also a favorite vacation spot for the decadent American infidels. It will send a message to them about the effect of their lack of morals, and because it hosts an annual computer show that brings in over one million visitors from across the world in just over two weeks from now."

Captain X's eye s lit up as he understood the target reasoning. In three weeks time the show would be over, but the first effects of the weapon would just begin to be felt. By the time the million plus visitors returned to their homes, the virus would begin in earnest, and hundreds of millions of people would be getting sick without knowing it. Inside of four weeks, people would begin to die. By the time anyone realized what was happening there would be close to a billion people, all western unbelievers, that would be fatally infected.

There was still something gnawing at the back of his neck: the fear of transporting this terrible biologic agent inside the confines of his new submarine. As he began to voice his concerns, Macmoud raised his hand to silence his obviously simple-minded new partner.

"Let me assure you, my dear captain," he said reaching inside his coat for a small flask of the agent.

The captain pushed away in shock and fear as this dead-eyed scientist apparently lost his mind by playing with this deadly virus! Macmoud laughed out loud at the reaction of the captain as he unscrewed the lid.

"Let me explain, oh fearless one," Macmoud chided, "This is completely harmless until it is put into a solution of water and consumed by mouth. In fact, if too much water is present, the virus becomes too diluted to be effective. That is another reason why Las Vegas was chosen. We have provided just enough agent for the weapon being loaded on board right now for Lake Meade to be contaminated. By the time they realize there is a problem, it will have been contaminated for over a week."

The captain could see the excitement in Macmoud's gleeful movements and in his dancing black eyes. He continued to back away from the now-open container, saying "Yes, but what about that open container?"

"You still aren't listening, my captain," replied Macmoud. "Breathing this powder would be perfectly harmless to you or anyone else. It requires enough water to become completely soluble. If I were to dump this down the drain," he went on, "it would be completely harmless because it would be much too diluted by this small amount in the vast ocean. So you see, it is the perfect harmless weapon while on board this ship. It won't be until it reaches the confines of Lake Meade that it will become active."

As the knowledge began to sink into the captains still wary mind, he took offense to this little man's laugh at his expense. He puffed his chest out with bravado and told the scientist to "put away your toys, and be serious. After all, we must make sure that we make no mistakes in completing our sacred duty."

Macmoud smiled inwardly at the obvious bravado of the captain, but decided the best course of action at present was to put the cap back on his sample. He took great comfort in the vial of agent that he kept in his breast pocket. Patting it as he put it back into his pocket, Macmoud asked to oversee the loading of the tube-launched cruise missile.

The captain was glad to give his permission and be rid of the wretched little man. He shuddered inwardly as the self-confident dead- eyed scientist stood up, turned and left the cabin. He couldn't help but feel like he needed to wash his hands after having touched the evil—yes that was the word he was looking for—evil little man.

Las Vegas, Nevada, May 16, 2007

Naomi had come to Vegas two weeks early. She had to pay through the nose for a suite the week of Comdex, so she was staying at the cheapest, sleaziest dive she could find for the two weeks prior. She stared in amazement at what the definition of "dive" looked like. She sighed in disgust and decided that in the morning she would redefine "dive" for herself, no matter what it cost her. After all, she was the President and CEO of NB Software of San Diego, California.

She smiled at her own self-importance and laughed out loud as she studied her business card. I have to make this work, she thought to herself. If she could get Microcom's interest in bundling her database software into their suite, she'd really be something, not just the leader of a three-person company trying desperately to sell their wares.

It really was good stuff. She knew it was better than anything else out there; she just couldn't get anyone else to recognize it. Another sigh escaped her lips. At twenty-three, she was ahead of the curve.

She had gone to college in Hawaii and had spent three years involved in student government. Leader of the young Republicans, and President of ROTORAC—the college ROTARY club, she had business success written all over her. She was "cute"—that's how people described her. At 5'1", with long, straight dark hair, deep brown eyes, a curvy figure and dusky Hispanic features, people just naturally called her cute. But she was more than that.

Dad said she had a beautiful mind and a beautiful smile to go with it. She smiled as she thought of her father and mother. They were never too busy to help her out or listen to what she had to say, even as busy as their lives were back in Washington. She had known what she wanted since she was 12. How odd, she thought, that she had every last penny riding on this conference. She just couldn't fail! Not her. Heaving another deep sigh, she rolled over and grabbed the phone to call JD. He always could make things better for her.

Silicon Valley, California, May 16, 2007

In the offices of Microcom, the decision had already been made. The database was the best of the offerings out there; it was just a matter of whether they would take the offer or try to make it work on their own. The president was headstrong, no doubt about it, and smart. They'd have to find just the right spot for her. It was important that they get her along with the database software.

Microcom wasn't just in the business of software; they were in the business of developing the largest brain trust the world had ever seen, beginning with their own CEO, Martin Stanton. Stanton, it seemed, almost never slept. He had a plan that only he knew about, and it was coming together nicely, but for now he had to come up with just the right enticement to get Naomi into the fold. That was the problem with these really bright, driven people; they often didn't want to work for someone else. They wanted to be on their own. Getting them was much more difficult than getting the product they had built, but Martin was really good at finding the lynch pin that drove them and then exploiting it.

Finding it with Ms. Benson was proving to be difficult. He looked through the company data and the data his private detective had pulled together for the third time this evening and still didn't see the weak point... Perhaps the boyfriend, he thought... He was no slouch either. Maybe a two for one ploy. Well, he had another two weeks to find the answer. He punched the button on his desk phone and spoke. "Angie, get Mr. Jakees with security for me first thing in the morning. Tell him I want more information on Ms. Benson by the end of the week. I want to know everything, down to what color underwear she wears on Thursdays. Is that clear?" The computerized but gentle voice of Angie soothingly cooed a "Yes, Mr. Stanton" back. "Will there be anything else, Mr. Stanton?"

"No Angie," came his terse reply. He'd have to get someone to work on that software and tweak it to understand when he was upset. No one wanted to be cooed at when they were upset; they needed to hear the fear in their secretary's voice at moments like that, not cooing! He thought about making the note with Angie but decided that it would just make him more upset.

Back to Ms. Benson. What would it take? With people like her, it would take money and security for her underlings; she was that type.

He sped read through the data again, stopping at the appropriate spots and reading about the others in the organization. Only a three- man team. He could afford to sign them all and then whittle away the chaff after a couple of months. Most of them got the message and left on their own in a few months anyway. He wondered again about Naomi and what it would take to get her, but mostly, he smiled.

Beijing, China, May 16, 2007

Chaing Xau smiled an almost identical smile as Martin Stanton, half a world away. He had just received and read a report from one of his nation's operatives in Iran. President Ahmadinejad was the perfect puppet for the times. He really believed in his own ranting and raving. It took so little to stir up the man in the funny black suit. Just the right words had stirred the man to spend more than a billion dollars of his country's money on an outrageous plan that had more chance of failure than of success, all because of his fascination with America and the West.

By mentioning America he could get him to do most anything. So far, this little plan had put 1.6 billion dollars into his country's coffers. He had taken great pains to hide the ownership by his country of the Japanese ship builder he had recommended to the president. He again smiled at his own cunningness. On the other hand, if this silly little man did manage to pull off this wild plan, all the better for China. It could speed his plans for domination along all the sooner. It made him excited just thinking about it. At 10:00 in the morning, it was unusual for him to feel the excitement in his loins and he gave in to his stirrings. Pressing the button for his private secretary, he moved from the office to the door of his private studio.

As she entered the office, Li Ming was surprised to see Chaing moving toward the studio, and wondered what had gotten the randy old goat in such a mood this early in the morning. She painted a smile on her face, even though inwardly she felt like vomiting, but she knew how to get through this. She closed her eyes, momentarily visualizing her boyfriend's features replacing the sagging fat old man's, and then opened her eyes and smiled the smile she knew he liked. Tonight she would wash the stench from her body with a long luxurious bath with her boyfriend Hong Lee. She visualized once again how well hung Hong was and almost laughed at the difference in the two men's penises. Yes, tonight would be wonderful.

Twenty minutes later Li was back in her office. The fat pig had expended himself in less than 5 minutes, and the rest of the time had been taken in stroking his ego about his extreme sexual prowess. She had spent the last five minutes taking notes about the Iranian president and another of his stupid plans to kill Americans. It seemed that Chaing had little belief in the plan, but he was excited by the possibilities it offered. She knew he had a larger plan circulating in his twisted old mind, but he hadn't shared it with her yet. It was her job to document everything he said, outside of the amorous meanderings, but she had no idea that everything she wrote was being read twenty-four hours later by the British Secret Service.

That night Hong Lee whistled as he walked the three and a half blocks to Li Ming's apartment. When the CIA had recruited him for a position, he had dreamed of being 007 and making love to beautiful women while chasing down bad guys. Now here he was, being paid to sleep with a beautiful Chinese woman, although he hadn't killed any counter-spies or chased any bad guys. All he had done was slip Li Ming a program and modem for her computer, telling her that it would speed up her Internet connection.

In reality, it did speed up her Internet, but it also sent data to the small receiving unit he carried in his satchel every night. All he had to do was be within a mile of the sending computer and everything would work perfectly. On top of everything else, he got paid by both the Agency and Niike Data Systems, his cover company. It was a dream come true—a beautiful woman to make love to, an apartment paid for by Niike in Beijing, an apartment of his own in Tokyo, a great salary being paid by Niike, a second salary almost as good going straight into a 401K account back in the USA, and the excitement of knowing he was screwing the Chinese government.

Of all the perks, the last was his real motivation. His father had been executed by those creeps right here in Beijing thirty years ago for having the courage to stand up against tyranny in the Tiananmen Square incident. Although his mother had taken his brother and him out of China to Japan months before the incident, and from there to the US three years later, he still worried that the Chinese government would wise up and find out who he really was, but the Agency had hidden his past well. He'd flown through the background check without any problems. Now, life was rosy!

The data was transmitted by a low-level UHF transmitter every night at midnight. From there, Hong dialed in to his company Internet site and downloaded his daily work report. Included in the daily report was his timesheet, which had the "change data" from Li's hard drive encrypted within it. If looking at the image on the screen, a person saw a .jpg file showing Hong's daily activity, but after 4th generation decryption and key access, the file showed the changes to Li's hard drive since the previous day's file.

Back in Japan, a low-level secretary for Niike Data Systems working in the payroll department would slip a usb drive into the port on her computer, move the file to it, and replace it with a clean version of his timesheet. Taking the file back to her small apartment, she connected to an Internet dating service called "Shag Central"; a cheesy British dating service, supposedly based in ShangHai, that in effect was a front for MI6 and running off of a server in prestigious Scotland Yard. After logging on and checking her mailbox for any interested parties, she uploaded a new profile that included Hong's timesheet. After the upload was confirmed, she ran a special cleaning program on the jump drive making absolutely sure that no trace of the data would ever be found in her possession.

From there, MI6 sent a copy of the data to Langley, Virginia, and to the CIA, fulfilling their part of the joint effort necessary to get the data out of Beijing. By the time the data was read by an analyst in Langley, nearly 36 hours had gone by. Today, the data was more than routine monetary movements and obtuse plans for shafting the west with low- cost cheap copies. Today both the CIA and MI6 were buzzing with the idea of an attack of a US city by an Iranian submarine.

The White House, May 18, 2007

President Beechum looked over the security advisory she held in her hand for the third time.

"Bill, how accurate is this?" she asked coldly, wrinkling the paper with her grip. Sitting around the oval table in the office of the same name were Bill Elliot, the CIA Chief, Head of the NSA Dave Benson, FBI Chief Hamilton (Ham) Cordova, and Homeland Security Secretary Alex Rice.

"Well, pretty damn accurate, ma'am," Elliot drawled.

"The real question is whether or not they're pullin our chain with this," interrupted Ham Cordova, always the impatient one.

Alex Rice nodded with apparent agreement. "It does seem rather far-fetched, and even more so that they would drop it in our laps this easily."

Bill continued his slow-moving report. "It does seem odd that the old billy goat would be this reckless with something this important, but he is old, and that secretary of his is hotter than a five dollar pistol on Saturday night in Harlem." He paused, then added, "Pardon the expression, ma'am."

Alex jumped in again. "I don't think we should believe it. They've blown our operation and they're playing with us."

Bill sat up, "Now wait a minute, Alex, We haven't had those bastards catch onto one of our ops in over 7 years, not since the previous administration."

Ham jumped in as well, his face turning a little redder "Yeah, well I'm with Alex on this. It's just too fantastic. It has to be a hook to catch us and make us blow our own cover."

Debra Beechum lifted a hand, bringing a temporary silence to the escalating discussion. "Dave, what do you think? You're being awfully quiet over there."

"What do I think? Well, I think that this is an amazing piece of information that we can't afford to ignore. At the same time, we must make sure that we don't expose our agents to detection. If what is in this report is true, we have to raise our alert status for the Navy right now and begin searching for this submarine. I suggest orders to shoot to kill any un-identified sub in our waters. We also have to put our best people onto determining which cities would be vulnerable to such an attack and what kind of chemical or biological agent they might use. We have a whole host of things to do, but most importantly of all, we can't just ignore it. We can do a whole lot without showing our cards. I suggest we do those things and do them fast."

Bill started to jump in again. "Well, this is a national problem so we should be point..." but that was as far as he got before Ham and Alex jumped back in again.

Debra held up her hand for quiet once again and said, "Dave will be running the show on this one, but I expect full cooperation from each of you! Is that clear? There is no room for any departmental political crap on this one, gentlemen. I expect to hear from Dave how well you each are handling your individual assignments and how well you each are sharing everything you hear, gather, or just come across by dumb luck. This is more important than anything any of you have done to this point, so let's get it right." As usual, the president had cut to the quick, as was her reputation. She dismissed them all except Dave, whom she motioned to stay behind.

"Dave, give me everything you're thinking on this one, will you?"

"Yes, Madam President," Dave replied, with a furrowed brow. "This could be bad, Debra." He slipped back into the familiarity he had with this woman whom he respected greatly. They had been friends back when she had been the Freshman Republican Senator from Florida, and he the DDO of the CIA. He had been instrumental in tracking down the Al Qaeda hit squad that had proclaimed they would kill her and five other freshman senators.

Though it had never made a single paper or TV news feed, the pretty young senator from Florida had never forgotten Dave or his professional handling of the situation. Fourteen years later, she had repaid that kindness by passing the Senior Elliot, Cordova, and Rice and promoting Dave to the NSA top spot.

"It could really be bad," he continued. "We don't know an awful lot, like when the attack is supposed to come, where it will happen, or what the weapon is, and how it will be released. We'll have to get the Navy going right now searching for this submarine. We can hide it under the angle that we're running a big ASW exercise off all three of our coasts. We've just got to pray that we don't accidentally sink one of our own ships. On top of the Navy, we'll have to get the best of our CIA analysts into determining if they can glean any other data from our friends in China, or perhaps if we can get someone into the Iranian Secret Police. The FBI and Homeland Security will have to combine their efforts into determining which of our coastal cities is the most vulnerable target. If we can reduce the area of susceptibility we can put more of our Navy ASW assets into the place most likely for the sub to be. Once we've done all of that, I'd say we have at least an even chance of stopping them before they deploy their weapon."

"Even!" The president's mouth opened and seemed to flop soundlessly. "Even? We've got to do better than that," she said.

"I'd like to give you better news, Debra, but you know I won't sugar coat it for anyone. I'd say even is the best we're gonna get."

"Dave" she said, then paused, "run this thing to ground and kill that damn sub and anyone associated with it. I consider this a danger to the United States of America and her citizens. Do you understand me?" she concluded.

"Yes, Madam President," came his reply, all familiarity gone. His orders were clear.

Between the Maldives and Chagos Islands, May 17, 2007, 18:00 Zulu

Macmoud was treated as a leper aboard the confines of the Sword of Allah. At least the captain was civil to the scientist. He had been invited to eat with the captain for the first time since they had sailed early the day before. It was hard for the little man to get used to the constant conditions aboard the submarine. It seemed as if there was no day or night, just a constant evening time, or early morning, depending on which you liked. Even the food gave no hint as to the time outside the sub. Six times a day the call to prayer sounded instead of the normal three, adding to his disorientation.

It seemed that the first shift acted as if they were the day shift, as did the second shift. Macmoud was at a loss. As he joined the captain at the dining table, it seemed that the captain was doing everything he could to further disorient him when Macmoud ordered an evening meal of lamb and greens, and the captain ordered a big breakfast. Macmoud opened his mouth but decided better about asking his question.

"What seems to be the problem, brother scientist? Are you not enjoying your cruise?" the captain asked with an inward grin.

"I would if I could only find out when we will be surfacing. I am having difficulty in knowing day from night," replied Macmoud.

"Surfacing? Not in this ship, sir," came the instant reply. "We will spend the entire cruise below the surface with this magnificent ship."

Suddenly, the ship seemed to squeeze tighter around the small scientist. He hadn't realized that they wouldn't be surfacing.

"But how will we survive? Our air will surely run out in a matter of days. We certainly can't run for more than three days without coming up!" The scientist's voice raised from normal to almost a full octave higher as the fear became apparent in his visage.

It was the captain's turn to play the game of superiority with his visitor now, and he relished the opportunity to do so. Raising his eyebrows just so and mimicking the scientists own lecture voice, he began a detailed explanation of how the ship used hydrogen scrubbers to re-generate oxygen within the ship and allow it to spend as much as six months below the surface of the ocean without replenishing its oxygen supply. With fewer sailors on board, the time could be stretched to an even longer period. He also explained that by keeping the ship at a constant temperature and lighting level the sailors would always feel more comfortable and not like they had to sleep during the daytime as on other vessels.

"Trust me, dear academian," he blithely continued on, "it is perfectly safe, much more so than your vial of death!"

Feeling chastised, Macmoud stood abruptly, threw his napkin to the floor, and started for the door to his cabin.

"Please, sir", the captain said in mock appeasement, "let's not get off on the wrong foot."

Macmoud turned toward the captain, not knowing if he was being baited, but wanting to believe the captain had returned to his senses and was going to tell him that he was only teasing about the air purification.

"Okay, captain," he replied, "I must confess I was a bit startled by the outlandish claim of air purification, but I see no reason for you to attack my biological masterpiece." He managed to regain his composure and air of superiority.

"Oh, I'm sorry," the captain quickly replied, " I didn't mean that I was kidding about the air purification, Doctor. Only that I didn't want you panicking while in control of such a dangerous substance." He smiled at the other officers in the galley as he spoke down to the small man.

Suddenly the air seemed to grow instantly stale in Macmoud's lungs and his collar two sizes tighter around his neck. Besides feeling air sick, he felt the heat of shame burning his neck and cheeks as the officers laughed at his expense.

"We shall see," was all that he could muster before weaving his way back to his cabin. As he reached the door, he patted the vial in his pocket, stroking it, as if by doing so he were stroking his own ego. Calming himself down, he let himself into the cabin. It seemed awfully warm and confined. Somehow, the captain must have changed cabins on him. It seemed to be a foot smaller in all directions. It was as if suddenly he could reach out and touch all the walls and ceiling from one spot in the center of his room. It must be smaller. And the heat—it felt at least 5 degrees warmer. It was a plot by that idiot captain to shake him. Well, he'd show the captain who was superior! He'd show the captain, all right. He reached into his shaving kit for the pill case he kept with him and took two Valiums. Almost instantly he felt better, but maybe just one more would make him feel even better.

By 21:00 Zulu he'd consumed copious amounts of alcohol and four Valiums. He no longer felt anything. He paced back and forth across his room, praising himself for his magnificent invention. He stroked the vial one minute and cursed it the next. He didn't need the vial to be superior to the captain; he was naturally superior. He told himself over and over how important he was, how he was the one who had given this gift to the president and to the enlightened one: Osama. He boasted to himself of his standing in the inner circle, how Osama himself had called him by his first name. Surely when the enlightened one knows you by your first name you are most important. Just one more pill and he'd have all the importance he needed. And so he took just one more... He was getting really sleepy now, but he wanted to show the captain just how important he was. He didn't need the vial any more to feel superior; he knew it inside of himself. So with one final stroke across its steel exterior, he dumped the 3 and 1/2 grams of powder down the toilet in his room and flushed it away forever, or so he thought, then he lay down and slept the best sleep he'd had in months.

Maybe it was the drugs, or the alcohol, or maybe he just hadn't been listening to the captain as he'd spoken of the sealed water system, but during that moment, and with that single action, Macmoud condemned the entire crew of the submarine to an agonizing death. He had literally flushed their lives down the toilet. Only time now would tell whether they would reach their destination and perform their final jobs before they met their demise.

Indian Ocean, 00:00 Zulu, May 18, 2007

Captain X entered his coordinates into the computer, setting the destination for the middle California coast line, just north of the San Diego harbor. He set the time to arrive for June 1st at 22:00 Zulu time. If everything went well, he planned to fire his weapon as soon as it was dark after he arrived on station, making sure that his weapon had plenty of time to work on the residents of Las Vegas and the million or so visitors to that desert resort town, set to descend upon it the first week of June. The steward brought him a magnificent cup of coffee that he half swallowed in the first gulp. It was truly a wonderful ship. And so it began...

Las Vegas, Nevada

Naomi had moved up to a small room at Sam's Town Hotel and Casino, paying only $32 dollars a night for the two weeks leading up to Comdex, and then moving into the ultra suite at the Maxim the next week at $500 a night. She had it all on the line. Her booth at the show was in a great location, just off the main set of conference rooms in the Las Vegas Convention Center. She was getting everything set. Her booth and her presentation looked great.

She was set to speak during the third breakout session of the first day at 3:30. Her topic was fifth generation databases and the odbc compliant real life language capability that was built into her new database. It was a real breakthrough that had everyone talking, but no one had seen the voice interface in action yet. She knew it would be the topping on the cake, but still she worried. Microcom had shown some interest, so maybe hope still lived.

JD had promised to come up this weekend, taking time off of his research project, so maybe they'd both be able to relax and enjoy the time before the conference this weekend. He was working so hard to finish his Master's and he was a pretty fair programmer himself. If things continued to work out between them and everything went well with Microcom, maybe she could convince him to come work with her, but somehow she doubted it. He really hadn't told her what he was going to do after graduation. Somehow, he always seemed to avoid the question, but she suspected that he'd never be able to leave the ocean. It seemed like it was just a part of him. The relationship he and Isaiah were building was one she didn't know how to compete with. She could fight another woman, but she could never fight the call of the sea and the adventures that it promised young men like JD and Isaiah. Even so, she knew that there was no other woman between her and JD, and there never would be. It was an unspoken thing that never would be spoken. She knew he loved her in the only way he could right now, and he knew that she loved him in the only way she could. For two driven individuals, the question always was: was it enough? She closed her eyes and decided that for today, it was!

The Southern Indian Ocean, 12:00 Zulu, May 18, 2007

Captain X was in good spirits but feeling sleepy. He didn't wish to relinquish the helm of this wonderful ship for even sleep, but the 12:00 call to prayer had sounded, and with it, the end of his shift. He went to his cabin and knelt upon the carpeted deck facing northwest from where he currently cruised 500 feet beneath the waves. Making only twenty knots, the Sword of Allah made virtually no sound whatsoever. Her two generators were running at 1/4 output and the ship had warned them of a submerged contact at 05:00 at a miraculous distance of nearly 100 kilometers— over 60 miles. The ship had then presented them with an optimal course change that would take them away from the contact and with a new speed to make up for the lost time. She was truly marvelous. Had the crew been confident and familiar with the system, the changes could have been made without the crew having to input the changes, but that would come in time, the captain mused as he continued mouthing the words of his prayer.

The Sword continued to track the contact for three more hours until it had disappeared to the northwest of their position. There were fifteen other surface contacts that the Sword continued to plot and watch, including seven that had been identified as an Indian Aircraft carrier and her six escorts—two cruisers, and four destroyers, all classified as diesel ships—loudly beating their way around Sri Lanka, headed for Bangladesh. As the Sword moved westward, she suggested new depths as the thermo clines changed, making sure to keep the boat beneath the line and keep them invisible.

12:00 Zulu, May 19, 2007

Slowly the Sword crept through the islands of Indonesia, heading westward toward the Marshall Islands. The crew was not used to being submerged for this long a period of time. Even during their training, they had come up for a few hours each night to make sure the crew felt comfortable, but now it was far too risky to come to the surface. Even the captain could sense the sourness of the air. He felt a tightening in his chest, but managed to keep himself under control. The crew, however, was not quite as successful. Several of the young men on the second shift had been murmuring about the mission and the death powder that was on board the ship. To them, the musty air was a sure sign that it had escaped its confines and was floating about the ship's air supply. Little did they realize that it was not the air that was contaminated, but the water instead.

The captain realized that he would have to do something soon. On top of everything else, the little scientist was preening around the ship during his waking hours, adding to the fear among the men. If he were not careful, one of his sailors, or worse, one of his officers were going to knock the little man's head clear off of his neck.

What even the captain didn't realize was that Macmoud was nearly beside himself with his own fears. He was having a terrible time dealing with his claustrophobia. Snapping and speaking down to those around him was his way of dealing with the fear he felt, but as his fear continued to rise, his nasty disposition continued to worsen, and as it worsened, the crew's disposition got worse as well.

The captain needed to do something to alleviate the situation, but he was not sure what to do. He finished his prayers and decided to sleep on it for another night.

America's Eastern Sea Board, 16:45 Zulu, May 19, 2007

Admiral Davidson was taking no chances. If the Iranians were stupid enough to try and sneak by the line of sonobouys running roughly along the Mid-Atlantic ridge, he had deployed every attack sub in the Atlantic fleet to sea not far from the rise, just waiting for any sign of their noisy subs. They wouldn't last long, but just in case, the rest of the Atlantic fleet was stationed in a picket line roughly 100 miles east of the American coast, pinging actively. Only a fool would try to get by the line of death that he had placed along his country's border.

At the same time, Admiral Franklin, Pacific Fleet commander, had a much larger area to defend, but he was putting similar orders in place to protect America's west coast. This would be difficult with the cutbacks he'd had to endure during the previous administration's reign. Seven years of the current administration would have normally been enough to get the fleet back up to acceptable levels if it hadn't been for the War on Terror that they were currently engaged in. A desert war had pulled funds from normal Navy coffers and was causing the slow dwindling of the Pacific fleet's operational capabilities.

While the Navy wasn't hurting, by any stretch of the imagination, it was taking quite a bite out of his submarine budget. All of his money seemed to be flowing through the aircraft maintenance and ordinance budgets. Today's bombs were not exactly cheap, and they were running through quite a few every day. But that was his problem for another day. Today, he needed to shut down his western borders, including surrounding Hawaii, without letting the world know what was going on. The Russians were already starting to get fussy. Davidson, out in the Atlantic, had seen to that by pinging everything under the ocean. He was making so much noise that there were ships as far away as South Africa picking up his racket. The president's explanation of a massive ASW exercise was beginning to fall on deaf ears. Franklin was taking a more stealthy approach. The best experts were telling him that the attack would be an East Coast attack, but he was going to be sure not to let anyone get inside his perimeter.

12:00 Zulu, May 22, 2007

The Sword continued her Southern crawl across the Pacific, headed on a path directly toward the French owned Austral Island. As she continued on her path, the crew was now openly questioning the captain's orders to remain submerged. Tempers were flaring several times a day and the captain had to use coercion, as well as threats, to retain command of his ship. He scheduled a meeting for all crew members at 00:00 Zulu on May 23rd to have the little scientist explain to the crew all he knew about the deadly powder. He also would explain in detail their glorious mission. It was time to call upon the superior faith of these men. He would unite them in their duty for Allah. As he closed his eyes to rest, he took solace in the belief that they were unstoppable. He knew they too would feel the same solace and soon they all would pull together.

At 00:00 the crew came together in the ship's dining room. Dr. Hossein looked ragged as he stood beside the captain and addressed the crew. Try as he might, he was not having a calming effect on the crew. He told them about how safe the weapon was, as long as it was not in the water supply. He raised the empty flask, telling them that he himself had been subjected to the powder any number of times and was still alive to show them.

This began to have the effect that the captain desired. It was the captain's turn next. He began with praises of his wonderful new ship. He described the mission that this marvelous boat had been built to accomplish. By the time he reached the conclusion to his presentation, shouting out "Death to the Infidels," the crew had been whipped into the frenzy that he had expected. They could care less if they were dying or not, or so they appeared. They were excited to be there to help make history. The captain was sweating with the exertion he had put into his histrionics. Soon they would make history. He had succeeded in exciting himself as well. Soon, very soon, he would make history.

His mind began to examine the efforts of Dr. Hossein... He really hadn't helped much at all. Standing there sweating like a pig hadn't helped either. He had half a mind to eject the stupid little man out of a torpedo tube. As if in response to his thoughts, his first officer appeared at his side, asking to speak to him privately. Captain X turned over the helm of the boat to the chief and stepped into the map room/library just aft of the control room, and closed the door.

"What can I do for you, Achmed?" The captain turned to his subordinate while putting on a happy face.

"Sir, despite all that was said in the meeting, the crew is still a little edgy about carrying this stuff with us. We'd all feel much better if "the shark,"—I mean the scientist—had looked a little more confident during his time in front of the crew."

"I know, Achmed," the captain replied, "but I cannot help his obvious fear of confined spaces. He hasn't been normal since his first night on the ship. Keeping to his own cabin, never stepping out for anything more than to get his food, and then back to his cabin as soon as he receives it. I'm not as worried about him as I am about his importance to the mission. We must keep him going long enough to prepare the weapon for firing."

"Perhaps, Captain, we should prepare the weapon now, and then we wouldn't have to worry about keeping the little man alive," came Achmed's reply.

"I've thought of that," the captain responded, "but think how that would affect the crew. They are already nervous. No, I don't want them worrying about an accidental exposure, especially now that they seem to be somewhat back to normal."

Tehran, Iran, 10:00 Zulu, May 22, 2007

President Ahmadinejad smiled inwardly as he read the reports coming across his desk. The Americans obviously had found out something, but not enough to stop the attack. Well, they were looking for something along their east coast; he'd give them something. He called his secretary and ordered his naval commander to report immediately. Within minutes, Navy Admiral Mobarrak was standing stiffly at attention in front of his nation's president.

"Admiral Mobarrak," Ahmadinejad exclaimed, "I need you to do something for me. Something difficult, but necessary. I need you to send our submarines to the east coast of the United States."

"But sir," Mobarrak countered, "that would be suicide right now. Our remaining submarine fleet makes too much noise to try and sneak up on the East Coast with all that searching going on along their eastern coastline."

"Admiral Mobarrak, that is exactly what I'm depending on. Think of it as a sacrifice we are making. If they sink one of our submarines in international waters, we will destroy them publicly, using their own 'free press' "—he spat the words out—"against them. And if they don't, we'll drive them crazy watching us move in and out of their territorial waters. They'll be so busy watching what we want them to see that they'll completely miss the real danger. Either way, we win." Ahmadinejad felt very self-satisfied. There was no way for him to lose!

Immediately following the short meeting with the president, Admiral Mobarrak called his submarine commanders together and gave them the orders just as he had been given his orders. Cat and mouse. What a dangerous game to play with a country as fearsome as the United States. To be perfectly honest, the admiral believed that the president had always been a wild-eyed fanatic, but he hadn't made it this far by "rocking the boat" with any of his fanatical leaders. He knew when to keep his mouth shut and do what he had been told. After all, it wasn't going to be him playing cat and mouse this time, and if he knew his commanders, they really wouldn't be playing too hard either, except for maybe Hassid. He wasn't sure how Hassid had lasted this long, but now was his chance to tangle with the Americans as he wished. Either way, he had done his job, said the words he was supposed to, and he felt safe from the assassin's bullet for another day. Praise Allah for that!

Mid-Atlantic Ridge, 15:00 Zulu, May 24, 2007

Captain Hassid had listened to the words of his admiral and met the words spoken to him with a zealot's fire in his eyes. Much like Captain X, he was anxious to earn a spot in the history books. Two months prior, he and X had celebrated the news of X's promotion to the new boat that they had just learned about. They had rented a large hotel room and brought in twenty virgins, pretending that they were martyrs in heaven. Together they took turns with the young women, pretending they were gods, and enjoying the benefits of their martyrdom. It had energized both of them. Now he had the opportunity to enjoy the real thing, and no one was going to stand in his way. He raced to the American coast and his appointment with destiny.

At the same time, an American Ohio class-hunter/killer sub waited for the noisy old diesel sub. It was like shooting fish in a barrel, Skip Hutchins thought. He was accustomed to hunting the ultra quiet boomers of the Soviet Navy, not these clunkers the Iranians were throwing their way. Were they mad? This was impossibly easy. He called for a quiet surface, knowing he had plenty of time before the contact was anywhere near enough to hear him. He needed to make a report before he took any further action.

Upon making contact, he learned that six other Iranian submarines had left port and were making their way toward the American coast in various states of slow headway. Only his contact seemed to be in a hurry. His orders were clear: follow the noisy Iranian and watch him closely. If the Iranian attempted to fire a torpedo or entered the American 12-mile limit, sink him before he could get a shot off. No questions asked. Skip wasn't keen on this. It was too easy a job and a waste of their time. What did the Iranians have that warranted this kind of fear? Skip didn't like it, but he had his orders, and he wouldn't hesitate to follow them. He took his sub back down to 300 feet and waited for the slow, noisy Iranian sub to cross his path like a wolf waiting for a rabbit to try and sneak past his lair on its way home. Only he still needed to be careful, because as noisy and stupid as this rabbit was, he still had quite a bite.

Half a world away, 500 miles south of Pitcairn Island, the Sword of Allah was making steady turns for 20 knots. Some of the crew had complained about not feeling well, but everyone was excited. They were inching closer to the western coast of South America, and they were feeling indomitable. They had avoided detection by two submarines, identified by name by their wondrous new ship. What amazing feats they would be able to do in this vessel. The captain had won them over, and they were excited. Even so, the captain himself was not happy with the temperature control systems; even though the thermometer read a constant 71.8 degrees throughout the ship, everyone on board was complaining of sweats and shivers. It had to be a malfunction, since all of them couldn't be suffering the same illness.

Inside his self-appointed isolation, Macmoud took his temperature for the third time in as many hours. Despite the aspirin he'd taken, his headache had not gone away and his temperature remained one degree higher than normal. The charts of the sample groups played over and over through his mind. It was just a silly thought, he tried to convince himself. Just the next phase of insanity that he was going through caused by the closeness of this terrible ship, his mind told him. With that thought, he buried himself in the sleep of two sleeping pills and a liter of alcohol.

In the captain's cabin, he also took aspirin for a headache and convinced himself that everything was going according to plan.

Chilean Coast, 12:00 Zulu, May 26, 2007

Something was definitely wrong. Three of his men were confined to the infirmary, and the rest of the crew, except for the cook, were all sick with an obvious virus. The evil little scientist refused to answer from his cabin and the door was locked. The captain was furious. He knew inside his heart that this was it, yet he couldn't make himself believe it. He ordered the speed changed to full speed and the course for the shortest possible route to the firing position. He had the door to the doctor's room opened by the chief engineer. What he saw upon opening the door frightened him. The good doctor sat bloated in his private bathroom. He had obviously injected himself with something to end his own suffering.

Sometime in the previous 24 hours the doctor had reached the same conclusion that he had reached—the virus was loose and they all had it. He ordered the doctor's body jettisoned through the escape hatch, cutting his nose off before sending him to meet Allah, and then called the entire crew together.

"My dear brother martyrs," he began. It was not what they wanted to hear. "The death virus has obviously been loosed by that terrible little man," the captain continued. "At this point we must believe that it is Allah's will that we will all become Martyrs of the Kingdom. In the coming weeks we will meet our God. How we meet him in Paradise will be up to each of us. You can be with me with twenty virgins to serve me, or you can beg for food in the streets of heaven as a coward." The crew didn't quite greet this news with the same vigor they had three days earlier. They had heard this kind of rhetoric before, but now it was for real. They were really dying, and all the words of rhetoric couldn't fix that.

The captain recalled the words that the doctor had spoken that first day: If the virus was loose on board the sub, it had to be in the water system. He decided that if there was any chance of survival, it would begin with cleaning up the water and the air. He ordered all the water dumped to the sea immediately, and new, desalinated water put into the system. He stopped the sub in the middle of the night and surfaced. The air was replaced and the crew given an hour-long chance to breathe fresh air again.

The crew needed the work to keep them busy, so they jumped with vigor that they didn't feel. Unfortunately, six of them also jumped ship, stealing a small rubber raft. What they didn't realize was that the currents in that portion of the Pacific pushed them to the southwest and out to sea. They would never be found. That afternoon, the first of the crew died. By then they were on the Peruvian coastline, making their way north.

Twice they had to stop for American warships actively pinging just outside of the twelve-mile limit. Fortunately, they were looking for ships to the west, not to the east. They continued to make their way toward America. Captain X was sure that they would make it to the firing point before they all died. By 12:00 Zulu time of May 27th, the cruise, which began with 27 crew members including the doctor, now consisted of 5 officers and 11 crew members still alive. Captain X was not quite as sure as he had been.

100 Miles East of Virginia Beach, Va. 12:00 Zulu, May 28, 2007

Skip Hutchins and the SSN Skip Jack were less than 800 yards astern of an Iranian diesel sub, captained by Captain Hassid. Skip couldn't believe that this could actually be construed as an attack of any kind. The boat they were trailing was behaving as if it were an invasion, not a sneak attack. They made so much noise that they could be heard by anyone in the vicinity. As well as the Skip Jack, three

Aegis class destroyers had been assigned to watch the noisy little ship.

Inside the Hand of Mohammad, Captain Hassid believed that he had been fortunate enough not to have been seen by his enemy. They had submerged just four hours prior, and while their radar had caught the shadows of two, and possibly three of the picket ships that were supposed to be at the 100-mile line the Americans had put in place, but it was obvious that they had slipped through by keeping only the conning tower above the water line as they slowly made their way through the line.

He took this time to give the crew the good news. Opening the intercom, he spoke to the crew, telling them of their good fortune, how they were now within 80 miles of their destination and had been, so far, undetected by the over-rated Americans. He laughed at them, and called for prayers to Allah for thanks. He then turned to the dive officer and called for him to set a depth of 300 feet, just below the thermo cline.

As the Iranian ship made it to the depth of 300 feet, Skip Hutchins took the opportunity to raise its radio buoy and send another message to ComSubLant. He asked for further clarification on his orders. He felt almost bad about this turkey shoot, but he was determined to follow orders.

After only 7 minutes of waiting, his request for clarification was returned. Follow the sub; sink it if she crosses into American Territorial waters, or if she attempts to fire any weapon of any type inside the 100- mile limit. Sink the target if she opens her torpedo doors or any type of water tight hatch while submerged. Further orders were to remain behind the target and remain undetected. His orders were now extremely clear. He reeled in the buoy and shook his head. He felt bad, but he understood that these men presented a threat to the United States, and whether they were throwing rocks or nuclear weapons, his job was to keep them from harming any person or piece of property of the United States of America, and he was going to do his job.

On board the Aegis destroyer Arliegh Burke, Captain Ernst Bergland watched the noisy signature of the Iranian submarine and knew somewhere behind it was an American Ohio-class submarine that he couldn't see. He was amazed that with all his superior ASW equipment, he couldn't see the American sub. He shook his head, not believing his eyes. He slapped his ops commander on the back and said, "Keep him targeted, Ted, and we'll kill him the second he crosses the twelve mile limit." He was sure by the actions of the sub so far that it would continue until it crossed the line, and when he did, well, that would be the end of the threat. He had no concerns of it being too easy, as his counterpart on the Dolphin did. He liked the idea of painting a conning tower on the side of his missile silos.

10 miles Southwest of Isla del Coco, 12:00 Zulu, May 29, 2007

There was hysteria on board the Sword of Allah. The cook had locked himself in the pantry, and refused to come out. Only six crew members and two officers remained alive aboard the doomed ship. The captain had died six hours prior, and with him all sense of order died. Two of the remaining crew members were beating on the pantry door with what little strength they had remaining, yelling for the cook to come out. The cook, an older man originally from Tehran who had spent nearly 25 years in the Iranian Navy, who couldn't read or write, but who was magical with his chosen tools—pots and pans—was scared out of his mind. He alone seemed to be immune to the terrible disease.

He shouted for his comrades to leave him alone and go away, but they continued to pound on the door with their puny strength. The officers that were left were huddled in the control room, trying to decide what to do: turn around and return to Iran, continue on their mission, or scuttle the doomed ship and find peace at the bottom of the sea. The captain's final orders had been to continue the mission, but they were afraid. Finally, they called for all living crew members to assemble in the control room. All but the cook came forward. The decision was to abandon ship, take a life raft and try and make it to the Isla del Coco and ask the government of Costa Rica for help, but they were determined to let their ship continue its automated mission on its own.

And so it was decided. Surfacing that night, the five crewmen and two officers left the ship. Thinking that the sub would submerge by itself and sink because of the open hatch, they gladly left the fore and aft escape hatches open, but what they didn't understand about the magnificent boat was that it was smart enough to close the hatches itself before submerging. The crew and officers gladly made their way to the island, thinking the sub had sunk just off the coast in the deep water surrounding the island.

The seven were rescued by a friendly fisherman and brought to the island's only hospital. Within eight hours all seven were dead. The doctor had the bodies cremated because he feared the virus they died of. Their internal organs were literally bursting apart. It was a terrible way to die, and the doctor feared that it might already have spread to the island. He immediately called the fisherman who brought them in, as well as his family, and put them into confinement. He also put the entire island under quarantine, but it was too late. The good doctor did manage to keep the death toll to only the 82 people living on the island.

On board the Sword of Allah, only the cook remained. Still afraid to leave his pantry for fear of a trick, he knelt next to a large leg of lamb. Ordinarily, he enjoyed the quiet of isolation. He was one who didn't normally mind being alone, but suddenly he felt as if he were the only person left in the world. His mind played tricks on him. He heard doors closing. The submarine had submerged again and picked up speed. More than that he could not tell, but someone must be driving the boat, he surmised, so someone else must be alive on the ship. Suddenly, he realized that it was so quiet.

Word had gotten out to San Jose, Costa Rica about the quarantine of Coco Island. The nationality of the seven men rescued by the fisherman was unknown, just that they were middle eastern. Costa Rica didn't exactly have the best relationship with the Norte Americanos, so they kept the quarantine quiet for the next week while they determined how bad it really was and if the doctor, despite his good reputation, was simply over-reacting.

Aboard an Aegis class destroyer off the coast of the French Island known as Clipperton Island, a faint echo was picked up just north of Coco Island. The captain turned his ship and made full speed to intercept the contact, but almost as soon as he'd turned his ship to track it, the contact had gone quiet. He had a track and a speed, so he made turns to intercept it as if it was still there, and he intended to intercept it in just less than four hours.

Four hours later, the Aegis destroyer sat listening for the contact 600 miles due west of San Jose. Unbeknownst to the captain, the Sword of Allah sat silently hovering in just over 1000 feet of water almost directly beneath the destroyer, silently waiting for the warship to continue on its way so she could continue with her mission. On board the Sword of Allah, the cook opened his pantry door for the first time in two days. He feared what he would find.

What he found was an empty submarine. The crew had thrown the dead crew members overboard before leaving the ship. It was obviously not moving at the current time, but there was an eerie hum of electrical equipment in the control room; nowhere else was there any sound.

The cook began to sing, softly at first, but louder as he became more frightened. As he went from cabin to cabin, room to room, he searched for someone who was running the ship, but no one remained. He went once again to the control room and began to look around. The maps on the monitors showed that they were off the coast of South America somewhere. He wasn't sure of the name of the country, just that it was a long way off. He saw the two marks on the monitor showing his submarine in blue, and a red surface ship almost on top of him. Then he noticed the depth marker of his blue ship and his heart almost stopped. 1020 ft. Over 300 meters deep. The first thought that went through his mind was that he was sinking, but then he realized the depth was not changing. What an amazing thing, he thought to himself, over 1000 ft. under the water. His calm was short-lived as he realized he had no idea how to get the ship to surface. All he wanted to do was to get to the surface and surrender. He had no qualms about telling anyone about the mission they had been on. He'd be happy to spill everything if someone could just get him out. He grabbed the microphone he'd seen the captain use many times and shouted for help, hoping that his voice would be transmitted to the ship above. Instead, his voice boomed across the decks of the empty ship, heard by no one.

Aboard the ship, only 1000 feet away, no noise escaped the quietness of the well made submarine. The warship cranked up its engines and headed southwest to return to its picket station, hoping to pick up the contact again sometime soon.

The cook watched as the red contact ship headed off to the southwest. His yelling was obviously not working, so he stopped. He sat dejectedly in the captain's chair, not knowing what else to do. He waited for an hour before going back to the galley and cleaning up the mess made by the crew before they had left. After cleaning the galley and making himself a meal of lamb and rice, he felt the deck shift slightly under his feet. Running to the control room, he eagerly searched for whoever was responsible for starting up the submarine again, but to magnify his fear, the boat seemed to have a mind of its own. On the screen was writing that he couldn't read, but it must mean that it had decided that it was safe to continue, so it had done just that—continued heading northwest along the Central American coastline. The cook saw that they were moving at a speed of 40, and were at a depth of 800 feet. He sighed disgustedly and went back to the galley to finish his meal. He didn't know what to do except wait.

Chapter 2

Attack on the East Coast, a Diversion

100 miles South of Washington DC, 18:00 Zulu, May 29, 2007

The Hand of Mohammad was just 20 miles east of the Virginia coastline. A scant 8 miles outside the 12-mile territorial limit. Captain Hassid still believed he was invisible to the rest of the world and was reveling in his invisibility. The crew, on the other hand, was becoming very nervous. Captain Hassid's orders had to be repeated several times before they were carried out. He chided the crew for being afraid. He laughed at their fear, saying that obviously the Americans would have been picked up by their sensors if they were anywhere close. Hassid tried appealing to the crew's patriotism, saying how he would soon be in firing distance of the American coastal city of Virginia Beach, and he looked forward to sending the evil Americans a two-thousand-pound surprise package that they would never forget. He also let the crew know that it was obvious that if they could get this close, then the real attack sub would have no trouble in getting their weapon launched at the evil Americans. He himself had no doubts that his brother, Captain X, at this very moment was preparing to launch an attack on the infidel Americans. Suddenly, his sonar operator heard something somewhere close. He yelled for his captain, but the sound was gone by the time the pompous Hassid reached the listening post. He called for battle stations and called for all stop. The listening match began.

On board the Skip Jack, Skip Hutchins was furious. The pressure had not been equalized in the torpedo tube before the door had been raised. A rookie mistake by his torpedo operator, but now was not the time to bawl the young man out. He just hoped that the other submarine hadn't heard the flooding of the tube as the result of the imbalance. The answer came a moment later as the target submarine went silent, her engines dead, and she disappeared from Skip's scopes. As the target went dead, so did the Skip Jack. It was time to play the game that the Skip Jack was so good at—hide and seek.

In the meantime, Skip took the opportunity to lie down for a while. If the captain of the target vessel was any good at all, it would be several hours before there would be any movement. Knowing that, Skip decided to enjoy the quiet aboard the ship to get some shuteye. The COB took the con from the captain and stared in disbelief at the coolness of his captain. To be able to sleep at a time like this? This kid Skip was one cold customer.

On board the Arliegh Burke, Ernst Bergland also heard the sound of the flooding tube and became aware of the silence of the target sub. His orders were clear: if the tubes came open he was to kill the target, but according to his sonar operators, the tube that had opened was not on the target. He scratched his head and wondered, could it be his own American sub that he'd heard? For three years he'd been playing hide and seek with those squibs in the submarines, and in those three years he'd never heard one of the American hunter killers unless they'd wanted to be heard—usually after being found by active pinging. Was it possible that they'd opened a tube without flooding it? It hardly seemed possible, but his own men were saying they were sure that the sound hadn't come from the target. Every second he waited to respond was another second the target could be escaping. He decided to go active and see what was going on. He fired off his active sonar, pinging in the target's direction. To his surprise, the pinging painted two silhouettes: the target, and what had to be his own American submarine.

Just as Skip reached his bunk, the first ping hit his ship. Knowing that he had just been found, he grabbed the microphone on the wall and called for flank speed on a heading 180 degrees away from the target vessel, wanting to know who had pinged them. The response—the American destroyer a few thousand meters to their starboard.

Just as surprised by the ping was the Hand of Mohammed and Captain Hassid. The operator of the sonar yelled out the discovery of a surface ship doing the pinging and a submarine 5000 meters to their stern that had suddenly appeared in the waves of sound, illuminating them both. The submarine to their stern reacted first, turning and heading away from the smaller Iranian sub. That action cemented Captain Hassid's actions. Yelling for flank speed, he also turned to chase the retreating submarine, ignoring the surface ship.

As the two submarines turned, the sonar operator on the Arliegh Burke identified the first as an American sub and the second as the target ship.

It was then that Captain Hassid made his last mistake; he ordered the torpedo doors opened and a snapshot to be made. The torpedo tube doors slid open in response to the command, and two deadly fish slashed away from the ship.

At the moment the doors to the torpedo tubes came open on the Iranian vessel, Skip entered the control room and ordered his own torpedoes, already targeted, to be fired. Before the Iranian torpedoes could clear their chambers, the two torpedoes from the Skip Jack were already making a U-turn toward their target.

Aboard the Arliegh Burke, an excited sonar man shouted "Fish in the water...1, 2, 3, 4..."

"I make it four torpedoes in the water, two headed for one sub and two headed for the other."

Captain Bergland shouted out to fire his own two torpedoes at the Iranian target sub.

Now six torpedoes were in the water, and both subs were moving at flank speed. Captain Hassid never had the chance to turn his sub away from the onrushing torpedoes. Both of the torpedoes fired by the Skip Jack hit the submarine— one hitting the bow and exploding, while the second exploded as it reached the conning tower. Captain Hassid never heard the second explosion. The two torpedoes from the Arliegh Burke found no remaining submarine at the target location and so began to circle, actively pinging, searching for a new target. At the same time that the two began pinging, they found the Skip Jack making turns for 40 knots and trying desperately to throw the two torpedoes, stalking her off track.

The Skip Jack's captain called for a hard turn to port, causing a knuckle of bubbles to form at the rear of the ship. At the same time, Skip ordered two decoys released from the rear of the sub, making the sounds of an Ohio-class submarine, headed 90 degrees to their starboard. Calling for another turn to port he released two more decoys. The first of the two torpedoes took the bait of the first decoy and exploded, shaking the Skip Jack like a rag doll in the mouth of a large dog. The second torpedo was shaken as well and passed through the knot of bubbles and came out the other side, losing track of the American submarine. Like the other torpedoes in the water, it would not wait long before actively pinging and re-acquire the American sub.

Now there were two torpedoes actively pursuing the American sub, roughly 8000 meters behind, and one torpedo 2000 meters starboard, lost and beginning to circle slowly to the left. As the two torpedoes locked on the American sub they began their quick acceleration to 60 knots. As the Skip Jack retreated, she had roughly 40 seconds before they would catch her. Skip shouted for the reactor to be pushed to 110 percent, giving them another 20 seconds of life. He searched for a thermo cline to hide under. He was fully alive. As he pushed the boat, he prayed that the remaining decoys would do their job. As he pushed his boat below a thermo cline, he released two more decoys and made a hard turn to the port.

Aboard the Arliegh Burke, the sounds of the Iranian ship imploding told Captain Bergland that his country was safe, but he wasn't so sure about his brothers aboard the American submarine. He ordered his two torpedoes to self-destruct. In response, there was a loud crash of one torpedo blowing itself up. What he didn't know was that the destruction of one had destroyed the second as well. The water suddenly vaporized by more than a ton of TNT. As the second torpedo fell into the void left by the vaporization of twenty tons of water, the crashing of the water into the void smashed the second torpedo, breaking it into four harmless sections. Still, the ringing of a single torpedo tearing through the ocean echoed in the ears of the sonar operators of both the Arliegh Burke and the Skip Jack. The remaining torpedo from the Iranian sub had now locked on to the Skip Jack and was accelerating to its top speed of 55 knots.

Aboard the Skip Jack, the captain asked for time to impact.

"2 minutes 30 seconds," came the reply.

The Skip Jack streaked away from the torpedo as fast as she could run. Skip felt more confident than he had thirty seconds earlier. He prayed that he could get the torpedo to go below the thermo cline before it got too close. He ordered more depth. As the sub responded, the torpedo also increased its angle of descent. The timing would have to be perfect. As the torpedo crossed the thermo cline, he would have to cross it in the other direction at exactly the same instant. He continued to wait, raising his depth to just below the line of temperature. As the torpedo crossed the line, he pushed his sub above the line, releasing a single decoy to head downward and to the port side while he called for a quick ascent and a hard starboard turn.

The torpedo wavered in the water, staying below the thermo cline and then settling in on the decoy. As it passed through the spinning decoy, it was confused to not find a ship to destroy. At the same moment that the torpedo passed through the decoy, the Skip Jack shut down all power and played dead in the water. The torpedo went back to its programming and began searching for another target. Finding nothing but empty water, it circled below the thermo cline for another twenty minutes before running out of energy and slowly falling to the sea floor. The Skip Jack came back to life and collectively sighed in relief as it moved slowly back toward the surface so it could report the activity to ComSubLant.

Washington D.C., 21:00 Zulu, May 29, 2007

Admiral Davidson was not a happy man. He had almost lost one of his submarines and had been involved in the sinking of Iran's military assets in international waters just off America's coast. While he was sure that his men had acted per orders, it wouldn't help them when they were being accused by the Iranians of sinking their ship "without provocation," as he was sure they'd say. He had the tapes of the incident on the way, and the audio tapes of the incident were already in his hands. He knew no matter what he said, his side would never make the evening news. Only what that crackpot little Iranian said would be treated like truth stated by the pope. This was not going to go well, no matter what information they had. He didn't like where this was no doubt going to go.

The White House, 10:00 Zulu, May 30, 2007

President Beechum hadn't slept well and was up early to deal with the impending crisis. She had half expected a call from the Iranian president all night long. To her surprise, CNN hadn't gotten hold of the story yet. They seemed to have a quicker tap into the events affecting the Middle East than did her own NSA. But not this time. Dave Benson sat opposite the president, eating a danish and swishing it down with Earl Grey Tea.

"Dave, I still don't know how you can drink tea instead of coffee like everyone else," the president said, breaking the silence.

"Nasty habit I picked up while I was living in England," he responded. "I just never liked the taste of coffee and didn't see the need at the time to force myself to drink it for the caffeine. When I did need the caffeine, all I could get in England was tea. Perils of the trade, I guess."

"What are we going to do, Dave?" the president asked for the first time this morning.

"We can't wait and let CNN break it as a story before we say something, Debra. If that happens no one will ever hear our side of it," replied Dave.

"You're right, of course, but I don't have a clue how to make it sound reasonable without detailing everything we know. If we do that we will endanger all of our assets as well as our ally's assets in the Middle East," the president lamented.

Her NSA chief rubbed his eyes and then brushed the final crumbs from his lap into the napkin. "If they haven't contacted anyone yet, it must mean that they're not sure he's dead. Maybe we can handle this differently."

"How?" came her terse reply.

✠

Across the pond, the Minister of MI6, Sir Dalton Brand, wondered why he hadn't heard from his counterpart at CIA. Thirteen hours and no contact, they almost certainly knew that the Royal Navy had assets in the area and had heard everything. Maybe it was time to make a call himself, he half decided. At almost the same instant the phone rang. "About bloody time," he said aloud.

There was a leak in the CIA. Dave Benson was aware of it, and knew that they had at most another day before CNN would be running the story of a submarine lost just off the Virginia coast. Maybe he could run it to ground and make things better for themselves. He called Bill Elliot first, giving him a blow by blow of the events but telling him that it occurred inside US territorial waters just 4 hours prior, when in reality it was outside territorial waters nearly 14 hours ago. After setting the trap, he made sure to tell Bill not to let anyone else at the CIA or elsewhere know. This was going to be handled by the president herself, and she wanted it quiet. Bill smiled and drawled out a slow, "No problem, Dave."

Dalton Brand visibly blinked in surprise when Dave contacted him and relayed the information at hand. Dave didn't hold anything back, including the leak at the CIA that they were hoping to clear up. He told the minister to expect a call from Bill, and not to blow his story. Dave knew that the Brits would know exactly where the ship was sunk and exactly when. He asked for their help in chasing down their mole, and to please not blow the story but to contact him when and if it came to the minister's attention. The minister put down the phone and gasped at the audacity of the NSA chief to not trust his own CIA chief. Things are obviously not going well across the pond, he thought. He scarcely had time for another thought before the hot line rang again. This time it was Elliot.

Bill probed the minister for corroborating data. He plays the game well, thought Dalton Brand. Bill Elliot hadn't made it to his current position by being stupid. He smelled a setup, but he couldn't see it yet. Dave is being entirely too helpful, he thought. Even Dalton Brand was being too forthcoming. Then again, maybe he was being too paranoid. Slowly, he let down his guard and decided he was worrying too much.

Bill Elliot hung up the phone with Dalton Brand and was sure that he had the full story now and he had what he needed to put some real pressure on that damn woman in the White House. It would have been better if the sub had been sunk outside the 12 mile limit, but inside was good enough, he thought. A few leaked phone calls to the appropriate Democrats and the right press rooms and Debra Beecham would soon be turning in her resignation. He'd never gotten over the sting of being bypassed for the NSA position, and soon he'd extract his revenge. According to Dave, the CIA, FBI, and Homeland Security had all been notified and his leaking to the press could have happened by any one of the agencies. What Bill Elliot didn't know was that each agency had been given a different story, each with a different twist, and each agency head had been given strict instructions not to divulge the story to anyone in their organization or elsewhere. The trap had been set. Bill Elliot turned to his DDI and shook his head, motioning him to go ahead.

The DDI went to his office and called an 800 number that was guaranteed to be anonymous for CNN contributors in the Washington D.C. area. CNN had set up the line just for people like himself who wanted to let the news agency know something confidential without revealing their own identification. After two rings a young man answered the phone, with a bored sounding "hullo."

After listening more intently for the next minute, he excitedly interrupted the DDI saying, "Hold on a minute. I've got to get an anchor on the line with you—please!" he pleaded.

"No way," the DDI said. "Just listen and get it right. The US Navy just sank a submarine inside our 12-mile territorial limit four hours ago. It was an Iranian naval submarine, and it was attacked without warning by assets of the US Navy. The question is, did our president have reason to attack that submarine?"

The DDI then hung up and felt oddly sick at his stomach. He didn't like the games being played by the CIA director, but stiffening his back he took a deep breath and knew that it was the only way he'd ever make it to the next step up the ladder. If Dave Benson were pushed out, then Bill was a shoe-in for NSA chief, and he'd already been promised by Bill that he'd be the one promoted to CIA Director.

11:30 Zulu, May 30, 2007

CNN interrupted their regular morning news to break the story across the nation. Soon not only CNN but every news agency was clamoring at the door to the White House press room, begging the president's staff for any information or confirmation of the story. CNN, having no concern for the confidentiality they promised, had analyzed the tape recorded voice of the DDI and had already identified who the man at the other end of the phone was, and was identifying him as a "senior CIA official" instead of a confidential informant.

Debra Beecham and Dave Benson were watching CNN together in the president's personal office. She turned to Dave, rubbing her hands together, and said, "From being told not to say anything to CNN live in less than one hour, which has to be a record Dave?"

"You're right, Debra. We've got Bill dead to rights. The real question is, is there anyone else in the loop?"

"How will you find out?" Debra questioned her NSA Chief.

"He'll tell us!" Dave said emphatically. "We've got him cold, and if I know Bill, he'll do anything we ask to save as much of his skin as he can. Just know that we won't do anything illegal, but we'll push him as far as we can to get everyone involved. In the mean time, we've turned this into an incident inside our own territorial waters, instead of having to deal with it outside our waters, as long as the Brits continue to play on our side."

"That's a dangerous game, Dave," Debra Beecham replied. "You know I'll have to disavow any knowledge of this deception should things go wrong. You'll have to take the fall yourself."

"I understand, Madam President," Dave replied. "It's my game and I'll play it as long as it doesn't hurt you or your administration."

"Dave, be careful," the President said, showing more concern than just a boss to an employee. "I don't want to see you hurt either," she said with real concern in her voice.

The phone rang on her desk just then and her secretary informed her that both the FBI chief and the Director of Homeland Security were on the line looking for Dave Benson, both saying it was an emergency. Dave took the calls together. Hamilton Cordova and Alex Rice were both confused by the CNN reports and were worried about the misinformation. Both Ham and Alex had been told the event had happened inside the 12- mile limit, but Ham had been given the time of 2 hours prior and Alex the time of 8 hours prior. Dave put the phone on speaker and addressed both men.

"Ham, Alex, I'm sorry that I had to mislead you on the truth of what took place, but as you know, we've been dealing with someone passing information to the press before we were ready to deal with it so I gave each of you, as well as Bill, loaded information."

Silence engulfed the other offices that could only be described as being beyond quiet. "Dave, I swear I didn't tell anyone I swear," Hamilton Cordova spoke quietly and grimly, "but I sure don't like being used this way!"

"That goes for me as well, Dave," came the terse reply of Alex Rice. "Was Bill told the same thing we were?" Rice asked.

"Not exactly the same thing," came Dave's reply.

"Was he told 4 hours ago?" This time it was Ham.

"Yes!" Dave replied tersely. "Ham, I'll need you to go with me to visit Bill this afternoon. What he has done could be construed as treason."

The words struck both men with the reality of the situation.

"I know that you gentlemen have followed my instructions not to speak about the incident, but unfortunately, Mr. Elliot has proven himself to be the leak. I plan on using that information for the best use I can for this administration and for our country," Dave opined.

Both men felt mildly better about not being accused of being the leak, and a bit more fearful about how easily they themselves might have been in the same situation that Bill now was about to find himself in. They both now realized that Dave was playing hardball, and they both made a mental note not to put themselves into Bill's position.

"Okay, Dave," came Ham's reply. "Do I need to bring my handcuffs?"

"Bring your handcuffs and at least two good agents. I'm calling the Attorney General next to find out what all we can charge him with. And gentlemen, don't speak of any of this to anyone. Got it?"

"Yes sir," came the dual reply from both Ham and Alex.

"Dave?" Alex spoke.

"Yes, Alex."

"Don't ever use me that way again." Alex's voice sounded low and hard.

"Alex, I'll do whatever I need to do to get my job done and to catch someone who hurts this administration by leaking information. If that bothers you, let me know and I'll find someone who is willing to do whatever it takes to do your job as well." Dave's voice was non-threatening, but carried a sense of fact, not threat. His voice softened just a bit as he said, "I didn't like having to play anyone, but it was necessary to catch the person who was doing this. I hope you will think about it and understand, Alex. It's just the way it is today."

Alex grunted an "okay," but it was obvious that Dave's relationship with both Ham and Alex had been strained.

The sound of two phones hanging up unceremoniously sounded in the ears of both the president and her NSA chief.

Tehran, Iran, 11:30 Zulu, May 30, 2007

President Ahmadinejad knew the time was close for the firing of the missile. He had heard the CNN broadcast telling the world that his submarine had been killed inside US territorial waters at lunchtime, but his mind was more intent on his billion dollar attack than on the loss of an old diesel submarine that couldn't sneak up on a deaf man. He knew an opportunity when he saw one, and this was definitely an opportunity.

He asked his personal advisor Jimji, "What is the mood of my people this fine day, Jimji?"

"The mood is somber and quiet, Oh Mighty King," came his reply. Quite often Jimji would refer to the president as "my King" to make it clear that Jimji knew who was in command and for how long. Even if there were elections every 8 years—and there were—Jimji and everyone else knew today who would be elected until Ahmadinejad passed away.

Ahmadinejad shook his head in disbelief. "Must I always tell my people how to think?" he asked rhetorically. "A submarine of our mighty country is destroyed by those imperialistic demons in the US, and our people are somber? Jimji, make sure that our people realize the importance of this event and that they have the motivation they need, as well as the signs and flags that they need to show their proper mood."

"It will be done before nightfall, Oh Great One!"

"I want it for the evening edition of the Al Jazeera news so the Americans will be watching it on CNN during their lunches."

He called his writer, Adjahadeen, to him as well. "Amir, my fine writer," he spoke flowingly, "I need the story that we discussed last week," Ahmadinejad said.

"Which one, Mr. President?"

"The one that talks about how it is a lie that the submarine was inside their territorial waters," Ahmadinejad responded.

"Yes, Mr. President. I have it ready for transmission as we speak and I can have it in the offices of CNN and Al

Jazeera within 5 minutes, sir," he responded, clicking his heels together in an unconscious mimic of the little German bootlickers of the 1930s and 40s.

Jimji almost laughed at the obvious brown-nosing that Amir couldn't help but lay onto the President. Jimji knew when to lay it on, and did so frequently for the self-aggrandizing president, but he also could tell that Amir couldn't help himself. Amir was really in love with the man. It is almost sickening, Jimji thought. Amir really believed the crap that Ahmadinejad said. Even being this close to the lying little despot had not dissuaded Amir from believing the lies that this president spewed forth continually.

"Make it so, Amir," Ahmadinejad said. "Let the world know that we have been wronged by the Great Satan, and that we will not allow it to happen. We will take our revenge upon her as we wish, and when we wish!"

"Yes, my president!" Amir replied glowingly. He turned and rushed back to his office. Good to his word, the prepared document was faxed to Al Jazeera, and e-mailed to CNN within 5 minutes.

Washington DC, 11:45 Zulu, May 30, 2007

CNN interrupted the hot debate just getting started between a washed up Republican ex-speechwriter, and one of the new Democratic sharp-tongued up-and-comers that everyone loved. The Iranians had already responded. The announcer loved this.

"President Ahmadinejad has obviously taken this very seriously to have responded so quickly and so vehemently," the announcer crooned.

"Yes, Ted," the co-anchor chimed in, wanting to be heard from as well. "Looking at the verbiage he uses and his beautifully flowing dialog, the intelligence of President Ahmadinejad is obvious."

"How our own US Navy could have made the mistake of sinking an Iranian submarine outside the US territorial boundaries for no reason is beyond me," Ted responded.

The Republican speechwriter pointed out that CNN themselves had reported the incident as having taken place inside territorial waters only to be ignored by the Democrats who were already smelling blood in the water.

The co-anchor jumped into the conversation again, saying, "Ms. Beecham is obviously behind this debacle. It has her Wild West gun slinging signature all over this."

"I agree, Charley," said Ted. "We'll have the entire 10-page response from the Iranian government and President Ahmadinejad available on our website for everyone to read at your convenience."

"In the mean time, here are a few of the pertinent points made by President Ahmadinejad." With that, the screen rolled with the inflammatory lies from the Iranian president. He spoke of the riots already happening in the streets of Tehran that were supposedly a response to the deaths of the Iranian heroes of the Hand of Mohammed.

The microphone of the lone Republican had been silenced after his last comment, and even though he fought to be heard, his Democratic counterpart made point after point of how lost the current administration seemed to be and how poorly it was handling the situation. It mattered not what the truth was or what was actually happening, CNN made sure that as much political fodder as could be made was being made.

The White House, 12:00 Zulu, May 30, 2007

"It's just a little strange, isn't it," said Dave.

"What's that?" Debra replied.

"Fifteen minutes from announcement to 10-page response to both CNN and Al Jazeera with obvious refinements by his best speech writer."

"Superman couldn't have responded that fast with a written document." Dave smiled.

"And those dolts at CNN are licking it up just like Ahmadinejad knew they would." Debra responded, though not smiling as Dave had done. "They're crucifying us," she continued.

"Not to worry, Debra, I've got my own counter in the making. I just hope we got the one that was going to attack us. We still have another one to find—the one with the real weapon aboard."

Debra's brow was furrowed as she responded. "I'm counting on you, Dave!" She turned back to the TV sets in her office, switching between the news channels. Only FOX News was doing a halfway competent job of reporting facts.

CNN had quit reporting news back during the first Clinton administration and had gone into trying to promote the Democrat's into ownership of the White House. Now they were little more than the Democratic party's political slander wing. The other "Big Three," as they used to be known—ABC, NBC, and CBS—were not much better. With 98 percent of all the reporters and news anchors being registered Democrats, the nightly news had long since quit being news and had become the nightly commentary on what the Republicans had done wrong and how much better it would be to have a Democrat making the decisions.

FOX News did jump to the same conclusions that Dave had. At least someone there is thinking, Debra thought. She pushed a button on her desk, alerting her secretary. "Doreen, contact my press secretary immediately and clear some time for me for a press conference as soon as possible."

"Yes Ma'am," came Doreen's reply.

For the next six hours the news media did a blitz on how and why the president wasn't responding. As promised, Jimji had rounded up some 500 "outraged" Iranians that he used the last time he'd needed them, and supplied them with puppets modeled after the American president, and lots of American flags, along with gasoline, torches and plenty of pre-printed anti-American signs. They had paraded around the gates of the American Embassy in Tehran, and thrown rocks at the American soldiers, and culminated the riot by burning the president in effigy while draped in an

American flag. Jimji had outdone himself by coming up with 50 or so wooden boxes, actually too small to be coffins for adults, but shaped correctly, that he had presented to the mob with the intent to pretend that they were sons and daughters of the sailors who had killed themselves in anguish over the loss of their fathers at the hands of the Great Satan.

While pundits of the political left kept asking why the president hadn't responded, the president herself was spitting nails. Her air time had been pushed back 4 times because of "scheduling conflicts," first by CNN, and then followed in suit by ABC, CBS, and NBC. It was a game, one that the News media knew far too well how to play. Now CNN was up to bat again, saying that they needed another delay for just one more hour. Debra Beechum had had enough.

"Not just no, but hell no" she all but screamed at the CNN head when called to make the request.

"But Madam Pres—" was as far as he got before she silenced him with her own words.

"You can just not be a part of the news conference if you can't make it now." She calmed herself. "In fact, sir, I don't want you or any of your staff to be there. As of this moment, you and your NEWS team are persona-non-gratta in the White House."

She could hear the strangled-sounding words just escaping the CNN news chief as she hung up the phone.

She turned to her press secretary, whose face had just changed from red to white to ashen all in the matter of the last 30 seconds. "Madam President," he stammered, "you can't be serious."

"I can, I am, and I will," she replied back without blinking. "Make it so, Joseph," she pushed further.

"Yes Ma'am," came his dubious reply. He shook his head, already hearing the complaints and tantrums he'd have to endure for this decision. As with most Washington bureaucrats, he was more concerned about getting along with those he had to deal with every day so when the current administration left power he'd have a job to go into when it went out.

"You scratch my back, and I'll scratch yours" was more than a slogan in Washington DC; it was life. It was what made DC go around. If you didn't play ball with the media, you'd never make it here, and Joseph—with college loans, two kids, two ex-wives, a large home, and a desire for the finer things in life—needed to make it here. He was an up-and-comer—everyone said so—and he'd be darned if this president's temper tantrum would ruin his career while things had been going so well for him. With that in mind, he placed a call to the news head for CNN, using his cell phone's speed dial.

After two rings, the CNN chief answered. "Well, Joseph, did you hear that lunatic?"

"Yes, John, I did, and don't worry. I'll have you in for the entire thing without a hitch."

"You'd better hope so, old boy, or you'll never work in this town after next year again!"

"Calm down, John," came the soothing voice of the press secretary. "I've got it all fixed right now," he lied. "No one will dare press me on what I say." He almost believed in his own self-importance.

"Okay then, Joseph. I knew I'd be able to count on you. You've got a real future here, my boy, a real future," the old Englishman soothed, lying just as easily as had the young press secretary. Both men hung up, feeling equally full of themselves.

The White House Press Room, 18:30 Zulu, May 30, 2007

The press conference began with the introduction of Dave Benson, who would be laying out the facts, then would be followed by a statement by the president. Dave started his presentation by replaying the "breaking story," as told by CNN. The CNN news chief grinned broadly at the "scoop" his agency had gotten ahead of the others seated in the room. He looked around the room for his "source" and thought it odd that Bill hadn't made it to the briefing; it wasn't like him. Dave called attention to CNN's scoop.

"CNN really got there first on this story, Ladies and Gentlemen. It got there so fast that it failed to check into the facts of the story, as has been their typical modus operandi. Ladies and Gentlemen, here are the facts: Dave played the tapes from the un-named submarine skipper and destroyer skipper. He detailed on a map the exact location of the Iranian submarine, and even managed to produce some muffled but understandable dialog from on-board the Iranian submarine, giving away the plan Hassid had for firing his two-thousand-pound weapon at Virginia Beach, Virginia. After detailing the entire event from start to finish for the press, he opened the floor for questions.

John, from CNN, his brow well furrowed, was furious. He jumped up immediately, yelling from the back row. Dave noticed him and pointed in his direction.

"John, I'm surprised to see you here," he said calmly.

"I'll bet you are," snarled John, his two anchor's sliding down in their chairs not far away. "I want to know why you lied to the American public this way!"

"Why, what ever do you mean, John?" came Dave's reply.

"You told us that the attack had taken place within our territorial waters and gave us the wrong time. Trying to make us look bad?" he almost shouted.

"I beg to differ with you, John. If you will listen to your own newscast, you'll hear your anchor say those things. Not once did a representative of this administration say any such thing. You've got to quit believing your own made-up news flashes, John."

John turned purple and almost choked as he spat out the words Dave had hoped to hear. "But we got that information from Bill Elliot on the confidential line. We've paid him well for that information in the past," he sputtered before his own admission was realized.

"You mean to tell me, John, that your confidential line isn't confidential, and that you've been suborning members of the United States Government to give you information that can only be described as State Secrets?" Dave purred. I'll be contacting the Attorney General's office to see if you and your organization have violated the Laws of Treason and if further action need be taken in this matter." This was better than he had hoped for. "By the way John, I believe the president made it clear to you earlier that you and your staff were no longer welcome in this briefing room. You need to leave now. You may pick up your equipment at a time when it is convenient to us, and after we've had an opportunity to examine it to make sure it conforms to all FCC guidelines and rules."

John sputtered another threat in the general direction of Dave Benson and stared icily at Joseph as he tried desperately to regain his composure. CNN's feed was cut and a group of Marines appeared from out of nowhere to escort the CNN contingent out of the building. John shouted as he left the room, "You can't silence the press, Madam President."

But silence was exactly what met his ears as he was bustled out the door, silence that was so loud that the remaining press was dumbfounded.

Dave broke the mood with "Any other questions? From a reputable news agency perhaps?" That met with a few scattered but muffled laughs. It was no secret within the news world that John was a pompous ass that played the game unfairly, but he was powerful, and most of the people in the room feared his power. Even so, everyone there felt a little lighter and bubblier as a result of the encounter.

"Frank Hill of FOX News," came a new voice. "How did you get the feed from the Iranian submarine?"

"Needless to say, Frank, the assets we had in the area were very close indeed. Without giving away our own secrets, we do have the ability to capture the signals from internal closed circuit systems if we are very close. We were very close," came Dave's reply. "Next..."

After several more questions about the technology used in the briefing, the press seemed to have been quieted, and

Dave introduced the president and she read a prepared statement.

The statement was succinct and to the point. "Any foreign vessel making an attempt to hide from view within our territorial waters or making an attempt to do harm in any way to the United States, her citizens, or her military assets, no matter where they are, will be deemed an enemy of the United States and will be prosecuted by whatever means we deem necessary to deal with the threat without further warning."

It was clearly a warning. The reporters looked solemn and scratched notes as they sought to define their own angle on the story. After reading the statement, the president turned to go, but she was immediately inundated with questions.

"Madam President, please, why this change in policy?" It was ABC's anchorman.

"This is not a change in policy, sir," she responded coldly. "This is the same policy we've had for generations. I'm just reiterating it for those such as Mr. Ahmadinejad, who seem to not take our policies seriously. Perhaps he will realize that our policies, whether we state them regularly or not, are not to be tested. I hope so, because we will protect our shores by whatever means we may wish to do so, whenever and wherever we deem it necessary."

"Madam President, if it's not a change in policy then why the press conference?" This time it was NBC.

"You're not listening, Elizabeth." Debra shook her head. "We just sank another nations asset of war, just twenty miles off of our nations shoreline, boasting how they would destroy an American city with their technology. This is not a small incident over lost luggage or mineral rights or even trade deficits. They wanted to kill American citizens right here on our own homeland...and we have stopped them—this time. The press conference is to allow you, the press, to do the job you are supposed to do—to report the true facts and to warn our own citizens of the dangers posed by foreign governments to our people. We need you to let our people know that we, the US Government, are doing our job and are protecting its citizens as promised, and also so that you can warn the peoples of foreign nations what their own governments are up to. Hopefully, they will see the deadly games their governments are playing and will overthrow the yoke of tyranny that holds them constrained. I know that it is much to hope for, but if you, the keepers of the fourth estate, will hold firm to your role in presenting truth, this country and others like it will prevail in giving government, by the people, to the whole world."

Silence swept the room again, this time from the effect of the president's words. She turned again and headed for the door but slowed and stopped as the silence was broken by first a single man's clapping, then followed by others as the press corps stood together en masse, saluting their president the only way they knew how, with a standing ovation.

As she exited the press room, she motioned for Joseph and Dave to follow her into her office. Joseph had been trying for the entire time of the press conference to come up with a suitable excuse for why John and the CNN crew had been allowed in. He was sure that he had a good alibi, but he was still curious as to how he was going to fix the problem of getting the president and CNN's news chief back on the same page. He couldn't have been further away from what he needed to worry about.

"Joseph," the president began, "before I react, I want to know if I have been misunderstood in any way about what I wanted as far as CNN and John were concerned."

"No Ma'am," came Joseph's reply. "It's just that..."

"Joseph, I don't care about excuses. You were told that they were persona non gratta and that they were not to be allowed into the press room."

"Yes Ma'am, I know, but I didn't think you really meant it in those terms, Ma'am. I just knew you couldn't really mean that CNN wasn't welcome in the press room." Joseph was still incredulous at the very idea of it.

"Joseph," the President stated, "you work directly for the President of the United States of America. Does that not mean anything to you? Do you not recognize that the office of the President of the United States is a bit more important than CNN?" Now it was the president's turn to be incredulous. "Joseph, I'm very sorry that it has to be this way, but I can't have someone working for me that can't follow my orders, especially orders given so directly and so firmly. I want your resignation on my desk within the hour."

"What?" came Joseph's reply. "I can't believe you mean this. I've smoothed over so many problems for you with CNN and the other networks. I've been there to help you be understood by the news agencies when they wanted to crucify you. And you treat me like this? I can't believe it!"

"Believe it, Joseph. If I'd wanted you to smooth over things for me, I'd have asked you to do it. What you're really saying is you've mislead me as to what is really going on in the hopes of keeping a friendship going between you and the news agencies. Well, now you'll be able to devote full time to getting in close with those agencies. Maybe John at CNN will have a job for you, since you obviously chose to answer to him over your current boss. Good luck, Joseph— and I really mean that," she said. "I wish you no ill will, only that you might learn loyalty to your employer in your next job."

Joseph turned in a huff and marched out of the office toward his own office to collect his personal items.

"That's two direct employees today that I've had to fire. I'm not going to win any popularity contests tonight, am I?" she quipped.

"Not to worry, Debra, you're doing fine with the people that matter. Reports are already coming in on your Q & A after the statement, and all reports are great. The people of this country of ours love the fact that you care about them and that you are working to save them from terrorists like Ahmadinejad. Now if we can keep the spin doctors of the left from trying to make us look like cowboys trying to start a war..." Dave replied. "By the way, we still have yet to locate our other sub that the first sub commander talked about. He must be just about in position."

West coast of the Baja Peninsula, 00:00 Zulu, May 31, 2007

Three more times the submarine had come to a stop and had started itself back up. Three times the ship's cook had yelled and pounded on the doorway to the command center with a wrench, hoping to draw attention to his plight. But it was not to be. The sword of Allah was too quiet and too stealthy to let it get into close range of another deadly submarine. The cook looked at the screen for the 100th time since being marooned alone on board the ship, but this time he reached up and touched the blue ship on the screen. To his astonishment, it began to flash as if it understood he wanted to talk to the ship. He cried out and spoke in rough but understandable Farsi. No effect. He shouted out for the ship to surface. Again, no change took place, only the constant feeling of silent movement through the water. To his dismay, the blue ship on the screen quit blinking, so he reached up and touched the screen again this time touching the numbers that indicated the 1000-ft. depth. As the number began to flash, the cook went to the keyboard and typed in "40," having heard that forty feet was surface depth during the training runs. To his astonishment, the ship began to rise. He watched the number climb ever so slowly up to 40 ft. He then walked to the escape hatch and opened the door.

To his surprise, the door opened easily and a fresh sea breeze blew into the hatch, but he was still traveling at nearly 25 knots. He walked back to the control room and touched the screen again, this time slowing the boat down to 0. He then went back to the escape hatch, donned a life jacket and jumped into the warm waters of the Pacific Ocean. Knowing he was only a few miles from the coast of the Baja peninsula, the cook decided to take his chances with making it to shore. He didn't care what happened to the submarine; part of him wanted it to sink. He had left the hatch open and he prayed to Allah that a wave would fill its contents and it would sink. Twenty minutes later he finally lost sight of the submarine's superstructure. He continued slowly but methodically, swimming to the east. His father had shown him how to spot the Northern Star, and he used that knowledge now to guide him eastward. Each stroke, taking him closer to the peninsula of Baja, and to Mexico— who knew. Maybe he'd survive and lose himself in the country of Mexico. He had nothing to return to in Iran, and after all, he'd heard stories of the beautiful Mexican women... Maybe he'd find out for himself.

Thirty minutes later, at approximately 00:50 Zulu time, the Sword of Allah, now abandoned completely, closed its hatches, submerged, and continued on its course to a point just north of San Diego Harbor, not far off shore from La Jolla, a perfect path with well viewable alignment points that would take a cruise missile from that point to its ultimate target of Lake Meade. There were quite a few ships in the area, and that was what had prompted the Sword of Allah to submerge and continue on its mission. It was on its way once again.

San Diego Coast Line, 01:00 Zulu, June 1, 2007

Twenty four hours later, the Sword of Allah reached its firing location, exactly twenty-one hours ahead of schedule. Upon reaching its firing location, the Sword of Allah found a level portion of sea floor and came in as close as it dared, then sank slowly to the bottom, turning all its systems to a sleep state and making sure that all electronic systems were turned to a sleep state as well. Several US Navy ships passed within a mile of the sleeping predator, actively pinging and listening for any sound that might give away a sneaking death ship so they could kill it, but it was of no use while the Sword remained at rest. Even going right over the top of it, even the most sophisticated of sonar would have had a hard time spotting the ship. It would have taken a side-scan sonar moving slowly back and forth along with a magnetometer in conjunction to determine that something was down there. And so the sword remained undetected by the US Navy's best ASW gear.

Chapter 3

Las Vegas, a Convention in Town

Las Vegas Nevada, June 1, 2007

Naomi looked around the auspices of her new suite at the MGM Grand Hotel. It is beautiful, spacious and huge, she thought to herself. The week had been full with getting everything ready for the presentation. She was thrilled at how well the simple language interface was working. Her presentation was just a few hours away and JD had spent the week working with her on the slides, as well as tweaking a few lines of code that had really sped up the interface. What a glorious week it had been for them both. It was almost like a vacation away from the stress she had put on herself for the past two years. Even though they had shared a room, they hadn't shared a bed. It was something unsaid between them; they both felt the love for each other, and on more than one occasion they had come close to succumbing to the pleasures of the flesh, but both respected each other too much to fall into the trap of easy sex. There had never been any pressure by JD to push her into that, and she had made it clear that she respected his abstinence and she found it even more enticing for her.

She shook her head to clear it of her thoughts and to try and focus on her immediate issues. JD would be staying for the breakout session but would be leaving soon afterward.

"JD, do I have a chance with you, or will you always let a mistress stand between us?" Her frankness took JD by surprise.

"Naomi, you know how I feel about you. How can you think I have a mistress somewhere else?" His face was flush and his voice tinged slightly with anger.

"The sea, JD, the sea..." She laughed.

"Oh, I understand," he said sheepishly. "I don't know, Naomi. You know that I love you and I don't have any problem saying so, but right now I need to know that I won't be hurting you or leaving you in the lurch when I need to be away doing my research. I won't be the one to hurt you ever." He seemed to be tormented by the question she'd asked.

"JD, don't you worry." Naomi smiled. "I'm not pushing, and I was just being wistful for the moment. It's been such a wonderful week with you and I wish we could go on without it ending." She sighed.

"I know, Naomi, and I feel the same way. That's why I'm tormented, to love the sea and to love you as well tears at my heart, especially at times like these, but I have work that I must do. It calls to me. There is more. I feel it, I just don't know what it is yet, but I do know that when it presents itself I'll know it."

"Enough of this somber mood," Naomi said and smiled. "Lets go get a bite to eat before the breakout session. The last thing I need is to have my stomach grumbling in front of 500 potential customers."

"Naomi", said JD in mock disbelief, "I've never seen you holding back this way. Why don't you quit hiding your thoughts and say what you really mean?" he said, laughing.

She laughed along with him.

"You know you always start thinking of food when you're nervous," JD chided.

"I know. You'd better keep me satisfied or you'll end up with a two- hundred-pound girlfriend by next week." She punched him in the side.

"Yeah, right." He pushed her back. "I'd like to see you gain a hundred pounds in a week." He eyed her sleek figure behind the form- fitting dress she had chosen for her presentation. "If you looked any better I'd start to get worried about some slick-talking millionaire coming and sweeping you off your feet." JD half joked.

"Don't worry about it handsome," Naomi cut her eyes enticingly at JD, and leaned toward him to give him a kiss.

"Naomi," he stammered, "you complete me," he cooed, copying Tom Cruise.

She giggled and replied, "You had me at hello, you handsome hunk you, but you've got to promise not to jump on Oprah's couch over me." She laughed again and said, "Take me out for lunch now, you big hunk, and I'll follow you anywhere."

"I promise," he responded, and then made a beeline for the couch in the corner of the room, acting like the goofy actor on the Oprah show.

The two locked arms and headed out of the room and down to the buffet at the back of the hotel. Neither one would have believed the drama unfolding around them.

San Diego Coast Line, 04:00 Zulu, June 2, 2007

The Sword of Allah came to life at the prescribed time for mission completion. Lights came online and a warning claxon was sounded as 8:00 PM on the west coast signaled the beginning of a new day for the world, and the end of the mission. It was the end of the mission for the Sword of Allah. The Sword raised itself slowly off the sea floor. It listened for traffic in and around the area, and then silently slid a tube-launched cruise missile into the first torpedo tube, then opened the outer doors, a compressed fist of air pushed the torpedo out of the hull and into the warm waters of the Pacific.

Closing the door, the Sword of Allah monitored its deadly fish. As it sank back to the bottom of the bay, the torpedo circled until it reached maximum speed and then turned straight up, heading for the surface. As it broke free of the water, a jet of compressed air pushed it further from the surface of the waves, where a rocket motor kicked in. Now airborne two stubby wings and a tail popped out as the rocket motor pushed its speed to nearly 700 mph. The identification section of the cruise missile began searching for landmarks to take it to its predetermined destination. Five seconds later, it had found its first landmark and was headed toward its goal, accelerating to mach 2.

JD planned on leaving the conference after listening to the successful presentation by Naomi. The crowd listened intently and had asked question after question, which Naomi fielded as easily as if she were a queen on a throne. She spoke with the confidence born of years of hard work and methodical effort. Microcom's CEO had disguised himself, as he was famous for doing, and watched the presentation, undisturbed, in the back row. JD hadn't noticed him, but he had noticed JD, who also sat on the back row.

He sidled up quietly to JD and commented, "This really is great software."

"Yes, it is," said JD, "and Ms. Benson is the force behind it," he said knowingly.

"Really?" said the odd looking gentleman. "You know her personally?"

"Yes," came JD's reply. "We're good friends."

"Is it true that her father is the Director of the NSA?" he questioned.

"Yes, it's true," JD replied, "but she's made it this far on her own work. I don't want anyone to think she relied on him to be successful," he said.

"Maybe you could set up a meeting for me," the man said. "I don't usually come to these myself, but this was of real interest to my company," he said without pretense. The man turned and walked away after handing JD his card.

To his surprise, JD read the name "Martin Stanton, CEO Microcom" as the man walked away. As Naomi fielded the last of the questions and a small group of rather nerdy looking computer experts gathered around the podium where she stood, the Marine engineer elbowed his way to the front of the pack. Standing a good six inches taller than most of those around him, she picked him out and made eye contact.

"I thought you were heading out after the presentation," she said and smiled at him.

"I just thought you'd like this," he said, extending his hand with the card. "Just a little something from an adoring fan at the back of the room. He wants to talk," JD said as he released the card.

Naomi took the card and smiled as she read the name. "Really?" she said, trying to contain her excitement.

"Really," said JD. "I've got to be going, but I really wanted to let you know how proud I am of what you've accomplished."

"I'll call you later," she said. She blessed him with another one of her smiles, lighting up his day once again. He couldn't help but smile back. As he drove away from Vegas, back toward San Diego, his mind wandered back to the discussion they'd had earlier.

✠

As the cruise missile headed off toward its destination, the Sword of Allah had completed its mission and shut itself down again. Sinking slowly to the sea floor and turning its systems to sleep mode, it sat, awaiting commands from a non-existent crew.

Ten miles out and three miles north of the position of the Sword, a Navy cruiser, the Benedict Arnold, was listening with all of her new equipment for sounds of a submarine.

Suddenly, and without warning, the sound of a torpedo in the water was heard roughly ten miles to the east. Without hesitation, the captain of the Benedict Arnold turned the cruiser away from the wind and pushed her with all her speed to find the torpedo. Before she had traveled more than a mile and a half, the torpedo had gained speed and seemed to be circling, then without warning, it headed straight upward. As it jumped from the sea like a dolphin, the torpedo, now a missile, took off.

As it had now become a radar target, the Benedict Arnold fired a group of five anti-missile missiles, hoping to destroy the cruise missile before it found its target. It also loosed two torpedoes that were designed to search for and destroy any submarines in the area. As it loosed the anti-sub torpedoes, the weapons were set on fire and forgotten as the more pertinent task of destroying the missile was at hand. The five missiles each chased after the presumed target of the cruise missile: two took a northern track, hoping the cruise missile would turn north toward them, while two others took a southern track hoping that the cruise missile would turn south toward them, while the fifth missile followed the same track, hoping beyond hope that it would catch the cruise missile from behind.

Seconds later, the cruise missile passed the easternmost edge of San Diego and made a sweeping turn to the north-northeast, headed across the mountains and desert toward Las Vegas, Nevada. As it did so, the two missiles taking the northern track gained several miles of distance on the cruise missile. At the same time, the two southern missiles continued their track, but they had lost all chance of exploding the cruise missile at this point. The fifth missile continued, its pace slightly faster than that of the cruise missile, slowly gaining on its target. Minutes passed and the cruise missile continued on its path. The two southern missiles were terminated over the desert by the captain of the cruiser, while the fifth anti-missile missile was continuing to make headway on the cruise missile. The two northern missiles were getting very close now, but suddenly, on the closer of the two missiles, the shaking from its bumpy ride, and because it's solder joints had not been checked well enough at the factory where it's guidance board was manufactured, caused the 12 percent failure rate to catch up to the missile. As a soldered joint broke apart, the signal to keep following the radar-return was lost and the missile lost its target and began a series of spectacular loops and turns, traveling at nearly mach 3 until it crashed harmlessly into the desert night. The other of the northern missiles appeared to now be the only chance for knocking down the cruise missile.

✠

Twenty-five miles to the northeast, JD watched the night sky as he drove back to his apartment. Just after 8:00 PM as he watched, the fire of the missile caught his attention in the distance, curling around in circles like no falling star had ever done. As it made circles in the night sky, JD pulled over to watch it, and he noticed another flash coming his way. To his surprise, he counted a second light following the lead light. He watched in amazement at what had to be two missiles chasing each other across the southern sky. Further off in the distance he thought he saw a third light chasing the other two.

One hundred feet beneath the waves, the two torpedoes had reached their destination, the point closest to where the cruise missile had first appeared, and were beginning their search patterns. They began to actively search for any sonar return from their active pinging. The two torpedoes began circling, one to the left and the other to the right, in ever-expanding circles. As they continued to circle, the Sword of Allah monitored the deadly torpedoes and calculated that the southern-most torpedoes would cross within 1545 meters of its current location on its third pass, and then would pass again within 1668 meters of its location on its fourth pass. Any pass before or after that would be irrelevant, it considered. The engine was brought online and the power was made ready to be put to the screws if the torpedo showed any signs of coming toward the ship.

Two minutes later, the remaining northern missile moved into position and exploded just twenty meters behind the cruise missile when it blew. As fragments of the exploded missile flew forward at mach 3, the speedy cruise missile was shaken slightly off course from the compressed air bubble that hit the missile first, then its tail section was visibly thrashed by shrapnel from the exploding missile. The cruise missile wobbled visibly, but not enough to tumble end over end and cause the destruction of the missile's body. As it wobbled and strayed from its path, it seemed to have made it through the second missile's attack. That left only the fifth missile, which continued its pursuit from now only ten miles back. As it continued its pursuit, the question now was whether there was time enough left to catch the cruise missile, and whether the anti-missile missile had enough fuel to catch the cruise missile before it died.

As JD sat and watched the oncoming streaks of light, he saw the northernmost light explode somewhat behind the lead light. It had failed to shoot down the lead missile, but the light trailing behind it was gaining with rapidity on the lead object. It just had to be a missile. He wondered why the military would be running missile tests this close to the Interstate. He'd never heard of such tests being held this close to a major city. He made a mental note to check it out with the newspaper next weekend when he got back from his time out with Isaiah. He continued to watch the rapidly approaching rockets, each streaking forward on its own mission of death.

On the third pass across the Sword of Allah, the torpedo wobbled momentarily as if it had picked up a return from the hull of the submerged submarine, but as it continued on its way without turning downward, the submarine watched patiently as the torpedo moved further away again on its ever-widening path.

Two minutes later, the fifth and final anti-missile missile detonated just thirty meters above the surface of the desert and eighteen meters behind the cruise missile. The cruise missile was now within sight of Lake Meade and was starting its downward descent when the missile behind it exploded. The force of the explosion, along with the slight downward tilt of the cruise missile's nose, caused a wobble that was too pronounced for the missile to correct.

As its rear end lifted above its nose, the cruise missile began to tumble in mid-air, causing the nose and rocket sections to separate from the payload section. The payload section, with its two stubby wings, now minus a nose and a tail spun wildly slowing and falling to the sandy earth below. The nose-cone hit next, planting itself into a muddy hole twenty meters from the lake. The engine section, with its heavy weight and still turning tail, was the last to hit and skipped over the waves of the lake before sinking silently to the bottom of the lake.

JD could scarcely believe his eyes as the missiles came together, seemingly just over his head... They were so low. The two had zoomed over his position scarcely 100 feet in the air. As they passed by, the explosion seemed to take place. JD shook his head at the sound of the explosion, and his eyes widened as the huge blast rocked the night sky. Pieces of missile flew in all directions, but the force of inertia pushed the main pieces toward the reservoir. Again, JD shook his head. He'd never heard of the military running a test this close to a public water supply. The rocket motor itself seemed to have fallen into the lake. With the final explosion, the night sky seemed to have fallen back into silence. JD took a final look around and decided to get back out on the road. It had been quite a night. He sat back in the cab of his truck and jotted down a few notes about what he'd seen and then started the motor and continued on his way. He didn't think twice about the possibility of any further danger.

The payload section broke open upon impact with the hard desert floor. The contents of the payload section were nothing. The captain, in all his planning and forethought, had been worried about the payload accidentally going off early, so had decided to not load the payload until just before launch. Before his demise, he had been too far into delirium to realize he'd forgotten to load the powder into the payload section. The doctor had been too intent on his own demise to load it as well. The end had come and the "would-be martyrs" had failed miserably in their attempt, primarily because of their own self-absorbed failings.

On board the Benedict Arnold, the captain and crew cheered the demise of the cruise missile. A message was sent out immediately to ComPacFlt, describing the odd missile attack. They were still feeling a bit odd about the obvious target of the cruise missile. Who in their right mind would fire cruise missiles at a lake? However, their own Clinton administration had fired nearly two hundred cruise missiles all targeted at caves and sand dunes just a scant ten years earlier. Oh well, thought the captain. We got it before it hit its target, and hopefully we'll get the sub that shot it off as well. As to that end, the Benedict Arnold was not having much success. The fourth pass yielded no better effect for the southernmost torpedo than the others. The Sword continued to lie at rest, with no movement and no work left to do. She was a deadly fish, with power and grace, and no one to take her in harms way. As the Benedict Arnold reached a point one mile northwest of the location of the Sword, she began her own search pattern, moving to the north and east. She did not find the sub after searching for nearly four hours. Afterward, she moved back off-shore, continuing to watch for any more submerged activity. By the time she was moving off shore, several more Navy ships had joined in the search, sweeping the coastline for a hundred miles north and fifty miles south. The captain of the Benedict Arnold was whisked away by helicopter to Fleet HQ in San Diego as more ships came into view. After relating the experience to several different admirals, a general, and the NSA director, he was finally allowed to return to his ship.

Washington DC, 06:00 Zulu, June, 2, 2007

The president and Dave Benson were at the same positions they seemed to have been in for the past three days—sitting and listening for any further word of attack. They believed that the second submarine must have been somewhere near San Diego Harbor, with a target of Lake Meade, but something was still wrong with that. While the cruise missile had been taken out, it had been too close for comfort. The payload canister had been found by a military helicopter a scant 100 yards from the shoreline of the lake, but it had been empty. Not "empty" as in the contents had blown away, but "empty," as if the contents had never been loaded into the canister. Could this also have been a taunt by the Iranian government, or had the Iranian crew just screwed up and fired an empty shot? If that were the case, why hadn't they fired another shot with a full tank? It was all very confusing, and both Dave and Debra were at the brink of exhaustion.

Too much to do and too little time to accomplish it. Dave looked at Debra, her head lying cradled by her slim hands, and said, "That's it, Madam President. You need some sleep. This country can't go on without a president to guide it, and you, Ma'am, are it."

"Thanks, Dave, but what about you? I can't let you handle this crisis by yourself."

"You're right, Debra. That's why I'm going home to get some sleep too. If anything else happens, my staff will let me know and you'll know as soon as I do. In the meantime, we've both got to get some sleep."

"I still can't believe we haven't heard any more from our old friend Ahmadinejad," Debra said. "He usually will be a fly in the ointment any chance he gets, but since our press conference with all of our facts and proof of wrong doing, he hasn't let out a peep."

"I know," said Dave. "It really is a bit spooky to have him not saying anything. I just feel like he's waiting for his project to take off, like he's waiting for his masterpiece to be unveiled for the public."

"That's it! He's waiting to hear that the missile made it into lake Meade," she said triumphantly. "He can't wait to goad us. How can we get the word to him that the missile made it to Lake Meade, without letting him know it's a set up?"

Almost immediately a plan came to Dave. "We'll use Bill," he said.

✠

Bill Elliot wasn't his usual cocky self as he sat sequestered in the small holding room inside the offices of the NSA. He hadn't been home in two days, and the threat of a treason charge hung over his head. The shame of being hauled out of his own office in handcuffs while his subordinates looked on still turned his skin a hot red. His head swirled with emotion. Every emotion—from fear, to shame, to hatred, and even angst—swirled throughout him, charging him to a point where his world of normalcy seemed a million miles away. Soon afterward, the key to the door of his small spartan room clicked its way to the open position and the director of the NSA pushed his way into the room and sat on the bed opposite Bill.

"Dave," Bill began, "this was a one time thing. I'm not even sure who it was that sold us out."

"Bill, you sold me out," Dave countered. "I told you very specifically not to tell anyone. I even warned you about speaking to MI6. Even then, I was specific to tell you not to give out any information to them that they didn't already have, and you couldn't wait to spill all the information I'd given you. Bill, you make me sick. I know that in that sick mind of yours you think that this is the way it's supposed to work: tell a secret here or there to gain the acceptance of someone important or to get a little spending money and no one gets hurt, but that's not how we work in this administration. In this case, loose lips really do sink ships," Dave replied.

"But Dave, all I did was tell my DDI." Bill broke, his eyes tearing up. "It was him, not me," Bill insisted, continuing down the path of blame.

"Bill, we know about the DDI, and he has already given you up, letting us know that he leaked the information at your direction. He has tendered his resignation and we are still reserving the right to file charges if we deem it necessary," came Dave's quiet reply.

Bill was shaken; he was depending on being offered the first opportunity to give up his contacts for consideration in the matter. Now he realized for the first time that there was no one above him to turn in, and he felt really alone.

"Dave, this can't happen to me," he almost bawled. "My wife, my kids... What will people say? I can't... I don't know what to do," He stammered.

"Bill, those are the questions you should have thought of before you committed treason," Dave replied coldly. "I know I wouldn't know how to face my wife and children either if I'd done what you've done! The difference between you and me is that I couldn't face myself in the mirror having committed this offense. You, on the other hand, can't seem to face yourself only after being caught committing the offense. Bill, I can't understand how you could do this after the way you've been treated by your government." Dave got that far before being cut off by an angry Elliot.

"Done for me?" he almost screamed. "Done for me? I was passed over for your job for no reason. I suppose it's because of your relationship with her." He implied impropriety with his voice.

Dave sat quietly and said without raising his voice, "you are an idiot. You know there is no relationship between the president and myself except for a professional one, and as far as being passed over... look at where you are and what you're capable of and tell me that the president didn't show good judgment in passing you over. Bill, you are in no position to complain right now. Your failing is this: you aren't sorry for doing wrong; you're sorry you got caught. You are an idiot, Bill. Do you know what your wife's response was when we spoke to her regarding why you weren't going to be home last night? It wasn't to ask if you were hurt, or if you were going to be all right, or to rush to your aid. She wanted to know what you'd been caught doing. Then she threatened to go to CNN with company knowledge of certain things that would be embarrassing to the administration. I had to set her straight that in your position, Bill, you should never have spoken to her about anything that happened within the confines of the company or the administration, and by spilling her knowledge to CNN she would only be burying you deeper in the hole of treasonable acts and she would be dragging herself into it with you. And here you sit, Bill, trying to tell me that it only happened once, and that it'll never happen again. Bill, you are an idiot."

Bill hung his head in shame. Damn her! he thought. She'd been the one to suggest making use of the things he knew for profit in the first place. She was the one who wanted the summer house down in Florida, and she was the one who wanted a full time maid, the new cars... It is all her fault, he thought. Even now his true colors were showing through; he had to blame someone besides himself for what he'd done. His only conscious thought was that it wasn't his fault.

"Now Bill," Dave began, "here's what you're going to do and what you're going to tell CNN next." Handing Bill a two-page bio on fictitious events resembling the shooting of a missile into Lake Meade by an unknown submarine and the sinking of that submarine in US Territorial waters off of San Diego.

Bill smiled and said, "For a break, Dave, I'll give you someone in the DNC if you want him."

Dave said, "Now you're thinking, Bill. Let's talk about it."

The month of June passed unceremoniously. President Ahmadinejad had thrown his fit in front of the cameras of Al Jazeera and had continued to deny any culpability in the obvious stunt that had cost Iran a submarine. Even though he denied that his submarine had been on a mission of war, the president couldn't quite get past the loss of his other secret weapon. All he had was a leak through the DNC saying that a weapon had splashed into the water supply of Las Vegas. He had smugly posed in front of the Al Jazeera cameras, stating that Allah would soon punish the evil Americans for their sinfulness and their attacks on the "defenseless research ship," as he was now calling his submarine. He even went so far as to say that Allah would strike the Americans in their most sinful city—the City of Las Vegas. This last he said in his most prophetic sounding voice.

Across the Middle East, Ahmadinejad had been praised for his belief and strength of purpose. Behind his back, however, most of the Middle Eastern rulers laughed at the ravings of a mad man. To predict the demise of an American city, he was loony, they were saying behind the scenes. Ahmadinejad heard the whispers and silently kept track of those casting dispersions upon his name. I'll have the last laugh, he thought, smiling at the vision it brought to his mind. After June 8th came and went without word of an outbreak, President Ahmadinejad began stepping up his rhetoric. By June 15th he was anxiously scanning every news agency, looking for a hint that things were happening in the desert city.

He grew irate, and his ramblings in front of the press were even more unbelievable than before. He accused the American president of covering up millions of deaths in the American Southwest. Even his own people were looking at him with raised eyebrows. On June 21st he rose from his slumber and scanned the international papers, looking for an outbreak report. Finding none, he shouted loudly,"Jimji!"

"What has gone wrong, Jimji? All my planning and all of the work—three years of time, money and planning—all for naught." He almost cried.

"My President, perhaps it was not your fault at all, but the fault of those you trusted." Jimji planted the seed.

"Perhaps the Chinese gentleman that helped you so much wasn't really helping you at all. Perhaps he was setting you up to fail." Jimji stroked the president's ego, as he knew he needed to do so before his wrath fell upon Jimji himself.

"Yes, Jimji." Ahmadinejad saw the opportunity to save face with his generals and advisors. He called for an advisory meeting, and prepared himself to blame the Chinese for the obviously bad idea that he had followed over the past four years.

✠

At almost the same time in Washington DC, President Beechum smiled across the table in the oval office at her NSA director, her new CIA chief, Tom Putnam, as well as Alex Rice and Hamilton Cordova. For a week there had been an uneasy peace between Rice, Cordova and Benson, but now, after things had obviously turned out so right and the Iranian President had turned out to look so silly on national TV, Rice and Cordova were coming around. Even CNN had made their apologies to the administration, begging for a place back at the table. President Beechum was feeling pretty good for a change.

"Dave, is there any chance that you'll take the extra responsibility of being my press secretary as well as NSA director?" Debra asked.

"Not a chance, Madam President," he laughed as he replied.

"But you handled it so well when duty called," she went on.

"Maybe so, maybe not," he replied, "but I do know that the press would soon tire of my rudeness. I could scarcely sit through a single announcement without throwing half of them out on their self-righteous left wing ears." He smiled knowingly.

Alex turned slightly to look in the eyes of Hamilton.

"I thought for a while you would throw all of them out a few weeks back," said Hamilton, offering his first unsolicited comments in two weeks.

"Why Ham! You're back among us." The President smiled at him.

Hamilton looked down, but returned the smile. "I must admit, Dave," Hamilton continued, "I was afraid we'd have no one left to leak our own undercover leaks to by the time you were through with our good network contacts." He laughed slightly.

Dave did laugh at the thought of having no one to leak information to in Washington. "That'll be the day, Ham," he said and chuckled. He shook his head at the thought of what politics had come to in Washington DC. What a mess, he thought.

Alex continued to look somber. He was the only one not laughing at the mess of intrigue that politics had come to. "And what of Bill?" Alex asked darkly. "Is he to hang for treason for the very thing you sit and laugh about now?"

"Not at all the same thing," Tom interjected. "He didn't give out false information intentionally to serve the government, but instead gave out information that could have hurt this government for his own willful gain, or for the hope of hurting this administration, which by the way is this government!"

His words stung Alex, causing him to turn his eyes away from the group.

"Well said, Tom," said Dave. "You have hit the nail on the head. We must not lose sight of the fact that we serve this administration, and in so doing serve the Government of the United States, since they are one and the same. Too many people have lost sight of the fact that through our own free elections we have elected this administration to be the Executive Branch of the Government of the United States. By working to undermine the administration, they are working to undermine the Executive Branch, and thereby the Government."

Alex turned to look at Ham, but got no return glance. It was obvious to everyone in the room that Alex was not a happy man, but he was too smart to throw away his position by making any comments at this time. He simply straightened his tie, picked up his cup and hid the grimace he couldn't reveal behind it as he took a sip of the excellent coffee.

It was quiet for several heartbeats until Debra broke the spell by turning to Tom and asking for his analysis of the loss of the second submarine. She listened intently to the words he spoke, but her mind was on Alex and what she would have to do quite soon. She couldn't ignore the fact that Alex was not happy and was not forthcoming about his own feelings. I will give him one last chance, privately, she thought, to come clean and be honest with me. If he doesn't, I will ask for his resignation. She steeled herself for the unpleasant task

June 26th, 2007

The world was a mess. JD and Isaiah lay on their backs, examining the beauty of the stars above them. Gently, the boat rocked to and fro and the two men drank cola and discussed their shortcomings, as well as all the rest of the world's flawed governments.

"You should hear some of the stories Naomi has told me about the willful lies that are told right on the Senate floor. These men lie to each other and to the world in order to put gold into their own pockets, and when they're not filling their pockets, they're setting themselves up for another term or to strengthen their party. They're willing to destroy their own government to win another seat in Congress."

"I know, JD," replied Isaiah. "I think the whole world has gone mad." He took another swig of Coke. "The news media poisons the minds of everyone. They take the side of the Democrats and seem to work incessantly to make the Republicans look bad."

"Isaiah," JD said, "how is it that you, being one half Hispanic, aren't a born Dem?"

"Two reasons, JD," Isaiah retorted. "One, I have a mind of my own that no one is going to whitewash with the brainless crap the news media tries to shove down our throats, and two, my Poppy—that is my Granddad—taught me to think for myself and not to let those talking heads on the boob tube think for me."

"Yeah, me too," said JD. "I just don't understand how come so many people don't seem to be able to see through the obvious lies the news anchors shove at us. They get some heartbroken housewife who lost her soldier son to a terrorist in Iraq to get on the news and bad- mouth the president, and all the while no one seems to ask the obvious question: If her son hadn't joined the Army voluntarily, he wouldn't have been there to be killed. If you were to check with his buddies, I bet you'd find that he was proud to have been there and gave his life honorably and now his mother, not able to deal with her own grief, is running around dishonoring him in a way that he would have hated."

"Yeah, I'll bet you're right," Isaiah replied. "What would you do if you had a few billion dollars to throw around?"

"I don't know," JD replied. "You can bet I'd find a way to try and save the world somehow." He laughed. "Look at me. As it is, I'm broke and still trying to find a way to save the oceans from man's pollution."

"Yeah", said Isaiah, "I'd like to save the world too, man, but I'd like to do it from my own yacht!" He grinned at JD.

The two remained quiet for a while, slowly digesting their own wandering thoughts and feeling the enveloping greatness of the starry expanse above them. Moments like this seemed to come far too few times in life, but they seemed to occur between these two "brothers of the sea" more and more often. They had reached a point where they could almost finish each other's sentences. They knew each other's minds as well as they knew their own. Both had strengths that the other admired. Together, they worked in a most invincible harmony. JD's thoughts ran back to the weekend with Naomi. He smiled, but remained quiet, not wanting to spoil the moment.

Isaiah felt, more than saw the smile on his friend's lips and asked, "Why don't you marry her?"

"Whoosh! Where did that come from?" asked JD.

"Come on, man. Here we are in the deepest of thought and you can't help but think of her. You two belong together."

"Yeah, well, you know, man. We belong together, but we—well, we have this understanding. You know, man. We just understand each other so completely that she knows not to push me, and I know not to let her down. Isaiah, man, I love her. I really love her, but the timing isn't right yet. I'll know when it is, and so will she."

"Yeah, well man, just don't let someone else slip in and steal her from you, man. She's the real deal. You know what I mean?"

"I know, man," JD replied. "I don't know what I'd do if I ever lost her."

"Yeah, and on top of that," Isaiah said, "her old man must be loaded."

They both laughed and clanked their bottles together in a mock toast.

San Diego Harbor, July 13, 2007

As they stored their gear like they had done a hundred times before, the two young men yawned, stretched and made their way down into the boat. The morning dew was already disappearing as the heat index was climbing above one hundred, and it promised to be a beautiful but hot day. Little did the two young men realize what they would be pondering before the day was over.

"Cast off the aft line," Isaiah said to JD as he himself cast off the forward line.

He used his foot to push the forty-two-foot hatteras away from the dock. JD pushed away the aft portion of the boat at the same time. Isaiah started the engines and checked the fuel in the tanks and the oil gauge, as well as the battery power, to make sure there would be no problems during their trip today. As the engines coughed to life and the ship began to make slow steerage through the main channel and out into the harbor, Isaiah turned on the GPS, the bottom monitor, and the radar.

For a smallish boat, the LeiLani had it all. Below deck was a main cabin, as well as a secondary berth that Isaiah had fitted out like two beautiful salons, each with its own plasma screen that had inputs for antenna, DVD, and from the control room. While taking rest, the young owner could keep track of a front and rear camera, as well as the radar and GPS outputs. While he couldn't control the boat from his cabin, the control room could be enclosed by sliding a hatch across the top and closing a sliding door at the rear.

All told, the LeiLani was the most beautiful ship Isaiah had been fortunate to fall into. He had worked aboard another research vessel on weekends during his high school days, and had gravitated to it full time after graduation. His mother hadn't been happy, for she believed him capable of being an engineer. She was right, but Isaiah had never been happy cooped up in school. While he had excelled, he never liked being indoors. He had heard the call of the sea from the first time his parents had taken him to the beach.

It was just two years after graduation that the original owner of the LeiLani was tragically killed in an auto accident. The owner had been the brother of his current employer. The owner's wife had no desire to keep the boat, and had offered to sell it to her husband's brother. Being a gambler, his boss did not have the money to purchase the boat, but knowing that young Isaiah never spent his own money and still lived at home, he offered the same deal to his young deck hand: $88,000.

At the time it seemed like a world of money, but it was more than a fair deal, and he'd prayed and begged and made every deal he could with his mother to get her to co-sign the loan for the boat. He put down the $15,000 he had saved of his own money, and had done well in making his payments ever since. In the four years since purchasing the boat he had managed to pay off another $30,000 of the debt, leaving a little more than $42,000 to pay. According to his plan, he should have it paid for in two more years.

JD had been a large part of that. Isaiah was close to missing his first payment in two years when he'd run into JD. That was two years ago.

During that next two-year period JD managed to acquire three grants that had funded their adventures to the tune of nearly $60,000. Half had gone to reduce his debt, and the other half had gone to pay for upkeep, fuel, and a few additions to the boat to make it more comfortable and more adept as a research vessel. JD had all the data he needed to finish his doctoral thesis, but he enjoyed the work. He felt more at home doing his work in the small guest cabin than he did at his desk back in his apartment building. He was nearly through with the last of the grants, and was technically done with his doctoral thesis; he had turned in the last of his requirements and expected to hear from the review board by the end of August.

Straights of Gibraltar, October 21, 1307 AD

Tristan's lead ship, the Templar Valiant, had undergone significant refit in the previous eight days. She no longer looked like the dirty troop carrier that she had been for the previous five years since her creation in the shipbuilding port of La Rochelle. She had served the purpose well of bringing Knights to the front lines of the Crusades. Now she had been re-fit as a cargo ship. With only enough men to keep the ship sailing, the rest of the crew's quarters and open space were filled with cargo, hidden in boxes and wrapped in oilcloth. The top deck no longer had cabins to house troops; instead, the top deck was stacked with heavy boxes of cargo. She sat low in the water and had been renamed the Demeter, the Greek Goddess of the Earth, and repainted a ghastly dark brown. Her sails, which had been dirty but emblazoned with the red Templar cross, were now new and a crisp white.

It took eight days to sail the length of the Mediterranean, and they were passing the great Port city of Gibraltar as

Tristan stared from the starboard rail, the wind blowing his dark hair across his face and causing it to stream behind him. He prayed to God that the fair winds would continue to blow him on a righteous and expedient path. So far, God had blessed the voyage. None of his twenty-four ships had reported seeing another craft, nor having been seen by any. That, he knew, was about to change, but he had prepared for that.

All the ships had been repainted and the sails replaced with plain white sailcloth. The previous night they had scattered and would each pass through the narrow confines of the channel, leaving the Mediterranean and entering into the great sea. Tristan's ship would be the first, and would linger around the eastern shores until all twenty- three of the others made it through. Only the most trusted among his friends were brought on board to captain the ships. Only the most trusted among his guards were allowed to guard each ship. Even so, the biggest defense that he had on board was speed, speed to guard the treasury of the Templars.

Now, no longer in existence, many of his Templar brothers had headed north to the Hinterlands, with a substantial amount of treasure with them. Even if the money they had lent to that pompous French King Edward were lost, their treasury was still vast, and many of his brothers had been entrusted with setting up their banking empire in a location protected by the mountains on all sides, away from French domination.

As the last of his ships made it through the narrow confines of the pass at Gibraltar, Tristan turned his ship into the wind and began an arduous journey. Pushing his ships on a southern trek far enough out to sea that it was with great difficulty that he, even with his magic magnifier—a gift from the great King of the Arabs, could scarcely see the shoreline. His plan was simple. He had heard the stories of a great land to the east, discovered by the Norsemen, but reachable by sailing south along the African lands until the water drained from the water bottle in the wrong direction. At that point he intended to sail due west until he found the new lands. It was a trepidacious trip, to be sure, but one he did not fear. He trusted God to protect him—God and his sword and shield—but his sword and shield would not carry him safely to his destination. He had to rely on God and a swift ship to take him to his new home. Twenty-four ships now prowled the East African coastline. In the coming days, their numbers would provide safety for them as they moved further to the south.

Three days later, the group of ships stopped for fresh water after spotting a group of islands off their starboard side. Turning to the islands, the ships scared the small group of blacks occupying the islands and the even smaller group of Spanish officials who claimed ownership of the land by parading around in fancy clothing and keeping the black islanders subjugated with superior weaponry, and an air of superiority that the natives feared more than the weapons themselves.

After negotiating for fresh water and food, the islanders began bringing the supplies to the dock and wanted to bring it aboard the first of the ships, but a small group of English knights took control of the small pier and allowed no one on board. The Spanish looked on in amazement, but because of the small fortune they were making on the loading of 24 ships they looked at the gold in their pockets and decided to shut up and take the money. Scarcely 8 hours later the ships were back in formation and headed south again.

Before leaving the island, Tristan met with Governor Ferdinand De Cordova. The governor was quite interested in the destination of such an armada, and he was nobody's fool. He knew these had to be the missing Templar ships that had caused such a fuss the previous week. Ships leaving Spain had brought the news of the missing ships just two days prior. After a short conversation with De Cordova, Tristan was sure that he was too great a threat to leave in the open. As Cordova began bantering, hoping to "shake down" the Templar Knight, Tristan offered the Spaniard a simple offer: Come along, or die. The blood drained from Cordova's face until he regained his composure.

"I'll die before being threatened by you," he said, almost spitting in Tristan's face.

"As you wish," was Tristan's only verbal response.

Fifteen minutes later the new governor of the Islands, a young black man, sat wondering at his great fortune at having been promoted in such a startling fashion. His first order was to have the pompous peacocks' bodies burned. According to the tall man in armor, they had died of the pox and their bodies had to be burned to stop the disease from spreading. In the mean time, he put another woman to work cleaning the floor in his new office. It had blood all over it.

Accra, Friday November 3, 1307 AD

Seventeen days since their last landfall had the men a little on the jumpy side. They had not seen the desert for at least the last seven. They had seen very little of life for the past week and a half. Even though the land had become lush and green once again, it was hot. As they approached the shore, the backs of great serpent-like beasts swam in the briny waters of the rivers they passed. They varied in size, but some of them came up and took large oxen with a single bite.

Tristan wondered in awe at the size of these beasts and if they might be relatives of the crocodiles he had heard of along the Nile River. Certainly these were much larger than any he had ever heard of. As the heat continued to climb, the men became more and more spooked. Tristan needed them to be calm and clearheaded and afraid of nothing. He decided that they needed another stop, this time for more than just food and water.

As they continued following the shoreline eastward, Tristan scanned the shore for a good place of shelter for his armada. A day and a half later, the lead ship spotted an island off the coast of an island the natives called Malabo.

Dropping anchor off of the eastern side of the island, three boats from three different ships each took a small contingent of knights to the island to negotiate with the natives. The natives were, as it turned out, none to friendly. They had dealt with slave ships from the England before and thought that they were here for a new shipment. Knowing that they didn't have a shipment of slaves to sell, they feared the retribution of the English and hid themselves in fear.

Not finding native help, they returned to their longboats, signaling an all-clear by flags. The rest of the boating parties left the shelter of their ships and came to the island. After searching in and around the village, a source of fresh water was found, and after several attempts, two of the large river crocodiles were killed and provided wonderful meat, not to mention leather.

Tristan, who had been in on one of the crocodile kills, cut several sections of the rough hide along the back of the monster and was intent on making himself greaves that would be the envy of any knight of the European realm. That's when he stopped and laughed at himself. He knew he'd never see Europe again. It was time to speak to the men and make that clear. Until now, even he had been living in the world of false hope that they would return one day. If all went well, they would start a new world of their own. He smiled and reached for the shield around his neck. To have such men as these to begin a new world... He smiled inwardly; he was a lucky man.

That night, as the first of the villagers returned to their huts, they were astounded to find that their village had been completely overrun by these white men. They realized that they seemed to not be looking for slaves, but only foraging for food and water. Soon the entire village was back in place and a peace had been struck between them and the strange white men. The natives offered the slaves they had, about twenty, and offered to collect more. Tristan only laughed at them and said "no" through his interpreter. Instead, he offered to give the natives a dozen long steel-tipped pikes with which they had killed the crocodiles, and miscellaneous beads and silks from the Eastern empires when they left the island.

The natives had never seen such a treasure trove and were in awe that the white men treated them seemingly as equals. While the natives seemed to be friendly, Tristan made sure that the small beach area they had landed on was secure and well guarded. He also made sure that the boats in the small harbor were left with guards that would be swapped out every 12 hours while they were at anchor. Tristan checked the perimeter of his encampment and surveyed the area for possible points of attack, and then rejoined the chief and the rest of the celebrators at the village. The chief felt as if he had a new brother in Tristan and gave him his most prized possession, a huge slave that was young and fair- skinned. The chief swore to Tristan that the young slave was only 15 years old. Tristan studied the averted gaze of the young slave and gave the chief a jewel-encrusted dagger that had come from the Holy Land. The chief was ecstatic—drunk, but ecstatic.

That night, following the party, Tristan and his men returned to the beach. While the natives had drunk their strong native brew, Tristan had made sure his men had not partaken of the beverages offered, but drank from the fresh water they were steadily loading instead. Tristan gathered his captains and with the steady beat of the waves upon the open beach, he laid out his plan. Each of these knights had been with him throughout the past twenty years; many had been there even longer. Tristan told them of the opportunity to create greatness in a new land. He told them that they had the opportunity to own kingdoms of their own in a new world that had not been spoiled by the greed of kings or corrupt politicians.

"We have the opportunity, my brothers, to do it right!" He lifted his sword in the air. "Are you with me?" he shouted.

"To the death!" came their stalwart and unanimous reply.

He knew that he would still need to speak with each one alone, but he also knew that the group needed this bonding. As the meeting broke up and men wandered away in twos and threes, Tristan headed to a small knot of his closest friends, and wrapping his arms around them, he pushed his way into their midst and asked them, "Well, now that we're alone, tell me what you really think?"

It was the same all night long as he made his way from tent to tent. The answer was always the same. His men were excited—excited enough to fight for the opportunity. Around midnight he came back to his own tent, exhausted, but pleased by the reception his men had given him.

Upon entering, he was at first surprised and then a bit shaken by the large young black man standing guard just inside his door.

"What am I to do with you?" he asked into the darkness in what was supposed to be a rhetorical question.

"I do not understand, Master!" came the reply from the native.

Shocked by the response, Tristan stammered, "You speak English?"

"Yes, Master, I do," came the reply.

"But how?" Tristan still couldn't believe it?

"I was taken as a slave at the age of 3 by an English sea captain to serve as his personal cabin steward, and later as his translator. The chief of the village we just left murdered the ship's crew and stole their weapons several years ago."

"What?" Tristan almost yelled, "No!, Not what, but why are you telling me this?"

"Because, Master," said the young slave, "you have the face of a good man, and because the chief is a bad man."

He said it so matter-of-factly and without any sense of malice that it struck Tristan with a sense that this was not a foolish boy talking nonsense. Without wasting further time, he called together guards to keep watch, then he sent a man back to warn each of the boats. Tristan felt better about having withheld the alcohol from his men during the celebration. Upon re-entering his tent, he looked closely at the young man and asked his name.

"My name is whatever you wish to call me," he said to

Tristan. "I have been called by as many names as I have had owners," he said.

"I want to know what your parents called you," said Tristan. "You are a man and worthy of a name. Free or slave—you were born free and thus have the right to a name."

The young man was taken aback. "My parents... I don't remember what they called me. I was too young to remember much about them... except that my father was very tall man. As for a name, I have always liked the name Sama," he said. "Will that name please you, Master? Sama?"

"If it pleases you, Sama it is," said Tristan. "Now, Sama, have you no loyalty to the chief?"

"No, Master. The chief is a very bad man who has beaten me many times, but I showed him. I never let him see me cry out, not even once. He would not have given me to you if he had known that I could talk English. In fact, he wanted to get rid of me because he thought I be lazy, but I am not lazy. I just no want to do things for lazy bastard chief," said Sama, breaking out in a toothy grin.

Tristan smiled also at the infectious delight of the boy who'd been forced into manhood too soon. "Well, Sama, tell me, do you think the chief will try to take our boats or try to attack us?"

"No, Master. Not tonight. Tonight he will have big headache. He thinks that all English men are stupid and will get drunk, but I saw you not take the drink he offered. He will know that tonight is not the time, but he also knows that you will be here two, maybe three days to get food. He will let you feel safe with him and then attack your camp, not the boats, when you are weak."

"That is good to know, Sama," said Tristan, "but all the same, I think I'll put up a few extra guards for the rest of the night. And don't call me 'Master'," said Tristan.

"But you are my Master!" came the instant reply from Sama. "What shall I call you if not Master?"

"Call me Sir, or Tristan, or friend," was Tristan's sleepy

reply as he headed out of the tent for a final chat with the guards.

Ten minutes later, Tristan returned from his final check of the guards and found Sama standing at proper attention like a soldier in the ranks; with Tristan's battle sword at the ready should anyone come through the door unannounced.

"What are you doing with that sword, Sama?" Tristan asked, his own hand finding the pommel of his own sword.

"I will guard you, Master, while you sleep," came the reply. "Even if I do not think it will happen, I will never let anything happen to you...Tristan," he said, holding the proper name as if it were glass on his tongue. "Twice in this very night you have treated me like I was important, like I was your friend, once by letting me name myself, and by letting me call you 'friend'." His voice almost broke at the saying of the word, "friend." "For that kindness, I will be your man for all time and you will always be able to rely on Sama as if our hearts are linked together." Sama's eyes glistened, and Tristan felt moved by the boy's obvious hero worship.

"All right, Sama," he said, "but let's get one thing clear. You may serve me as any servant might, but you are owned by no man. I will teach you much that you need to know, but it will be as brothers in this great adventure of life."

Sama stood speechless, then knelt at Tristan's knee.

"None of that, my brother," said Tristan, helping Sama up. "You've got guard duty for the next six hours, then I'll be on duty while you sleep."

Fifteen minutes later, Tristan was fast asleep and Sama kept watch just outside the tent's open flap and pondered the strange Englishman. He looked at the sky, not knowing who to thank for his great good fortune at becoming this man's slave.

The next two days were spent in sending his knights around the island on hunting expeditions. They found that while there were many of the crocodile around the island, there were very few of the cattle-like animals to be found. The chief continued to try and get Tristan to use his men as guides on the hunting trips, but per Tristan's orders, the soldiers managed to always send the guides back to the village before the first hour had passed. Each night Tristan's men were invited back to the village for a party, but each night Tristan politely turned the invitation down citing the "illness" some of his men had contracted, hoping to scare the old chief with the fear of a plague.

On the morning of the third day, the chief met Tristan at the edge of his encampment. Tristan recognized that the chief was not going to be put off today. The chief had brought six men to go along on the day's hunting party. Tristan realized it would take another full day of good hunting to fill the larders for the rest of his ships. He had hoped to get the hunting done today and slip out after midnight. According to what Sama had told him, the old chief liked to wait until several hours after the sun set, while the crew was eating or had just finished an attack. By doing so, the old chief felt that the men would move slower and with blindness in the dark, having been around a campfire.

Tristan had also found out from Sama that it was a trick of the chief to ambush the hunting parties to reduce the number faced that night. So far, Tristan had been able to keep that little trick from happening by sending the "guides" back to the village, and thereby keeping the spy from telling the chief where they were hunting, or keeping the spy from leading the party into the ambush. Tristan realized that since the mice weren't going into the trap, the old chief was more than likely moving the trap to the mice. He agreed to take the chief with his hunting party that day, as well as two of his best hunters. The other four men, he told the chief would be needed by their own families to provide food. Sama stood by Tristan's side, remaining as stone-faced as ever, but as Tristan turned the attention of the chief toward the boats in the harbor, Tristan smiled and winked at Sama. He sent the chief and his men to the other side of the clearing and pulled Sama aside.

"Don't let on that you can speak English, Sama, and don't worry about anything I might say about you. I might have to say some things that are not true to gain the chief's confidence and to set my own trap. Do you understand, Sama?" asked Tristan.

"Yes, Master," said Sama. "I understand that sometimes you have to lie to a liar so that you aren't caught in his trap."

"Good. Now you'll have to find a way to let me know if he says anything in his native language that might be important to me," Tristan said, huddled with Sama in strategy.

"If it is important, Master, I will point at the ground and yell Gutu," said Sama. "That is the word for the wild pigs that live in the jungle."

"Good, Sama. We make a good team, you and me," he said, patting his friend on the shoulder.

Sama grinned his silly grin momentarily, then went back to the stone-faced look the chief was used to seeing.

The chief and two men meandered back to the huddle of knights that Tristan was speaking to.

"Ah," said Tristan, "here are our guides now. Chief, I thought we'd do something a little different today. I've decided that since we're still a good deal short on what we need, we'd send out three teams today. You and I will lead the hunters. I'm sure your men will be of great service in directing us to the best hunting grounds, and my other two teams will gather fruit to be put in our wooden barrels for our trip."

"How many men come hunt?" asked the chief in his broken English.

"With your two, I figure we'll only need five others to hunt and bring back the kill," Tristan lied. "Oh, and of course the manservant you gave to me."

"That good idea, Captain," the chief replied, all but licking his lips in anticipation.

"Let's get started then," said Tristan, picking up a pike and checking his sword. He sent his shield and armor back to the tent and instructed his other knights to do the same.

"We may need to move fast on our hunt today, men," he said. As they headed toward a game trail leading into the jungle, Tristan asked the chief what they'd be hunting today.

"We hunt the big wild cow," the chief smiled broadly at his description of water buffalo.

"Good" said Tristan. "That will give us enough meat for a whole boatload of men." He smiled broadly. "You know, Chief, that servant you gave me, he doesn't seem too smart. Never says a word," said Tristan, his finger tracing a circular pattern beside his temple.

"You right, but him servant. Not need to speak," he said smiling his picket-fence smile. "He good at hard work. Him work when everyone else give up. Him got strong muscles, but he be lazy. Sometime gotta beat him whole lot to make him work, but when he work, he work hard." His grin changed to a frown, as if he had just realized the boy was lazy for the first time. Then his face changed to a grin again as he remarked, "But you got no problem, Captain. You know how to beat him real good, I bet!"

"Yes," said Tristan, turning his head so the chief wouldn't see the disgust he felt written all over his face. As he turned, he caught Sama's eye and saw Sama wink knowingly, and Tristan felt instantly better about the lies he'd been spinning.

Ten minutes elapsed before the chief pointed to the right and said, "We take the path that way. Got much cows that way."

As the team headed down the right path, Sama jumped up and yelled "Gutu," gesturing wildly down the left hand path.

"What's he say, Chief?" asked Tristan, feigning stupidity.

"Him say pig that way, but I no see pig. We go this way," he said pointing to the right.

Without waiting, Sama headed down the left hand passage as if he were chasing a real pig. Tristan jumped after him, leaving the startled chief standing on the trail with nothing to do but follow.

As Tristan caught up with Sama, the boy spoke. "That path is no good. It leads to trap just around next bend.

Rocks on left side are good place to trap you."

The two continued to run, outdistancing the chief until they were alone. "We'll turn the tables on him, Sama. How many men can the trap hide?"

"Ten, maybe twelve," said Sama. "How do we trap them? There are only six of us."

"No, Sama, there are twenty good men behind us ready to aid us," said Tristan.

"Ah, you are a clever man, Master."

"Well, I hear them thrashing about for us, Sama; I guess we should go back and walk into their trap now."

Sama grinned and hurled his pike just to the soldier's left, impaling a squealing pig that weighed in at around fifty pounds.

After making their way back to the split in the trail, Tristan tapped one of his men on the shoulder and nodded secretively, and then walked back to where the chief was waiting impatiently. None of the chief's men noticed as the man Tristan had nudged silently dropped a bright blue piece of cloth in the center of the path some distance behind them.

"We got the pig, Chief." Tristan pointed to the impaled Gutu. Sama had clubbed it on the head shortly after retrieving the pike, making sure to end the pig's suffering.

"Good," replied the chief, his eyes never leaving the right hand trail. "Him make good supper tonight," he said distractedly.

"You mean when we eat him on the ship," Tristan corrected.

The chief's head came up quickly as he realized his mistake. "Um, yes, on board ship," he corrected himself. "We go this way now!" the chief said as he moved forward.

As Tristan turned to look back down the path the way they had come, he could see the movement of the undergrowth, revealing that his men were close by. "Yes, Chief, we go this way now," he said, making an exaggerated move to point down the right hand path.

Tristan purposefully walked slowly. The chief was itching to move ahead and kept looking back to see what was taking Tristan so long.

"You hurry now," said the chief. "It long way to where we go."

"Don't worry, Chief. You're not afraid the cows will be gone by the time we get there, are you?" said Tristan with a laugh.

The chief wasn't laughing though. "We go ahead and check path," said the chief, making a movement to his two men to follow, and he quickly darted forward down the path, disappearing around a bend about a quarter mile up the path.

As soon as the chief was out of earshot, Tristan huddled his men and let them know that the trap lay around the bend. He had Sama quickly give them an approximate layout of the land, then sent one man back to bring the others in from behind the evil chief.

"Well, men, here we go into the fox's den," said Tristan as one of his men headed back up the trail to contact those trailing them. They continued to march down the trail, but they were now alert to each noise and they watched for the rocks to their left that would constitute the trap.

As they rounded the bend, the chief leaned against the largest of the three boulders that formed a wall about ten feet high. As he stood there smiling, Tristan stopped short of the clearing and spoke.

"Well, Chief, I see you, but where are your other two men? Out ahead looking for the cows?"

"You come into clearing. I show you," the chief replied.

"In a moment, sir, in a moment... There is something I have to do first," came Tristan's reply.

"What do now?" The chief's voice was clearly elevated. "You come here, I show you."

Scarcely before the last words were out of the chief's mouth, Tristan rushed across the clearing and held a long dagger against the chief's belly. Almost at the same time, several arrows whizzed through the clearing behind Tristan. As the knife came to rest just above the chief's belly button, Tristan turned the chief and used him as a shield from the arrows.

"What's this?" shouted the chief, then he shouted some unintelligible words to his comrades behind the rock, and the arrows quit flying. "What you do?" the chief stood motionless, but obviously a bit afraid of losing his own life.

"I don't like it when a chief tries to kill my men," said Tristan. "Have I not treated you with respect? Have I not traded with you honorably? And yet you try and set a trap for my men and me."

"No! No! You all wrong," said the chief, "We just playing game. We no kill good friends."

Just about that time there was a scream of pain from behind some trees in front of the rocks, and a native with a pike through his shoulder fell into the clearing. Upon seeing this, a dozen other young native men turned around and found themselves facing twenty of Tristan's knights. They backed into the clearing and stood, facing six knights inside the clearing.

"Chief, you are lying to me. You had hoped to bring my men into the clearing and have your twelve hidden men cut us down with arrows as we were pinned against these rocks," Tristan said, pointing to the rocks. "Now it seems that you and your men are the ones trapped in this little ambush. What should I do with you, chief?" Tristan's voice turned almost evil as he spoke the final words.

"No, you wrong, great captain." The chief turned to begging. "It was idea of that man," he said, pointing at Sama. "He tell chief that we steal all spears, not just ones you offer us. He tell chief to do this."

Tristan laughed openly at the chief. "You really think I'm a fool, don't you, Chief? Well, the biggest problem with your story, Chief, is that it doesn't matter who told you to do it. It was you who tried to do it, not him." The blood drained from the chief's face as he realized that the knife against his belly was pressing even harder than before. He tried to move away, but Tristan's grip was like iron.

"What you do with me?" the chief asked, almost crying.

"You will die very soon," came the cold but very calm voice of Tristan. "Who else in your men speak English?" he queried the man.

Instead of an answer, the chief fell at his feet, seemingly unable to lift his head. The other natives, now fully aware of what was going on, dropped the pitiful excuse for weapons they had and fell to their knees. It was clear that they all expected to die.

The men were tied with their hands behind them, and a short stride of rope between their legs so they were hobbled, much like a horse. They marched back to the encampment where a table had been set up in the open air. Much of the equipment had been taken down and returned to the ships, and only a contingent of forty men remained. Tristan sat behind the table, while the chief and his men were told to kneel in front. Tristan had Sama translate for the men. The chief went pale when he realized that Sama could speak English better than he could.

"Sama, I want to know from you, who were the ones that took part in the murder of your former master?"

"It was the chief, Master. He did it himself with a knife after he got the Master drunk."

"Now, Sama, think carefully. Are any of the other of these men bad in the way that the chief is bad?"

Sama walked slowly down the row of men until he stopped in front of a man with a wicked look about him. "This man, Master. He is a bad man too. The same night my master was killed, this man killed many, many men with his knife as they lay drunk with the drink."

The wicked looking man didn't understand the words, but obviously got the idea, for he leaped up and jumped. Grabbing the knife in Sama's waistband, he reached high to stab him. It happened so quickly that all Sama could do was fall backward.

As he fell, two pikes appeared through the front of the man's chest, piercing him from behind. He fell forward and to the right, dropping the knife in the process. While this was going on, the chief had managed to get to his feet and started to run. Started, but the hobble on his legs tripped him up and he fell face-first into the sand. As he was dragged back into place, Tristan continued.

"Sama, please translate for these men. Chief, you are charged with murder and attempted murder. You set a trap to try and kill my men when we treated you respectfully and with kindness. We dealt fairly with you and your tribe, hoping to give you what you needed while taking only what we needed in return. Instead, you returned evil for the kindness we offered. As a result, we find that you are not worthy to lead such a noble tribe of people, and you are not worthy of continued life on this earth. Have you anything to say on your behalf that might change this court's mind?"

The chief looked angry. "You no say I not chief. I am chief. I am good chief. I get many slaves for English. I big man! They not big man like me," he said, pointing at the other natives. "I give you boatload of slaves by next moon. Agreed, Captain? I chief. You get slaves. We be friends!" he said emphatically while shaking his head up and down.

"No, Chief, we will not be friends," said Tristan. "Sama, make sure that these men understand what I'm going to say. Chief, you are an evil man, and we, this court, find that you are bad, and are bad to all people that you see. You make slaves of your own people. You kill people for the things they have that you want. You show no mercy to anyone, and then ask for mercy for yourself when you are caught. You are evil, and evil needs to be removed from this earth. Chief, you are to be hung from this tree until you are dead." Tristan looked down. "And may God have mercy upon your soul."

Sama finished translating, then one of the others timidly asked Sama a question, which Sama translated for Tristan.

"He wants to know what will happen to them now"? Tristan turned to face them as one of the knights threw a rope over a limb of a nearby tree.

"Which of you is the best of men?" Sama translated. There was jabbering between three of the men as a fourth man was pushed forward.

Sama said, "They say that this man is, Master. And they are right. He fed me many times when the chief tried to starve me."

The chief snarled at Sama, saying something in his native tongue, but Sama ignored him.

"Will he be a good leader, Sama?" asked Tristan.

"I think he will be, Master. He has a kind heart."

"So be it," said Tristan. "This man is your new chief. If any man says different, he has to answer to me." Sama translated and it was obvious from the expressions and emotion that the remaining men were very pleased to have a new leader.

The time had now arrived for the hanging. A table was placed beneath the tree limb, some twenty feet in the air. The chief was placed on the table and the rope tied around his neck.

"Have you anything to say?" asked Tristan.

"I will kill you all." The chief glared back at Tristan as he spat out the words.

"God, I pray that you will be merciful to this heathen, who has not been taught about your grace, or your commandments. Even though he sought to do evil unto us, we hold no malice in our hearts, and do forgive him, Lord. We cannot, however, in good conscience let him live to continue his evil ways on others that might not be as capable as are we at protecting ourselves. And so, it is with these thoughts that we commend his soul unto your hands, oh God. Amen."

Tristan prayed these words, then he kicked the table out from under the old chief's legs. The fall did not break his neck, but he twitched and gagged as the rope stole away his life's breath. After about a minute, the man quit moving.

The other tribesmen watched the grisly display. They were silent as the man continued to sway from his twitching movements earlier, then they turned to their new chief, with smiles. It was easy to see that they felt no loss at the passing of the old chief, but instead were filled with hope. Tristan had the men cut loose from their bindings. He spoke to the new chief, using Sama to translate.

"Chief, we will continue to honor our word to your tribe as we gave it to the old chief. You will be given the treasures we promised you three days ago when we landed if you will fulfill your bargain with us and help us to get our supplies."

The new chief replied, "Oh wise Captain, we would be honored to have you stay among us as long as you wish. Your wisdom is such that we will sing about it for generations to come. I myself am going to name my next son in your honor, and we will always welcome you to our village. Please, oh Great One, honor us whenever you return again this way," the young chief gushed.

Tristan smiled at the thought of a black child in darkest Africa running around and being called Tristan.

"We will miss your friendship, and will return to greet you if we should ever return this way again," he replied.

That afternoon, a dozen of the large cattle were driven into the encampment by the happy villagers. More meat than we need, thought Tristan, but he knew better than to turn down his new friends for fear of insulting them. The beef were slaughtered, butchered and packed away in salt drums for keeping. The old chief had been right about one thing though—the pig killed by Sama made for a wonderful dinner that night. It was eaten by the men who remained on the beach, and just as he had planned, Tristan slipped back aboard the ship before midnight, and the journey continued.

Chapter 4

Remembering a Strange Light in the Sky

San Diego, California, Home of Isaiah's Mother, July 13, 2007

"Isaiah Diego!" His mother's voice carried well, he thought absently.

"Yes, Mother?" Isaiah replied.

"Why didn't you tell me you were bringing JD with you for dinner?"

"Please, Mrs. Diego. If it's any trouble..." was as far as JD got before his friend's mother cut him off.

"No JD, it's not trouble. I just want to teach that son of mine to call before bringing someone home to dinner. Heaven forbid that he ever get married and do the same thing to his wife. He needs to know these things, JD. I know that you'd never do that to your mother, or your wife. Speaking of wife, how is that lovely girl you're dating? Naomi, isn't it? She is just the most precious thing, don't you think so, Isaiah? Well, don't you? What do I have to do to get you to answer me, Isaiah Diego?"

The whole speech had taken her almost a whole 10 seconds to spew out. Isaiah was fond of saying that his mother was not a speed walker, but a speed talker. He thought it was funny, but for some reason, she didn't. JD just nodded to her as she continued to alternately praise him and roast Isaiah. Finally, coming to Isaiah's rescue, JD pushed back from the table.

"Mrs. Diego, that was a wonderful meal. I can't imagine that you could have done any better on that steak had you known I was coming. But right now, Isaiah and I have a lot of work to do, if you don't mind us working in the living room."

"Of course I don't mind. You boys go and do whatever it is you need to do. I just hope it will help my Isaiah get the idea to get back to school. You know, JD, that he could be a great engineer..." Mrs. Diego never missed a chance to push Isaiah back at the school angle.

"Yes, Ma'am. I know he would, Ma'am, and I'm doing my best to help him do that, Ma'am."

They finally made it away from the table and into the living room. Isaiah had a printer set up on the table and the results from the side scan sonar displayed on the television. As they looked at the charts and the sonar data, JD dug through television and newspaper web sites, looking for any information he could find about a missing submarine.

"Nearly a month ago there was a big hubbub over that Iranian sub that was sunk off the east coast. You remember that mess, JD?"

"Yeah, but that was on the east coast off of Virginia." Suddenly, JD recalled the night in the desert. Dropping his pencil, he jogged off out the front door to his truck, which was parked outside. Moments later he returned with a folded scrap of paper.

"Six weeks ago I was coming back from helping Naomi with her presentation in Vegas. Remember? Well, I saw something in the night sky that I thought was a missile test at the time. I remember thinking it was strange that the military would fire missiles at night, but get this—the missile that I saw was killed by a rocket and fell into Lake Meade. Now put that together with the sound track that the president played on CNN from that Iranian submarine, and what do you get?"

Isaiah scratched his head. "I don't know, man. Are you saying that your missiles and the Iranian sub are related?"

"Yes, Isaiah, they are. That Iranian sub was some kind of decoy or something, sent to make the US, who was obviously aware of their plan, think that they were the bad guys, when in fact the bad guys were in a sub, shooting their bad stuff into Lake Meade."

"Okay, Sherlock. If they weren't the real bad guys and the real bad guys were shooting at Lake Meade, then why and where are the real bad guys now?" countered Isaiah.

"Well, I'm not sure, but its got to be either about a dirty bomb supposed to poison Lake Meade, or maybe even a biologic weapon meant to spread disease by poisoning the lake. Yeah, that's got to be it! And the where? They are north of Point Loma near La Jolla, just sitting there under 150 feet of water."

Isaiah nearly fell over. "Are you saying that the thing we found just west of La Jolla is an Iranian submarine?"

"Yes, I am," replied JD, "and furthermore, I think the Navy found it and sunk it that night I saw the rockets in the sky. I think the sub got its shot off, but the Navy saw it. They launched anti-missile rockets to kill the bomb, and then, while I sat on my truck and watched the air show, they moved in for the kill and whacked the sub that fired it."

"Okay, I'll buy most of it, but why didn't they stick around to clean up the mess? Why let us find it at all?"

"Because, my dear Watson, they figured a couple of torpedoes like the ones they have now, and there wouldn't be anything larger than a dishwasher left in one piece."

"Guess they were wrong about that, huh Sherlock?" Isaiah replied.

"I guess we'll have to dive to see for sure," said JD. "Are you up for it?"

"Are you kidding?" said Isaiah excitedly. "There's no telling what we might find down there that's salvageable." He had no idea how right he was.

✠

JD walked groggily toward the boat, his legs guiding him along the path he'd walked a hundred times before. He took another pull of the hot coffee that he knew would eventually wake him up. As he stepped aboard the LeiLani, he saw that Isaiah was already there, hustling around the foredeck and messing with the diving gear. Both were experienced divers, and since JD had access to the Institute's diving equipment whenever he needed it, they had some of the best re-breathers that money could buy stacked on the front of the boat. With a regular double tank of air, they'd only be able to have around 15 minutes of air time at the 150-foot-depth mark, but with the re-breathers that Scripps had let them use they'd be able to stay and work for nearly an hour before coming back up to the surface. The re-breathers were good for four hours of downtime, but with a dive of 150 feet, they'd have to take 15 minutes or so getting down, an hour to work, and two and a half hours of ascent time because the longer you stayed down, the longer it took for your body to get rid of the nitrogen in your blood stream on the way back up.

He hoped for a long dive, because that meant they would find a real sub with salvageable equipment. His mind wandered at the thought, but it could be that when they got to the bottom they'd find a smashed hull and little else. In that case, the dive would be a short one, and they'd only have to take 45 or so minutes to re-surface. Either way, he would get to dive in the fairly clear water just outside the bay, and that always made for a good day.

As these thoughts ran through his mind, he absently held a second cup of coffee out toward Isaiah, asking, "Hey, man, you want some?"

Isaiah was obviously pumped up. "No thanks, man. I've had two already. You know I hardly slept all night, thinking about this dive, JD. Do you really think we'll find an Iranian Sub down there—intact?"

"Well, judging from the sonar pictures, I'd say that there's probably only one hole in her about the size of an oven. I figure that's what we saw with the magnetometer—the portion of the hull where the torpedo or missile or whatever hit her. That is what is giving her away. The rest of the picture is just a lack of data, like there's a hole in the ocean floor there, but we know there isn't."

JD was wrong about the reason for being able to see the sub, but right on target with the size. The image being picked up by the magnetometer was indeed an oven. When the Japanese had assembled the Sea Wolf, they had ordered all non-magnetic devices for use inside the submarine so as to avoid this very issue, but somewhere in the order process the wrong oven had been sent and installed without the mistake being caught.

An hour and a half later, the two men were parked almost directly above the GPS location they had marked the day before. Just like the day before, they were being monitored by the sleeping sub just below them. Without further orders, the Sword of Allah sat where she had been told to stay, pending any updated orders. Self-preservation was still built into her priority schema, but without specific orders she would stay and monitor the boat above her until it was proven she was at risk of being attacked. Reading the signature of the boat as she approached, the Sword knew the boat above carried no weapons but would be classified as a threat only if she tried to send a message that might give away her location. So the Sword remained on the sea floor, playing dead.

JD and Isaiah chatted idly as they threw out the buoys that marked the area as a dive spot, both at the fore and aft of the boat. "So, JD, what ever happened with that rich dude who was so interested in Naomi's software? Is he gonna buy it to bundle with his suite of tools?" asked Isaiah.

"I don't know, Isaiah. She's got a meeting with him again next week, Monday I think. Yeah, I'm sure it's on Monday the 16th. Just a week from her birthday. Wow! Wouldn't that make a great birthday present for her? A few million bucks in the bank and her name on an office door as "Vice President" of Microcom or something like that. Wouldn't that be wild?" JD was temporarily carried away.

"I'll bet the old geezer takes the bait, man," responded Isaiah. "He'll get one look at Naomi in a tight dress, man, and he won't be able to say no to her." Isaiah laughed.

"Hey, dude—not cool!" came JD's instant response.

"Don't cloud up, man. I'm just yankin your chain. Chill, JD. It's just a joke."

"I know, Isaiah, but there really is something in the way he looked at her that day at the conference that I didn't like."

"Well, don't worry, man," said Isaiah. "I've seen the way she looks at you, man, and you got nothing to worry about!" Isaiah smiled as he said it.

JD knew Isaiah was right, but it was hard not to worry about a man only fifteen or so years older than himself with billions of dollars of net worth. "Isaiah, they say he just turned 40 this year and is worth something like 6 billion bucks. I've got a long way to go, and a short time to get there, man."

Isaiah busted out singing the "Smokey and the Bandit" tune, "East bound and Down," made famous by Jerry Reed. As he sang, he made sure that he really got into the portion where the words his friend had spoken were repeated..."We've got a long way to go, and a short time to get there," he crooned, pulling the cap off of his head and bowing to no one in particular. He really did have a terrible voice for singing, but ironically, he seemed to know the lyrics to almost every song that JD could name.

"Okay, man, enough already. You gotta promise me no singing while we're under water, Isaiah," said JD seriously.

"But I love the acoustics, man," came the teary reply from Isaiah.

"No singing. You'll scare away all the fish again," JD said, again in mock seriousness.

"Yessa, Massa. I be your good slave boy. We'uns who can't sing shouldn't sing, I guess," said Isaiah, pretending to be wounded to the core.

"The wisest thing you've said all morning," JD chided.

"You're just jealous 'cause you don't know the words to any song all the way through," said Isaiah. "All this self-righteousness from a guy who thought they were saying something dirty, instead of "Its Mag-ic... you knoo-oow, Never believe its not so-oo." Isaiah crooned the words to "Its Magic."

JD ducked his head sheepishly and turned red. "You'll never let me live that down, will you, Isaiah?"

"Not in this lifetime." Isaiah grinned back at him.

They finished putting on the gear, checked their Doxa dive computers, and did a com check on the full face masks. Satisfied that everything was working as it should, the two stepped off of the back of the boat into the warm waters of the Pacific. Pulling themselves down the aft anchor line, they slowly descended. As they reached the 75-foot mark, both men turned on their helmet lights, and JD turned on the extra bright hand-held dive torch that the Scripps Institute had been kind enough to loan them, along with the rest of the fancier gear they had. As they reached the 100-foot mark, the silhouette of the submarine seemed to spring into view. Both men gasped at the same time at seeing the sail looming up at them a scarce ten feet below their fins.

"God in heaven!" said JD. "Do you see that?"

"See it? How could I not see it?" came Isaiah's reply. "Its huge!"

As JD played the light fore and aft along the boat's hull,

its length and width became apparent. "She's got to be 400 feet long," he said.

"Yeah, and look at her beam," said Isaiah. "She's wider than a normal sub by nearly twice."

"And she seems to be flatter as well, not the tube shape of a normal sub," said JD.

"I'll bet she's 80 feet wide at her widest point," said Isaiah.

"And the sail seems shorter as well and no wings on the sail," JD added, "and what's that hump behind the sail?"

The two swam back and forth like kids trying to make up their mind in a candy store. Finally they calmed down and checked their time; nearly 30 minutes had elapsed.

"What do you think, JD?" asked Isaiah.

"I can't find a hole in her anywhere, not even a dent. She looks as clean and new as if she were just launched."

"That's what I thought too," Isaiah said, running his hand along the top of the sail and feeling the rubbery surface. "I did notice that there are slots just below us, about mid-way up the sail, for wings to slide out, and there seems to be an escape trunk at the back of the sail where it meets the deck."

JD cut in. "Really? An escape trunk? Are you thinking what I'm thinking?"

"No way, man. We need to come down with a fresh re-breather set if we want to do any exploring inside this thing. No way I want to get inside the hull and have to come back out in fifteen minutes. We need more time," Isaiah said.

"You're right, man. Lets get back up to the surface and do this right," came JD's response.

As they ascended to the surface, they had plenty of time to chat about what they had seen. They buzzed back and forth about the condition of the ship. JD had found no marks on her hull, and was puzzled as to why she had sunk.

"You don't suppose she's dry inside, do you?" Isaiah threw out.

"No way, Isaiah. She has to be wet. By the look of the silt built up on and around her, I'd say she's been on the bottom for at least a month. No crewed ship would be on the bottom that long without moving."

"Well, if she's a wreck, then where's the hole?" Isaiah questioned.

"Maybe underneath her. If we're lucky, the hole is on the bottom and has been sealed off by the way she lies on the bottom," responded JD.

"How do we get in then?" asked Isaiah.

"Through the escape hatch. If the pressure is equal on both sides we should be able to open both the outer and inner door and swim on into the interior of the boat. We're liable to see some pretty spooky things though, if the crew went down with her," said JD.

"You mean like they'll still be manning their stations and everything?" queried Isaiah, shivering at the thought despite the warm water.

"Could be, man, so buck up and get ready. We may be able to salvage this ship yet. Wouldn't the US government pay a pretty penny for a ship like this?" JD speculated.

"You think we can weld the hole in her hull shut and pump her out, maybe even float her again and bring her home?" Isaiah said, thinking out loud.

"That's exactly what I was thinking," said JD. "No reason why we shouldn't be able to do it," he said, his confidence growing. "Let's hurry up to the top and call someone to bring us out a welding rig." JD said, wanting the time to pass faster.

"Let's talk it over during lunch," said Isaiah caution tingeing his voice.

Even on the surface, they were scarcely able to contain their excitement. As they tore open a bag of chips and took two bottles of cola out of the fridge they talked about what it would take to close up a hole that size, and what kind of pump they would need. Isaiah made a couple of his famous deli sub sandwiches and they took all of it up to eat under the canopy of the top deck.

"I think I can get a pump from Scripps that will pump her dry," said JD between bites, "but I don't know about under-water welding gear. I think we'll need to bring someone in for that. In fact, we should call the Coast Guard right now and report what we found."

"No!" Isaiah shouted. "No, by the law of the sea. If we want to claim her as salvage, we have to bring her in. If we call in the Marines we'll lose everything."

That thought silenced JD. "I guess you're right, Isaiah. I'm getting the cart before the horse, huh?"

"You bet, mon," said Isaiah in his best Jamaican accent. "Let's just see if we can get into her before we do anything else."

"Okay, Isaiah. I'm glad you're here to temper my quick leaps of action. I'd probably have called the Coast Guard and gotten a hearty 'Well Done' for all my time and good work."

"You're right, JD. You gotta be slow to act when life throws something like this at you or you're liable to make the wrong decision."

JD stuck the wise words in the back of his mind for use at another place and time.

After lunch the two busied themselves on deck for another hour while the re-breathers were recharged and fully checked out for another dive session. Suiting up again, they both felt the adrenalin from the excitement of another dive on the submarine rush through their bodies.

"Slow and steady," said JD.

"You bet. It wins the race every time," replied Isaiah.

With those words, they stepped off the back of the boat for the second time that day. Following the same line as before, they were once again startled by the size of the submarine.

Shaking his head as if to clear it, Isaiah said, "I still can't believe how big she is."

"Me either, man," replied JD. "Where did you see the escape trunk?" he queried.

"Back side of the conning tower, right at the base," replied Isaiah.

As the two swam to the location, Isaiah, the more powerful swimmer, arrived slightly ahead of JD. They both looked at the sealed hatch but saw no handle or access plate with which to open it. As JD ran his hand around the edge of the door, two lights suddenly lit up on the right hand side of the door as it opened.

"What's this?" JD almost jumped as the lights—one red, one green—came to life.

"I guess the batteries are still workin', dude." said Isaiah. "Could be we can just walk in and turn the pumps on inside her and pump her out ourselves." He smiled cockily behind the faceplate.

"Well, here goes nothing," JD said, pressing the green light.

As he did so, there seemed to be a stirring of silt at their feet and the sound of water rushing in. As the sound decreased, suddenly the hatch popped slightly ajar.

"Well, I guess we're being welcomed in," said JD.

"Just so long as we can get back out," said Isaiah nervously.

Swinging the door open, both men swam into the trunk, which was big enough to hold eight or so large men. Leaving the door ajar, they tried the buttons inside the trunk that would release the inner door, but it was to no avail.

"Maybe you've got to shut the outer door first," said Isaiah to JD.

"Oh, yeah, I guess that makes sense. You wouldn't want to flood the submarine." JD laughed at his joke. To his surprise, as he closed the outside door, the escape hatch began pumping the seawater out of the hatch. "Now what do we do, smart guy?" asked JD.

"Just don't take your hat off, friend. When the inside door opens, we're liable to need to breathe again in a hurry." A small waterproof screen showed percent empty, and had a group of words in what looked like Farsi scrolling across the bottom in red.

"Wonder what that says," said Isaiah.

"Lets find out," said JD, touching the far right menu bar word, and was rewarded with a drop-down menu, also in Farsi. After fiddling around with a few taps on the screen, the Farsi text changed to English.

"Hey, how'd you do that?" asked Isaiah incredulously.

"Elementary, my dear Watson. The last word on the menu is always the help screen. I figured anything this fancy had to have a menu button to change between languages and the help screen is the place to find it."

"Amazing, my dear Holmes. Amazing," Isaiah said.

They looked down as the screen asked them how long they wanted to decompress before entering the sub. There was a mandatory 15 minutes on the clock already. "Well, looks like we get to wait here for at least 15 minutes," said Isaiah.

"Neat. That's exactly what the Doxa dive computer says too," said JD.

"Oh well, open the outside air valve and breathe the air it's giving us, but be ready to close the valve as soon as the inner door seal opens. We're liable to get a real hard shower when that inner door opens," said Isaiah.

They both did just that. At 14 and 1/2 minutes, both men went back onto the re-breathers and moved to the back of the chamber as they prepared for the door to open. To their surprise, the door made a small PSST sound and swung gently open into the interior of the sub.

"I can't believe it," said JD, still on the headset intercom.

"Me either," said Isaiah.

Turning off the re-breather's again, they pushed open the door the rest of the way and stepped across the threshold, pushing the door closed behind them. It sealed itself automatically with another PSST. The two men slowly removed their bulky helmets and re-breathing equipment, looking around the smallish room as if they had stepped into another world. Now, just wearing their swim suits, they found two unused hooks beside a half a dozen others that held full drysuits and full face diving gear, and they hung their gear on them. Testing the hatch, they moved out of the dive room and into the main deck. Looking forward, they saw a whole lot of doorways, many water tight doors, all open, and lights. To the aft was much the same. Just ahead of them and to the right was a spiral stairway, with deep blue pile carpeting leading up into the conning tower, and also down to the next deck down. They looked at each other silently, afraid to say anything lest a crew of crazed Iranians should materialize from the rooms and kill them. Slowly, they made their way up to the conning tower, where they fully expected to find a control room.

As they came to the end of the stairway, they turned around a carpeted wall to find the control room, complete with a raised chair that looked like it was made for Captain Kirk, and five other control stations, situated comfortably around the center chair, obviously for the other officers to sit at.

"JD," Isaiah said, finally breaking the silence, "what's going on here, man?" His voice was almost a whisper.

"I'm not sure, but it looks like the crew must have abandoned ship or something. Maybe we can look at the captain's log and find out," said JD.

"Lot of help that'll be. It's probably in Farsi," Isaiah said dejectedly.

"Maybe it's electronic, like the menus were," said JD, snapping his fingers. Without wasting another breath, he jumped into the captain's chair, swinging the flat panel in front of him. "Hey" he said, "whoever designed this really knew how to make it comfortable. Whooee! Is this a classy set up or what?"

"It's even better than the control room of that aircraft carrier my mom took me to in Hawaii," said Isaiah, finding a chair and sitting at the station just in front of JD. "Hey, this looks like it might be the steering control station," he said as the screen lit up in front of him as he sat down in the chair. "Did you see that? The screen came on just because I sat down."

"Yeah, mine did too," said JD absently, pressing buttons and pulling down menus as he had before. To his right, Isaiah could see everything that JD was doing as a large monitor came to life, showing the actions the captain was performing. As he swiveled in his chair to face JD, Isaiah noticed the large three-dimensional view screens that came to life as well. There he saw a blue ship obviously at the bottom of the ocean, and a red blinking boat almost directly above it. Both had pertinent data associated with the contact. At the bottom were the obvious longitude, latitude, and depth readings for the submarine. All at once, the information on the screen changed from Farsi to English. At the same time, he heard JD whoop with his success. "Did it, man," he yelled.

"Yeah, well, look at that man," said Isaiah, pointing at the screen behind JD.

JD swiveled in his chair and exclaimed, "Far out, man! That is the coolest display I've ever seen. Its so three-dimensional...and look, here's the sub, and here's the LeiLani and..." He stopped momentarily as he realized the line he was pointing to was the target track for a torpedo. "Here's the target track to destroy her." He gulped.

"This ship was targeting us, dude," said Isaiah.

Just then a new target appeared on the surface. According to the computer, it was a yacht of similar size and shape to the LeiLani, but was a good twenty miles to the north.

"Man, this is a cool ship," said JD.

"Yeah, but we haven't even had a chance to look at the whole thing yet. What are we going to do with her? Let's go together and check out each room to make sure there is no one on board, then go on from there," said Isaiah.

"No problem, but first let's locate the armory and see if we can't liberate a few weapons," said JD.

"Good thinking, bro," said Isaiah.

With a few clicks of the mouse, JD had located the armory, two flights straight down, but he also read that their were two hand guns located in a compartment beneath the captain's chair that could be unlocked from the console. Pressing the correct button, he was rewarded with a quiet "pop" as the drawer beneath the chair opened up. They both took a weapon—a Glock 45 cal, with two clips of ammunition each.

"Okay Sundance," said Isaiah in a mock western drawl, "you ready to ride?"

"Ready when you are, Butch," came JD's reply as he pulled back the slide, chambering the first round.

Almost an hour later, they made their way back to the control room. The ship was a ghost ship. All the hatches were sealed and watertight. The rooms were all devoid of life, but it was obvious that something bad had happened in at least one of the cabins, and it was also obvious from the mess in the ships infirmary that there had been a bad sickness on board.

"So what do we do now?" asked Isaiah. "No one on board and everything seems to be working."

"I guess someone needs to stay the night," said JD. "I guess what I'm saying is that I need to stay the night just to find out what happened here. In the morning you can come back, and I'll either meet you on the surface or you can dive down and come back on board like today. By then I'll know what happened here and we can decide what to do next."

"Okay, JD, but look, man, don't drink the water. If you have to drink something, they've got to have sealed food and water in the galley; drink that. And be careful about what you touch. This thing seems to have a mind of its own," Isaiah cautioned.

"Good advice, man," said JD, "but here is something I want you to do for me."

"What is it, JD?"

"Take these bottles. I've captured an air and a water sample. Take it to Marisa Hartman, You'll have to look up her number, but she should be able to run a full set of tests at the Scripps lab. Tell her that I think there might be toxins in the water and possibly the air. Tell her it came off of a ship we found sunk inside the bay, but that we need a full toxicological screening. Tell her it was Jap boat sunk in 1944. Heck, man, tell her anything you want to, but find out if the water and air on this thing are infected."

"What if it's the air, JD?"

"Well then, Isaiah, we've both got a problem. If it is the air, don't infect anyone else, and bring Marisa back here with you any way you can. Use your best judgment, Isaiah, but be careful."

With that said, they both made their way back to the escape hatch room. Putting on his own gear, Isaiah finally broke the silence.

"Until tomorrow, dude."

"I'll be waiting," said JD in response.

"Just don't push any buttons marked 'nuclear death,' man," Isaiah said and laughed.

"No way, Isaiah. I promise I'll be here when you get back."

Silently, he entered the air lock and stood there quietly as the water filled the room. Suddenly, he heard static, and then JD's voice. "Thought I'd see how far we can talk across these head sets."

"Good idea, JD," said Isaiah. "I'll be back first thing in the morning, unless Marisa can't do the tests until then. In that case I'll be back at noon."

"Okay Isaiah." The outside door opened and Isaiah stepped out and began his climb to the surface. "Isaiah, can you still hear me? The door has closed and it pumped itself dry again. No need for you to be slow going up. Just remember to exhale all the way to the surface and you should be able to go straight to the top without decompressing," JD told him.

"Right-O, old chap," came Isaiah's reply. "See you in the morning. I'm almost to the surface and I can still hear you. I'll let you know if I'm coming through the headset when I get here. Okay?" said Isaiah to his companion, now a hundred feet below him.

"Okay, Isaiah, I'll be waiting to hear from you. TTFN," he said jokingly.

"TTFN," replied Isaiah.

With that he climbed back aboard the LeiLani, took off the dive gear, placing the two vials safely in his dive bag, and then pulled up the dive markers and the anchor. Suddenly he felt very alone. He put the dive mask back over his head and called to his friend.

"JD, JD! Are you there?" But there was no response. "He must have just turned off the headset," he said to himself. Starting the motors, he pushed the throttle forward as he engaged the props, and the LeiLani left, with a lone passenger after having arrived with two.

One-hundred and fifty feet below the surface, JD watched on the screen as the LeiLani moved across it, headed for the safety of the harbor and the dock. "Well," he said out loud, "back to work." With those words, he began digging through the logs, looking for the captain's last thoughts. After an hour's digging, he finally came across the log he was looking for. The words he read were astounding. He couldn't believe the audacity of the plan those terrorists had in store for his country, and yet his country was handcuffed by world opinion. Reading in between the lines, he saw for the first time the inadequacy of it. He saw clearly now how the terrorists played the media and world opinion against the US, making themselves out to be poor, mistreated freedom fighters, when in reality they were nothing but thugs and mongrels who were trying to hurt everyone else in order to win their own nearsighted political goals.

They were willing to kill millions, possibly billions, of innocent people all over the world just to win the praise of some wacko religious nut living in a cave somewhere in Pakistan. At least he'd found that much out—Osama was behind all of this. Reading in between the lines, he'd seen that the Chinese were also doing everything they could to make things worse. It is so clear, he thought to himself. It really was a war of religion, even if the West wasn't playing the game like the East was. This was about everyone else against the Christians—the Muslims, the Atheists, and every other religion or anti-religion out there. They were all out to destroy the western world and the Christian way of life. Slowly, he pushed the touch screen away from him. He had to make sure that there was none of that crap still on board, and then he'd... "No, slow," he said to himself. Decisions like this needed time to be made correctly. He reminded himself of Isaiah's wisdom. Slowly, he pulled the touch screen back toward himself, thinking...

"Okay, Sport," he said to himself, "let's learn to fly this thing." Making himself comfortable, he said aloud, "First I need something to eat and drink." He headed down the stairs and to the galley, singing "Do Wa Ditty" as he went forward to where he remembered seeing the somewhat messy galley. Searching the pantry, he looked around, thinking there must at least be a pack of hot dogs somewhere in the freezer. As he dug through the large portions of frozen meat—Lamb, Lamb, Lamb... Then it hit him. He shook his head at his own stupidity. "These guys aren't gonna have a hot dog." He laughed at himself. No hot dogs, and no pork. He did find some bottled water and some left-over soup in the fridge. He got a portion of the soup and heated it up in the microwave. He took it and headed back toward a table in the dining room. Sitting down, he blew on the hot liquid, unwrapped some crackers and crumbled them into the soup. Something was scratching the back of his mind. He looked back at the monitor on the wall, thinking, and then Wham! it hit him and he backed away from the soup like it was death itself—and it was! Dumping the soup into a trash container, he put it into a barrel sized plastic container. Emptying the rest of the food out of the refrigerator, he put it all into the plastic barrel. Cleaning out every prepared liquid and food substance, he thought hard about where anything else might be that might have been prepared by the cook with the tainted water supply. He cleaned everything up while wearing his full facemask. Several times food splattered the mask and he was glad he wore it, even though he felt rather silly. After spending nearly an hour and a half cleaning the galley, he finally felt safe about even being there. It was nearly 7:00 PM and he was still hungry. He grabbed a bowl, some cereal and a self-contained single serving container of milk and headed for the control room.

Sitting down in the captain's chair, he ate his supper while reading the operating manuals for each of the functions situated around him. He devoured the manuals, touching the controls alternately as he read about the functions available to him. Turning on different functions, he realized the power that he held at his fingertips. He reached out with the long-distance sonar, listening for traffic. To his amazement, the view on the 3D monitor evaporated and a map of the Pacific from Alaska down to the tip of South America and stretching west to Hawaii materialized in front of him. Scattered around the expanse of ocean were at least a hundred red points, each with a designation around it. About fifteen of the red points flashed brightly and were marked as warships. Three of those fifteen also gave the third dimension of depth with their information, indicating they were submarines. There seemed to be a line of warships about 30 miles out from the coast. Six of them were within 200 miles of his current location. Obviously, they had an idea that this submarine was still somewhere in the vicinity.

It was an amazing testament to the builders of this vessel that they hadn't been able to find her. Even more amazing was that he had. It made him feel comfortable. He checked the weapons status. The sub carried sixteen Mark XII torpedoes forward and eight more in the rear torpedo room. It also carried 4—three of which were left—sea-to-land cruise missiles. Ten of the forward torpedoes had conventional 2000 lb. warheads, but the other six carried something called a "low level neutron magnetic charge." From all he could gather about it, there wasn't much information, it was supposed to explode approximately 8 feet below the hull of the ship it was fired at, with a low-level neutron explosive that had the power of around 20 tons of dynamite, enough power to break the unfortunate ship, no matter what size, in half and throw the pieces in different directions. It could kill a Nimitz-class aircraft carrier with a single shot, and probably take three or four escorts with it. Two of the rear torpedoes were also of the same type.

The two sets of torpedoes were arranged in a self-loading mechanism that replaced the need for manual loading and unloading of torpedoes. It looks very much like the drums of an old Thompson sub- machine gun, he thought. The difference was that these "shells" could be loaded and unloaded at will without being fired. The final weapons platform available to the submarine was a group of four missile silos, grouped just behind the sail. Inside each of these four silos were four rockets, four of which were anti-ship missiles with a range of 70 miles, four were anti-air missiles with a range of 120 miles, four were mid-range (1500 mile) tomahawk sea-to-land based missiles, and the other 4 were small intercontinental ballistic rockets with ranges of up to 4000 miles and a payload that could be swapped out with a weight of up to 1500 lbs. Currently, they had conventional warheads on each.

The sub had an array of defenses as well, including over a hundred decoys that, with the click of the mouse could be set up to sound like different types of submarines and ships. There was also special set of pores around the leading edges all over the submarine that would disperse an oily substance much like silicon, that when used, would make the surface slippery enough to give the sub a predicted extra 10 knots of speed. This had not been tested yet, but the calculations looked right. Add that to the sub's already impressive 65 knot top end rating and she should be able to outrun any torpedo known by at least fifteen knots.

The sub also had a new electronic fiber-optic rubberized skin. While being radar absorbent to keep it invisible to surface radar and undersea sonar, its fiber-optic pores allowed it to present a view on its surface that made it look like what was 180 degrees from it; literally, it could be almost invisible to the human eye. This had been tested for several years by the United States, but the Japanese had stolen the technology and taken it to new heights. According to the documentation, when turned on, the black-skinned submarine would be virtually invisible to the naked eye unless someone opened a hatch.

On top of the SAM (Sonar Absorbing Material) that covered the exterior, it also had a new invention that was a SJS (Sonar Jamming Skin). Upon receiving a sonar "ping" or sound, the computer would send out a canceling tone, the opposite in amplitude and strength, effectively canceling the wave and stopping any return. Inside the submarine, in areas where noise generation was constant, a similar system had been put in to cancel internal sound as well. The theory was effectively the same as used in noise-canceling headphones. The skin was not smooth like most submarines. Instead, the skin was pitted and almost rough to the touch, like the skin of a shark. These pits along its surface caused water to build up in the grooves, making for a slick surface. As water passed along its hull, the pits filled with water and became a place for the water to build up, making the slickness of water against water instead of water against rubber. This made for at least five more knots of speed. Along with the impressive electronic intelligence-gathering capabilities and defenses, it also had two deep submersible subs that could seat two and leave enough cargo room behind them for a dozen men. As he read more about these two submersibles, he was amazed at their capabilities.

Along with the normal submarine weapons, he also read about an anti-matter ray that had a range of up to 5 miles. Supposedly, it excited the atoms in whatever it hit and they literally shook apart, leaving dust as the atoms fell apart. This ray was fired through what appeared to be another radar mast that was extended up through the conning tower and fired a beam that started out 6 inches in diameter and lost effectiveness at five miles at a diameter of 8 inches. It was radar-driven and appeared to be for defensive purposes.

If radar could see it, then this weapon could put a hole through it in less than a microsecond.

Smaller versions of the beam were also mounted on the mini-subs. They had much less bandwidth and were effective to no more than 1000 yards. The diameter of the beam was a scant two inches.

The sub also had within its arsenal of weapons a group of 10 drones, each of which could remain aloft for up to a week. These drones, though small, could fly unnoticed above and relay tactical data back to the submarine. A small hump just aft of the missile silos served as a launch bay for the small drones. With a 10' wingspan, two at a time could be assembled in the launch bay, and when the ship surfaced, the bay opened up allowing the drones to be launched. They could pass data in scrambled format to the ship in three modes: UHF, ULF, and HF frequencies. Even though it was slow, the ULF format could penetrate the depths of the ocean easily, but it could take hours to send the data intended. The drones could fly independent of control by using self-contained programming, or could be controlled by virtual control consoles located in the next room over from the control room. The drones could also carry two air-to-surface missiles that, although small, could take out strategic targets—like leaders.

The ship had power to spare, literally; the two reactors on board could light up a small city each. And it was quiet. Really quiet, JD thought as he stopped and listened. He couldn't hear anything except the movement of air through the ductwork. He smelled the air—cool and clean smelling. His thoughts went back to the samples he'd left with Isaiah and he said a silent prayer that they both would end up okay. After having read the log and how the captain had emptied the water systems and flushed the air systems, he felt better about it, but still he worried that he and Isaiah may have succeeded in infecting America where the Iranians had failed. He prayed that was not the case.

Isaiah had made a point of avoiding all contact with people. He even avoided the dogs and cats, just to be careful.

He was anxious about meeting with this Marisa Hartman, but he knew he needed to get the vials checked right now. Stopping at a pay phone booth on the corner of a gas station, he rifled the pages of the ragged copy of the phone book. Twice he was afraid that a car was stopping beside him, but they had paused momentarily and kept going. Finally, he found her listed, along with 25 other Hartmans, and jumped back into his car. Pulling out his cell phone, he parked the car and dialed the first of three M. Hartman's on the page.

"Are you Marisa Hartman?" he stammered as a woman answered on the second ring. "No, I'm Mary Hartman," came the reply.

"I'm sorry, Ma'am," he said quietly. "I was looking for a Miss Marisa Hartman. Sorry to have bothered you."

"Please wait," the woman said quickly. "She's my daughter. May I help you?"

"Yes Ma'am, I'm looking for her for a friend—Mr. JD Gilhooley. Could you help me to get in touch with her please?"

"If you give me your number I'll have her call you when she comes in," the nice woman replied.

"Certainly, Ma'am, I'll do that, but if you don't mind, I really need to speak to her urgently. Could you perhaps call her and give her the message please?"

"All right, young man, but only because you have been so nice and polite while speaking to me."

"Thank you, Ma'am, very much. My name is Isaiah Diego, and I'm calling on behalf of JD Gilhooley. My number is 867-5309. Have you got all of that?"

"Yes, Mr. Diego. I'll get the message to her right away."

They both hung up. Isaiah could hardly contain himself. Now, he thought, what else do I need to do?

Starting the car, he drove to a burgeraunt and ordered a meal. He was careful to avoid any contact as he put the money in the tray and had the girl put the food on the edge and asked her to back away. She looked at the young man behind the rolled-up window oddly, but then did as asked.

As she backed away from the window, he rolled his car window down, picked up the food and quickly left.

"Well, that's one girl who'll never date me." He laughed at how odd it must have seemed to her. But, he thought, I'll be doggoned if I'll be the cause of a worldwide plague. He didn't realize that if he were already infected, going to a burger joint was the worst thing he could have done. He parked his car in a church parking lot a mile from his house and curled up with his food, and the phone, praying for a call. Fifteen minutes later, it came.

"Hello," he shouted into the receiver.

"Yes, I'm looking for a Mr. Diego," a friendly-sounding voice at the other end of the phone replied.

"Ms. Hartman, I presume?"

"Yes. This is a bit odd. Any chance you can tell me what it is that JD needed from me?"

"Yes, Ma'am. I have in my possession two vials—one of air, the other of water, that JD and I need to have tested for toxicity—poisons, you know, that kind of stuff."

"Well, Okay, but why doesn't he just bring it to me tomorrow at the lab at school?" she asked, thinking the request a bit odd.

"Well, you see," he said, "we've—that is he and I—well, we've kind of gotten ourselves into something. You see, we found this sunken boat, and it kind of had some trapped air and water on it. Well, the water isn't really the problem any more, it can be dumped, but both he and I breathed the air, and it might have been subjected to biological warfare, so I left him to guard it and I brought the samples to you for testing."

It had all spilled out so quickly that Marisa could say nothing but "Oh." Finally, she grasped his urgency. "Well, then, I guess you need to know right now if you might be infected. Right?"

"Well, that would be nice," said Isaiah with a slight chuckle.

She smiled at the other end of the phone. "You can joke at a time like this?"

"One has to keep his sense of humor," said Isaiah as his real personality began to shine through the conversation. His nervousness was gone. She seems like a nice person, he thought. "Can I meet you somewhere, Marisa?"

"My, you do move fast!" she said, sounding slightly affronted.

"That's not what I meant. Well you know...I mean, I just meant..." Isaiah stammered at her obvious distrust.

That's when she laughed. "Just wanted to see how well your sense of humor really was." She laughed again—really a giggle.

"I can't believe you got me," Isaiah said. "Well, now that you've had your laugh at my expense, how about it? Can I meet you somewhere?"

"Sure. Meet me outside the school at the burger joint parking lot and you can ride in with me."

"But what about the chance I'm contagious?" he asked.

"Don't worry," she said. "Chances are if you were infected today you wouldn't be contagious for at least a week. Even if you were, I'll be able to isolate the virus and I'd save the world for you and me inside of a day. As long you haven't been to too many places, we could fix this and contain it without too much effort." She had managed to assuage the young man's fears.

"Okay, Dr. Hartman," he said obsequiously.

"Not yet, but soon," she said laughingly.

"I'll be there in ten minutes." He smiled and hung up. In the back of his mind he thought, I sure hope she's pretty.

An hour later they were talking and laughing with each other as if they had known each other for years. Waiting for the results from the GC and the slides had given them time to get to know each other quite well. I really like her, he thought, looking at her as she picked up the used equipment and took it to the sink for cleaning. She had an easy way about her. And she laughed easily too. Good sense of humor, smart, very easy on the eyes, he thought.

In turn, she was analyzing him as well. He is tallish—at least 5'11", and so good looking, she thought. But it was more than that. He was good looking, but he seemed to have gotten more so after she had met him. He has a good sense of humor, and he's smart—real smart, she thought, but not conceited. I think I might like to see him again sometime real soon. As the thoughts crossed the room in unheard vibrations, she broke the silence.

"Well, I can tell you that the water is drinkable, but it shows very small traces of small pox. I'd say that someone had used small pox as a carrier for something else. If it was the Japanese from World War II, it was probably just small pox," she said. "I'd really need to know who the perpetrators were before I'd know what to look for..."

She was fishing, and Isaiah knew it. He didn't know how far to take it or what she might say to people, so he fished a little for himself. "Can I trust you, Marisa? I mean, really deeply trust you to keep what I have to say between us?"

"As long as it's not morally or ethically wrong," she replied.

"Okay," he said. "Everything I've told you has been the truth. I just haven't told you that the wreck we found wasn't old."

"I thought you said it was... No, you didn't, did you? You just implied it, didn't you? Okay, so whose wreck was it then?"

"It belonged to a group of Iranian terrorists sent to drop a biological weapon into the water supply of Las Vegas. At least that's what we've deduced so far. We've managed to get on board, but we are afraid of doing the job for them if we aren't careful." He laid the cards on the table.

"Okay," she said somberly, "if it was the Iranians, that means Ebola."

The word hung in the air like a nasty odor. "Ebola. That's the nastiest of all the viruses out there. Right?" he asked.

"Yes, but it has only been thought to be air borne in one case, and that was manipulated, just like this," she thought out loud. "God in Heaven! I hope not," she said. "The water supply, that fits with Ebola as well. Well, the good news is that I can tell you right now that the water is no longer carrying Ebola, and I'll know with just one more GC test if the air carries it, but I really doubt it. It wouldn't last more than a day in a closed environment."

Ten minutes later the test was done and it was clean. Isaiah's whole body visibly relaxed. "That's really good news, Marisa, not just for me, but for JD as well."

"Not to mention the whole world." Marisa laughed. Isaiah joined in. "Well," she said smiling, "can you really deeply trust me?" She laughed again, and her eyes danced.

Isaiah reached out and embraced her warmly, and their eyes locked for a moment until he kissed her willing lips. As they held the embrace, her eyes closed and her body felt every touch of his body against hers. Never before had a man made her feel like this—like a school girl one minute, a best friend the next, and then a woman, all in the space of an hour. Or was it a minute, two, or thirty seconds? She wasn't sure, but as they pulled apart their eyes locked again.

"I'm sorry, Marisa..." Isaiah stammered. "I'm not usually forward like that—ever. I guess it's a combination of the news, and the way you smell, and, well...the way...well, everything about you. I just, well, I'm sorry," he ended, but his eyes said that the only thing he was sorry about was rushing. His eyes said all the right things, she thought.

"Me too," she gushed. "I'm not one of those women who kiss a fellow on the first date, much less on a lab visit." She smiled.

They both ducked their heads, and felt silly. "Look," said Isaiah, "I like you, but I don't want you to be scared of me, so how about we start the last few minutes over again?"

"Okay," she said "By the way, Isaiah, before we forget everything, I like you too."

Isaiah blushed, but he took her hand and kissed it elegantly, saying "Thank you for an entirely lovely evening, my dear."

Together, they walked back across the parking lot to her car. With some chitchat along the way, they managed to keep it loose and easy. As they got to the car, Isaiah asked her to have dinner with him. She agreed. It was nearly eleven before they left the restaurant and headed their separate ways.

"I'll call you on Monday or Tuesday," he said.

"Two day rule?" she asked and smiled again.

"No, I just know that JD's gonna have me busy for a few days now that we know that we're not going to spread the virus accidentally."

"Okay," she replied. "I have late class on Tuesdays and Thursdays, so not then, but when you can, give me a call."

They both smiled as Isaiah leaned in close and gave her a soft kiss on the cheek, and whispered "good night." She nearly melted again. Wow! she thought, A real gentleman too.

Later that night, Isaiah went back to work. He had much to do. His first act was to go to the all night grocery store down the street. He was shopping, two carts full, when his cell phone rang. It was Naomi. As he answered the call, he knew that JD would want her to know he was okay.

"Hey, Naomi," he answered.

"Hey, Isaiah, have you seen JD? I've been trying to get him at the apartment, and on his cell, but haven't been able to get him all afternoon."

"Yes, he's umm, he's out of cell range right now, Naomi," he said, trying not to lie, and yet not to say too much.

"Well," she said waiting, "where is he?"

"Well, he's out in the bay right now. I'm supposed to meet him there again in the morning."

"Oh," she said. "What's he doing out there at night?" she asked, not understanding.

"Well, we kind of found some strange things while we were out there yesterday, and he wanted to stay on top of them until we figured out how to best utilize the information," he said, still not lying but sounding a little odd to himself.

"Isaiah Lemuel Diego!" she said sternly. "What is going on? You know you can't lie to me. I know you too well and you're keeping something from me. Now, what is it, and is JD okay?"

"Okay, Okay," he said ducking his head from her tirade while standing in the potato chip aisle. "You have to meet me, because I can't really talk about it over the phone, Okay? I'm at the grocery store right now, so I'll meet you in an hour at JD's apartment, Okay? But don't worry, he's fine."

"Okay," she said. "His apartment in an hour."

✠

At about the same time, JD was busy trying out different capabilities of the sub. Being ever so careful, he decided it was time to try out the engines. He checked the maps—nothing around for over 20 miles, so here we go, he thought. Making note of his current location, he decided to go on a little test drive. Making a few clicks on the console screen, he switched to the drive screen and using the virtual controls, pulled up on the planes and forward on the thrusters, and he was rewarded with the feel of the ship lift slowly from the dust of the sea floor, and slowly move forward. Setting a course, he moved the sub toward the mainland just north of La Jolla, keeping her speed at less than ten knots. He kept the sub a mere 50 feet off of the sea floor, wanting to make sure he avoided any activity. As he started feeling good about himself, a flashing signal caught his eye on the 3D screen and he realized he was going to cross under a fishing ship unless he made a quick course change. Not wanting to snag a net, he turned the ship sharply to the port, not realizing he would be entering an area of shallow water by going in that direction. Soon his conning tower was running slightly above the water, and he realized he was visible. Turning hard to port again, he headed back into deeper waters and was once more below the surface. He decided it was time to get back and stay out of trouble until he had more help. He realized that being near land wasn't the right place to try out a submarine, so with a heavy sigh, he headed back to his originating spot.

To his surprise, the warships had moved closer in now. The two Aegis-class destroyers had radar systems that could see the splash of a shell in the water from nearly 50 miles away. While not being able to see the reflection of the conning tower, one of the two had spotted the wake the conning tower had made and it had struck the operator as odd to see a wake without a reflection of a boat making it. After relaying the information to the other destroyer, they both headed to investigate.

As his sub settled back into its spot at the bottom of the sea, he put the sub back into sleep mode. The two warships, both identified to be of US origin, had caught his scent. They were moving back and forth, headed generally into the area where he had gone above the surface. They were now within 5 miles. As they moved in an obvious crisscross pattern, JD asked the computer for a projected plot. Instantly, a plot showed, moving out from each ship, indicating that they were crossing in front of him and moving into the port, never getting closer than 1 mile.

Without being asked, the computer also put up torpedo tracks so they would hit at the closest point where they would cross in front of the sub. The plot scared JD. He made sure that the weapons system was locked offline. The two ships continued following the predicted plots, and as JD watched, they passed him, went into the harbor, and then headed back out into the open ocean. After an hour of sweating out the two ships JD relaxed and decided to do some reading while catching some sleep in the captain's cabin. To his amazement, almost anything he could see from the control room could be seen from the screen in the captain's cabin as well. What a ship! he thought. Setting an alarm for 6 hours, he drifted off to sleep.

✠

At the same time that JD was cruising around just off of the coast, Isaiah was sitting in JD's apartment, telling Naomi a story she could scarcely believe.

"Now, Naomi, you have to promise me that you won't say a word to anyone, especially your dad, about this," Isaiah begged.

"I don't know, Isaiah. This is really a big deal. Why don't you just raise it, tow it into the harbor and claim it as salvage? I'm sure the government would pay you well for it, and then it wouldn't be your problem any more. Besides, if it had a biologic weapon on board, the government would be able to use that proof to hold Iran responsible."

"You really believe that, Naomi? Remember a month ago when the government sank that sub off of the east coast? They had that sub dead to rights, in their own voices they said they were going to attack Virginia Beach, and we still have people attacking the president, as well as your own dad, for sinking it—and those are our own senators!" he said hotly.

She shook her head sadly. "You're right, Isaiah. We'd probably have to turn it back over to the Iranians again as their property, and let them use it to sneak up on us again. It's disgusting!" she said. "Really disgusting. You're right. I don't think you should turn it over to them. I think you ought to use it against those terrorists. Use it the way the US government can't."

"What are you saying?" asked Isaiah.

"Well, with the right inside information, you might be able to use their own weapons against the terrorists without the US being involved. You could be kind of pirates for justice." She smiled.

"Pirates for justice!" said Isaiah. "Well, it sounds good, but we need to talk it all over with JD."

"We'll talk to him in the morning then," she said.

"What's this we stuff?" asked Isaiah stiffly.

"We'll talk to him tomorrow, Isaiah, or I'll talk to my dad tonight." She smiled sweetly at him. "In the mean time, you take his bed and I'll take the couch," she said, pushing him off of the couch with her feet.

"All right, all right. I know when I'm beat. I just can't believe I could get beat so easily by a woman. Sheesh!"

"Just wait," she said. "By the look in your eyes when you talked about Marisa, I'd say you were beaten by more than one woman tonight!" She laughed.

"I knew I should've never told you about her. She's too nice to be mean to me like you." He laughed also.

"I'll bet."

"Hey, Naomi, what were you so hot to get hold of JD for anyway?" he questioned.

"Oh, nothing much. I just wanted to let him know I made my first couple of million today." She smiled and turned over, fluffing the pillow.

"What?" Isaiah said, almost fainting.

"My software," she said. "I got a big offer for it this afternoon, and I had an offer for JD too. Now I'm not sure whether to take mine or his?"

"His offer, your offer—what are talking about?" said Isaiah.

"We'll talk in the morning. Now go to sleep. I've got to get my beauty sleep, you know," she said, turning her back to him.

Isaiah shook his head and walked to the bedroom, scratching his head both mentally and physically. "Goodnight," he mumbled, more to himself than to her as he left the room. Women! he thought. Boy, was JD gonna be pissed at him when they both showed up tomorrow. Oh well, what could he do?

Chapter 5

Knights of Truth and Honor Cross the Equator

Friday, November 10th, 1307

Tristan and his fleet of heavily laden ships had reached a point where the water in the bottles swirled out into the cups the wrong direction. It was time to head west. For November, it was still quite warm, but God had blessed them with few storms, and they were light, so far. Normally in November in the Mediterranean they would be experiencing wicked storms that blew cold winds to the east, but where they were was like a new world.

According to one of the books salvaged from the great library of Alexandria, found as a treasure of the ancient Jewish temple, the beaten brass and gold plates that formed the pages of the book told of a route to a new continent, one inhabited by the distant descendants of a tribe of Arab and Jewish travelers, supposedly guided to the new land by God's hand before the conquering of the Jews by the

Emperor Nebuchadnezzar some 700 years before the birth of Christ. Following the same path, the men fleeing the Templar persecution felt they could make the trip as easily as had the fearful Jews 2000 years earlier. According to the plates of brass and gold, the crossing would take two months. Tristan figured that with the changes in technology they should be able to make the trip in no more than 6 weeks. He sent word to each ship in the fleet, making sure they all had enough supplies for a trip of at least that long. As a positive response was gotten from each of the ships, he sent word to follow him west for a long journey. The next day they passed an island on the port side that appeared to be deserted. Continuing west, they all felt a little anxious about their journey.

For two days the sea was calm, with minimal waves and a beautiful westward, gentle breeze that everyone hoped would continue throughout the remainder of the journey. Unfortunately, that changed early the next morning. Waking up to a darkening sky, Tristan looked all around the ship and found nothing but sea for as far as the eye could see. The waves had gotten larger during the night and looked to be at least 10 ft. tall. The ships, large for their day, suddenly seemed quite small and inconsequential, but Tristan bent his head and knelt. To Sama, the actions seemed strange. As Tristan prayed to God for leadership, Sama watched with some consternation.

"Master Tristan, what are you doing?" asked Sama worriedly.

"Don't worry, Sama. I'm not afraid or lost. I just need to pray to my God for guidance to make sure I make good decisions for all of the ships," he replied.

Sama nodded slowly, but it was obvious that he was worried that his friend had lost his confidence.

"Listen Sama," Tristan said, recognizing his young friend's fears, "Over the next weeks, I will teach you much about my God so you will understand."

The next day they set up several hours to study the word of God and to explain Tristan's strong beliefs. The day continued to look gloomier. As noon crept upon them the weather seemed to get worse each hour. The waves were now 14 ft. high and the wind was swirling and hard to gauge. By 2 o'clock word was passed to the fleet to go to minimal sails and to put out the sea anchors to keep them facing the approaching wind and waves.

The night was frightening to everyone. God seemed to be testing each man's faith. High waves crashed over the decks of all the ships. The once trusted ships seemed to be ready to break apart, leaving the crews lost at sea. More than one of the seasick knights cried out to turn around and go back to Africa. The more tried and true sailors knew that this was a bad storm, but not one to be afraid of yet. The morning found the ships scattered. Of the twenty-four ships in the armada, several smaller groups were now in existence: two groups of ten each, a group of two, and two individual ships that felt exceedingly lost.

The day and the storm seemed to break at the same time. Tristan ordered flaming arrows shot into the air to attract the attention of the lost ships. By noon, the twenty of the ships had come together and two other groups of two were still looking for help. The ships continued their westward route, firing arrows into the air, looking for the wayward ships. By evening two more ships were back in the fold, and Tristan had begun to fear the worst about the remaining two ships; nevertheless, he ordered arrows to continue to be fired in hopes of contacting them.

Around 10:00 PM the signal was seen by the remaining ships and returned by them. After a full day of fears, the fleet was back intact. It led to a meeting the next day in which a message was sent out to each ship, letting them know the plan for continuing should they become separated: continue west as close to the original course as possible. Upon reaching land, head north, slowly waiting a day between sailings. The larger group would send scouting parties both north and south for a week in search of straggling groups.

With that decided, the voyage continued. They all felt better now that they were all still safe. Tristan gave praise to God for their safety, and prayed daily for their success. During the previous rough days and nights of sailing, young Sama had ported himself well, but was still struggling with seasickness. Daily, Sama spent his daytime hours trying to get fresh air in his lungs and the feeling of queasiness out of his mind. Nightly, he dreaded the rocking of the ship. By the end of the first week at sea he was getting used to the rocking of the ship. Even though he was becoming accustomed to it, he still feared another storm. Tristan did his best to quash his young friend's fears, and he gave him many duties to keep his mind and body busy.

After sailing for three weeks and six days, land was spotted. The trip had been more or less uneventful. The only storm they had run into had been the bad one the third day out. The land they spotted was a small island. Upon finding safe harbor in a small but protected bay, Tristan and a group of knights took a small rowboat to the island. The island was small and uninhabited. No water was found, but the island was lush and inhabited by birds, snakes and small animals of all description. Within an hour it was decided that staying on the island for any length of time would not be safe. The ships were given time for any repairs, and for the capture of any birds or small animals that they wanted for eating, and then they'd be heading farther west. The next morning all twenty four ships left the safe port and headed westward toward the unknown.

By morning of the second day after the island stopover, land was again sighted—another island, this time on the port side of the armada. Deciding to pass this island up, Tristan continued due west. After another two days, the mainland was sighted for the first time. Upon sighting land, he also sighted the signs of people. Although they had not yet been spotted, Tristan knew they would soon be either the guests or the captives of the people of a new land. Tristan prayed that it would be the former and not the latter.

It was now mid-December and the weather was still stifling, but it was better than the cold windswept islands in the Byzantine Empire. He noted that in places the mountains seemed to rise right out of the sea and continue inland forever. He wondered what type of people might inhabit such a lush green world. Deciding to continue the northern route that had been the original plan, the ships hugged the coastline, continuing in their northwestern route. Within a days sailing, a safe harbor was found. A beautiful sandy beach lining the cove of a natural inlet beckoned to the knights.

Still not having seen any people or fishing vessels, Tristan was beginning to believe that the new land was uninhabited. He was not, however, foolish enough to believe his own feelings. He knew he had to be very careful if he was to protect the legacy he carried hidden in the depths of his cargo holds. The people of these lands must have never heard of Christianity, or of Islam, for that matter. They could be more pagan than the blacks in Africa. With some trepidation, he ordered a small group of his men to gather. Along with Sama, Tristan and 10 knights went ashore. There were trails leading to and from the beach. Footprints up and down the trails gave proof that they were indeed not alone, and beyond that, certainly not unknown to the residents.

Their immediate reconnoiter showed that there was no one present upon the beachfront. Wasting no time, he signaled for more men to come ashore. Gathering the men together, he and the knights knelt together on the beach and gave thanks to God for their safety so far and their continued safety forthcoming. Then, arising, Tristan began to give orders.

They needed to restock their water and food supplies. The men were restless as well. Having been at sea for the better part of three months now, they were desperate to reach a place to call "home." Tristan knew that it would be important to find just the right location, one that they could occupy as well as one that would have natural protection should the local inhabitants decide they wanted the riches that they traveled with. This was not it. It would be a temporary stop, but a necessary one.

The "riches..." He smiled to himself again. They were not important because of the gold they contained, although it was an immense amount; they were important because of their history—the History of Christianity. He knew that if the kings of Europe or the pope were to get their hands on the vast golden treasure in his holds, the history of Christianity would be melted down into gold coins bearing King Edward's likeness. Lost to the world would be the Ark of the Covenant and the vast golden books of Moses and Joshua. Also hidden in his holds were vast amounts of golden bricks, and a map made of thick gold, imprinted with the path to the mines of Solomon. Along with the map were thin pages of gold that detailed the destruction of the entrance and where and how it was hidden along Africa's eastern coastline. Included were beautiful green emeralds the size of a man's palm, and rubies bigger than the pommel of his sword, encrusted with gold, and a promise of more should one but follow the path promised in the map.

It was a history he carried. In his hold was the most important of the relics found hidden beneath the temple mount: the death clothes of Christ himself, along with the crossbeam of the tree upon which He was crucified. Also found in the ornate golden box was a history, written on ancient scrolls, a first hand account by Joseph of Aramathea, detailing the night of Jesus' death, his burial in Joseph's own tomb, and his subsequent resurrection three days later. Joseph had begged for the body of Christ from Pilate, and he, with the help of several of the local women, had prepared the body and wrapped it in accordance with Jewish tradition and law, and buried it. This testimony had been translated to brass and golden plates over the next several centuries, in Greek as well as Hebrew. There were three witnesses, all saying the same thing, all verifying the death and resurrection of Christ. With this, there could be no doubting the story that Christianity held most sacred.

Along with the other remnants of that day was also the spear, supposedly the same spear that pierced the side of Christ after his death. Tristan knew he had to keep this "treasure" safe with every last breath in his body, and so he took only the chances he must.

By now it was four hours past noontime. Tristan decided that it would not be wise to spend the night ashore, but to build fortifications the best they could for today and sleep onboard the ships, then begin a better temporary home again in the morning. The men were set to work building walls and digging trenches that surrounded the landing location.

The walls were made of anything they could find—tree trunks, rocks, even the odd seedpods dropped by trees. They looked like date trees, but instead of dates they had clusters of large seed pods that appeared to be falling off of the trees at random. Upon breaking them open, a smaller, but still the size of two men's fists, inner seed was found inside. This seed was much harder to break open and when it was breached, was found to have a sweet milky liquid inside. Coating the inside was a pure white meat about half an inch in thickness all around the inside of this strange seed. Upon tasting the white coating, the knights found it to be delightful, as was the sweet nectar that it contained within it. The knights had found coconuts for the first time in their lives, and they were amazed by them.

Tristan wondered what other discoveries lay ahead of them in this new world. After building a fire and roasting open some of the shells they found in abundance along the shoreline, they ate from the abundance that the sea offered to them. Several turtles were also caught and slaughtered for the meat they offered. It was good to be back on land, and by nightfall it was difficult for the group to climb back into their boats and row back to the ships, but that is what they did. Before leaving, Tristan ordered them to resupply the fire with wood, and stoke it so it would burn throughout the night.

Around 10:00 PM, Tristan was summoned to the topdeck. A lookout had been watching the shoreline, and had seen movement around the fire. Using his looking device, he tried his best to see what and who was moving around the fire. With his crude telescope, Tristan was able to make out several human shapes, poking around and searching for clues about the foreigners. Nothing had been left ashore, and the only thing that the crudely dressed natives could find was the walls and trenches that had been made.

They were dressed strangely, with dark hair and a funny slope to their foreheads. Tristan noted that they carried spears and wore breast plates, grieves, and shiny armor on their upper and lower arms in sections. It was difficult to see, but they also seemed to have a reddish tint to their skin. While it could have just been the firelight, these men seemed odd to Tristan. He clutched the shield of gold around his neck and instinctively rubbed it. They may be different, but they carried spears and wore armor, and that worried him.

Tristan praised the guard for his good eyes and made sure that the guards on deck were aware of the movement on shore, and they were told to be doubly sure to watch for any boats that might carry natives to their ships. He especially ordered the seaward watch to be extra careful, for if he were to attack sleeping vessels, he would do it from the side least expected—the seaward side.

Word was passed to the other twenty-three vessels in the fleet by means of signal lamps. The night passed tensely, but uneventfully. By morning, when Tristan appeared on deck, it seemed the whole crew was standing at the port side of the boat, looking at the sandy beach. As Tristan moved to the railing, he understood why.

"When did they arrive?" he asked the lookout he'd spoken to the night before.

"They just sort of materialized out of the mist this morning, sir."

"How many?"

"Last count was 120, sir."

"Well," said Tristan "you can bet if he has 120 on the shore, there are more in the jungle waiting."

"Yes sir." the lookout replied, turning a bit white.

"Have you seen any boats?" Tristan again probed.

"No sir, none. They seem to be a land-only people. Haven't seen anything close to a boat yet."

Tristan took out his viewing device for a closer look. With the sun now up he could get a better view. "There, in the front—the one in the middle seems to be the chief. He's wearing a feather headdress that is much fancier than the others, and he has much more shiny breastplates and carving on his grieves and armor," said Tristan, pointing to a central figure in the line of men. "They seem to be carrying spears and clubs of some kind I've never seen," he continued. "Their skin is definitely reddish in color, not black like our friend Sama here, and not brown like the Islamic people, and not white like our own. While they don't appear angry or to be waving their weapons in hostility, they definitely have weapons, though made only of wood. Strange. It would be best if we are very careful in our dealings not to antagonize them." Tristan put away his telescope and went back below.

Putting on his most pompous and pretty armor, and carrying a various array of weapons, he reemerged from his cabin. Ordering a group of five long boats, each with ten men, to prepare, he set out to meet the inhabitants of this land. Ordering a group of archers into two of the boats, he had them remain close enough to shoot their arrows, but far enough to escape if necessary. Six boatloads of knights, ready to fight, were to stay in their boats, and only to come forward if called for. Tristan and a group of 15 knights were to follow him on shore and greet the leader of these people in the most non-threatening way possible. Sama begged to go with Tristan, to protect him, and was allowed at the last second. Sama armed himself with a bow around his naked chest, a sword about his waist, a strange bag of rocks, and an odd belt-like device with three ropes tied together at one end and a fist-sized rock at the other end, which he hung about his neck.

The ten boats set off from ten different ships. Each one had its orders, and followed them like the fighting men they were. Each was anxious about what might occur in the next few moments, but they were unafraid. Each man prayed, as did Tristan. Even Sama was now a firm believer in Tristan's God, and he prayed as well. As the two lead boats pushed ashore, just twenty or so yards from where the chief stood, Tristan was worried by the lack of movement of this wall of men. Stepping from the boat, he waited for his men to pull the two boats further onto the beach. Six boats remained, scraping against the sand, with the sixty men in them ready to jump and run at a moment's notice.

Here I Am

Tristan assembled his knights in a four-deep pattern behind him, with Sama trailing slightly behind and to his left. As Tristan approached the line of men, he could see that he was correct in assuming that there were others in the jungle, but not as well dressed and protected as the obvious fighting force on the beach. Tristan continued his slow walk toward the chief until he stopped just five feet away from the small man. All of them were small in comparison to the English and French knights. They stood no taller than Tristan's shoulder, and next to Sama they looked almost like midgets. Tristan started to bow, but realized that the chief had already begun a bow of his own. Not knowing what to do, Tristan halted his bow and waited. The chief lowered his eyes and began speaking in a language that none of them had heard before. Looking at Sama, Tristan asked, "Sama, do you understand him?"

"No master! It is a language I have never heard." Upon speaking, the chief looked suspiciously at Sama and began pointing at his dark skin. Fear showed in the chief's eyes, and he again averted his eyes downward while speaking to

Tristan. Bowing again, he called something out. Coming forward were four men, carrying a large wooden box by means of two poles extending past the length of the box. Each man had one end of a pole. As it was placed before Tristan, the chief made a motion that he was giving this as a gift to him. With a proud flourish, the chief had the top removed and to Tristan's surprise, inside were beautiful emeralds and golden bracelets and artifacts that were made to look like grinning serpents with feathers around the neck. Eagles with snakes grasped in their talons, and large cats with emeralds and clear white stones where the eyes were supposed to be. Looking closer at the chief, he now realized that the breastplate and armor the man wore were also made of gold. Tristan was stunned. The chief again bowed before Tristan, this time prostrating himself on the ground. His men did so as well. Tristan reached down and grabbed the chief's hand and helped him up. As he did so, a man to the chief's right jumped up threateningly and was about to swing his club when the chief yelled at him. Instantly, the man fell back to the ground in obvious fear. Tristan and the chief walked arm and arm down the beach front, with Sama trailing slightly behind. As they walked, Tristan reached inside of his waistband and pulled out a large gold chain made with intricate workmanship by the gold workers of Izmir. At the end of the chain was a beautiful cameo the size of the chief's palm, also set in gold. The cameo displayed a Roman-looking man sitting at a table inside a Roman-columned temple. Tristan bowed before the chief and placed the prize around the neck of the somewhat startled chief. Examining it, the chief again fell to the ground, almost in tears. Again, Tristan helped the chief regain his composure. To the chief, it was the most amazing thing he had ever seen, or even heard of.

Several weeks passed as Tristan remained a guest of the chief. Though the chief offered more riches, Tristan politely refused, but the chief was affronted by the refusal so Tristan accepted, but limited it to only one such chest of riches for each of his ships. Tristan asked only to be allowed to refill his food and water supplies. The chief, with a wave of his hand, had several hundred of his people bring the supplies to the waiting boats. As the weeks went by, Sama, who seemed quite adept at learning the language, began working as a translator between the chief and Tristan. As they began to speak together, the chief told Tristan that he was not the leader of his people, but only a leader of an area the size that a man could walk around in one year. He said that his king, who ruled the land as far as they knew, had been sent for. It also became clear that this king had been sent for because only he was worthy to speak with a God such as Tristan. As Sama interpreted, his eyes met with Tristan's, but did not betray his surprise. Tristan replied to the chief that he was grateful for the sending for of the king, but was not able to stay and wait. He had a great distance to travel yet, and he needed to be on his way. The chief would not hear of it. He would be put to death if Tristan were to leave before the king arrived, he said, and the fear in his eyes showed him to be telling the truth. Tristan did not quite know how to handle this odd situation, so he decided to follow his conscience and to tell the truth to the chief. "I am not God," Tristan began, "but His emissary. Much like you, Great Chief, I am not the one whom you should worship, but instead the protector of the God you talk about."

The chief could not quite comprehend what Tristan was saying. "Are you not the bearded white God we have been waiting for?" was the chief's reply. "We have passed the stories down for many, many generations—how we came as one people to this place on a boat guided by our God, how we became split as a people and how God punished us for our wickedness and sloth by changing our skin. Then we learned how great battles were fought between the white-skinned people and the red-skinned people, and how in a great battle all of the white-skinned people had been killed. We knew that a great darkness had covered the land one day and the mountains shook and volcanoes spewed their ash all over our lands. Soon after that, the white-skinned bearded God visited us, showing us the wounds in his hands and feet. We were told many things, things we no longer remember, but he promised to return to us one day. Is this not that day, and are you not him?" the chief asked, his voice raising as he relayed the story.

"Listen, Good Chief," Tristan began. "I am his messenger, sent to tell you that He has not forgotten you, and that He Himself will return again to you soon!" Tristan realized he was on the verge of losing an ally and being forcibly removed from his place of honor. "I am God's servant, and He expects you to treat me as you would treat Him," Tristan finished.

The chief nodded his head as Sama translated, but it was obvious that the chief was a bit less impressed than he had been when he thought Tristan was a God.

"When do you expect this great king to arrive?" asked Tristan.

"Soon," said the chief. "Before the next full moon."

According to his calculations, Tristan knew that to be within three days. He was worried. Perhaps he had made a mistake, not lying to the chief about his godliness. Somehow; he just couldn't do that. He prayed that he hadn't doomed his men to another Holy War. Tristan realized from his own experience that men would fight for gold or honor, but they would die for their religion.

Tristan was struck by the story the chief told him about his God and the wounds on his hands and feet. Was it possible, he wondered, that Christ had somehow made an appearance here in this whole other world? After having seen the image of Christ in the blood of his death shroud and having read the stories over the past twenty years, how could he not believe that it really was Christ who had appeared to these people? But still... He'd have to really look into this. Perhaps when there was more time. He made a promise to himself to make sure that he would follow up on this when they had reached their new home. In the meantime, he went again to the chief and asked to have someone who was well versed in their history to come and be a guest with Tristan for the future, to travel with him as an interpreter and as a man to document for the chief his own dealings with the people of this world. The chief was honored by the request and brought a young man of roughly the same age as Sama to be his representative. The young man's name was Lem-u-Hi, or at least it sounded like that. To say that Tristan was nervous about meeting the king was an understatement, but he managed to remain calm in front of the chief and his men. The two of them had had many discussions from the time they had landed until now, but now the chief asked about Sama.

"How is it that this giant man," he pointed toward Sama, "is here with you, and why does he have black skin? Has he been painted by God for doing something evil?" the chief asked.

"No, chief, he has not done evil, just like you have not done evil. Is not your skin also painted red? Did you do evil to make it so? No." replied Tristan. "His skin color is black because of his forefathers, just like yours. You believe that God changed your forefathers' skin color because of their sins, not yours. You have the skin of your forefathers because of it. So it is with Sama. He has the skin of his forefathers. Did they do something to God? Only they know the origin of their skin. Perhaps they were blessed by God, as were you," said Tristan.

The chief smiled at the answer. "Never before have I thought of it as a blessing from God," said the chief.

Tristan replied, "In this climate that you live in, with the sunshine so bright every day, it is indeed a great blessing to have skin color such as yours so that the sun does not burn you each day, as it can to a white man."

Again, the chief's smile turned into a radiant beam. He felt wonderful inside, and it showed in his countenance. "I'm sure the great king will want to take you back to his great city—the city of Tenochat'lan, the city of God," said the chief.

"That will be decided when he arrives and after I have spoken with God," replied Tristan, reminding the chief that while he wasn't God, he was His representative.

✠

The king's entourage began arriving the next morning. By noon the king had still not made it to the clearing. Tristan was amazed at the procession and the glitter of gold and bejeweled slaves that kept moving through the beachfront, now adorned with several large open-air huts that made up the compound. The stream of members of the kings procession moved into the compound through one gate, passing in front of the open-air room where Tristan and a small group of knights sat, and out of the hut and through another gate to the outside of the compound. As each group passed through, they lay an offering at the feet of Tristan, bowing lowly as they lay it down, then continued on. At each gate was a group of the chief's guards who were there to protect Tristan. Finally, around the first hour after noon, the king's litter was brought to the gate. Tristan arose and went to meet the king. The king ordered his litter lowered and arose and stepped forward to meet Tristan. Together, they faced each other for the first time, halfway between the gate and the common house. The king bowed slightly, as did Tristan, each measuring the other for weakness, or for royal bearing. It was an important moment, and Tristan was well aware of it.

Having learned enough of the language from Sama and from the chief, he spoke to the king in the king's own tongue. "I bring you greetings from God on high, oh great and powerful King of the Aztec people. Your God is pleased, but He wants to speak to you about many things," said Tristan.

The king surprised Tristan by replying in acceptable English " I am an honored servant of God, and am pleased to greet you as an equal servant of He who knows no time and fears no man."

Tristan listened to the words and bowed slightly, as did the king. The two men proceeded back to the open-air house, where they stood as the entourage continued, this time bringing with them chairs and rugs and soft furs to lean against so their king could speak in comfort with their God's representative. As the house was now "properly" adorned for a king, the two sat side by side as the parade of people continued to stream through the house, laying treasure at their feet. As the two sat there, the king began to speak.

"You were thought to be the God when you arrived on our shores. Why did you not let that lie continue?"

"It was not a lie", said Tristan holding the gaze of the king. "Your chief made the assumption that I was the God because of the way I looked. I could have made the same mistake by assuming that he was the king. When I realized that he was mistaken, I made sure that he knew the truth. It is what God would want."

The king shook his head in understanding. "You could have made it appear as if you were God and I would have bowed at your feet."

"King, I am not looking to have any man bow at my feet. God is the only person to whom any other man should bow. I don't have any problem in acknowledging that you are the king of this great land, and that you are to be honored as such, but only God is the Savior of each man." Tristan launched into an explanation of how Christ died for the sins of each man and how each man was equal because of it.

The King looked deeply into Tristan's eyes, shaking his head slowly as he mulled over the words in slow understanding. A light went on behind those eyes. He understood the meaning of equality for the first time. All men owed the same debt to the same man. Without His death, they all would go to the hell that waited below. The same hell, that the king and his people believed so strongly in, awaited all men without the God. It all made sense.

"I understand..." The king smiled. "I fully understand. For years I have struggled to understand why the God came to my forefathers and spoke to them. I now understand why he said we were brothers. I am the king of this great nation, but also I am a brother to my fellow man."

"Yes, King," said Tristan. "you are beginning to understand, and that is why I am here, to help you fully understand so that you and your people will live in happiness."

The king smiled at Tristan and clasped him arm to arm. The members of his court were shocked at the display. The king had never touched another person publicly since his childhood. To the members of his inner circle, this man Tristan was to be feared. No one had affected a king in such a manner since the God had come to them. For that reason, they feared and were jealous of him.

Within hours of meeting, the king and Tristan were close friends. Tristan wanted to give back the piles of gold and gems that had been laid at Tristan's feet by the king's people. "Surely, your highness, your people need these riches for themselves," said Tristan.

"Please, my friend, allow them to honor you with this. It is just a small amount compared to the rooms full we have in the palace," the king replied.

Tristan was amazed at the thought of such vast wealth, and he thanked the king. The king asked for Tristan and his men to come to his capital city and be his guest at the palace. While Tristan was flattered, he kept in mind the importance of his mission, and respectfully declined. Instead, he inquired if the king could provide some men to help him in the building of some new ships, and perhaps safe passage to the lands to the north. After much discussion back and forth, the king and Tristan had reached a decision on what needed to happen. Both were happy, as were the members of the king's court. Two new ships were needed to hold the amazing amount of gold and jewels that had been presented to Tristan and his knights. The new ships were built with the aid of the ingenious little red men. While they did not look like the ships of the fleet, they were floated better in the water and were much easier to guide. They were longer by half than the existing ships and wider abeam, but there were outriggers on both sides of the main ship, with a planking across to the outriggers, enabling structures to be built upon them above the water. The combination of English and Native engineering had created the first Tri-merran. The speed of the two ships was amazingly fast for their size and they were each able to hold more cargo than any two of the other ships in the fleet. They were completed and ready to sail within two weeks. Tristan was amazed at how fast the ships were built, a testament to the fact that with a large enough staff, anything could be done quickly. The king and Tristan spent the two weeks speaking deeply of the belief in God, and how God was watching them. There was great understanding and friendship between them. As the time neared for Tristan and his knights to be on their way, the king was saddened, and he again asked them to accompany him back to the capital city. He brought out maps and drawings of the city to impress Tristan.

Tristan was indeed impressed. According to the layout and span, the city must be at least 10 miles by 10 miles in size, with the king's palace in the center, with huge pyramids, reminiscent of Egypt's pyramids, surrounding the palace grounds. Water was moved about the city through aqueducts that provided everyone with access to clean water and sewer. A huge arena was located to the north of the palace and was used for what the king referred to as "religious games."

As much as Tristan was engaged by the drawings and the description of the city, he knew his future lay to the north, so he again respectfully declined the offer and promised to return one day when he had more to offer to the king.

The next day, Tristan and his crew loaded everything onto the new ships and weighed anchor for the continuance of the mission. It was January 1st, 1308, the beginning of a New Year.

Lem-u-Hi waved at his father, the king's youngest brother, and his mother from the deck of the new ship. He had become very close to Sama over the previous two weeks of tension and excitement on the shores of his homeland. He felt extremely lucky to have been chosen by the chief and accepted by the king himself to be the emissary to this representative of God, Tristan. Many times Sama and Lem, as he was now called, talked in depth about Lem's world, and the differences between it and Sama's world. While Sama was not completely sure about Tristan's world, he knew that Tristan had rescued him and had shown nothing but kindness to the young black man. He had treated him as an equal when no other white man did, and that had made Tristan almost godlike in Sama's eyes. Soon after spending time with Tristan, Lem also shared Sama's feelings for Tristan. While he had never had the feeling of inferiority that Sama had been raised with, Lem felt more and more in awe of Tristan after each conversation with him. It wasn't fear or superiority; it was something else, something that Lem had never felt before—equality without animosity, friendship without any desire to use it. Tristan was—a friend just because he was a friend, for no other reason—not to use as a stepping-stone, not to take advantage of. Lem didn't really know quite what to think of it. In his society, one used his position to gain a better position. Here was Tristan, with the opportunity to use his position, and he didn't seem to care. It was amazing. He had never met a man of power who didn't seem to want more of it. Tristan was really an amazing man, and Lem wanted to learn from him.

✠

A month later, the small fleet of ships had sailed up the coast of South America to Central America, always meeting with the king's people, and always being granted privileges as they went, thanks to the presence of Lem on board the ships with them. They were well provisioned and continued to hear of islands that no one inhabited off the coast. These islands intrigued Tristan. He believed that if they could find the appropriate untouched island, they could prepare a place of safe haven, protected for the future and safe from the greed of mankind. Tristan continued to sail along the coast, finally reaching a place that looked perfect for his men. There were several small islands off the coast, and very few natives that his men might displace or have friction with. Also, not far away, were the hundreds of uninhabited islands that the natives spoke of. Yes, here would be perfect. Very few natives inhabited the area, and with the blessing of the king, any who were there were paid for the land and moved away, heading either north or south. The king set aside the land from south as belonging to his friend Tristan. He also gave Tristan any uninhabited island that he might want. Tristan was happy.

✠

On March 3ʳᵈ, 1308, Tristan and his knights began building the home they were so anxious to create. The knights spread out, each taking ownership of their land and carving out the space they needed; however, they remained loyal to Tristan and the ultimate goal. Tristan didn't build as many of his men did. He was still searching. He, Sama, and Lem, along with a group of twenty knights, continued their mission—to find the right place to hide the history that they were responsible for. And so they went sailing once again. This time they were looking for the right island.

They explored the Texas Coast. They were taken aback by the size of the Mississippi River as it exited into the Gulf of Mexico. They sailed down the Florida peninsula, and discovered the islands of the Bahamas. They all seemed too small for their needs. Sailing further south, he sailed around the island of Cuba and then south to Jamaica. Cuba was too flat and too large. Jamaica had real possibilities, he thought, but then he decided to look to the east again. There he found Haiti, Puerto Rico, and the Virgin Islands. Each of them also had great possibilities, although the Virgin Islands were probably too small. After much soul searching and prayer and discussion with Sama and Lem, Tristan finally decided on the island that had mountains and caves that could be used. Returning to the mainland, Tristan sent word once again to the king, asking for his help. He would require the service of five hundred men for at least a year, after which each would be well paid for their time, but also would be expected to never speak about the work again. The king, as good as his word, had five hundred strong young men ready and waiting for Tristan before the week was out.

Using his two new, now unloaded ships, Tristan sailed the group to the island that he now labeled "New Jerusalem." He had found a wonderful protected bay on the south side of the island. It was there that he dropped off the men and returned to get the others. After three trips with each of the ships, the feat was accomplished and all five hundred of the workers were safely relocated to the island. Along with his twenty knights, the work would now begin in earnest. The troop of men moved northward, following the beautiful little stream across the flat part of the peninsula they were on. As they followed the river, it soon took them up into the mountains. The traveling became tougher. By the third day, the contingent of men had made it to the area that Tristan had hoped to find. Upon a wide plateau, Tristan began by having the men build a base camp. It would be their home for the next year. It took only a week and a half for the crew of men to build suitable housing for the entire company. They were not used to living in housing such as Tristan proposed, but they seemed to like the wood-framed houses, complete with breeze ways and thatched roofs. While they were building, Tristan searched for just the right location for his next project. On the eastern point of the island were mountains, rising up over 7000 feet, although they were presently only about half way up. In a beautiful valley, covered with an odd variety of Cedar trees, Tristan found what he was looking for. Behind a waterfall was an area of the mountain, eroded by the constant flow of water. Hiking up and behind the waterfall, he was able to go back 50-60 feet into a cave that had been created. From his vantage point on the top of the mountain he could easily see his ships in the safe harbor, and he could see the twists and turns as the small river fell from the mountain and wound its way to the harbor below. Without wasting further time, he set his men about their arduous work.

At first it was slow work because only twenty or so men at a time could get back into the cave, so Tristan put the others to work building a castle and rampart at the top of the mountain. As the tunnel he was boring behind the waterfall began to grow, he expanded it with his workers. Keeping his knights in charge, Tristan supervised the whole of both projects. A group of twenty men were set aside to hunt and provide food for the small army of men. Another twenty were to fish and gather fruits each day. By now, roughly half the men were working on the tunnel and another two hundred were working on the castle and keep. Work continued smoothly on the projects. Tristan made sure the men were given adequate break time and sleep time, and he also made sure that they all were given Sunday off to rest. On Sundays, Tristan and his knights taught the Aztec workers about God and of Christ. Each day, lessons on mathematics, star charting, writing, and English were available to those men who wanted to learn. Much to Tristan's surprise, there were those among them that were quite learned about mathematics and the stars. Tristan was presented with the Aztec calendar, which was different than the Julian calendar the English were used to, but surprisingly began counting time from the same general date as the Julian calendar—the death of Christ. It had 13 months of 28 days each instead of the 12-month calendar he was used to. As it turned out, the calendar was actually more accurate, since it required a one-day adjustment only once every 10 years instead of once every four years like the Julian calendar. Once again, he realized that he needed to be sure and not underestimate his new neighbors. Although on the outside they appeared a bit savage and untamed, they were by no means stupid. He was determined not to anger these people.

By the end of six months, Tristan and his workers had created a wonderful mountain refuge, with walls 4 feet thick, surrounding a beautiful castle they had built into the side of the mountain. The stream emerged from underground in the middle of the castle's right-hand tower, which was piped into a cistern between the upper layers of the tower. The Aztec engineers, working with the knights, had developed a method of porting the running water into the rest of the castle where other stone cisterns held the water, allowing any turbidity to sink to the bottom, after which it flowed throughout the castle and was piped down below and back into the flowing river just before it cascaded over the falls. It also supplied water to a set of fountains in the courtyard. The flowing water provided clean drinking water for the kitchen area of the castle, as well as running water in ten toilet rooms found throughout the castle.

The castle itself had twenty-four spacious bedchambers, each with room for a small library and a table with chairs. There was a huge kitchen with four stone ovens and two pantries, each the size of one of the bedchambers. Also in the kitchen was a center counter, rising up from the floor and made of hand cut stone, with a black obsidian countertop running the entire distance of 25 ft. Storage for the cutlery and dishes was contained within three large cedar hutches that sat side by side, and the stone walls were adorned with beautiful hand crafted tapestries that the king had been gracious enough to present to Tristan.

There was a king's chamber at the highest point of the castle, taking up the entire top floor of the first circular tower overlooking the bay below, with a stunning view of the waterfall as it shot over the cliff. The round room had a diameter of 40 ft, with several portions walled off as a private bathing area, private toilet, closets and an anteroom. Tapestries hung on the walls here as well to ward off the dampness of the stone, though it was hardly necessary in the beautiful climate.

From the window and balcony, one could see for a hundred miles out to sea. Below the first king's chamber was a series of rooms, including a library, a meeting room with a round table, and finally on the ground floor, a huge hall. Each floor was larger than the one above it, as it was closer to the ground, with the bottom floor being a combination of the base of the tower, and the base of an adjoining building and then another tower. On each floor at the side closest to the mountain rising behind it was a fireplace. Though they would probably never be used, the English knights just couldn't bring themselves not to include it in the building. The Aztec engineers couldn't fathom why they were needed, but they allowed the strangers their whims, so each floor had a huge fireplace large enough for even Sama to stand in without worry.

On the opposite corner of the castle was a second tower, similar to the one just described. It was connected to the first with a building two stories high that acted as the outer wall on one side. This two-story "Long Building" was open from one tower to the other on the bottom floor, creating a "Great Hall." The two towers had a diameter of 100 ft. each and the length of the Long Building between was 300 ft, making the entire length of the Great Hall a whopping 500 ft. The width of the Long Building was 50 ft, not including the 4 ft. thick walls. In the second tower was a second "King's Chamber" at the top, followed below by a private dining hall on the third floor, and the kitchen on the second floor. On the second floor of the Long Building were the twenty-four individual bedchambers and the six toilet and bathing rooms. From each of the two towers ran a two-story wall with a walkway along the top from the tower to the edge of the cliff, some 600 ft away. Inside the walls were hidden passageways that led to tunnels on both sides of the outer perimeter.

In the courtyard were walkways paved with the beautiful blue-green stones that were found in the area. Granite was used to channel the water into different locations across the grounds and a series of ornate fountains were built, to the amazement of the Aztec engineers. Low granite walls were also constructed to manage the flow of the water the remaining distance to the waterfall. There were two large gates created in the center of the walls on both sides, although the gate on the right side led only to a small path that a mountain goat would have trouble navigating. On the left side was a much wider pathway that Tristan had widened and smoothed so that it would be an easy path down the mountain and to the harbor below. The path wandered by the waterfall, but never came within a distance close enough to see what was going on behind it. Inside the First King's chamber was a secret stairway, hidden and accessible from inside the fireplace. By pushing a certain stone block, a cantilevered wall gave way to a hidden stairway leading down. Unlike the regular stairway, this one didn't stop on the ground floor but continued down into the mountainside. Deeper and deeper it went until it joined the cavern that had been excavated behind the waterfall. Nearly 100 feet beneath the surface of the castle above it, the stairs had been cut.

Behind the waterfall a tunnel had been cut, angling upward by ten feet, and then downward and back into the mountainside. For nearly 300 feet, the tunnel dug into the mountainside, angling first up and then down, then straight and level. The tunnel was wide enough for five men across and about eight feet high. It was there that the stairway from above came into the side of the tunnel below. It was also there that the Aztec workers began their final portion of the task before them. Using ropes and pulleys and steel tools that the Aztec had never seen before, they dug out a cavern from deep inside the mountain. Using the natural geologic formations wherever they could, they cut out granite and were even rewarded with emerald and the beautiful blue stone that was so rare. After six more months of toil by the entire force of workers, a multi-floored cavern had taken shape. Roughly square in shape, it was two floors in height. The bottom floor, where the tunnel entered into it, was two hundred by two hundred feet in size, with a ten-foot ceiling. A stairway led upward in the center of the room to a second floor that was roughly one hundred by one hundred feet in size, also with a ten foot ceiling. There was at least ten feet of rock ceiling between the two floors. Along the walls of two sides of the bottom floor and all four sides of the second floor were shelves dug out of the natural rock. An oak door was fitted to cover the entrance into the cavern, blocking entrance from the tunnel and the stairs. The door was made of heavy oak and set in place by a stone lintel around it.

One day, while working to complete an alcove room being built on the Southwest corner of the bottom cavern, one of the worker's chisels disappeared. Shouting to the knight in charge that he had gone through the mountain, the knight and a small group gathered around to see what the man was shouting about. Instead of "digging through the mountain," he had instead discovered a natural fissure in the mountain. Tristan and his men decided to take their time and explore it further at a later time. There was plenty of space in the chamber already, so the fissure was closed off with a door and a stone lintel.

After the construction was completed, it was time to release the workers and move in. Tristan thanked each man individually and rewarded them each with a brick of silver that weighed almost twenty pounds. As he thanked each one, he extracted a promise from them to never speak of the work they had done on the island or the things they had been involved in building. They were amazed at having been paid to do the work; they had expected to work without pay. Even so, they were exceedingly grateful and each promised on their own lives to remain quiet. Tristan had still not shared the contents of the ships with anyone outside his own hand-picked knights. Now numbering twenty-six fully laden ships, Tristan called together his ships and his men once again. After sailing for three months, weathering the terrible storm, and spending a full year building their new lives in this new land, Tristan was pleased that his men responded so quickly when he called them. Tristan sent runners to each of the new buildings his men had begun and asked them to once again help him to safeguard the history they had rescued from under the temple mount. All of his men came at his call, and a group of twenty-five knights agreed to come and stay with him on the island and to aid him in his purposes once again.

Using the twenty-five knights, two ships at a time could be sailed to his new island home. The two ships took just a day to sail to the island. They were moored in the harbor. The path that had been created took them to a hidden second path that led behind the waterfall. From there the men moved the treasures from the ships into the cavern. It was very difficult, heavy work. Tristan had some special wheeled devices made that aided in the moving of the heavy items. Using ropes, pulleys, and the attachable wheels made moving easier, but it still was time-consuming and difficult. The twenty-six men managed to unload and move the contents of one ship in four days' time. After improving the road and learning the best way to move things, and by building a few low carts with four wheels, the men managed to unload the second ship in only three days. They were getting better. It took one hundred and fifty days of hard work, taking Sundays for rest of course, to unload the entire twenty-six ships. While unloading the ships, Tristan had thought of another plan. He intended to speak once again to the king and he prayed that the king would remain generous to his desires. That will come in time, he thought. For now, he still had much work to do.

Occupying the castle, Tristan kept fifteen of the knights, as well as Sama and Lem, inside the castle with him. Of the group of five hundred Aztec workers, some three hundred had decided to continue living on the island as well. They had never lived in such homes as had been built for the workers. The village was five hundred feet below the castle and about a half mile walk to get to the gates. Many of the native workers continued to work inside the castle for Tristan. Tristan occupied the first Kings Chamber, with Sama living in a separate room just off of Tristan's chamber. While it was much smaller than the rooms in the Long Building, Sama refused to leave the proximity of Tristan. Lem wasn't as particular. He enjoyed the large room that was first on the left from the first tower. The second King's Chamber was left unoccupied for the current time.

His other permanent knights each had their own bedchambers in the Long Building and were very comfortable with them. Construction of the servants' quarters was begun and soon a two-story building with very comfortable rooms lined the eastern wall of the castle. Two hundred workers could be housed easily without any concern of overcrowding. In the mean time, Tristan, Sama and Lem went to work each night through the secret stairway down to the cavern. They put the books together into the shelves that lined the walls of the lower cavern. They arranged and straightened the statues and artwork, putting each magnificent piece in a place where it could be examined and admired when the time came.

The upper floor was reserved for the most important pieces: the Ark of the Covenant, the death shroud of Christ, the cross, and the spear. Scrolls from John, Andrew, Joseph of Aramathea, Mary Magdalene, and even from Mary the Mother of Jesus were placed in stone jars and sealed with wax. There was even a book written by Joseph, the husband of Mary and father of Jesus, that they had found partially destroyed, but stored in a stone amphora. All these, as well as the tons of gold given to Tristan by the king, were carefully placed for safekeeping. Walking into the rooms was almost unbelievable, even to Tristan. The three workers also hung a large tapestry on the wall, concealing the doorway into the caverns. A large statue cut from the blue stone, shaped like a bearded man rising from the ocean waist high in a beautiful blue green wave, holding a torch in one hand and a scroll in the other which pointed upward toward the stairway, with a wreath of gold upon his head and a gold chain encircling his neck, stood in front of the tapestry, further obfuscating the doorway. Upon reaching this point from the tunnel, one would instantly conclude that the statue, used for lighting, was there to point the way upward, and thereby help the non-educated to reach the wrong conclusion.

After fully arranging the relics and making sure they were safe, Tristan felt as if he could relax for the first time in nearly three years. It was now August, 1310. This odyssey had begun in October, 1307, with the decree of King John asking for his head. Now, three years later, who would have believed that he would have successfully hidden the Templar treasures in a continent unknown to all but a few people in Europe, and that he would have escaped from under the noses of the pope's spies, located all across the Mediterranean.

He took a deep breath, thought of his son in Lorraine and prayed that he was safe. It was now time for the final step. He hoped that the fissure they had found would lead them down to the protected bay below. He had seen many cracks opening into caves along the shoreline of the cove. He hoped that one of them would lead upward to his cavern… If so, he could have a protected route all the way from his castle to the cove below. It will be perfect, he thought.

Tristan, Sama and Lem began exploring the next day. Using ropes and pulleys with torches every fifty feet, they began the descent into the bowels of the mountain. Twice along the way they entered into great natural hallways, some big enough that Tristan couldn't see the end of the cave from his torchlight. The caves seemed to be completely uninhabited—no bats, and not a sound except for the water that made its way ever downward. The other thing Tristan noted was that the cave was very dry, not like the caves he had seen in England or in France, but more like the dry sandstone of the tunnels under the Temple mount. The three decided that they had explored enough for one day and they could continue on the next day. They followed their trail back up to the cavern, then back up to the tower room, leaving their ropes and climbing gear in places where they would need it tomorrow.

The next day they entered the cave more prepared. Ready for an adventure that could last a week, they headed back down the way they had come the day before. Easily reaching their stopping point from the previous day in a scant three hours, they pushed ever downward. The natural caverns they came to were smaller each time. Most were roughly the size of large rooms. Sometimes they came across the water that was flowing ever downward through large fissures and openings in the mountain. Sometimes they had rough, very steep openings they had to contend with, but usually it was sloped in such a manner that a man could walk slowly, but safely, down a path that looked as if it had been worn by running water. After a full day, they camped in a room about the same size as Tristan's bedchamber. The three of them ate a meal of dried beef, corn and "sweet cane," as the knights had come to call the sweet bamboo that grew wildly about the island. They also followed it with a delightful drink made by the natives from the fermented sweet cane, along with wild berries found nearby. It was quite a delight. They slept well that night.

It was odd, thought Tristan, to wake up fully rested, and find it is as black as midnight on a moonless night. That's exactly what it was like, waking up in the cave. Lighting the torches helped. The three washed themselves in a small pool at the back of the cavern, then continued on their way. Downward, ever downward... It seemed longer than just a day. About an hour later, the three men entered another natural cavern. This time, however, they found no easy going. There was a crawl space leading to another chamber, but something was different. Tristan stopped and listened. No sound. The sound of water running had disappeared somewhere in the last hour. In these two chambers, the sound was gone. In searching the second chamber, another fissure was found, leading down, and they continued, wondering what it meant. As they headed downward, the three men grew very quiet. What had been active discussion the day before had gone silent, like the cave over the last hour. Each was worried.

After a nice easy walk down a slope for about twenty minutes, they came to a spiraling hole, going almost straight down. Pulling off the rope, Lem dropped a torch down the hole and began counting. It hit the bottom as he reached four. Looking at the light from the torch burning below, it appeared to be at least two hundred feet down. Sama made the decision to climb down. The others would be necessary to help him make it back up. The three set up a pulley on a tripod over the hole and tying him off, they lowered Sama into the hole. Fifteen minutes later, Sama's feet touched the floor of the hole. The hole opened up into a massive natural cavern. It stretched for thousands of feet in every direction from where he stood. Near where he stood was what appeared to be a beach. No waves splashed the shore, but sand led down to a pool of water that extended into the blackness of the massive cavern. Sama looked at it and thought that there was room for twenty of the sailing ships in this secret port inside the mountain. He touched the water, smelled it, and tasted it. It was salty. They had made it to the ocean, as Tristan had wished. Tristan would be pleased. Calling for help, Sama tied himself off again, and with the aid of his two friends above he began the climb back to the top of the hole. Upon reaching Tristan and Lem, he was caught up and began babbling about the huge cavern below and how there was room for many ships. Tristan listened, still deep in thought, but he didn't smile and laugh with Lem and Sama. His thoughts were more worrisome. Finally, Sama stopped his theatrics and asked Tristan what was wrong. Why didn't he share their joy?

"It is simple, Sama. We are too deep," was his reply.

"What do you mean, too deep, Master?"

"Sama, we have descended below the depth of the ocean inside the mountain. We are several hundred feet below the water."

Sama and Lem both had trouble understanding how that was possible, so Tristan pulled out a piece of charcoal for drawing and on a flat stone he drew a diagram of how the air inside the cavern was trapped, holding the water outside from flooding the inside of the cavern, much as a cup held upside down under water remains full of air. They understood, but they didn't know what to do.

"Do?" said Tristan with a wistful smile, "We go back up and remember that it's there so that if for some reason we find a need or a use for it we'll know it's there."

Puzzled by his reaction, Lem and Sama decided to follow along and go back.

After an hour's climb back to the two low caverns they had found earlier in the morning, Tristan began exploring the first of the two, looking for an exit. Not finding one, he went to the second. There also, no luck. He remembered the sensation from earlier about how quiet it was. He surmised that they were just below sea level here. He needed to continue upward. As they climbed, Tristan listened attentively for sounds. About halfway between the small cavern and the cavern where they'd spent the night, he heard the sound of dripping water again. Following the sound, he used a steel-tipped pole to push and dig his way toward the sound. After an hour's work, the three men pushed a hole outward into the sunlight. Then, disguising the exit, they left the confines of the cave system. Tristan was exceedingly happy. They were within five minutes' walk from the beach where two of his ships were moored. As they walked onto the open beach, a group of Aztec workers who were busy building a dock that could be used by the boats looked at them as if they had materialized out of nowhere. After many questions, Tristan just smiled and said they had come down the mountain the back way. That was all that was needed to be said.

✠

Five years later, Tristan was truly a happy man. Many advances and changes had been made to his island. His castle had many new buildings along its walls. The walls themselves had been reinforced to eight feet in thickness and nearly thirty feet high. Buildings lined the inside walls of the castle, further fortifying them, and a soldier could walk the perimeter of the castle on a stone path from one side to the other without fear of the weather. The entire top level had a wooden roof over it. The remarkable thing was that the wood for the roof was almost fire proof. It contained enough moisture that a flaming arrow in it would eventually just burn itself out. Tristan had learned to engineer lots of breezeways into the design. After dealing with the heat the first year, windows had been cut into the castle structure at key points to allow for the natural wind currents to provide air conditioning for the large manor, after a massive storm wreaked havoc on the pier and many of the homes that had been built on the beach. The homes in the upper elevations and the castle itself had withstood the storm without too much problem.

Now a great number of families lived on Tristan's island. Sama and Lem were both fine young men, around the age of twenty-two or three. He wasn't really sure about Sama, but he was as proud of them as he might be of his own son. The knights he had left back on the mainland were enjoying productivity of their own. They had married into the population, and had land and farms of their own. Many had mixed-race children and were as happy as they would have been on their own lands back in Europe. During the big storm, half his fleet had been caught offshore, and many of his original men had died at sea. Of the other half, only ten survived the murderous winds of the giant storm. The natives took the storm all in stride, saying that they were used to rebuilding about every ten years. Tristan had built well, though. His farms on the other side of the mountains were doing well. He and his people were growing enough crops to export back to the mainland. They had set up a distillery for making fine wine out of the sweet cane, and a fine white powder resulted during the refining process that was sweet to the taste. When mixed with other wheat and flour, the most delicious sweet breads were created.

The path from the inside of the cavern rooms down to the bay had been finished and provided an interesting walk all the way up to Tristan's chamber now. A separate path from the stairway leading downward had been cut that intercepted the path down to the bay. The other path, leading up the treasure rooms, was sealed and hidden so no one would recognize it was there. At the bottom, the entrance into the path leading up to the stairway was also hidden from view. A very narrow entrance existed, and only he, Sama, Lem and six workers knew it was there. Tristan had decided that if trouble ever erupted on the island, he would seal off the entrance from behind the waterfall and use only the entrance at the bottom.

The central grounds of the castle were beautiful. The natives had helped him plant beautiful bushes with red, blue, and purple flowers all around the compound. Large mimosa trees had been transplanted into the grounds as well, and tall pines were sprouting up almost as high as the new buildings in half a dozen places around the walls. The underground stream brought fresh water to him, and the beautiful stonework the natives had done created a lovely path through the center of the garden area, where fountains flowed, and knee-high bushes bloomed in vivid color. The steps beside the aqueducts were painted with the artwork of the Aztec people. The feathered serpent, and Chac Mool could be seen everywhere. On the edge of the cliff, overlooking the pretty little bay, was an open-air church. Unlike the cathedrals of Europe, it had no massive steeples and walls to contain the worship; instead, it was open to the air, with a thatched roof rising in a circle nearly three stories high. With huge cedar beams holding the roof up and a circular design as you looked upward from below, the beauty and grandeur of nature itself was enough to inspire a worshipper. No need for man's definition of God, one had only to look out from the rail protecting the edge of the cliff to see the magnificence of God and His creation.

The new pier he'd had built was large enough to anchor eight boats at a time, and he kept most of his remaining armada there in safe harbor most of the time. He had decorated the castle inside in the fashion of the Aztec people—lots of carved wooden statues set in and amongst the large heavy tables and chairs made from the cedar forest down the mountainside. Instead of the heavy tapestries found in the castles of England and France, Tristan had thin, beautiful silk tapestries that told the story of their escape from the Holy Lands across the sea and to the beautiful new world, hanging along the walls of the Great Hall. Starting beside the massive fireplace and moving from left to right, the story of their crossing was told as an epic adventure on a quest sent forth by God Himself. It told of the meeting between the Aztec king and Tristan and how the two had become close friends. It told how after five years of friendship the good king had accepted Christianity and was pushing his people to do so as well. It was a beautiful story, but the reality was that there were storm clouds on the horizon and Tristan could see it coming. The old guard was pushing back. They didn't like it that the king spoke so freely to Tristan. Just as distance makes the heart grow fonder, closeness breeds contempt, and that is what was happening with the old guard. They were beginning to believe that Tristan was not really God's emissary, but that instead he was just a man that was taking advantage of the king. Had they really been listening, they would have realized that Tristan had never claimed to be anything more than a man. He had claimed to be God's emissary, but then again, he had been. Look at the changes that had been wrought as a result of his work. All the same, murmurings were beginning, and that was bad for the king, and if it was bad for the king, it could be bad for Tristan too.

His people were happy and healthy and successful. Tristan knew that with success there would come envy by others, but he had a plan for that. Because of the success of Tristan and the islanders, Tristan began giving away the excess food and grain his farms produced. His wines were unknown to most of the Aztec people, but the king and Tristan traded yearly, and the wine was a favorite of the inland peoples. The king in turn traded a brown leaf to Tristan that when rolled and lit on fire at one end produced an enjoyable product the natives called bac-co. They also had stone pipes in which they placed a ground up version of the bac-co in that created a soothing sensation. Corn was also one of Tristan's favorite new finds. It could be dried, ground and mixed with water and then cooked in the oven to create a delicious flat bread. The kernel could also be removed from its seedpod and dried and then put in a pan over a fire. The result was a loud pop and the kernel would open up to reveal a white puffed tasty meat, or it could be soaked in water and boiled to produce a moist and tasty meal. Yes, corn was definitely a favorite. Tristan's ranch was also doing well on the other side of the island. A large area had been cleared and fenced with wooden rails. Inside, some of the wild cows from the northern lands the king had given Tristan had been successfully bred. He also raised cows, pigs and chickens.

Once a month Tristan would load a shipload of his produce up and sail to the mainland, sharing with anyone who wanted or needed his surplus. Twice a year Tristan loaded four of his ships with his finest wines and grains, along with salted pork, cheese, butter, and sweet breads to be taken to his good friend, the king. Each time he went, he spent at least a week with the king. They spoke of many things, and Tristan taught him the things of the Bible, and told him the stories of Christ. In turn, the king told Tristan the stories of his people, and how they had come to know "The God." Each time, the king became closer and closer to Tristan, and each time the political insiders became more jealous. Tristan did everything he could to alleviate the problem. He gave more and more to the troublemakers, trying his best to lure them into his camp.

During each trip, Tristan took copious notes of his conversations with the king, writing down both his own history and the history of the king's people. Strangely, for such a literate people with so many intelligent ways, they lacked a written language, so Tristan was the first to scribe the history of the Aztec people. As he wrote down the history of the mighty people, it struck him that as it was in his own lands, so it was here. All fighting and wars were essentially caused by one group of people either trying to force their religion and ways on another group or one group trying to free themselves from the religion of the other and practice their own ways. At an even lower level, he found that there were a few individuals, usually a king, a pope, or someone like them that was behind the "outrage" of the masses. In reality, the masses weren't outraged; they were simply stirred up by this single person or small group of people. And always, it was the common man who was destroyed in the end. Whether it was tens, hundreds, thousands, or even millions, it was the quiet masses that ended up dying in the fields of a battleground, slaughtered en masse, while the king or pope or whomever sat in a comfortable palace somewhere giving the orders to go and die for his cause. It was the same, no matter where he went. He almost wept, knowing that in time this good people would do the same.

Right now, he had a history of a people that had gone from good to bad, then back to good, through a series of good and bad kings, and a series of wars that could only be described as fights of good against evil. Currently, the Aztecs were a peaceful people, living in a wonderful time for them. They were building and growing. Their crops were bounteous and people were happy and had everything they needed. Even so, the king told him about those among him who wanted to worship the old gods—Chac Mool and others. As the king told Tristan about Chac, his face went sour. "Chac is an evil God," said the king. "He craves the blood of humans as a sacrifice. At the highest point in the worship of Chac, there were as many as one hundred people sacrificed a day by the ruler of this city."

Tristan was shocked by the number, and by the revelation about Chac worship. "A hundred people a day? How is that possible, my king?" asked Tristan. "How is it that there are still people alive?"

"There very nearly were not," said the king. "My grandfather's father was the king at the time. Things were not good; the plants would not grow and for five years in a row the great storms came and destroyed many villages, twice in one year. The people were afraid and the priests told the king that it was happening because they had been unfaithful to Chac. They demanded that Chac's thirst for blood needed to be slaked. As sacrifices were made, more and more were demanded. The priests became very powerful. The people began to fear the priests as much as they did Chac. The priests demanded that gold, silver and precious stones be brought to be sacrificed as well, but the priests kept the gold and silver and killed the people and dumped their bodies into the sacred waters. After the death of my grandfather's father, my grandfather became the king. He spoke openly about the greed and wrongdoing of the priests. The people rose up against the priests and thousands of the Chac Mool priests across our country were killed in a single night. Those who one day believed in and were priests of Chac Mool, the next day acted as if they didn't know who Chac was. All across our nation, blood was shed. The king sent out a decree that all the treasures of the Chac priests should be brought to the palace. To his astonishment, the treasure came for months and months. We have vast rooms filled with treasure that the Chac priests were hoarding. Today it belongs to my kingdom so if we need to buy food or deal with other nations we may do so. Mainly, it just sits in its room, taking up space," laughed the king.

Tristan sat, fascinated by the story. One small group's quest for power led to the deaths of hundreds of thousands of their fellow man. All the while, they sat idly by while it continued, all because they wanted to "own" something they couldn't eat, drink, use to build with, or protect themselves with, or ultimately take with them. It was only useful within their own minds to make themselves believe they were better, or richer, than everyone else. It was the same story told over and over again across the entire world. How easy it was for man to order the deaths of his fellow man if it gave him more "power." Whether the power came in the form of gold, or in the ability to order men to their deaths, it mattered not. Men were willing to do the most evil things in the quest for it. May God help them, he thought.

As if punctuating his story with reality, the king snapped his fingers and a group of twenty men came out of a side chamber. Each man was laden with the weight of a golden chain that encircled them. The king said, "The length of this chain I am not sure of, but there is in it one link for every time that I have prayed for your safe return to my presence, and for each time that I have been in deep thought over the things that you have brought to my attention, and for each time that I have thought about you, my dear friend. I believe that there are those in my country who fear you and would do harm to you. I hope that it will not be so, but I want you to know that a chain exists that ties both you and me together for as long as I live. Because of it, you will be under my protection as long as I am alive. I have spoken also to my sons, and they feel as I do. I pray that we will live our days in harmony for many years to come."

Tristan was in awe of the chain. It was easily a hundred feet long, with each link the size of a man's hand, made of rolled gold nearly an inch thick. "Oh king, I cannot possibly take such a gift from you. Your friendship is the only gift that I could ever want. Why do you ask me to take these things, especially after we have just spoken about the greed and corruption of others? Are you testing me?"

"No, my good friend," said the king, laughing. "It is because you always try to turn it down that I see that you know its real value. The gold is not of value to me. I have rooms full of it. The value to me is what it represents—my commitment to my friend. Tristan, my good friend, I can't give this to just anyone, because they only see it as wealth. With you, I know I can give it as a gift of friendship and not worry about any other message. You understand the real message."

Tristan dropped his head and thanked the king for his wisdom and his gift. "King, now that I have accepted your gracious gift, I still worry that others will not understand and will use this gift against you."

"They would not dare," said the king. "What kind of king

would I be if I didn't bestow a gift upon those who gave to me such riches?"

Tristan looked puzzled. "What great riches have I bestowed upon you, my king?" he asked.

"Why, you do not know? You have brought to me the gift of understanding and of God. When you landed on our shores for the first time, I was leading a nation of lost people in circles, with no direction. Even though some of the old people don't like it, we now have a direction. I have a job to do—to lead my people to the understanding of God. You have given me purpose, Tristan, the greatest gift a man can give to another. The only greater gift is that which God gave to each of us. And Tristan, I have no doubt that if it were in your power to give, you would give even that away to me as well."

Tristan was moved beyond words. With those closing statements, the king got up and went back to his chamber, leaving Tristan to ponder his own purpose and whether he had been successful. Today he felt as though he had arrived.

That evening, with the boat loaded, Tristan said farewell once again to the king and headed back to New Hope and his castle in the mountains. Tomorrow he'd have another treasure to put into the rooms beneath his castle. As for tonight, he'd spend it writing down the account of the day, and he'd do well to put a copy of the king's words on a plaque next to the chain's resting spot in the treasure room. Two days later, the chain had been moved to the treasure room on the lower level. A whole separate area had been created for the gold and silver treasures, as well as the precious gems that had been given to the knights by the king. The chain was coiled up around the base of a statue of one of the previous kings. A plaque was put in place at the head of the chain, explaining what it was, when it was given, and for what reason. Just inside the main door to the lower chamber, Tristan had a large oak desk made with a top that would close and lock with an ingenious locking mechanism that didn't show from the outside at all. It simply looked like a polished wooden box on legs until a key area was pushed while another was pulled, and then the lid opened to reveal it as a desk. Inside the desk, Tristan had catalogued each item as well as it could be described, using a hammer and stylus on sheets of hammered brass. Each sheet described, as well as Tristan was able to, the contents a box, or each statue, or whatever was there within the described area. It had taken a great deal of time, but the accounting was up to date, and with each addition, a new plate of brass was added to the book so it would always be current. Brass was used in case a fire should ever break out within the room, the writings would not be lost. Also inside the desk was another of Tristan's most prized possessions: a set of logbooks that he had begun keeping the week he was given the assignment to protect the artifacts. Since that time, he had written some each day in the logbooks. Upon opening the magic desk, there were now twenty-one leather-bound volumes, each with one hundred pages of various types of paper. Most had come from a collection he had brought with him onboard his original ship, but the more recent volumes were made while he had been here on the island.

His group of men had become quite sufficient at creating whatever it was that was needed. A year ago, it had been paper. Tristan had given the order, and his men, working along side the Aztec engineers and scientists, had come up with a type of paper very similar in looks to the papyrus created by the Egyptians. The Aztecs had been very interested in the new product, but ultimately found it of little value, since they had never developed writing as a skill. Even so, they had successfully produced what he had needed, and now he had a limitless supply of paper and leather to bind it with. Ink had also become scarce about a year ago. That was solved quickly by using the dyes the Aztec used to color their feathers and skin with during the days of their festivals. They had produced many colors of ink for Tristan, and now he found that his writing came to life with not only words, but with drawings of things to help with the descriptions, done in vivid color. In these log books, Tristan put down his innermost feelings and thoughts. They represented his life, and he was proud to share them with the ones who would read about his life in the future.

Later that week Tristan took Sama and Lem with him into the treasure rooms. Upon entering it, he lit the first of the nearly four hundred torches that lined the walls or that were self-standing throughout the lower chamber. The upper chamber had almost as many, each one waiting to be lit individually as needed. He had long since taught them that the only worth these objects held was as historical items, not their value as gold.

Lem asked him, "Master, why is it that these items are made of such things as gold and silver if it is the history that makes them valuable?"

"I can answer that better by showing you than by telling you," Tristan replied, "but I'll tell you the answer as well." Leading them upstairs, he showed them a spear, broken and rotted by time, whose brass tip was pitted by age, the death shroud which lay in tatters, and a clay cup whose handle was broken. "What do you see?" asked Tristan.

"I see worthless scraps of a bygone age," said Lem.

"Wrong," said Tristan. "These are what are left of some of the most important historical items ever found on this earth: the spear that spilled Christ's blood on the cross, the shroud that he was wrapped in during his three days of death, and the cup which he drank from his last night as a mortal man. Each item has an unbelievable historical value, and each has been bought with the death of more than a hundred thousand knights. See how common materials corrode and rot through time? For that reason, man has learned to make items that are going to be of great historical value out of the metal that doesn't spoil over many years, the material that can withstand the salt water depths—gold. Because of that, there are always a few greedy men who are more interested in the value of the gold than they are in the history it represents, so it is a struggle to hide it away from those who would destroy it, and in so doing, destroy history."

Both young men were quiet as they thought about what Tristan had just said. "I think I understand," said Lem.

"As do I," said Sama. "That is why, my friends, my knights and I were sent around the world to find a place where this history would be safe from plundering fools like the King of France and the pope. That is why I am here—to protect this history until the right time, when man can be trusted with the history this gold represents and the true story of Christ that is evident to those who see it. The pope would take these artifacts you see before you and stir up another war that would maim and kill thousands, maybe millions more. In turn, the Ottomans would claim it to be false and use it to incite their peoples to further bloodshed. Right now is not the right time to bring out the truth. Truth cannot be distributed to everyone equally right now. When that time comes, it will be time to release the real evidence of Christ's holiness and let each man decide for himself, without some religious fanatic standing on a street corner or in a mosque telling him how to interpret the facts. Facts speak for themselves and should be presented to individuals so they can see and think for themselves, not so one person with an agenda can tell them how to think. That's why we need to hide this and keep its secret between only two or three trusted people from now until that time comes.

"Gentlemen, you are the ones who will be the guardians of this secret after me. I suggest that you come down from time to time and look at these few truly sacred objects so you might always remember why we guard them so strongly. This is the reason we are Templar Knights." Reaching into his belt, he removed two chains made of gold; on the end of each was a shield exactly like his. "These are for you two. I'm sorry that I can't officially knight you the way it was done by the King of Jerusalem, but in my status as the keeper of these treasures, I request that you kneel."

The two men knelt in front of Tristan wordlessly. Reaching out to each, he touched them on the shoulders, then removed his sword. Holding it point down in front of the two, with his hands resting on the end of the pommel, he spoke. "You are hereby charged into the Holy order of the Temple Knights. Do you solemnly swear to protect the secrets of the Holy Temple with your life and unto the death of the enemies of Christ? Will you keep these holy vows of silence and protection unto the end of life itself and swear to adhere to all the rules and obligations set unto you by God and the holy order?"

The two young men both swore the oath. Tristan touched their shoulders with the tip of the sword. "You are hereby appointed and accepted into the order of Temple Knights. Never forget your promises and always honor God in the performance of those duties you are assigned."

The two young men stood quietly, letting it sink in to their understanding. After eight years with Tristan, they finally fully understood his calling and his quest, and they were committed to it as well. Placing his sword back in its sheath, Tristan quietly placed the chains around each of their necks. "Not all Temple Knights have this chain and shield to protect them. It is a symbol I have chosen as my own for you. I give to you my name as your own, should you choose to accept it. I dub thee Sir Sama of New Hope, son of Tristan of Lorraine." Turning to Lem, he repeated the words, "I dub thee Sir Lem-u-Hi of New Hope, son of Tristan of Lorraine." The two were quiet and still as Tristan swept his cape in a flourish and turned, leaving the cavern and heading for his room. "I have doublets that are the same as my own waiting for you in your chambers," he said as he walked away. Never before had either seen such emotion in Tristan's eyes, and they both recognized the gravity of the moment. Clasping each other's arms, they smiled and said together "Brother!" They instinctively looked at the shield around their necks: "Truth and Honor" it read. They were proud.

Chapter 6

The Dock at San Diego Harbor, Sunday, July 15th, 2007

It was 4:30 AM and Isaiah and Naomi were both bent over, untying the forward and aft lines to release the LeiLani from its grasp of the shore. They both fumbled their way back to the top steering cabin and Isaiah turned the key, starting the twin engines and idling them as he engaged the clutch and allowed the props to push the boat slowly forward into the open water. By 5:00 AM they were leaving the marina. Isaiah looked at Naomi and asked, "Did you really say you'd sold your software yesterday?"

"Not sold yet, but I got a great offer from Mr. Martin Stanton of Microcom himself yesterday. It would mean at least 2 million in my pocket tomorrow and stock options that would mean another 10 within the next five years. On top of that, a million-dollar-a-year salary as the president of the database division at Microcom. To make it even better, he knew about JD and offered him a job as vice president of the private engineering section."

"That's some offer," said Isaiah, feeling a little dejected. He wondered, how could either one of them possibly turn down such offers? While happy for his two friends, he knew in his logical mind that no one in their right mind would turn it down.

As if reading Isaiah's mind, Naomi punched him in the arm. "Don't look so glum, chum. I can negotiate a new deal with Martin, and we could run around the Caribbean as the new pirates of justice."

Isaiah laughed. "Justice, you bet. I can live with that." He smiled. "Right now, though, I'd like to rain a little justice down on the head of that jerk living in the caves of Afghanistan."

"Me too," said Naomi. "You don't have any idea how much information goes unused by our military because of politics on the hill. The sniveling little puppets in Congress use the information they're given to gain a little power here or there and to put money in their own accounts at the expense of letting people like Osama keep running around free. I'll bet you didn't know that back in '96 the president was given perfect strike information that would have killed the creep with a single warhead shot from a waiting sub. Instead of taking the shot, he basically sold the information for political capital and campaign contributions for his wife's election to Congress in 2000. Osama was warned and got out. The president made a mockery of firing a war shot from the sub into an empty hole in the desert, and the Steel Magnolia got her campaign contributions. Now she's the distinguished lady from New Jersey, elected by fools who know she never lived in New Jersey a day in her life."

Isaiah was speechless for a moment, then asked, "Is that really true?"

"Yep," said Naomi.

"I can't believe it's really that bad, Naomi."

"Trust me, Isaiah, it is."

"If the president hadn't waited he would have killed Osama in '96, then all those people in the World Trade

Center wouldn't have died," said Isaiah, putting the pieces of the puzzle in place in his mind.

"That's right," she replied.

"How could he do that?" asked Isaiah incredulously.

"Its easy," she said. "He's one of those little weasels I was talking about. He'd rather put money in his bank account than serve the people, and she's even worse. It's not about money for her. It's power that she craves. She'd do anything, and I do mean anything, to replace Debra as president in the next election. As it is, when Debra was elected in 2000 she was supposedly so pissed off about not getting to be the first woman president that she wrecked the White House living quarters and broke a dozen irreplaceable settings of china from the Lincoln presidency."

"Are you kidding me?" asked Isaiah incredulously. "Why didn't the press let everyone know about that?"

"Because they're so far behind her they don't dare tell anyone about her tantrums or some of the other stupid things she tries. They're out to get her elected too. You remember the health care crap she tried to ram down the country's throat back in 93? When ABC ran a story saying she might be using flawed data to prove the need for change, she blew up and threatened to kill the anchor. After she calmed down somewhat, ABC was barred from White House press meetings for nearly a year. The truth was that she had made up wholesale lies to back up what she was saying. Even so, ABC had to sign a waiver saying that they'd pass all stories mentioning the White House, her, or the president through her before they ran them in the future. She never let the facts get in the way of what she wanted. She ran the White House, not her husband," said Naomi seriously.

"How come no one knows this stuff?" asked Isaiah.

"Because the news media controls what you know and she and her liberal friends control the media," she replied.

"How do you know all this stuff?" asked Isaiah.

"My father is an insider. He gets to see it and hear it all from first hand witnesses. That part about her threatening to kill the news anchor—the anchor was so worried, he was out sick for two months, and still wears a bullet proof vest under his wardrobe everyday. That should tell you how serious he took her threats. They say the road to the White House left more than 10 people mysteriously dead in Louisiana where he was governor and she was a partner in a law firm, and 5 others that have never been found. No one doubts how much she desires the White House, nor what she'll do to get there again."

"What does that mean for us?" asked Isaiah.

"It means," said Naomi, "that when she's elected in '08, the military will be neutered again and terrorists around the world will have a heyday. They will go unchecked by any government and they will have free reign to persecute the small countries of the world, pushing their religion on the poor masses that have no one to protect them from these evil men."

"You mean if she's elected in '08," said Isaiah.

"Yeah, yeah, if, but take it from me, something big is going to have to happen to change things to make it an if instead of a when."

"As for the us—you and me, us—it means that I think we should take the opportunity God has dropped in our laps and make the best use of it we can to try and make that change happen. Maybe, just maybe, we'll be able to do something with it that will save the lives of people who need help all over the world."

By now they had cleared the markers and were in the main channel, heading around Point Loma toward La Jolla. Within the hour they'd be approaching the spot where the sub lay submerged. Funny, Isaiah thought, it only took an hour to reach a point where he couldn't see the shore any more, where he felt almost alone and free from the rest of the world. He wondered if men all around the globe felt the same way. He imagined a fisherman in China pushing his boat to the limits and escaping his world of domination and feeling free for a short while. He shook his head to clear away the thoughts. Both of them sat back as Isaiah opened up the throttles to full speed. Settling back, Isaiah punched the coordinates into the GPS, plopped his feet up and scanned the area in front of the boat, making sure there was no chance of running into anyone else. Not much chance of that at 5:00 AM, he thought. No one else was out this early on this quiet stretch of the ocean. All the marina's serving yachts and pleasure boats were on the other side of Point Loma. The working vessels would be coming out from the southern end of the Point. He wouldn't see any of them out this way; most of them stayed in the shallower waters south of the Bay. Naomi was snuggled in a blanket, half lying on the couch at the rear of the wheelhouse. Isaiah scanned above the wheel, looking for lights, and then checked the four monitors just to the right of the wheel that were visible from the port, forward, aft, and starboard wide angle cameras mounted on the boat. All quiet.

Naomi stirred a little. "Want some coffee?" she asked.

"Sure," he replied. "You know how to make it and where the maker is?"

"Yeah, I'll get it started." She moved from the couch, sliding lithely down the stairs into the galley. Eight minutes later she emerged holding two cups of steaming coffee.

"Sugar or cream?" she asked.

"No thanks. On the sea we only drink it one way—straight," he replied.

"I could only find these broken cups to drink out of. Looks like someone broke the handles off of all your coffee cups," she said questioningly.

"Those are naval-style cups." "No handles. It's a British thing," he said, shrugging.

"How long before we get there?" she asked.

"About another hour," he replied. "You might as well get comfortable."

Without questioning further, she settled back onto the couch. After another five minutes she broke the silence again. "So what about Marisa?" she asked, smiling at Isaiah.

"What about her?" he replied.

"Wow! You really do like her."

"Why do you say that?"

"So sensitive, Isaiah. You're never this sensitive when I ask you about a girl."

"Well, she's different I guess."

"What do you mean, different? Go on, tell me about her and why she seems different to you."

"Well, I just mean—she's nice, you know Naomi, and...I don't want to talk about it."

"Sure you do, Isaiah. Tell me why she's so special."

"Naomi! I didn't say special."

"Maybe you didn't, but your eyes, your voice, and your actions did. Tell me why she's so special Saiah."

"Okay, Okay," he said, turning to face her for the first time, his eyes lighting up as he spoke. "She's smart, and funny, and Wow....have you looked at her? I mean, Wow, she's gorgeous! And did I tell you how smart she is? She listened to me like what I said mattered, and she knew how to use all that lab equipment to find out if the air was poisonous or not. She really knew just exactly what to do. And she'll be a doctor by the end of the next semester. And on top of all of that, when I kissed her I thought I was going to fall into those lips and eyes forever."

"Wait, wait..." said Naomi, "When you kissed her? When did you kiss her?" She jumped up on the couch. "You only met with her to get a couple of samples checked—maybe an hour. How is it that you kissed her?"

Isaiah smiled, turned back toward the monitors and kept quiet.

✠

By now JD was monitoring the outside traffic. He saw a small boat, which he identified as a private fishing class, headed straight toward him. Five miles away there were two Aegis-class destroyers parked—one 10 degrees starboard and the other 15 degrees to port. He didn't like it that they were there. He worried that Isaiah might tip them off. He had to find a way to warn him off. He hoped that Isaiah had his own radar on and that he would see the two warships waiting out there in the gray dawn. He had spent the night reading and studying the electronic manuals on the magnificent ship. He found that the ship's name had originally been the Sea Wolf, and that's what he thought it needed to remain. He knew he had a decoy in his armory that would be perfect for this situation, but he was very hesitant to shoot a torpedo in the general direction of a US Naval Ship.

Isaiah, almost as in answer to JD's thoughts, flipped on his radar and swept the distance around the LeiLani, searching for any boats in the area. Only a faint echo returned off one of the two destroyers parked two miles from JD. Isaiah's radar wasn't nearly as strong or up-to-date as the modern military radars in use. Even so, there was a faint return coming from the destroyer on the port side. Isaiah saw a return, but it seemed too small to be anything to worry about. In reality, it was the return presented from an open hatch that a young cook's helper had left ajar as he stepped outside to smoke a cigarette. Five minutes later, Isaiah took notice that the return had suddenly disappeared from the scope. He scratched his head but didn't worry any further about it. The sun was just peeking over the tops of the rapidly disappearing mountains in the distance. The shoreline was now discernable from the sea and it sparkled as the sun glinted off of the water where it hit the beach. Half an orange ball was visible above the mountains. Eighty-five degrees and rising... By noon it might be pushing a hundred, he thought. By noon I'll be 150 feet below the waves, was his next thought.

JD had brought the dive mask into the sail, hoping he'd be able to transmit to Isaiah before Isaiah said anything to him. JD knew he needed to speak first so that he could warn Isaiah about the ships in the distance.

Isaiah slowed the engines to half speed. Turning to Naomi, he said, "Naomi, would you get me the full dive mask that's laying down in the bow of the boat?"

"Sure," she said, pulling herself up and heading down the steps once again. She stopped and turned back to him. "If you tell me how it is that you kissed her."

"Will you drop it?" He laughed nervously. "I'm not telling you any more, Okay?"

She turned, feigning disappointment. "Okay, but you will tell me. You know you will."

Isaiah shook his head as she disappeared down the stairs. He knew she was probably right. He wondered how JD had fared during the night. He hadn't slept a wink all night. So many things went through his mind, and there was so much to think about. He was worried, thrilled, excited, confused, and in love, all at one time. Life just can't get any more complicated, he reasoned. He scanned the horizon; it was still grey out to sea and the sun was too bright for his eyes when he looked back toward shore. He pulled up to a stop, dropping anchor and heading down to get the dive gear. As he took the first step down, Naomi was coming up the stairs. "Here's the helmet," she said, handing it to him. He flipped the switch to open the com and heard JD's voice come over the earpiece immediately.

"Isaiah! Isaiah! Are you listening? Turn on the set. Yeah, there on the side. Do you see it?" JD was talking as if he were standing on deck.

"JD," was all Isaiah got out before he was again cut off.

"Good, Isaiah! Did you see the ships off the port bow? I think I can see him there in the mist," said JD, telling Isaiah why he was being so secretive.

"No, I didn't, but now that you mention it, I think I do," said Isaiah, taking the cue.

"Good. Now we go for a little dive and then do a little fishing later?" said JD.

"Right. Let's go."

On deck, Naomi was anxious to put the headset on and speak with JD, but she noted the odd conversation and Isaiah's sudden interest in the darkness to the left side of the boat.

"What's going on?" she asked.

"He's tracking a ship, probably a US warship of some kind, off our port bow. He was warning me not to say anything over the helmet com."

"Why not?" she asked.

"Because, Smarty Pants, the Navy has ways of monitoring any kind of electronic signal there is. They probably were listening to everything we said." As he finished checking out his gear, he explained how she should wait there and they'd both be back soon. He gave her a headset and microphone, telling her that she could keep in touch with them on that when he started his dive, but that she should be very careful of what she said so as to not give away the fact that they were separated or that they were in a submarine, or use their names. "If that happens," Isaiah said, "you'll find out just how fast a Navy destroyer is and what it feels like to be held for questioning by the United States government."

"They don't scare me." She lifted her chin mockingly. "I have friends in high places!"

"They can't help you if you aren't allowed to call them," he said and smiled back at her.

"You make an excellent point, my friend." She lowered her chin and then said, "So I guess I'll be extra careful."

"Thanks," he replied.

Two miles to the southeast, and to the northeast, two sets of radio operators were listening for any more conversation between the men on the small boat that was anchored over the interesting spot they were watching. The captains of the two destroyers had been notified of the boat parked in their watch-zone five minutes before the LeiLani stopped her engines. When she parked almost exactly over the area they had been watching, they both got very interested.

Stepping off of the stern, he spoke again to JD. "Boy, that water is cold, man. By the way, I showed Naomi how to talk to us over the onboard radio. She should be monitoring us after all as we head down."

JD was silent for a moment and then replied, "Look. Are you sure she knows how?"

Naomi broke in. "Yes I do, and yes I can, Mr. Skeptic."

"I was just wondering if...never mind," JD said, thinking quickly and not wanting to sound too odd.

"I'll tell you, JD, these are beautiful waters. What is it you wanted to check on the bottom this time?" Isaiah said, acting as if JD were right next to him and giving any spying ears a reason for why they were here.

JD took his queue and began giving a lecture. He stepped into the role so well, Isaiah, who was quickly becoming bored, swam as quickly as he could to the hatch just to get JD to shut up.

"JD, okay, I get it. We're looking for the reason for the anomalous reading from the other day. All you had to do was tell me that you think someone threw a stove overboard."

"Well, I just wanted you to understand the ramifications of litter to the legitimate marine research community and how it costs the researchers like me tons of money over our lifetimes."

"All right, all right. I'm suitably outraged," said Isaiah, faking a yawn through the faceplate.

Onboard the LeiLani, Naomi giggled. "You two should go on the lecture circuit," she said. JD, you could be the straight man, and Isaiah could get the laughs!"

"Two against one, huh?" said JD. "Just keep the noise down while I, the research scientist, look for a stove somewhere," JD said haughtily.

"Great," said Isaiah. "I'm glad no one's taping this for posterity. Imagine how that sound bite would sound being played as you stepped forward to accept your FLOATIE award or whatever it is you get for doing research work in the ocean."

On board both destroyers, the radio operators smiled in unison, and both captains, who were also listening, silently agreed with the Zaya person. The other one, JD, had been putting them to sleep. Almost in unison, the captains of both ships dropped interest in the boat two miles away. Knowing that there were two men diving the shallow depths they were interested in was proof enough for them that nothing was there. By this point they would surely have spotted a submarine and would have flipped out over the radio if they saw it. Time to move on.

As the two ships began making turns for moving off to the south, Isaiah entered the air lock. Continuing their mock conversation, JD monitored the exit of the two destroyers. Inwardly, he sighed with relief. Fifteen minutes later Isaiah joined JD on the bridge. Still carrying on the deception, JD put an end to the farce by saying, "Naomi, we're gonna turn off the radio to conserve battery power. We'll turn 'em back on when we start to come back up. In the meantime, just listen and we'll be back on the air in a little while. With these rebreathers we've got another hour before we have to start up."

"Okay," she replied. Turning off the sets, JD and Isaiah got caught up. After letting Isaiah tell him the whole story, leaving out Naomi's news—he thought she should tell him—JD listened intently.

"So the water and air are both good then. How come Naomi's on the LeiLani?"

"Hey man, she called, and you know I can't lie. She knew something was up and jumped all over me, so—I had to tell her, and then she had to come."

JD smiled at the thought of his 5'1" girlfriend bullying Isaiah. "Yeah, she can be tough can't she?" he said.

"There's one more thing," said Isaiah. "I kind of had to tell Marisa more than I wanted to also, man. She had to know who was behind it to know what to look for in the vials. So anyway, one thing led to another, and anyway...she knows we found a sub out here."

"Well," said JD, thinking and sighing resignedly, "I'm not terribly worried about Marisa or Naomi, but I am worried that those two destroyers who were parked watching for me. They followed me all around the bay last night."

"Wait a minute. You sailed this thing last night? Just you? By yourself?" said Isaiah incredulously.

"Yeah, it was so cool. I went all around the bay and this ship is fantastic. There is so much it can do. You've gotta see everything. We've got to keep it," he said flatly.

"I agree," said Isaiah.

"What?" said JD. "I thought I'd have to convince you."

"Nope. After the conversations I've had the last 24 hours and the stuff I've learned about politics and how bad people can be and get away with it, I agree. We have to use this ship to go—to be Pirates of Justice, like Naomi says."

"Pirates of Justice, huh? Well, we'll see. As of twenty-four hours ago, you and I are co-owners of The Seawolf," JD said. "I felt like that was a good name for what we should become, raiders of the sea that live with 'Truth and Honor' as our watchwords and perform acts of Justice to the world as best we can."

"You and me, partners and pirates," said Isaiah, holding out his right hand.

"Partners and pirates, Purveyors of Justice in an unjust world," said JD, grasping the given hand with his own.

"But..." said Isaiah.

"But what?" asked JD.

"There's something else that Naomi has to tell you that might change all of this pirate stuff," said Isaiah.

Knitting his brow in confusion, JD said, "What are you talking about? She's not against any of this, is she? She didn't tell her dad, did she?" he stood at the last in fear.

"No, No, No! Don't over react. She just has something going that may change your mind, that's all. I won't say any more. You need to talk to her about it."

"Okay," said JD. "In fact, it's time to find that stove for the Navy and surface this tub."

"What?" said Isaiah. "You don't mean to tell me you're going to surface now?"

"How else can we get her on board?" JD asked.

The Navy ships were no longer monitoring the communications between the three boring scientists, but the trio continued the charade anyway. After warning Naomi subversively, they began the slow ascent of the ship. Before it broke the surface, the two turned on the invisibility screen for the sail of the sub. They were rewarded with a warning that it would automatically be turned on once it was above the water line. It would not operate reliably underwater. Accepting that, the two checked for any activity in the area. The two destroyers by now were more than thirty miles away and still moving. No one else was any closer, except for inside the bay, and they were all local traffic—no war ships. They surfaced the ship only 100 yards from the LeiLani. As the sail raised itself from the sea, Naomi gasped at its size. As it continued to come up, the wings folded themselves into the slots on the sides of the conning tower. Only a few inches of decking appeared above the waterline, and as it did, the sail seemed to shimmer somewhat, and then it almost disappeared completely. Naomi couldn't believe her eyes. Where there had been a submarine, now there was a floating deck and something indescribable above it. It was, for all intents and purposes, invisible. Turning on the engines and activating the anchor winch, she pulled up the anchor and moved it gently up to the floating deck. Dropping the bumpers over the side, she was amazed to see JD step out onto the deck and grab the bowline from her. Tying it to the inside handle of the hatch, she was stunned, but glad to see him. They dropped the anchor on LeiLani. Thirty minutes later, the groceries had been transferred to the Sea Wolf, the lines had been cast off, just in case, and the three were inside the control room, talking.

After the trivial discussions about how wonderful the ship was, the discussion turned to Naomi's news and the subsequent decisions that needed to be made. That was Isaiah's queue to go for a walk around the ship's expansive interior. Walking back to the galley, he grabbed a cold bottle of water out of one of the refrigerators. Taking it with him, he began a leisurely stroll through the upper part of the sub. In the section just below the control room he found a large library. Instead of books lining the wall, however, there was a huge screen covering the front wall, rounded like the sub's hull. At first he didn't recognize it as a screen at all; in fact, he had walked past it several times before he realized he was in a library and that was the screen to read from. Sitting in one of the ten chairs strategically arranged in the room, he tapped the view screen that rose up from the arm of the chair. Expecting that to be his private screen, he began going through the menu choices until he found a box that read, "Outside View." Touching it, he was instantly rewarded with the huge screen in front of him coming to life and showing him a view from the front of the conning tower as if a huge window had been opened in front of him. Looking further at the options, he chose "Rear View" and was rewarded with a view of the world to the stern of the ship. After playing a bit more, he found that all four walls were screens and that by setting them correctly he could stand in the middle of the room and see the outside world as if he were standing on the conning tower and looking in any direction. What was even better was that with the touch of the screen he could zoom in with what was marked a 20x optical zoom and a 200x digital zoom. Looking toward the port, he could zoom in enough to read the time on the clock at the tower of one of the fancier marinas. It was amazing. Looking further, he found that any book he wanted and any map he wanted to see was at his fingertips. Stepping downstairs, he went to the rear of the sub, tripping on a chair leg. He dropped his water bottle, spilling it on the thick pile carpet that lined the walkways. Almost instantly, a subdued klaxon sounded and the doors to either side of him at opposite ends of the room slid shut and a female voice said in a slight English accent, "Water alarm in engineering section 1. Please acknowledge." It repeated itself several times while Isaiah looked for some way to silence the alarm. After the fourth repeat of the message, the klaxon bell silenced and the voice went away. Instead, JD's voice resonated in its place.

"Hey dude, what are you doin' down there—sinking the ship?"

Isaiah kept looking anxiously for a com device to answer with. In desperation, he yelled, "How do I answer this thing?"

JD instantly replied, "Just speak, dude. Once I spoke to you, you can speak back to me without touching anything."

Feeling a little embarrassed, he said, "Well then, Mr. Know-it-all, how do I initiate the conversation?"

"Look at the light switch. There's a button to the right of it in every room that activates a hidden screen next to it, allowing you to pick who you want to talk to."

"Thanks, dude. By the way, I dropped a bottle of water on the floor. That's what set off the alarm."

"Okay, Isaiah. You want to head back this way? We've got some more talking to do."

"Okay, I'll be right there. Uh, what about the watertight doors?"

"Oh yeah," said JD. "There." As he said it, the doors opened with the familiar "psst."

Naomi and JD were still sitting at the table in front of the captain's chair. Isaiah entered and sat next to Naomi. "Well?" JD said, "here's what we came up with, but we need your input as well. We've decided that Naomi is going to take Martin's offer for the software and take the job as president of the database division. I, however, am not taking his offer to be VP of Engineering or whatever it was he was offering. I'm just not interested. Isaiah, we're going to need a lot of things to make this work: a place to park this thing that's hidden, about 20 men that we can trust completely. And we'll need a few others—a doctor, an engineer, and a couple of others to back them up. We also need a weapons expert, someone who knows how to use the things we have at our disposal. And you and I—co-captains who won't be looking for power or money or anything else. Two captains on the same page, working toward the same goal. Are you in this with me as co-captain?"

Isaiah sat back, considering the offer. JD continued, "If you aren't in this with me, Isaiah, we'll just sail this into the bay and give it to the government and hope we get a few million each for it."

"Don't misunderstand, JD," said Isaiah. "I'm not sitting here trying to find a way to say no. Remember what I said last week about making decisions the right way—slow and right? I just want to go over it one more time in my head before I say yes."

JD smiled and knew that Isaiah would answer when he was ready. A full minute later, Isaiah replied, "Okay, JD. You know that I want to do this, and my answer is yes. I just want you to know that even though we're co-captains, there can only be one captain on the ship, and that's you. I'll be your co captain on the ship, and you and I are definitely on the same page. I'll work with you, but let me be one of the engineers as well. It would make my mom so happy to have an engineer for a son." He laughed, and so did JD.

"Okay, Isaiah, but I want you to know that you and I make the decisions together unless it needs a snap decision, and even then you have the right to question me or give me advice at any time. Okay?"

"Okay, JD. We're in it together. And by the way, since I can give you advice at any time... Are you nuts? Turning down a VP job with Microcom? Are you loco, man?"

They all laughed. "Now," said Isaiah, "when do we leave?"

"Friday," came the reply.

"I've got some things to get done then," said Isaiah.

"Me too," said JD.

"I think we should move the ship somewhere else, somewhere quiet," said Naomi.

"Up for a short cruise?" JD asked.

"Let's go," Isaiah responded.

Twenty minutes later the two ships were under way, with JD and Isaiah in the sub, sailing south along the coast toward the Baja Peninsula. Six hours later the sub parked on the floor of the sea, in between two huge boulders and just inside the Mexican Territorial waters, just about twenty miles across the border and lying in only 100 feet of water. It was just deep enough to keep it invisible from above and far enough from the fishing grounds to keep it from drawing attention from hung up nets. Getting back into their diving gear, they waited another hour until the LeiLani parked above them. After diving back to the surface, the two climbed aboard and began the trip back to San Diego. They were challenged by a US Coast Guard boat as they entered back into US waters, but they were otherwise not bothered. They made plans and discussed the future and possible crew as they headed back. Naomi turned out to be the biggest help in that area. She addressed the subject carefully, but told the duo, "I have a father with access to some of the best people for this kind of work. With the proper persuasion we could end up with a team that has just the right talent. Certainly something to think about. She told them that if things continued the way they were, her dad might want to join the crew himself. They laughed about it, but suddenly, a new thought was churning through JD's mind. Perhaps Naomi could use her dad to get the right info for their missions. She might be the real captain as it turns out, JD thought. They agreed that she would carefully broach the subject and see where it led. They arrived back at the dock at 11:45 PM, and they were all exhausted. They all crashed at JD's apartment that night.

Morning arrived very early for the trio. An alarm went off at 6:30 AM. Isaiah, however, was already up and making pancakes. An early riser from birth, made worse by owning a boat, he loved the mornings. Flipping the pancakes, he watched as first JD staggered into the kitchen, soon to be followed by Naomi. Isaiah helped them find chairs, fixed the pancakes for them, and finally poured juice and then coffee to get them moving. By 8:00 the three were back to planning. With a little urging, the guys had convinced Naomi to call her father. Eleven AM on the east coast, she knew he'd soon be headed for lunch. He was a creature of habit— noon every day. She reached into her purse pulling out a rather odd looking cell phone and what looked like a dock to put it into, but it didn't have a base. She sheepishly looked at them and said, "This is a scrambler, only for special people. My dad forced it on me back when he took "the" job. I've never used it—until now."

"Hi, Dad," she said after waiting for the warbling to stop.

"Hi, sweetie," he said. "What's up... you know this is a special line."

"Yeah, I know. It's that...well I need something and its gonna sound a bit weird and I don't want any of the millions of computers that listen to the phone calls into your world to pick up on what I have to say. Okay?" she said.

"Okay," he replied. "You've definitely got my attention now. But I must say, I'm more used to having discussions like this with my operatives, not my daughter."

"Daddy, you have to promise me that none of what I say goes beyond you. Can you do that for me?"

"As a father, the answer is an emphatic yes. As the Director of the NSA, I'll promise you the same as long as it doesn't harm my country in any way."

"It will help protect your country, Dad, so long you keep it between us."

"Okay then," he said. "Shoot." Three thousand miles away, she winced at the euphemism.

"Dad, I'm in need of some help from some people that you know better than I do. I'm in the need of a few good men." She laughed.

"For what?" he asked.

"Don't ask that question of me, okay, Dad? I need twenty men, all specialists in some really dangerous fields, and all who are experienced enough to depend on, and all who know how not to talk."

"My goodness," he said. "Okay, go on..."

"Well, I also need an engineer, a doctor, and a weapons specialist who knows all kinds of weapons." Her intonation of the word all made her father wince.

"It sounds like you're putting together a mercenary team," he half laughed.

"Dad!" she warned.

"Okay, Okay, I'm not asking, but I need a little more info. What kind of specialties?"

"I need two communications experts, in fact two of each of these type men—communications, small arms, heavy weapons, navigation, food preparation, and at least 10 all-around infiltration and abduction experts."

The last really got her father's attention. "Okay that's it," he stated flatly. "Trust your old man or hang up. This is bordering on a bad dream," he said.

Looking at the other two, she took a deep breath and said, "Dad, I need to talk to you about this, but it just can't be over the phone. I guarantee it's worth your time. Please fly out here to San Diego and I promise to give you all the answers. Okay?"

JD and Isaiah looked a little bug-eyed.

"Okay ,Sweetie, but just to make me feel better, tell me you're not involved in anything illegal."

"I promise, Daddy, nothing illegal, and nothing morally or ethically wrong. Okay?"

"Okay, but you've really got my attention. I'll be there by—let's see, around 1:30 your time. Okay?"

"Where should I pick you up?"

"I'll meet you at your apartment around 2:00."

"Okay, Daddy. I'll see you at 2:00." She hung up the phone.

"This is it guys. What do you think, Naomi?" asked JD.

"I think he'll do it," she replied.

At two o'clock sharp there was a knock at Naomi's apartment door. She answered the door while Isaiah and JD sat, feeling a little awkward, on the living room sofa. After the initial hugs and greetings, Dave walked into the living room, and as he did so, both JD and Isaiah stood.

"JD, It's good to see you," said Dave, "and you're the friend— Isaiah, right?" he said turning and facing Isaiah as he extended his hand.

"Yes sir. We met last Christmas," said Isaiah.

"Okay," he said while removing his coat and placing it over the back of a chair. "Obviously you two are part of what my daughter was so covertly talking to me about on the phone this morning. So now that we're all here, what's really going on?"

JD was the first to respond. "Sir, it's like this. Isaiah and I found something that is pretty amazing. Well, let's just put it on the table. Before I do, though, I want a promise that you aren't carrying anything that would record our conversation or transmit it so that it can be heard by anyone else. Okay?"

"Done. I promise," he replied.

"Okay, we found a submarine."

"Let me guess," said Dave. "An Iranian sub, somewhere off the California coast line, with a dead crew, or something close to dead. You didn't try to save any of the crew or come in contact with them while they were alive, did you?"

The three conspirators looked at the man as if he were Houdini. "No sir. The sub was empty. The crew was gone, but how did you know?"

"We've been looking for it. You've done a wonderful thing," he started, and then stopped. "But that's not why you called, is it? You need men from me. You plan on using this ship…" His eyes narrowed and he looked at each of them.

"Sir," said JD, "we've got it and we sure could use your help, but we're not going to turn it over to the government and have it wind up back in their hands shooting more canisters of Ebola virus at our water supplies." Throwing a sheaf of papers on the table, JD punctuated his remarks. "This is a complete mission layout, including who ordered the mission, and who carried it out in both original Farsi and in English."

Isaiah spoke up, "We know what'll happen if it goes back into the hands of—pardon the remark—but bureaucrats like most of the people in DC. We believe that an elite group of dedicated men with a weapon such as this can prevent terrorism across the globe in a way that political maneuvering just can't do. It would also give our government complete deniability—no connection, unless you want to count Christmas dinner."

Naomi added her comments. "Dad, I can't tell you how many times I've heard you complain about the political nonsense that goes on while good men die at the hands of terrorists and corrupt political despots. With this opportunity, we are going to do something about it the only way we know how. With your help, we'll be able to get started on the right foot and will be able to do so, knowing that we can trust the men you send us. If you don't, we'll find those same men; it'll just take a lot longer, and we'll miss a lot of opportunities to do good while we look for them!"

Her logic again, thought Mr. Benson; it was why she did so well with computer languages, he had always believed. She had always had great logic. "Okay, let's just say I agree. Let me say a few things to bust your bubble. If you do this you'll have some of the best Navies in the world calling you pirates and thinking you are the other guy's asset and doing their best to kill you. I don't mean kill in the sense of a computer game... I mean a torpedo up your ass in 10,000 feet of water. A no-escape kind of death. All the Navies of the world, including the US Navy—and guys, our Navy isn't good; it's great..."

"I don't mean to be disrespectful, sir", said JD, "but a while back, on my first trip in the sub, without knowing what I was doing, I played cat and mouse with two Aegis destroyers and neither had any idea I was anywhere around."

"I'll admit that's pretty good, JD, but it won't be playing. If you do this, I won't be able to help you in any way that will show publicly or even in the White House. For all intents and purposes I'll watch you die if you tangle with our Navy, and I won't be able to stop it from happening."

"We understand, sir," said Isaiah, "but we aren't afraid of dying, as long as we are dying for the things we believe in. Sir, we—the US—are involved in a war that our own politicians refuse to recognize as a war. They stick their heads in the ground and hide from the truth. Our media lies to the common man, telling them what the liberals want them to hear. Our Congress, in fits of retaliation, send our men into harms way and then pull the carpet out from under them the first time they kill a terrorist who happens to be under 16. They lie to themselves, and then to the public, only for graft or greed or power. Sir, the world needs someone to be there, and not to report to a congressional committee who will not allow us to do the job that needs to be done. We need just a little bit of assistance to get us started and then get out of the way as we do what needs to be done."

Dave looked at the two young men wistfully. Somewhere far away, he wished it were he who had found that submarine. "You have my blessing," he said, somewhat reservedly, "but we have a lot of things yet to discuss."

After it was all said and done, JD, Isaiah, and Naomi were blown away. They had wanted a few good men; what they ended up with was unbelievable. "You understand that we aren't going to tell you where the sub is or give you any secrets from it?" said JD, still thinking that there must be a catch to Dave's offer to them.

"JD, I don't want anything. I just want to help you any way I can and then be able to deny everything. Okay, what you don't understand is that I won't be in public life forever. When the current administration ends, I'll be out of a job, then I will be available to help you full time," he said, hinting.

"You've got it," said JD. What Dave had offered them was this: he had in his briefcase a file of men who were either currently in Special Forces—mostly the seals, or who had been and were currently in special organizations around the country. All of them had shown dissatisfaction with their current roles and were actively looking for more decisive work. All of them were single. He also had similar profiles for the professional men they had asked for. Above that, he had knowledge of three secret submarine bases that had been abandoned during the late 80s, due to budget cutbacks and the death of the cold war. Those bases would be perfect to hide such a boat and could be theirs by simply taking over a 200-year lease on one of them, and the other two were completely uninhabited. These bases were unknown of by the younger group of commanding admirals who were now coming up through the ranks, and they had been forgotten about by most of the older group that were still left. Only he and a very select few even knew they existed. He also had the name of one man whom he wanted included on the missions. This man was a scientist who had quite a reputation for brilliance, but also a reputation for being entirely dissatisfied with the political dabbling done by Congress into his work. His name was Olaf Jakees. Olaf was a gift, one that Dave was hesitant to bestow upon the group, but he knew both the group and Olaf would be best served working with each other. In an environment where no one was sitting on top of the genius, but instead using the extreme ideas that he was continually coming up with to keep marching forward by technological leaps and bounds. He was better served helping this group, Dave was sure. On top of that, he promised to be able to deliver all the torpedoes and cruise missiles they might need to one particular base, but these deliveries could only happen once a year and only through a very clandestine budget in the CIA.

He also could give to them the transmission codes and scramble codes for the IUSS (Integrated Undersea Surveillance System). It combined the SOSUS, SSIPS, and SDS systems that provided the United States ears with which to listen for enemies across the oceans of the world. The SOSUS (Sound Surveillance System), SSIPS (Shore Signal Information Processing Segment) and SDS (Surveillance Detection System) were the ears of the ocean. Since the cold war had ended, the priority for these systems had fallen on deaf ears. New software and new hardware to run it could make the SOSUS lines virtually impenetrable, but budgets for such things had been cut during the previous administration and the liberal control of the House of Representatives since then had denied budget funds during the current administration. Dave hinted to his daughter that with access to the code and to the arrays, they could know what was going on in every ocean of the world from their ship should they have the desire and the wherewithal to do it.

The last thing he promised was probably the most important. He promised to return in a few days with a list of codes, frequencies and satellite hookup information and equipment, including six of his newest toys: satellite scrambled phones that could display and download data, video, internet links, and GPS data. What was really wild was the signal operated on ultra-low frequency as a carrier for an ultra-hi frequency band. The bottom line was that it would work inside buildings, caves, tunnels, and below the ocean. They could be used like walkie-talkies or like a regular phone, and with the scramble button, even the "techno-weenies" at the CIA and NSA couldn't break what was being said. But that wasn't it. The reason he'd need those would be to give them their assignments. He promised to give them the data they needed in a hurry so they could get the bad guys when it counted. He remembered all too well the last president's bumbling and how it had cost the US the World Trade Center and 6,000 peoples lives. He wasn't going to let that happen again, no matter whom the president was—Republican or Democrat, Liberal or Conservative. It wasn't going to happen on his watch.

The first of the bases he offered them was on the Island of New Caledonia, in the Coral Sea. The French-owned island was very laid back and inhabited by an odd mix of French and Fiji islanders. The base had been created originally back during the Second World War, and abandoned soon after. It was re-opened by the Americans in the 1960s in a completely clandestine move by the CIA. It had remained open until '88, when a congressman snooping through classified CIA budget documents started getting too close. It was decided that the sub base was no longer worth the risk, and all the men had been pulled out and the base left forgotten. It had been a rather ingenious effort to make it work back when it was re-opened. They had made it look like the sub pens had been destroyed by a rockslide from the side of the volcano above; in reality, they had created an undersea entrance to the sub pens that were in far better shape than anyone knew in '88 when they were closed.

The second base was on the island nation of Iceland. It too had been built under the noses of an unsuspecting government during the 1970s. It had remained open until 1993, when it fell to the axe of the president's wife's hit list of military targets. Not understanding its strategic importance or the hundreds of millions of dollars that had been put into building the place, it was unceremoniously closed because she didn't like the admiral who was trying to keep it open. He resigned not long after. Really, that was what she had wanted all along; the closing was just a way to get him to go. What it did accomplish, however, was to provide a huge place for them with doors that looked like a sheer rock cliff that opened in a hidden fjord on the most remote part of the island. There was a warehouse, currently owned by the CIA, that sat atop the cliff, overlooking the fjord, with an elevator shaft that ran down to the hidden base below. This was the place where Dave could guarantee weapons shipments, skimmed from weapons made available for CIA projects around the globe. The request to have it sealed and sold was currently on Dave's desk. Asking price for the warehouse—whatever he could get. Dave had an idea that he could get about $100,000 USD for it. He'd handle the closing of the place himself.

The third base was in the Caribbean. On the island of Jamaica, the US had acquired a 200-year lease on the land, mostly inland but including a beachfront east of Kingston. The land was worthless, for the most part. It extended almost completely across the island and had on it several mountains that were so thick with underbrush and trees that they were deemed unclimbable and worthless. The base had been built, like so many others during the 60s, under the Kennedy administration when the CIA had power and money to work with. They had found an undersea cave system that honeycombed the entire eastern end of the island. Using sonar techniques, they found the largest of the natural undersea caverns, and they began building submarine pens, hoping to have a fleet available if needed in the Caribbean. The pens had been done well, but the warehouse they built above the pens was now in complete disrepair. Only one road ran to that part of the island, and the CIA had pumped a ton of money into keeping the road open. Now it was closed and the warehouse was going to ruin. The lease had been negotiated during the problems with Castro, so it had been very good for the US. To take control of the lease, one needed only pay 1,000 US dollars a year, negotiable again in 2162.

After talking in great detail, it was decided that all three were available, and why not? By utilizing all three they could play the shell game with their sub if necessary, hiding it from the world. A base in the North Atlantic, The South Pacific, and a third in the Caribbean—all that was left was to have one in the Med.

"Don't laugh" said Dave. "I know of a place in Gibraltar that the Brits own now, but that could end up vacant in a few years."

"This is amazing," said JD. "I can't believe there are so many places across the world being given up without a struggle. Why?"

"Because," said Dave, "the world has gone liberal and no one thinks we need submarines and aircraft carriers anymore. They think we can just jump an airliner or something and go to where the problem is and the bad guys will just give up when they see the US flag. It doesn't work that way, but the news media has made it seem like that."

They all sat quietly for a moment, digesting what they had put together. "Dave, this could lose you your job," said Isaiah.

"Son, it could lose me my life if it came out, but it won't, because after I get you set up I'll wash my proverbial hands, and you're on your own. Besides, the only way it could come out is if you or he or she says something—and that's not going to happen. From now on, my code name is 'Daddy Warbucks.' Got it?"

They all laughed and agreed. He was Daddy Warbucks, JD was to be called Nemo, Isaiah was Rex—from a book called Rex, King of the Deep, and Naomi would be Matahari. They kidded about the names, but inside they all knew there was a certain truth behind them. They had to be careful and they were anxious to get started. And so they did... They went over each résumé together. By 7:30 they had a pile of information on 25 men and 6 professionals that looked promising. They headed for supper. Over supper, Naomi broke the news to her father about her software sale. It was a good reason to celebrate.

They all took care of their own issues during the next three days. JD went to see his advisors and set up an Internet site that he could be reached through. They were pleased with his work and virtually told him his PHD would pass the review board and he could look forward to it by mid-August.

Isaiah went to see his mother. After some deep discussion, a few tears and many hugs, she was okay with her son's choice. Digging in the closet, she came out with a gold chain. "This belonged to your father, Isaiah. He would want you to have it. He wore it always, and he said it had been passed from father to first son for many many generations," she said. "He was wearing it when he was killed, so I don't think it has the power to protect you, Isaiah, but your father always said it had the power to make him feel like a man inside. I know he'd want you to have it as you go off on this adventure of yours."

Isaiah took it in his hands and examined it. It looked very much like the one JD had. He smiled and thought that both of their dads must have shopped at the same jewelry store. Taking it from her, he assured her that he'd keep it around his neck forever. His next stop was to visit a certain Ms. Marisa Hartman. She opened the door to her house and bounced out to meet him as he started up the steps to her doorway.

"Won't you even let me have the pleasure of talking to your mother again?" asked Isaiah.

"Not tonight, you're all mine tonight," she said, with a smile on her face.

"Okay," he said. "Where to?"

"I think we're headed for a little seafood place I know out on the North Side," she purred.

"Okay," said Isaiah. "You guide, I'll drive." Thirty minutes later they were there, and in the middle of a lively discussion.

"I've got you over a barrel and you know it," said Marisa.

"Yes, but I've got a partner who'd have to agree, and besides, you're a woman, and women shouldn't be on subs. Not even the US Navy allows it."

"Look, Isaiah, you need a doctor. I'm as good as any around right now and on top of that I'm a trained virologist and biologist. If you've got a lab on that ship, I'm your man."

"Yeah, but you're not a man; you're a woman."

"The only one who'll ever know that is you," she said and winked at him. "I will be the coldest block of ice that will freeze any other man in their tracks," she pleaded. "Besides, this is the dream I've always had. I want to do this. Please, please, please," she begged.

"All right, I'll talk to JD tonight, but no more talk for now. Okay? Our food's getting cold."

Chapter 7

Dreams Come True

Naomi went back to visit Martin Stanton at Microcom's headquarters in Silicon Valley. After some loose negotiating, she got a better deal than she had hoped for—three million dollars for her portion of the software, plus two million each to her two partners. On top of that, she would get one million a year in Microcom Stock for every year the database was used in the Microcom suite of software. In addition, she would get one-point-five million dollar starting salary for her new job as president of the database division, and a great office on the top floor of the Microcom tower in San Francisco and another office in the San Diego satellite office, which she was now to run. On top of that, Martin had leased a huge home for her on The Bay in San Francisco and had paid the lease for five years in advance, with an option to buy it at the end of the five-year lease. Naomi was stunned. As she walked out of the office, Martin turned to her and said, "Oh, by the way, Naomi, there's a five hundred thousand dollar signing bonus that's yours as well. Enjoy."

With that, she walked out of the office, shaking his hand and promising to be at work the next week.

"No hurry, my dear. Take your time. I have some housecleaning to take care of so, don't show up until September 1st. Don't worry though, you're on the payroll starting today. The signing bonus and money for the sale of the product will be in your account today, and your first year's stock payout will be sent to your broker. Just give Julie, my secretary, your account info and it will be done by the end of the day."

Naomi checked her accounts that evening; the money was there. I am now officially rich, she thought. JD and Isaiah were supposed to come over to watch a movie and probably talk a bit more. She'd have a surprise for them.

Isaiah, Marisa, and JD arrived almost together at Naomi's apartment. As they walked upstairs, the discussion was headed toward Marisa's request to join the team.

"We'll talk about it inside," said JD, "where we don't have to whisper."

"Okay, JD, but don't think you can stop me," Marisa warned. As they entered the apartment, Naomi smiled and said, "You must be Marisa." The smile on Naomi's face surprised Marisa.

"Why yes. Do I know you?" she questioned.

"Oh no, no, it's just that I feel like I know you," she said.

"What do you mean?" asked Marisa.

"Well, Isaiah has told me so much about you—how smart you are, how beautiful you are, and, well how wonderful you are, and many more..."

That was as far as Naomi got before a red-faced Isaiah broke into the conversation. "That's quite enough Naomi. I'm sure Marisa doesn't want to hear what I had to say. After all, wasn't everything I said true?"

Naomi smiled a big smile again and patted Marisa on the back. "I don't know whether you know it or not, but you've got that one hooked, and I do mean hooked," she said pointing at Isaiah. "By the way, I'm Naomi, and the tall one over there looking confused is JD. But you know him, don't you?"

"Yes", said Marisa. "We've had a few classes together back in the day. I take it that you and JD are an item."

"Yes, we are," said Naomi, "and I've been trying desperately to find someone to take that buddy, Isaiah, off his hands so we could do some real double dates. I guess you are it!" she said, pointing at Marisa exaggeratedly.

"I can think of worse duty." Marisa smiled and pulled Isaiah close, looking into his eyes.

"Okay, enough about the love birds," said JD. "We've got another issue to discuss right now. It seems that Marisa wants to be our doctor. What do you two think?" he asked Isaiah and Naomi.

Almost instantly, the mood in the room changed. They went from casual friends to a board room of professionals. After ten minutes of back-and-forth discussion, including an impassioned request by Marisa, she was given a temporary acceptance, provisional upon her finishing her degree and on a trial basis to begin in January of the following year... plenty of time to finish her schooling. After a little debate, Marisa agreed to the terms, and the evening of enjoyment continued.

JD was excited. The only position that had been left vacant after all their work was the doctor's position, and Marisa had fallen into their laps like a gift from God. "How wonderful," he mused out loud.

It wasn't long afterwards that JD noticed the necklace around Isaiah's neck. He didn't typically wear one, and it struck JD as odd to see him with it. Isaiah related the story his mom had told, and the thought that perhaps JD's and Isaiah's dads had shopped at the same jewelry store. Isaiah laughed, but JD didn't. Noticing the somber look, Isaiah asked JD, "What's up, man? Is it really that rare?" Removing his own necklace and shield, he put them side-by-side on the table. "Look at this," he said. "Both chains are of the same basic twist type, but made of heavy 24-carat gold. Both chains are the same length, about 19 inches, and they both have a heavy gold shield at the end with the same two words—Truth, and Honor. Mine has the letters SAMA on the back, Isaiah's has the letters LEM on the back. Where did your dad get this, Isaiah?"

Upon the reading of the letters on the back, Isaiah turned white. "I didn't know about the letters on the back. My mom said that my dad got it from his father, and so on down the line. JD, my middle name is Lemuel. I'm supposed to be named after my great-great-great whatever grandfather. His name was LEM-u-something or other."

"Isaiah, I don't know how to tell you this, but mine was passed from father to son as well, from a great grandfather named Sama. The rumor was that he was a light-skinned black man living in the islands somewhere—Jamaica I think."

"Okay, JD, so how is it that a light-skinned black man and an Aztec from Central America both end up with matching necklaces written in English?"

"I don't know, Isaiah, but I can't help but feel that this is a very good omen of things to come. I feel like maybe our ancestors were as close friends as we are, maybe even brothers."

They grew silent as they examined the necklaces and then replaced them and set about trying to relax again.

✠

Thursday morning came early. They had much to do. Naomi transferred funds to Isaiah, who paid off the LeiLani and paid the rent for his boat slip six months in advance. He went online and set up mailboxes for both himself and JD with one of those mailbox express places. They in turn sent info to the e-post office, changing their addresses. Next, Naomi set up a hotel room in Las Vegas for the two of them for exactly two months from that day. They'd have a suite at the Venetian for a month, spanning September and October. Once the room was set up, they started calling the people on their list. They cut the names of those who seemed to only be interested in money or who were overly violent, and they were cautious not to give too much info about the real mission. After narrowing the list, they came up with only fourteen names, and they set up appointments for September and October, one interview per day. Time was running out, and it would be up to Naomi and Marisa to work with Dave for more people to screen. JD and Isaiah were getting anxious. So much to do and so little time... Marisa and Naomi were to meet them in three weeks at the base in Iceland. Codes for the opening of the hidden doors were in the information Dave had left with them. They hoped to make it into the main base and begin setting it up for their future missions. Marisa and Naomi hoped that by the time JD and Isaiah arrived that they would have purchased the warehouse and begun setting things up there as well. Dave had things already moving on the lease in Jamaica, as well as the sale of the property in Iceland. The next morning they met at the LeiLani, with all the groceries they could carry. The satellite phones had arrived the previous afternoon by special courier. They would stay in touch using those once a day. As they climbed on board and began the six-hour trip to the sub's new coordinates they felt excited by the prospect of the adventure that lay before them. Things were happening fast now and they had great hopes for the future. That's when the satellite phone rang.

As the boat rounded the spit of land enclosing the harbor and passed point Loma, Naomi thought, It has to be Dad of course. No wrong numbers on these things.

"Hi, Dad," she answered cheerfully.

"Hi, Sweetheart. How are things?"

"Great, Dad. How about yourself?"

"Going well for today, but I had some information that I thought you and your friends could use."

"So soon? Well, I guess things happen when they do. What have you got?"

"I'm sending a package to you by courier today. It should get there tomorrow. It seems that our good friend President Ahmadinejad is starting more trouble. He has stirred up his people against the US, as usual following his obvious meltdown on TV, blaming us for his problems. He's closer to the truth than even he imagines, but for all the wrong reasons. We have some contacts close to him that are telling us that he's very upset with the Chinese, and he is pushing the oil cartel to withhold oil from them. He blames them ultimately for the problems they had with us, and he is pushing to ruin their economy in retribution for his meltdown. China in turn is threatening to blockade the Iranians.

"Oh, I see," said Naomi. "You need someone to break the blockade and not be caught. Let me get this straight. You want us to help out the little creep who just shot a WMD at Lake Meade in an attempt to kill millions of Americans? Is that what you're asking us to do?" she asked in an incredulous voice.

"Naomi, things are going to go badly if he manages to talk them into following his plan."

"Can't this be handled through diplomatic means, Dad?" said Naomi. "After all, I don't know what we could do to stop an oil embargo."

"Its not that, it's the retaliation that I'm already hearing threats of. If it goes like our planners are saying it might, China would sink every oil tanker leaving port from the Middle East, not just from Iran, but every tanker leaving every port in the Middle East. The idea is to reduce the Middle East countries to groveling for anyone to help, in the meantime threatening any country that offers to come to their aid. This could cause a worldwide panic and ultimately destabilize the every region on earth and end with the deaths of millions of people."

"Oh, I see," said Naomi, understanding for the first time. "The enemy of my enemy is my friend, or something like that."

"More like the lesser of two evils," her father replied. "Its not that I want to help the Iranians, it's just that I don't want a nuclear war to start because oil is denied to the worlds' powers, and China is holding them all against the wall by a nuclear button. The way I figure it is that if someone—and deniability is key—keeps the gates open and the oil flowing, China will have no one to blame for their inability to stop the oil from flowing. With no one to blame and all US assets accounted for, the Chinese will have nothing to do but back off. If at the same time pressure could be put on the Iranians, say, let the Chinese take out their tankers, and theirs alone, then they in turn would have to acquiesce to the Chinese demands. Both sides lose, and the world wins," said Dave.

✠

Around noon, the LeiLani reached the narrow strip of ocean bottom, just 9 kilometers off of the Baja Peninsula that rose up to between 30 and 100 meters below the surface. Parked on an isolated peak just 100 feet deep made the Sea Wolf an easy dive of only 60 feet to reach her escape hatch. She lay under the semi-clear waters, blending in with the mottled sea bottom. JD and Isaiah took their dive suits and promised to bring the sub to the surface within the hour, after making sure all was clear. Stepping off of the stern of the boat, they swam down to the submarine escape locker and entered their new home-away-from-home. After decompressing for 10 minutes, they entered the submarine and began the process of checking their surroundings. Just as they had figured, US boats were giving the 12-mile limit wide berth and the Mexican patrol boats were virtually nonexistent in this area. The nearest threat warning on the scope was nearly 150 miles away and it appeared to be going north, away from them. Checking the state of the ship, they set the depth for surface and watched as the ship began the process of pumping water from the ballast tanks and it lifted its hulk from the bottom of the sea floor. Isaiah turned on the outside view and watched the undersea view turn brighter as the sub rose. It was interesting, as if standing in a bubble and looking around from under the sea. An altogether interesting view, they both decided. It would be great for monitoring sea life at various depths, depending on how powerful a light could be provided for outside the submarine.

As the ship broke the surface only a few meters from the LeiLani, both women were surprised by the slow-rising hulk and its enormous size. At the point its deck settled above the waves, the conning tower shimmered and then seemed to disappear. A door seemed to open out of nowhere, and out onto the floating deck stepped both JD and Isaiah. It was beyond belief for the two women, even for the second time for Naomi, to see the entire sail disappear before their eyes. They tied up along side and both began the process of moving the stores from one boat to the other. In a matter of an hour, the supplies had been moved to the ships galley, and it was time for goodbye. Pledging to meet them in Iceland in three weeks and to bring information from Dave and any planning that had been done between now and then, JD and Naomi went to the LeiLani for a serious goodbye, while Isaiah and Marisa went into the library for the same. A few minutes later they met at the steps to the LeiLani, both couples anxious for the time to pass quickly, yet anxious to begin this adventure. Saying goodbye, they pushed away and watched as the two went back inside the invisible conning tower and disappeared as the hatch closed. They pushed away from the floating deck and headed back toward the San Diego port and home.

Within the hour, all systems were checked and the course plotted and put into the system. At that point the ship could run itself. The two men decided to occupy the captain's and 1st officer's quarters across the hall from each other. The rooms were comfortable, and they had very little to do aboard the ship, thus they were able to read till their heart's content. Both became equally efficient and knowledgeable about the ship and her many capabilities. They decided to try out the mini-subs as soon as they got an opportunity. Isaiah had been in the simulator and felt confident that he could drive the mini-sub from inside or from without by using the remote control. He felt the same way about the aircraft on board. He decided to do a little recon, using the airplanes, the next chance he got. He was looking forward to using the viewing room to guide and fly the planes and the subs. Together, they worked on plugging in the information on the IUSS codes. In almost no time, the computer had a new display up, splitting the screen between the Pacific and Atlantic and indicating the SOSUS lines in both oceans, as well as any sonobouys dropped by airplanes, helicopters, or ships. It was amazing. With the information at their fingertips, they could literally see almost every ocean-going vessel in the world. They noted with delight that they could not see themselves. They were still a long way from any of the SOSUS lines, but it was still nice to know that the SOSUS line could see the warships around the world, but they could not see them. The other thing noticeable was that very few submarines were visible—only two American subs, and one of them was already blinking yellow, telling them it was not a certainty, but a probability plot, and that they soon would disappear from the screen. Only two Soviet subs were visible as well. That could be because of a lack of funds or that they were quiet. No missile subs were plotted, only attack subs. China had four submarines out—two diesel and two atomic. They were obviously of an older type, since they were quite noisy. Other nations had subs out as well, a total of 16 others. Most were quite noisy; all were easily plotted by the system and followed by SOSUS. The disquieting thing was that there were no missile subs being plotted. They both knew they were out there, and it would be a problem if they were ever sent out to launch. That evening, as the sub headed into the deep waters of the Pacific crossing, heading closer and closer to the SOSUS Pacific line, they decided that a nighttime launch of one of the remote planes would be the thing to do. The plane could stay aloft for a full week and had a range of nearly 10,000 miles.

Both went into the launch bay and began assembling the first of the remote control drones. In surprisingly little time, the plane was assembled, gassed up and ready for flight. In the room just below the launch bay there were missiles and cameras of different types, as well as special missiles that could carry the toxin that the Iranians had developed. They fitted both an IR camera and a long-distance video camera into the plane and waited for night to fall. During the darkest part of the night, the submarine made its twenty-minute assent to the open sea. Up above, the night was pitch dark, with no moon. The sea was relatively calm, but even so, waves managed to sweep across the bow of the ship. As the ship turned bow into the wind, a rail silently raised above the waves and the shell protecting the air hangar opened. As soon as the door opened far enough, the quiet engine started up, charging the onboard batteries. The batteries turned an electric motor that in turn turned the prop, and the plane took off from the deck, using only 25 feet to lift itself from its harness and tuck its pontoons up into the fuselage of the plane, then it was gone. Within two minutes, the submarine was once again below the surface and headed deep beneath the waves. In the viewing room, Isaiah could see very little from the video camera. From the IR camera, the cool blue surface of the ocean was almost black. As the plane rose higher and higher, reaching its cruising altitude of 30,000 feet, more became visible. In the distance, several small boats could be seen. The large heat signature of a cruise ship was visible in the northern reaches of the drone's view. Isaiah set the drone to cruise up and down the Pacific American coast and to rendezvous with the sub again in a week as the sub passed through the Aleutian Islands. Any time a contact was spotted, the drone sent a warning to the system, which in turn was set to warn Isaiah. The picture from the drone could be sent to any screen within the sub. This was just too cool, they both agreed. The plan was to go up around the coast of Alaska and under the Ice Pack, coming out close to Greenland and on to the port in Iceland. Three weeks to make the cruise was much too much time, but it allowed the two men to become accustomed to the running of the ship. They could see where in an emergency situation the two of them would be hard-pressed to avoid the dangers that awaited them under the sea.

Nearly twenty miles away, a very quiet US hunter/killer sub was playing a game of hide-and-seek of its own. For nearly an hour, the sonar operator had been proclaiming he had an itch that he couldn't quite shake. Nothing had shown up on the screen, and nothing was automatically alerting anything, but Bud Williams was a legend in the US sonar world. He had picked up Russian boomers when they had been able to run the SOSUS lines undetected. To him, it was just the way the fish turned away at certain locations, and how the ocean seemed too quiet in certain locations that made his "spidey sense," as he called it, tingle—and it was tingling now. He notified the captain. Captain Kevin Blake had just taken over control of the USS Tiger Shark and was captaining his first cruise. He had been given "friendly advice" from the previous captain to "listen to what Bud says." Kevin had felt it was a good omen, having been born and raised in Deer Park, Texas, that his first command was the Texas-built Tiger Shark. She was the newest of the sub fleet and was as quiet as anything in the fleet. She was also currently on loan to the Pacific fleet, having normally been stationed around the Caribbean Islands, but because of the recent events around the San Diego area, she was positioned to maintain a sweep pattern back and forth from the Aleutians down to San Francisco. The contact that Bud was "feeling" right now was off their starboard side and about 20 or so miles to their west-southwest.

Isaiah and JD were enjoying the quietness of the trip when suddenly the threat alarm wailed, calling attention to a new contact. Some slight cavitations sounded as a submarine roughly at their same depth turned to face them. Automatically shutting down their systems and slowly sinking below the thermo cline, the ship coasted to a halt. The new contact turned and a projected plot between the two subs was put up on the screen, and a shooting solution for a torpedo was flashing, ready to be uploaded into a tube. As the sub settled into a path, it began flashing yellow, and soon disappeared from the screen with the approval of one of the officers. Both of the young men were barely breathing as they watched the display.

"What now, JD?" Isaiah spoke first.

"We just wait. We knew the US had more subs out here than we were aware of. Now we're aware of them, and obviously they have a hint of where we are. If we sink below the thermo cline we'll lose them, and they'll lose us as well. It's time to play cat-and-mouse."

"Yeah, but who's the cat and who's the mouse?" asked Isaiah. They both got quiet. They watched as the sub headed in a direction that would have coincided with their own path had they not stopped the engines. To their amazement, the Sea Wolf was able to plot and watch the exceedingly quiet USS Tiger Shark. The secret to the Sea Wolf's ultra sensitive sonar was an array of three trailing antennas, set much wider than the normal array because of the wideness of the Sea Wolf, as well as the arrays on the sides top and bottom of the ship's hull. She even had listening arrays on the leading and trailing edges of the conning tower. While not as sensitive in the directions directly ahead and behind the ship, she was much better with her array than standard subs without it. Deciding that now was not the time to cross swords or wits with a submarine of near equal capabilities, the two set a new path heading almost directly west, a path that crossed the SOSUS line and would test the limits of their stealth capabilities. Isaiah went into the viewing/ library and regained contact with the drone. It was currently one hundred miles to their east, and it would take about thirty minutes to cross paths with the submerged contact to their east-northeast if they re-routed it now. Isaiah did so.

Light was just stretching its fingers across the first waves of the west coast as the drone passed over the area of the ocean where the USS Tiger Shark was still heading in a west southwest direction, slowly, very slowly chasing a shadow that even now Bud was feeling less and less sure of. On board the Tiger Shark, Captain Blake was anxiously waiting for something that could be classified as real to show up on one of the screens.

"Where are you?" said Bud to himself, looking at the charts and thinking.

"That's what I want to know," echoed Blake just behind him.

"Sorry, Captain," said Bud. "I think I've lost him out there somewhere. It was like I just got a whiff of him, and then he was gone."

"I know, Bud, but don't worry. If he was there, we'll find him. All stop! Emergency quiet on board the ship," he called out. The orders were relayed throughout the boat, the engines went silent, and the huge ship glided to a stop 150 miles west of San Francisco. Almost on cue, an EAM message flashed, calling the USS Tiger Shark to periscope depth. As the Tiger Shark slowly crawled to the surface, Isaiah and JD watched a simultaneous plot of the submarine and the infrared view of the ocean below the drone. First, a red spec appeared on the black map, but it grew and grew until the shape of the submarine became visible from 30,000 feet above. Both Isaiah and JD realized the power at their fingertips.

Inside the Tiger Shark, they were putting together an action message of their own, letting the ComPacFlt know of their "possible" submerged contact. At the same time, they received word that the search for the missing submarine had been canceled. Word from above was that the search had been called off from the very top. The Tiger Shark was being reassigned back to their regular watch area. Captain Blake shook his head in disbelief. That itch would have to go unscratched for now.

As Isaiah and JD watched the infrared images on the view screen, the Tiger Shark turned south and slowly disappeared beneath the silent sea. Both turned, looking at each other, and wondered how they could be lucky enough to have this threat turn and leave when it should be hanging around and waiting for them to reappear. They realized their power, and at the same time their vulnerability. They would have to be careful.

They decided that getting to their rendezvous quickly wasn't nearly as important as getting there without being spotted. They slowed the boat down to a crawling 20 knots from the normal cruising speed of 40 knots. They'd still make it to their destination with a few days to spare, but at 20 knots or 33 percent reactor capacity, the manual said they could not possibly be heard. Even so, they were determined to be careful.

On board the Tiger Shark, Blake and Bud leaned over the waterfall display, hoping to catch a hint of the "hole" in the ocean before they left the area. He knew he'd get approval to follow and monitor if he could just catch another glimpse of it, but if they couldn't find it again...well, they'd have to continue their mission. Onboard the Sea Wolf, both Isaiah and JD watched as the Tiger Shark turned and slowly headed south. Within 15 minutes she had disappeared from her extremely sensitive sonar and became a yellow possibility track flashing on the screen, headed south.

An hour later, aboard the Tiger Shark, Captain Blake gave up the hope and pushed the throttles forward and went to his standard cruising speed of 25 knots, using about 70 percent of their reactor capacity. As he did so, a brief flutter of noise was captured by the sensitive sonar aboard the Sea Wolf and the probability track went from yellow to green, with a green dot showing the exact position and time of last contact. From it, another probability track flashed forward, showing an increased speed and an updated path. The distance between the two ships had widened to 34.6 miles or 55.8 kilometers. Up above, the drone had been reprogrammed to meet them south of the Aleutian Islands in the North Pacific. They felt safer after ramping up their speed under the ice. That's where they planned to make up for any lost time.

Naomi and Marisa were spending a great deal of time together. They had a new batch of possibilities for life on the sub. To their surprise, eight of the twenty her father sent this time were female, but they were open to the possibility especially now that Marisa was set to be a crew member. She and Naomi had talked a little about her being the only female on a boat full of "mercenaries." While neither liked the idea of the word "mercenary," they had to admit that by definition, that's what they were well on the way to becoming. They had worked together on getting the land leases and sales completed. As was expected, the government had not hesitated on the sale of the land in Iceland to a civilian company. After a routine background check, the company that Marisa and Naomi had set up, Icelandic Exports, with CEO JD Gilhooley III and President Isaiah Diego, was sold—the Iceland property and warehouse—for the sum of $100,000 US. The lease of the property in Jamaica was also turned over to the company for the sum of $200,000 US. The lease had been pre-paid by the US government to the country of Jamaica, and as a nice surprise, all the mineral rights went along with the lease, as did the promise of no taxes, all compliments of having the US government negotiate your lease for you. It was too good to be true. After looking at the documents her father had sent outlining the specs on the Jamaica base, it seemed to be amazing, and the prospect of having a house built on the land overlooking the bay really appealed to the two women. They talked about building a tunnel from the base up to a house built above for clandestine movement to and from the base. Naomi had gone through roughly $400,000 of her sign-on bonus money and, after taxes, she had only $1.3 million left, and they still had a lot of cleanup to do on three bases. Thank goodness the base in New Caledonia had no cost associated with it. As excited as she was about the sub and what she was doing, she was also anxious to get to work at her new job. She still couldn't believe her good fortune at being bought out by Martin and Microcom. Even so, she didn't know enough about him yet. She'd researched the company thoroughly and felt good about, but Martin was a real enigma. He'd been more than fair with the deal, and the money seemed to have just come pouring in. With another million yet to be deposited, this time in her new Jamaican account, for the first year's inclusion in the Microcom suite of software there was no question about that.

Marisa was equally excited about graduation and the prospect of being onboard the submarine. She felt she could be a help onboard the sub as the doctor/biological engineer, but more, she was excited by the fact that they would be helping the world and hopefully ridding the world of some of the scum that had a hand in the murder of her sister on 9/11. What Osama failed to realize when he masterminded the plans for attacking the Twin Towers was that he was inciting the individuals of the United States. As bad a thing as it is to upset the United States as a nation, it was worse by far to upset the individuals of the United States. Once they were incensed, they wouldn't forget, and they wouldn't give in until they felt avenged or successful in getting even with those responsible. For as long as they had inhabited the land, phrases such as "Remember the Alamo," "Remember the Maine," and "Remember Pearl Harbor" had rung in the hearts and minds of Americans seeking retribution for wrongs committed against them and their fellow man. Osama hadn't any idea about the commitment of the American people and the desire to do what's right for the right reasons. Given the opportunity, Americans would find a way to take care of business any way they could. Marisa was a keen example of what Americans were made of. It wasn't steel; it was much more flexible, and much much tougher. The material that made up an American was unfathomable to someone like Osama. He believed that Americans were like his own people, easily threatened and bullied into a feeling of hopelessness and despair. Americans, when cornered or threatened, didn't respond with fear; instead, they responded by fighting back, despite the odds. Americans never quit believing that they could win, no matter what the cost. Marisa was excited by the thought that she could make a difference in getting the bad guys, and even though she didn't like violence or killing, she knew she could push the button or pull the trigger that "killed," as long as she was sure it was someone evil or someone who worked alongside the evil men of the world.

The two women talked about it for many hours during the week as they prepared for their trip to Iceland. Marisa's school was out now for the summer, and she was looking forward to the trip. Naomi began looking for a new place to live in near San Diego, somewhere with room enough for four. She knew that she'd have to buy a place that would house all of them when they weren't out saving the world, but she wasn't sure that buying was the right answer for now. They might decide to make their base in Jamaica, as they dreamed, or in Iceland, or maybe even in French Polynesia. On top of that, she needed to move her furniture into her new place in San Francisco. Naomi left and went to San Francisco to start putting things together there, while Marisa went apartment hunting for her in San Diego. By Saturday night they got back together, with Naomi having set up her condo in Frisco, and Marisa had found two possibilities for an appropriate place in San Diego. After looking at the two, Naomi decided on a condo overlooking a wonderful marina that included a private boat slip large enough for the LeiLani. Four bedrooms and plenty of extras made it a great place for them to call home until they decided where to make a permanent base. She leased it for a year, paying the lease up front for the whole year. Needless to say, the owners were thrilled.

The two girls spent hours going over the intel that had been sent to them by Naomi's dad. It was all so confusing. It looked like the Iranians were very soon going to be caught between a rock and a hard place. They were making threats against the Chinese without thinking about the consequences. It was like they didn't understand the power they were screwing with. "These people have a million-man army and enough chutzpah to send them into action anytime they feel like it," said Marisa.

"Do you really think they'd go that far?" asked Naomi.

"Without blinking an eye, if they really feel threatened," said Marisa. "But to invade...are you sure?"

"No, I'm not sure, but let's just play this out. If the Iranians manage to get an embargo against the Chinese, their dependency on foreign oil is at 60 percent, and Iran provides a quarter of that. With their reserves only being— what was it, 45 days? No, 60 days. They would be in a world of hurt real quick. Within a month, the Chinese would have to find either an alternate source or force them back to delivering. How do you force them back? By threatening violence of their own. First they shut down the embargo by putting a reverse embargo in place, making sure they can't sell their oil. With no money coming in, the Arab states could hold out for quite a while. After all, they have no compunction about their people. Their only real concern is their own royal family. So the Chinese disrupt the flow. The Arab nations wouldn't really panic about it. They've got plenty of cash to hold them in Rolls Royces for a few million years, so to get their attention, the Chinese have to put a threat on their future. That means killing their ability to produce oil into the future, maybe by sinking their fleet of tankers, and attacking their oil facilities. Even that wouldn't completely scare them. So how do you scare the self-confident bums? Steal their comfort. Drive them back into their tents in the middle of the desert, with no money and no future. Attack them and take their land."

"Okay, Marisa, how do they get away with that? Sadam Hussein tried it with just one little country back in 1991 and the whole world rose up and trounced him."

"Yeah, but that was Iran and Sadam Hussein. He didn't have a million-man army, more nuke's than you can shake a stick at and the will to use them."

"You really think the world would just turn a blind eye to letting the Chinese march in and take the whole Middle East?"

"No, they'd be up in arms in no time, but the key is what they would really do about it. Besides, they'd have to come in by plane or by boat. The US would have something to say about them coming across the no-fly zone in Iraq and Afghanistan, the Russians wouldn't let them through Kazakhstan, and they can't march their troops through the natural barrier made by the mountains between them and Iran. It basically leaves only one option—a sea based invasion. They wouldn't want to force the hand of any nation with the bomb, but they wouldn't worry too much about making them mad as long as those nations weren't hurt in any way. All they'd have to do is promise cheaper oil contracts to the major nations and most of them would find a way to overlook the invasion as a natural consequence of Iran's own stupidity. Of course India would be a little nervous, but then again, they've shared a border with the Chinese for centuries and know the threat, and they have learned to be threatening in their own right. I doubt they'd send their Navy, as formidable as it is, into the path of a Chinese invasion fleet so long as the Chinese promised them a non-aggression pact."

"So, Marisa, you think the president's advisors are wrong?" asked Naomi.

"Not wrong," she said, "just not complete in their scenario. I think they haven't gone quite far enough with it. I think they're right in believing that they'd start by attacking their ships, and maybe even their refineries. They just kind of stop there. They don't ask what if that doesn't fix it. They just assume that the cartel will crumble and fold to that pressure. What if they don't? What if the Chinese just start by invading without trying a blockade of their own? This is really a powder keg situation."

"Well," said Naomi, "I guess the best answer is to keep either side from doing something stupid." A light glistened in her eyes.

"You've got that look Naomi, what's going through your mind?" said Marisa.

"I was just thinking," said Naomi, "wouldn't it be great if someone were to get the attention of both the Chinese and the Iranians, say with a threatening message that would promise real problems for both of them if they don't calm down and quit threatening each other?"

"What kind of threat?" asked Marisa, confused by what Naomi meant.

"The kind of threat that they both worked together on in their recent shot at Lake Meade," she said quietly, "but not quite on that scale. We could spike the drinking water of the Chinese Capital building there in Tiananmen Square, and the drinking water in Tehran if they don't get along. They think they can drop these things in our water supply and not have us do anything in return. Well, they've got another think coming." she said flatly.

"You don't mean you'd really kill millions of people like they were trying to do?" Marisa was quiet, for a few seconds. "Do you?"

"I don't know, Marisa. Not millions…and I know I couldn't kill innocent people like they do, but look at what people at war have had to decide for thousands of years. What about the innocents that are in the wrong place? Literally millions of innocents were killed by the fire-bombing of Berlin and the cities of Japan."

"Yes Naomi, but they were killed to prevent a direct threat, to save the lives of hundreds of thousands of people that it would have required in order to invade Japan."

"Yes, that's true, but they were innocent and they died anyway. And Marisa, take a step back. Why invade at all? The invasion was because we were at war. We needed to win the war to stop the threat of continued aggression by Japan and Germany into other countries. They were not threatening the US; we were invading on behalf of other nations that were being destroyed by them. The difference is that today these nations are attempting to destroy our nation and our economy. Not someone else's—ours! If there is collateral damage, well, it's been a fact of war for a long time."

"Yeah, Naomi, but war is declared by nations, not by people."

"Not so, Marisa. Look at 9/11. If you look at what Osama did in 2001, you can't say that war is declared by nations. Osama declared war on the US by the Islamic people."

"And we—the people of who—are responding. Who, Naomi, who?"

"The Christian people, Marisa, us."

Marisa sat quietly, contemplating the words Naomi had spoken. Had she gone too far? Could Christian people respond in this manner? For the first time, Marisa started to realize, there was a war going on. It was a war of religions. Christians against a coalition that were non-Christians. Those who hated Christians and Christianity against those who wanted nothing more than to love their neighbors, and it was that "Love Thy Neighbor" part that the Anti-Christian coalition of forces depended on to allow them to attack with impunity the great Christian world. Marisa shook her head to clear her thoughts. "It's like when the Jews finally began fighting back. For thousands of years they had been slaves to whichever nation chose to take them as slaves until 1948, and their nation was reborn. Suddenly, their will to defend themselves was reborn as well, then they, the Jews, understood. It was either fight back or be wiped out by the same coalition of evil people that were now fighting to destroy the Christian world as well."

"Right, Marisa. Now those same evil people are at war with us. We have to fight back if we are to survive," said Naomi.

"It's war. Declared by a nation or not, it's war. Marisa, the people like Osama, and the Chinese premier, Chaing Xau, depend on the Christian people to be over-dependent on their parent nations. The fear is now that ours and other nations are being attacked from the inside by those anti-Christian forces, as well as from outside. The Christian people no longer have anyone to protect them from outside forces, willing to kill them at will, so we must become the protectors. The big difference is that we will attack only military targets, the evil men, and hope that there isn't too much collateral damage, instead of attacking civilians and hoping for an uprising by people to change the political climate as they do."

Marisa was teetering on the fence, then Naomi asked a critical question. "Marisa, who built the ship our two men are driving around the ocean in now, and why was it built?"

Marisa understood.

Chapter 8

Are We at War, or Aren't We?

Why should we fight?

The question is, are we at war or aren't we? There is a war going on out there that people like Osama Bin Laden are waging. It is a war with real guns, and real bombs, and real violence that kills real people. Unfortunately, there are at least half the people of our society that don't seem to realize that this war they are waging is a war against them. They hide daily behind the Wall Street Journal and the left wing television do-gooders, and the belief that everything is okay, that the violence they read about can't touch them. It stems from the "I'm okay, you're okay" philosophy. The reality is, there is definitely a war being waged and only one side is waging it. Unfortunately, this is like a hive of bees attacking a person. When a single bee stings you, it hurts for a while, and then it goes away. If two bees sting you, it hurts and may cause you to swell, but it goes away. If we get stung by a bee, typically we run away initially, and then come back later, find the source and attack it with strength enough to wipe out the hive. What would happen if we chose another avenue instead of running away? What if we decided that when we were attacked by the bees we simply lay down and didn't move, or simply ignored the bee's attack? It's possible that one or two or maybe even three bees might land on us and sting us and then leave. Or it's possible that if enough of the bees were angry and incensed, the whole hive might attack and sting us as we sat unmoving. In that case, we would surely be killed. After all, it only takes about 30 stings at one time to be fatal for the average human. Today, we in the US are big enough to withstand the bee stings. We might not like them, but we can withstand them. We may even swat the bees after they have stung us, but they have already done the damage. What we aren't doing and haven't done is run from the attack and come back in force to get rid of the hive. Some people believe we should just run away and leave the bees alone. Unfortunately, we've tried that and they just keep coming to where we are and keep stinging us. We are at war. We in the US don't seem to get it. We need to completely wipe out the hive that is breeding new bees to terrorize us as we relax. We can't ignore it and have it go away. These bees don't like us and they use their religion as the reason. This war has been going on since the Crusades, and even though it has had its quiet seasons, it has never stopped. These latest attacks—9/11, the Cole, WTC—the first attack, the embassy bombings, the beheadings, the '79 capture of the US embassy—those are just the things that have happened to the US. Britain, the Soviet Union, France, Sweden, Denmark, the Philippines, they all have been attacked by these particular bees, and the bees are still angry and still buzzing and still making new bees. I'm not saying we need to kill all non-Christians. We do, however, need to start treating this like a war and quit swatting individual bees.

You also have to understand that all bees aren't harmful, but the bee's that are harmful need to be destroyed and kept from repopulating. We don't need to go to war against Islam; we just need to stop the radical rabid bees who use Islam as an excuse for their non-religious, anti-Christian, evil designs. Unfortunately, sometimes non-rabid bee's that are too close to the bad hive get destroyed in the destruction of the bad hive. In war, those things happen. That's why innocent people tend to flee areas of bee infestation when they notice it, e.g. Britain's leaving London before and during Hitler's fire bombings.

Making Arrangements

Marisa and Naomi had decided to visit Jamaica and the new property they had purchased. Making travel arrangements for Jamaica and then to Iceland, they packed their bags and were off. They leased a four-wheel-drive vehicle for a week and took off to explore the eastern end of the island. They had rented a hotel for the week in Kingston, and put their luggage up and went out to find their warehouse on the first day they arrived. It took most of the day to find the right roads that led to the property. The roads were in complete disarray. They had been overgrown and left unused since the CIA had quit sending supplies to the warehouse. By late that afternoon they managed to pull up to the medium-sized warehouse, with no windows with a steel door leading to what looked like an office, and several steel garage type doors. They all looked as if they were overgrown with vines that now covered the concrete driveway. The sun was completely blocked by the thick overgrowth. It was dark and moist, and with the sun heading down, the heat of the day had been replaced by a cool breeze and the sound of ocean waves breaking only a half mile away. They stood looking at the partially fenced grounds. It had at one time been neat and clean, but now it was completely overgrown. Naomi held in her hand the only key that could be found when the property had changed hands. It was obvious that no one had been out to look at this place in quite some time.

A mere 10 miles from the edge of town, it had taken nearly 30 miles of driving to get there. Now, as they placed the key in the door, it took a minute and quite a bit of jiggling of the doorknob to free the tumblers. Amazingly, the lock finally gave and the knob turned in Naomi's hands. She pushed the door open, slowly at first, but then a little easier as she put her weight against it. The hinges screeched from the lack of oil. As they stepped into the silent warehouse, they couldn't believe their eyes. The place, while exceedingly dusty, was otherwise neat. There were crates neatly stacked and labeled as "tractor parts" throughout the warehouse. There was one other door leading out the back of the warehouse. Just outside was an old but capable looking generator.

Marisa couldn't help but open one of the crates that neatly lined a shelving unit next to the office. Prying the lid off of the two foot by six foot by one foot crate, she half expected to find rifles. To her surprise, it was neatly stacked with .45 caliber pistols, at least 25 of them stacked vertically, each wrapped in an oily paper and with a leather holster between its owner and the next pistol in line. Lifting one from its cradle, she unwrapped it and found the standard military issue 1911 model .45 semi-automatic pistol. She thought, looking around the room, that if nothing else, they could now run guns in Central America and get back everything they'd spent so far, judging by the number of crates in the warehouse. Naomi headed for the secret entrance. Just as described in the paperwork, there was an overly large column in the center of the warehouse. It looked like a point where four columns had met in the center of the building, creating a pillar roughly 10' square. According to the documentation, there was a switch hidden by the steel framework on the front right steel girder that, when flipped, would open the supposed concrete pillars and reveal an elevator that was 8' x 8' in size. The elevator led to the base below. After searching with her eyes, she finally resorted to feeling with her hands. About two feet from the floor, she found the switch.

It didn't work of course. No power, and the generator had been down for years. Putting the pistol back in place and the lid back on the crate, the two decided to rummage through the office to see what else they could find there. After going through an obviously bogus set of files that listed customers on the island, they found a file book with records indicating who had performed the maintenance for the building while the Agency had owned it. They decided to take it with them to look over that night. After moving a few desks around, specifically looking for the safe that they had the combination to, they found a flat panel that had been covered by one of those plastic floor protectors so frequently used in the 80s to protect floors from rolling chairs. Under the protector and under the panel it covered they found a counter-sunk wheel type tumbler for a safe. It took Marisa three attempts to get the tumblers to fall into place. When they did, a 3' x 3' door, with a handle marked "Diebold" made a faint "Click" sound. Grasping the counter-sunk handle and pulling it to the left, then lifting it upwards, it revealed the contents of a safe, approximately 4' x 4' x 3' in size. The inside had six hard-sided briefcases stacked on half of it, a key box, and a set of manuals filling about a quarter of it, 20 gold ingots, and several large stacks of $20 bills and $100 bills which occupied the last quarter of the safe. They were blown away. Each of the ingots were roughly the size of a 1" thick dollar bill and weighed between 5 and 8 pounds. They couldn't resist holding the ingots in their hands.

They both wondered how this could have been left behind without anyone remembering it. In effect, the man who had stockpiled the gold and money there had a plan in mind to use it, along with the stockpile of weapons, to support a revolution in Cuba, but his plan had died with him when he suffered a massive coronary embolism. No one else knew where his stockpile had been hidden, and with his death it had disappeared. Now it belonged to them to use for their own purposes. They replaced the gold and removed two of the briefcases. Inside was a rather strange-looking electronic gear with a key velcroed onto one side, and a slot to put the key into, obviously for use in programming it. Looking at the contents, it appeared to be some kind of unit for connecting to and programming a rocket, or missile, or maybe even a bomb. They looked ominous all the same, and the women closed the lids and replaced them in the safe. Carefully, they locked the safe, replaced the things covering it, and slid the desk back into place. Checking further, they found only a few other books in the back of the desk next to the door. When Naomi flipped through the two books, she noticed a correlation between them; one had the location, row, column, and box number for everything in the warehouse, and the other had a breakout, showing what each piece of farm equipment equated to. For example:

Tractor Part   JD1-8734B-74   MGL 20R

In the margin next to the MGL 20R was scribbled in pencil, "Mobile Grenade Launcher, 20 rounds."

The owner had used his own codes to keep up with the inventory of what was in the boxes around the warehouse. The first book told how many boxes there were, where they were, and what the outside label was. The second book gave them the truth about what was in the boxes. They'd inherited a gold mine—quite literally, it turned out.

The next day they made arrangements for the power to be turned back on for the property. They also made arrangements for a supply of fuel and a technician to work on the generator to come with them. They had a week to get the fence back in shape and the property cleaned up... All it took was cash, and they had plenty of that. Cash money always sped up the works. By Saturday evening, the two women were sitting in new chairs in a freshly cleaned office, with lights on from the power company, a generator outside that worked without anyone needing to start it up, and a brand new 10' hurricane fence with razor wire around the top, and a gate on wheels that used a punch down keypad to electronically open and close it. After the last technician had left, the two women went to the hidden elevator, a gun in one hand and a flashlight in the other, and they felt ready to finally see the inside of the hidden submarine base. The doors opened as the switch was touched, sliding silently, even though it had been years since it had been activated. The two stepped in, observing the keypad on the inside of the door, before the door closed, Marisa reached out and kept the door from completely closing. "Perhaps we should do this one at a time just in case there's a problem with the elevator," she said.

"Good thinking, Marisa. I'll go first and I'll send the elevator right back up if everything is okay. If it doesn't open on its own, then…well, you'll know something is wrong." She pushed the "down" button, as Marisa stepped out of the elevator. Nearly five minutes later the elevator door opened again, revealing an empty car signaling that all was okay. Two and a half minutes later she rejoined Naomi at the bottom of the excavated cavern, a half mile inland and nearly 500 ft. below the ocean's surface.

The power to the subsurface portion of the base was ingenuously connected to the power grid from the warehouse above. As the doors opened and Naomi stepped out into the base, a touch panel under the floor turned on a timer, illuminating the pathway leading to the glass enclosed control room that was built into the back of the cave. Most of the cave floor had been concreted over and it was obvious that there were pens for side-by-side subs, with a pier on either side, repeated four times, making the pen capable of holding 8 conventional-sized subs. With the size of the Sea Wolf, only one in each of the double spots could fit in, making it so that only 4 Sea Wolf Class subs could be housed. As she waited for Marisa, Naomi searched for the power switches that would allow for the lights to remain on. After walking to the control room, she found the switch marked "pen lights" and pressed it. To her surprise, almost all of the overhead lights came on. She saw what had to be a dozen torpedoes stacked and waiting on the far pier. Also nearby were several gas-powered vehicles used for loading and unloading torpedoes into the ships. There were several overhead cranes above each pen. This is a great place to park a sub, she thought. Just then the elevator opened again and out stepped Marisa. It wasn't long before Marisa reached the same conclusion.

Cleanup of the sub base when it had been abandoned had been thorough and effective. Despite the dust and cobwebs, there was nothing out of place. The desks and chairs in the control room were cleaned off and vacant, the lights on the control panel showed all conditions green, and they seemed ready to operate. Crossing their fingers and double checking their instructions for opening the outer submarine gates, they pushed the button labeled, "Outer gate." With a quiet whirring sound, the wheels at the exit of the submarine pen began to spin, moving the doors ever so slowly, showing a seam that widened as the doors moved apart. Both women expected to see sunlight. To their surprise, the doors revealed only a rock face behind it. After opening the doors to their completely open state, they realized that a slight glow seemed to come from the water. It was then that they realized that the doors, even though they were above the water on the inside of the pen, were hidden by the rocks on the other side, and the opening they allowed was strictly below sea level. A sub entering the pen must enter it submerged and then come up to the surface after being inside the pen. They pushed the button again and confirmed that the doors slid slowly closed. They were ready at this location and after much discussion were very happy with it. Naomi felt sure this was the place they would call home. All they lacked now was a home on the side of one of those hills behind them and they'd have Paradise as a home and hideout.

That evening they had really good news to report when JD and Isaiah called. They had gotten into a routine of calls around 12:00 midnight Eastern Time, and tonight they reported on how the recovery of the drone had gone according to plan. The two men decided that they had been fortunate. They had run the drone for six days and were down to less than a day's fuel. With that in mind, they decided they had been lucky that the weather had permitted the recovery of the drone. Weather in the North Pacific was tricky in the summer months, and they easily could have lost a drone by not having enough layover time at the pickup point. The women reported their luck at the sub pen that afternoon. They absolutely gushed about the ease of getting things back in working order. They had spent the previous three days going over the stock inside the warehouse, and found several surprises. They had in their possession a dozen 50 cal sniper rifles, 100 cases of M16 rifles, both 30 cal and 50 cal machine guns, hundreds of claymore mines, 10 cases of .45 cal pistols, 10 boxes of UZI machine pistols, 100 standard warheads for Mark 50 torpedoes, and 50 warheads of a type they were not sure what they were. They were labeled only "Mark 50 ND Warhead." There were more weapons that they hadn't checked yet, but they were excited by the bounty left behind by the government. All these things, and then they told JD and Isaiah about the gold and money they had found the first day. After checking, they found they were the proud owners of $750,000 in cash, and they hadn't looked up the value of the gold yet, but they were sure it had to be at least another $100,000. What they didn't know was that their twenty 10 lb.-ingots of gold were worth exactly $951,640.34 in US dollars.

That evening the Sea Wolf passed between the Aleutian Islands and headed north under the ice of the North Pole. Pushing the speed to 30 knots, they set a course directly toward the Icelandic coast. Taking the view and turning it on its head, they looked at the course plotted under the ice, taking them some 100 miles south of the pole. It was an interesting view, looking at the earth from the top. They were learning to view the world and think in three dimensions. The two men were becoming quite adept at using the systems of the submarine, and they saw the need for more eyes to watch what was going on all the time. The sub did a great job of keeping up with everything that was going on, but it had set points that it used to warn the operators of impending problems and dangers. They could see that if someone were monitoring the many ships and target points that the sub was watching, they could have more advance warning before shutting down the sub and waiting. Instead, they could take advance action and turn the ship so as to avoid the contact, and thereby not have to stop and wait. All in all, the sub was doing a great job, but they needed some help on board the ship. They hoped to get to Iceland early so they could get going with further interviews.

That same evening, Naomi and Marisa packed their bags and got ready to depart Paradise and head for the cool summer breezes of Iceland. They knew it was supposed to be nice this time of year and they were both anxious to see what it was like. They were also looking forward to searching through the warehouse left there. They joked about what the US had left behind in this one. "Maybe a Nuke," they kidded. A little more than 7 hours later they boarded the airplane, headed for Iceland.

They arrived six and a half hours later, after a brief stopover in Chicago, and they were excited to get off of the plane in Reykjavik into the 54-degree sunshine. While a cool breeze blew across the tarmac, the two ladies stepped off the plane onto a bus and headed into the terminal. After recovering their luggage and passing through customs, the two were eyed cautiously. Unknown to the two of them, their luggage had been set aside and sniffed carefully by drug dogs and the two were photographed by an overhead camera by both US and Icelandic customs agents. They had made the list of suspects because of their week long stay in Jamaica on "Business" and then coming to the shores of a US ally for another two-week stay for "Business Purposes." They looked very suspicious. The two seemed rather young and perky for drug dealers, and didn't behave like "mules." Quite frankly, their behavior was more like tourists than business associates. After asking the routine questions and picking the younger one—Marisa—for a "random" search, they found nothing of note in her carryon luggage and nothing on her person that they were worried about. Inside her bag they found a large amount of cash, $8,500, but not enough to break any laws. When asked about the cash, her reply was simply that she didn't trust credit cards or travelers checks and she planned to have a good time while she was here. The two were released and allowed to pass with what to them appeared to be only a passing interest. While not a major worry, their pictures were forwarded to Iceland's National Central Bureau (Iceland's equivalent of the FBI). The NCB wasted no time in sending copies of their passports and photos to Interpol, with whom they had a great working relationship. It took a little less than 15 minutes for a full history of Naomi Benson, who she was, and who her father was, to make its way back to the NCB. Along with the information in a manila envelope and the blank folder for Marisa Hartman was a note from Interpol to handle this business pair with kid gloves. This note struck a chord with Jenn Svygenborg, and the chord was off-key. He believed in his gut feelings and he really didn't like having anyone, much less a faceless organization, telling him to keep his hands off someone who had tweaked his gut-o-meter, which he joked was never wrong.

Jenn Svygenborg was not what you thought of when you think of a great detective, or a great mind. He was short, rather slouchy, and mildly overweight. His bald head was covered with a world-class comb over. First from the left, then from the back, and finally from the right. The long hair surrounding his bald head was combed and then oiled down to hold it in place. His nose was pudgy and a bit bulbous, his legs too short, and his arms too long. With a face marked with the scars of a bad case of juvenile acne and eyes that looked too large for his face due to the thick black-rimmed glasses that he hid behind, his looks belied the sharp mind that resided inside the cruelly unhandsome face. He had earned the gold shield he wore inside a worn leather billfold, which he liked to flip open like Kirk flipped open his communicator, by finding the key clues to more than half a dozen cold cases he had tackled on his own time. His peers had, at first, been standoffish toward the funny looking little man, but he had earned their respect by his quick leaps of understanding in difficult cases and by his uncanny "gut-o-meter," which was always keenly accurate. His partner was the other half of what the chief of detectives called the "odd couple." While Jenn was short and dumpy, Sven Larson, was tall and gangly, with rugged good looks and the ability to put people at ease. Sven could put his arm around a kid who'd just been robbed at gunpoint and who had just witnessed a triple homicide, and within five minutes they'd be telling jokes and carrying on like the oldest of friends. It was a gift, and one that he used effectively to help feed info to his human lie-detector partner. The two were now told officially by the chief detective to drop the investigation and find something else to work on, but the Jenn and Sven Show was in motion and very little could stop it when it was underway.

Marisa and Naomi checked into their suite at the Loftleidir Hotel, just 4 km northwest of Reykjavik. They arrived in their rented 4WD Mitsubishi and let the bell boys take their luggage up to their waiting suite. While money wasn't a real point of worry for the two, they decided to stay together to save a little money and to allow them to speak freely all evening long. They went out that afternoon and explored the sights and sounds of Reykjavik like a pair of tourists. While they checked out the local tourist stores and shopped for shoes and watches, the "Odd Couple" took turns following them at a distance and checking on purchases and questioning the staff behind the counters about what the two were looking for, and even going so far as to ask the cashiers what they may have overheard of their conversations. They were coming up empty in their one-day investigation, but they were thorough if nothing else, so they decided to bribe the concierge and wait to follow them tomorrow. That evening the two women stayed in and discussed their business. Tomorrow was going to be an interesting day for them. They had keys to their new property and they had been told to expect a security guard at the property. The CIA had kept a paid security service on retainer, even though the warehouse was supposed to be completely vacant. With that in mind, the two women got their ownership papers in order that night, complete with paperwork showing the creation of their company, Icelandic Exports, and their power of attorney privilege, as well as copies of the signed ownership deeds. The fee for the security company had been paid up in advance until the end of the year and they didn't intend on having any problems with them or with getting into the warehouse when they got there. They both felt pretty good about having a security guard present for their initial look around. That night they slept well.

Sven got a call from the concierge at 7:15 in the morning. By 7:45 the Odd Couple was on the road, following the two women. They traveled the main road leading northwest out of Reykjavik. Jenn and Sven knew they looked completely transparent in their attempt to trail the two women since there was no one else headed that direction on the road once they had left the outlying communities around Reykjavik. Two cars going up and down the mountainous terrain, the two men remaining 500 meters behind the larger, newer rental vehicle. Suddenly, the SUV pulled across the left lane, entering a scenic overlook. The men kept going. At the overlook, Marisa fumbled with her camera while Naomi hopped out of the vehicle, pretending to look at the beautiful fjord where they had stopped. As the dirty brown fiat went on up the hill, passing the entrance to the overlook, Naomi squinted at the car and saw the passenger straining to look back over the front seat and through the rear seat windows, returning her look.

"I knew it Marisa, they were following us."

"What do you mean? They went on by. If they were chasing us, they had the perfect opportunity to pull in and block us so we couldn't get out," said Marisa.

"I didn't say they were chasing us. They were following us. Ten-to- one says they're waiting in that ugly brown Fiat, pretending to change a tire or something, before we go another two miles," said Naomi.

"Okay," replied Marisa. "I'll take that bet. I think this spy stuff just has you wound a little too tight. You're not 'Pussy Galore' and I'm definitely not 'Plenty O'Toole,' " she said. She looked at the beautiful view and snapped a picture of the early morning mist covering the water at the bottom of the fjord. A cool breeze blew across the barren landscape and sent a shiver down her spine as both of them stepped up into the seats of the SUV.

Naomi checked the mirrors and the road behind them, seeing nothing for miles, and then looked at the winding road ahead, failing to see the brown Fiat.

"Okay," she said, "you're right, Plenty, I'm a little nervous about all this, but I still have a weird feeling that I'm being watched, and I'm sure that one guy was really staring at us when they drove by us a minute ago."

"Naomi, look at us. We're the only two women for probably thirty square miles. Two old geezers drive by, what do you think they're gonna do? Look the other way?"

"Okay, Okay, you're probably right, but let's just keep our eyes open. I don't like this feeling."

Naomi should have made the bet with Marisa. Just a little over one mile down the road, the SUV made a turn that looped back on itself and as they came around the blind side of the curve there sat the Fiat, with the two men standing by it as if waiting for triple A to show up. Marisa's mouth dropped open and Naomi pushed the throttle down and sped past the parked car, almost in disbelief. After 10 seconds of stunned silence, Marisa stammered, "I'm sorry. You were right. I'm so sorry. You were right, you were right, you were right."

"Okay, just a minute. Let me think," said Naomi. Continuing down the road, staying right at the speed limit, Naomi asked the important question: "What do they want with us? They certainly don't know anything about us. Do you think they're police, or are they creeps trying to rape us or something?"

"Well," said Marisa, "they can't be after us to rape or mug us, or they would have stopped and attacked us in that rest stop back there. That means they're either FBI or police, or whatever they have for FBI here."

"Okay, well it can't be the police, 'cause we haven't done anything to be chased by them, and they'd just pull us over if they wanted us, so that leaves the IFBI or whatever they are. What do they want with us?"

Naomi continued the reasoning line of thought.

"Okay, we arrived yesterday. They know I have some cash, probably more than normal. What else?" asked Marisa.

Naomi continued. "Well, we did just come from Jamaica. I wonder if they think we're drug dealers or something," she pondered.

"Hmmm, I'll bet that's it. We drew attention by our actions. Cash, Jamaica, business, two women alone... I guess we weren't thinking too well, huh?"

"Yeah. I know we were kidding about the .007 stuff, but we've got to start thinking more like we really are spies if we want to not look suspicious," Naomi said.

"Funny", said Marisa. "We have to think like spies in order to look like tourists, because when we think like tourists, we look like spies?"

"Yeah, real funny," said Naomi. "Now, who do you want to be Pussy Galore or Plenty O'Toole?" she asked in a humorless pout.

"Seriously, Naomi, what now?"

"Well, we have business to attend to for Icelandic Imports, don't we? So let's go check out the new warehouse we purchased for our business and not get shook up by these guys. If they knew anything, they'd be picking us up and sweating us at the local office."

"Okay, so let's get our story straight," said Marisa. "What does our company do?"

"We are in the import/export business," said Naomi. "Our business is buying and selling. We're the middlemen. We sell lots of things cheap to a whole lot of different companies worldwide, and buy them even cheaper. We need the storage to cover the float product. We're just getting started."

"Not bad for off-the-cuff like that," said Marisa. "What about customers?"

"Well, we're new to the business, so we don't have any today, but our two owners, JD and Isaiah, are on a month-long worldwide selling junket to find new customers."

"Good again, but what's our specialty? You know, what products do we really specialize in that we know we can sell like this?"

"Well, Marisa, how about software? Or maybe oil pipe. They do a lot of oil work in the North Sea, don't they?"

"Oil drilling equipment would be good. How about special computer equipment for drilling and software as well?" suggested Marisa.

"Great," said Naomi. "It sounds plausible and it's a story we can stick to. We don't necessarily need to know details since you and I are just the legal advisors and aids to help them look at the new acquisition and clean up the grounds so they can get started in the business. You see, we don't need to be terribly knowledgeable; we're just the hired help."

"Got it," said Marisa. "It still worries me that they're watching us. Kind of freaks me out, you know?"

"Yeah, me to, but once I'm past the shock of it, now I can deal with it."

"Me too, I guess," said Marisa. "I'm sooo glad you're with me on this, because I'd probably get scared and make mistakes with them."

"Funny," said Naomi. "I was thinking the same thing about you." They both laughed and then set their minds to the task at hand and watched the mirrors for signs of the Odd couple. It wasn't long before they showed up. They nervously watched as the Fiat remained attached by long distance to their bumper.

Reaching the town of Grundarfjordur, they knew they had about 75 Km. to go, so they stopped for petrol and grabbed some sandwiches and cold drinks, just in case there was nothing close to the warehouse. They passed just one other small town, Stykkisholmur, before spotting the turnoff for the warehouse. They couldn't see a warehouse from the road, but they had to stop, get out, open a gate manually, stop again, close the gate, and then continue about 2 Km. down a blacktop road. After all that effort, they thought they might have turned down the wrong road. Instead of a large warehouse, they found only a quaint two-story Icelandic style home, with a sign outside, proclaiming it to be the home of World Mining Services, Inc. It was the name of the company and warehouse they had purchased from the US government, but they were concerned that the warehouse had been torn down or demolished. Parking the SUV at the front of the house next to a small electric car, the two women walked slowly to the door, examining the property in hopes that they would overlook a large warehouse somewhere. Behind the house was a garage that looked like it was long enough and tall enough to house a semi-truck and trailer, but not what they considered a warehouse, by any stretch of the imagination. They went to the front door and knocked. As they waited for a response, they both turned and looked back to see if their Fiat shadow had followed them into the drive. Sure enough, the Fiat sat parked just on the top of a ridge overlooking the house about a kilometer away. As the two girls turned to look at the car, it backed slowly around and headed out. About that time the door to the cottage opened and a harmless looking man about 40 years old stepped forward and asked if he could help them.

"Is this World Mining Services?" Marisa asked.

"Why yes, it is," said the fatherly looking man. "How may I help you two?"

"Well" said Naomi, "we represent the new owners of the land and the warehouse. The problem is, we don't see a warehouse around here. Are we possibly at the wrong location?"

The man flashed a thin smile and said, "You'll have to pardon me if I don't just give you all the information without some proof of ownership. I've had lots of people over the years snooping around our ground. In fact, there was a brown Fiat registered to the NCB that followed you onto the property. Were you aware you were being followed?" he questioned.

The two women were a bit surprised by the middle-aged man. Looking closer, they realized that the frumpy fatherly look belied strength in his body. He wasn't the weak rent-a-cop they first took him for, but instead he was a real professional who wasn't going to just fold under pressure or give in to a pretty face.

"Yes sir, we did," said Naomi, "but we weren't aware that they were NCB. In fact, we don't know who the NCB are. We do, however; have the documentation you require as far as proof of ownership. We represent the owners who purchased the grounds two weeks ago under the name of Icelandic Imports. The owners are Mr. JD Gilhooley III and Mr. Isaiah Diego. Here are copies of the deed, the certificate of transfer, copies of the official tax IDs for the company, and here are the copies of our power of attorney and copies of our IDs."

"Well, I must admit, Ms. Benson, that you seem to have everything you need, but I still need to call my head office and let them know that you're here requesting to take possession," said the security guard. Without waiting for approval from the women, he turned, motioning them to follow, and walked into a room that should have been the dining room but was instead an office with half a dozen monitors and an array of phones on a small but tidy desk. Picking up the first of three phones on the desk he pressed 9, waited a moment, then dialed a number from memory. Moments later he was speaking with someone he had called only "sir" during the whole conversation. After relating the situation in precise language, the guard, who'd identified himself only as Rolf, listened and said "Yes sir," and hung up the phone. Turning to the women, he smiled that fatherly smile once again and said "I'll be happy to help you in any way I can. I've been instructed to show you everything about the facility and to aid you in whatever you need."

"Thank you, Rolf," said Marisa. "The first thing you can do is answer our original question. Where is the warehouse?"

Rolf smiled again and said "It's right below you. The warehouse was built before the house or the garage, you see. It's roughly a 200,000 sq ft. warehouse with access for trucks through the garage and a parking level. With a simple pull of the lever a ramp descends from the garage out back to the parking level. The parking level has a circular road that leads to the third level, which is the warehouse level. All levels are accessible from the main building, which we are in now."

The two girls looked at each other in disbelief. Without thinking, Naomi burst out with the first thing that crossed her mind. "Who built this thing, Al Capone?" She quickly put her hand over her mouth, realizing the gaff she had just made. As it turned out, it was the perfect way to break the ice with Rolf.

"No ma'am, not Al Capone, but quite possibly a group of his most ardent admirers," he said while letting that fatherly smile out once again.

"Okay, Rolf, spill it," said Marisa. "You obviously know who built this thing, so tell us what you really know," she coaxed.

"Before I do, you tell me how you managed to get your hands on this particular property. I've been here since before the place closed down and you might say I had a pretty good relationship with the prior owners. In fact, I worked for them after a brief stint in the Navy Seals." He rolled his sleeve up to reveal a tattoo of a black seal with a red ball balanced on its nose.

"Well, Rolf—is that your real name, Rolf? Anyway, I'm

the NSA's daughter. You may have heard of him—Dave Benson. I'm Naomi Benson."

"Oh, a family deal," said Rolf.

"It's not like that. We had a need for something of this nature and, well, it was available," said Marisa.

"Okay, fair enough. Yes, my real name is Rolf. I was born in Iceland to an American Air Force mechanic stationed here and a native of Iceland that he married. To make a long story short, I went into the Navy at 17, made it into the seal, was recruited by the company in 1984, and was sent here to oversee security for the…uh…secret things that were going on here. After being away from Iceland for so long, I kind of fell in love with it all over again when they sent me back. When the company folded up shop in '98, I was able to stay at a reduced salary as the—quote security guard, unquote. I've got a deal to stay at least till the end of the year."

"Come on, Rolf. What about the other layers to the warehouse?" Marisa prodded.

"I was waiting for you to bring that up before I did," he said. "There are actually six warehouse levels and the sub level. It can house up to four submarines in the pens at one time, and it has all the necessary equipment for dry-dock and repairs, as well as refit and reloading. The place is set for just about anything. The fourth level down, which is really the first hidden level, is protected by more than a hundred feet of solid granite between the third level and it. It houses offices and quarters for up to two hundred men, and I don't mean in cramped quarters; I mean in comfort. Individual rooms, cafeteria, game rooms, chapel, theater, the works. It's a hardened shelter with its own underground emergency generators, air purification, water purification, and with enough groceries down there to last those two hundred men a hundred years, if necessary. It was originally intended to be a shelter for our returning boomers to come back to after they delivered doomsday to the rest of the world. There's enough enriched uranium fuel squirreled away in those bunkers to keep four Navy subs in power for a long, long time. The generator is a nuke as well. It's running the power for the entire warehouse structure, and it has been for twenty-five years now."

The women were impressed. "What about you, Rolf? What do you want to do for the future?" asked Naomi.

"Well, I had hoped to ride this gig out until retirement in fifteen or so years, but I guess that's out the window now. I suppose they'll either force me to go back to doing real work in the company or let me go completely." He sighed.

"I'll tell you what," said Naomi. "Get me a resumé—and I mean the real deal, not just the cover stories—and if you're interested in keeping your job, or maybe coming to work for us, we'll put you on the payroll."

"Music to my ears," he said.

Within minutes the happy security guard was showing them throughout the depths of the warehouse levels. In the middle of the third level, a buzzer sounded on a pager-type device he wore on his belt. Picking it up, he pushed a button that activated a view/screen. Touching a button on the screen, he spoke into the device. "May I help you two gentlemen?"

"Yes, we are lost and we were hoping you could give us directions."

"Certainly, where are you trying to get to?" asked Rolf convincingly.

"Well, its not where, it's who we were trying to find," the tall one said.

"I'm afraid I don't follow you," said Rolf.

"We were looking for two young ladies that we thought might be lost, and we see that their car seems to be parked at your business," the tall one said.

"Well, gentlemen, unless the NCB has some fear for their safety, I can't for the life of me understand why you would be in search of wayward tourists."

Their cover obviously blown, Jenn spoke for the first time. "Actually, we do have our concerns and would like to speak to the two young ladies immediately." His voice carried authority in its tone. With that, Naomi took the device from Rolf.

"I haven't heard you identify yourself or your organization for me yet, and until you do, I have no recourse but to assume that you are the two men that were stalking us on the highway. I promise you that I will call the local police if you don't leave immediately or otherwise identify yourselves," she said.

"Ms. Benson—or am I speaking with Ms. Hartman? I am Detective Jenn Svygenborg and my partner is Detective Sven Larson of the NCB. We'd like to speak to the two of you if you aren't too busy at the moment."

"Now see how easy that was? It really beats sneaking around and playing spy games and scaring two innocent young girls to death, don't you think, Mr. Sylvanberg?" she replied, purposely mispronouncing his name. "We'll be there at the door in a jiffy if you'll just wait for us," she cooed.

Rolf smiled and led them back to the elevators, where they were whisked back to the house and to the front door in a matter of under 3 minutes. Rolf showed them into a proper sitting room and offered the small group coffee and tea.

As the four sat down, Rolf stood attentively to the side, playing the part of the fatherly old security guard to the hilt.

"Might we speak privately?" said Sven, looking oddly at Rolf.

"If you don't mind, we'd rather have Rolf stay with us. After all, we know him much better than we do you," she stated rather pointedly.

"All right, but please don't play games with us." It was as far as he got before Naomi jumped into Jenn's opening words. "Play games with you? May I remind you that it was you who followed us out to our meeting place today, scaring both Marisa and me to death. We even stopped to see if you were following us when we thought someone might be, and low and behold, if you didn't pretend to be working on a tire beside the road as we left the rest area. You frightened us to death. And then pulling up as we entered the house here, again trying to hide from us, as if you were some kind of stalker, and you have the audacity to threaten us if we play games with you? I've never seen such cheeky behavior!" she said, her cheeks flushing to almost the same color as her red lipstick.

"I'm sorry if we frightened you, Ms. Benson, but well, we uh had some questions is all," said Jenn, a bit flustered.

"Well, by all means, you followed us from the airport to our hotel, and from our hotel to here, these must be some really spooky questions, and difficult to ask." Naomi continued to grind the two's behavior into their faces.

"Please, ask away. I really can't wait to hear what these earth-shattering questions are!" Marisa added.

Jenn's lip twitched with the obvious unease he felt. "Ms. Hartman, you and Ms. Benson arrived yesterday from Jamaica. What is the real purpose of your visit?" he queried.

"Real? Did you say real purpose of our visit?" Marisa questioned. "I believe we answered the question first on our visa application form, which, by the way, was approved by your government, a second time when asked by the polite officer at the airports customs office, but I suppose I can answer it a third time for you as well. The real purpose of our visit to Iceland is business, Mr. Sylvanberg." Marisa snapped her response back to Jenn, again mispronouncing his name.

"The name, Ms. Hartman, Ms. Benson, is Detective Svygenborg and this is Detective Larson. I apologize if I have offended you with my questioning, I must admit to being a bit clumsy with my English," he lied.

"Oh, I see," said Marisa. "It is ineptitude in your language skills that is behind your hide-and-seek behavior as well, or is it just an overdeveloped desire to play James Bond that causes that particular habit?"

"Ms. Hartman, if you continue to be so antagonistic toward our questions and us, I'll have to take a more aggressive tack myself." Jenn's face remained calm, but his voice left no doubt but that his words were a threat.

"Mr.—excuse me, Detective Svygenborg, do you deny that you and your partner followed us as I said earlier?" asked Naomi.

"No, but that's not the point."

"And do you deny that you acted in the rather clandestine way as described by myself and Ms. Hartman a few minutes ago?" Naomi continued.

"No, Ms. Benson, but that is not why we're here."

"And when Ms. Hartman answered your question, albeit with contempt for the way in which you asked it, your response to her was to threaten her?" Naomi asked incredulously.

"If you two don't quit playing games with us right now, Ms. Benson, we'll make sure you get stopped for traffic violations every kilometer back to your hotel, and then I'll find drugs in your possession that will show everyone back in the US what you really are—drug dealers trying to start up a new business here in the clean confines of our wonderful nation," Jenn blustered, letting them know they couldn't play with the detectives of the NCB.

"Oh, I see, Detective Svygenborg," said Naomi resignedly. "And Detective Larson, would you also stoop to falsifying evidence and bullying defenseless women as well?"

"Lady, you're about as defenseless as a pit bull, and I wouldn't hesitate a minute planting a dime bag on you right now. Here it is," he said, pulling it out the cuff of his hat.

"But how can you threaten us this way in front of a security guard like him?" she said, pointing to Rolf.

"Because, lady, he won't say anything either if he wants to keep this nice cushy job. We're the government, and we can do what we want," Larson said patting himself on the back.

"Well," said Marisa, "it looks like you two hold all the cards. What is it that you want from us?" She looked very near to tears.

"That's better," said Jenn. "I know you're up to something illegal. Now, what is it you brought in with you from Jamaica, and who's the buyer?" He looked ready to burst he was so happy with himself.

"Detective Svygenborg, I filled out a declaration form when I came into this country, as did Ms. Hartman. Those declaration forms were accurate in every detail and in every way. We have broken no laws, and we don't intend to. We came to oversee the opening of a new office of our company, 'Icelandic Imports,' for the CEO and president, who plan on coming for a visit some time in the future. The cash we brought with us came from our petty cash fund and it is to be used for hiring the needed cleanup work and any extraordinary expenses that might arise from an office that has been closed for nearly ten years. Now I have explained what it is we are doing here, what we brought with us and why, and to be completely honest, I feel quite soiled by the conversation you have thrust upon my coworker and myself. I promise you, sir, that if you follow through with your threats, I will fight you with every means I have available, and I will win. Do you understand that, Detective?" asked Naomi.

"Now here I thought we understood each other so well," said Jenn.

"Me too, Jenn," said Sven. "I guess these two uppity Americans need a lesson in the facts of life. Facts like Daddy ain't here to protect you now," said Jenn. With that, Sven took the bag of drugs from the inside cuff of his hat and threw it at Naomi, causing her to catch it as it headed for her face. As she caught the bag, Jenn reached out and said "My, my, my, what do we have here, Sven? This American has a bag of cocaine in her possession with the intent to sell. Prints all over the bag and everything. It's an open-and-shut case. In Iceland, that's at least 5 years in prison with no chance of parole. You're under arrest. You too, Ms. Hartman. I saw both of you back in the last town trying to sell your smuggled drugs. It's a shame you two couldn't work with us."

"Work with you?" asked Marisa. "What is that you want from us?"

"It's too late to work with us now, Ms. Hartman. I'll have to confiscate that money you brought with you. If you hand it over, I might be tempted to help you out of your legal troubles," Larson said.

"I see," she said. "I can get you double the amount if it might help get Naomi out of her trouble as well," Marisa offered.

You could see the dollar signs floating in front of the two dirty agents. "Cash money, and today," said Jenn.

"Done," said Marisa.

"Maybe we're being too soft here," said Sven.

"Don't be greedy, Sven. These two lovely ladies will be working around Iceland for years to come. There's plenty of time to get to know them better," Jenn purred. "Now, Ms. Hartman, you say $16,000 US dollars? Now where is it?"

"In my hotel room safe," she said.

"Well then, let's be on our way. I'd hate for you to forget our deal and find the police showing up at your door in the middle of the night," said Jenn. Turning to the security guard, Jenn spoke again. "One word out of you, Rolf, to anyone, and you're family won't have a paycheck, because I know the owners of the security firm you work for. You won't work there or anywhere else in Iceland again. Got it?"

"Yes sir, Detective." Rolf spoke with reverence and deference to the powerful agent.

"Now what did you see here today?" Jenn asked Rolf.

"Well, these two dealers came in and forced their drugs onto the property I'm guarding."

"Well put, Rolf," said Sven, not realizing that was exactly what had really happened.

"Ms. Benson, in the car with me, and Sven, you go in the SUV with Ms. Hartman." No sooner had the four walked out the door then Rolf made a series of phone calls, the first to his handlers at the CIA, who in turn contacted the State Department, and within fifteen minutes to Naomi's father. The second call was to the NCB and the chief of detectives there. After speaking with him for a few moments and cutting through his protests about how his men wouldn't do that, Rolf played the audio portion of the tape he'd made over the phone. He also promised full video as well, after he made copies for the lawyers and the police. The chief of detectives quit protesting and started working out a plan to trap his two detectives. By the time Jenn brought in Ms. Benson to put her in the holding cell before booking, a full-scale sting was in place at the hotel. When Ms. Hartman opened the safe and turned over the $8,500 she had to Sven, he called Jenn to tell him that she hadn't come through with the full amount. Jenn led Ms. Benson to booking and started the process. As he laid the cocaine on the evidence table, the three booking agents grabbed Jenn instead of Ms. Benson, placing him under arrest. Simultaneously, Sven was grabbed by the sting agents at the hotel as he exited the hotel room. The money was in his possession, and he was charged on the spot. Within twenty-four hours, the President of Iceland was praising the two women, and had extended to them the country's highest civilian honor for helping in this sting operation planned by his country's FBI equivalent, the NCB. Of course, behind the scenes, a very sincere apology was extended to the two women and a reward of ten thousand dollars each was given to them in hopes they wouldn't file international lawsuits against their nation's highest police organization, especially with the evidence they had in their possession. No one would be trying anything with them again any time soon.

The ladies made their way back the next day to the base. Opening the door for the them, Rolf smiled his fatherly smile and said, "No one threatens anyone under my protection."

"You know, Rolf," said Marisa, "I believe you."

"Thanks for being on our side, Rolf," said Naomi.

"My pleasure, Ma'am. You're the boss now, and you can trust that I'll not let anything happen to you or anyone you say. Okay, Ma'am?"

"Okay, Rolf. You've earned yourself a spot on the payroll for as long as you want it."

"What I'd really like, Ma'am, is to keep doing what I'm doing when you're not here, but otherwise to be yours and Ms. Hartman's personal guard while you are here."

"How about being our guard when we're in San Diego or Jamaica? Could you do that as well?" asked Naomi.

Rolf smiled and said, "Yes, Ma'am. I'd love that."

"Then it's settled, Rolf. You are our personal bodyguard until you get tired of doing the job."

Evil...

Evil comes in all shapes and sizes and must be fought at all costs. Sometimes it is large and easily seen by the world, and sometimes it is small and hides behind the confines of normalcy and even the law. When such things present themselves the public cannot turn a blind eye nor allow it to continue. Failure to confront evil allows it to gain a foothold, to grow and fester like a cancer growing inside an otherwise healthy body. As it grows, it destroys the good around it, turning it into evil just as surely as if it was evil itself. Like the bee analogy, you cannot just let evil exist in its own element, for it will grow and consume and take over until rooting it out, and exterminating it will take years of effort and the lives of many good men. Our own war in Iraq is a prime example of letting evil go its way for many years. What could have been wiped out after World War II by a concerted effort to rid the Middle East of German collaborators. The BAATH party, instead, was left to fester without action. Hoping it would go away, instead it turned into decades of abuse and crippling evil thrust onto the backs of good people in Iraq, Afghanistan, Lebanon, Iran, and Syria. Not only have they terrorized their own countries, they have found ways to export their terror to their immediate neighbors first, and then to the far reaches of the globe as the cancer grew. Now, in an attempt to deal with the cancer of evil, the United States has had to make difficult choices and deal with the extended evil that seeks to fight them every step of the way. It's not easy, and it never will be, because evil holds on tightly when it has a foothold. So a word to the people of the world, don't let evil exist when you see it! Stand up to it and cut it out when it is small. It won't get easier by leaving it alone. It sees that as weakness and laughs at it. Never stop fighting evil where you find it.

That is the motto that Isaiah and JD, as well as Marisa and Naomi had taken as their own. They realized that the world was full of evil that no one was fighting, and they had been given the opportunity and the means to do so. The fight was theirs and they weren't going to shy away from it.

Three days later the sub arrived at the outer edges of Iceland's territorial waters. Finding the right fjord was difficult. They didn't have the exact pinpoint GPS location, so they had to depend on signals from the group ashore. They rented three large searchlights from a company in Reykjavik. From twelve miles out, the three lights made a triangular pattern, shooting straight up into the sky. JD and Isaiah spotted the signal by using one of the subs visible range scopes. Switching to infrared, the signal lights shone brightly against the cold stone of the coast. They steered the ship on a course for the center heat source. Being careful to use the guidance systems in conjunction with the radar and sonar, the sub slowly plowed through the waters of the fjord. It entered with just the conning tower above the water line. The ship continued broadcasting the signal as they had been told. As they moved around a corner, the wall in front of them slid slowly up into the rock above, leaving a hole wide enough for three normal subs to slide into the gap. Using a ship-to-shore low power radio signal, the men spoke to the women inside the control room. The women suggested that they back the sub into the pen, as there was little room to turn the sub around inside the pens after the door was shut. The men turned the boat and passed the opening. As the rear end of the ship centered itself on the opening, the propellers were reversed and the ship slowly and carefully backed into the opening. As the power to the engines was cut, Isaiah appeared on deck, tossing a heaving rope to Rolf, who stood on the quay. Pulling the rope until the heavier rope for tying her off was pulled out of the water and secured around the hawser. After about 10 minutes, the ship was secured, the outer wall was once again down, and the sub pens were completely invisible from the water. The floodlights were killed, and the small group of conspirators had left the Sea Wolf for the comfortable confines of the hidden base. JD and Isaiah relaxed completely for the first time in nearly three weeks. Marisa and Naomi also relaxed for the first time since their boyfriends had gone to sea three weeks earlier.

"Is this the way it's always going to be, JD?" asked Naomi.

"I'd like to think it will get less tense the more adept we get at using the ship and with more men to depend on," he replied.

"Well, we've got some time before we go back out again, and when we do, I expect it to be with a full compliment of crew members," said Isaiah. Introductions to Rolf were made by the ladies, and since they'd already heard the story of the sting, the two men shook his hand and welcomed him into the group. Rolf was thrilled to be a part of them, and he was excited by the size of the sub he'd witnessed pull into the first empty slot. With the width of the Sea Wolf, only two more normal-sized subs could be put into the pen on the other side of the quay from her. The conversation eventually turned back to the time left before they would have to depart again. "In the meantime, we can play around with the mini-subs if you'd like," said JD. "We've got enough room to do so around the Island nation, and there are lots of old Viking wrecks that are supposed to be in great shape, thanks to the cold water of the Greenland Sea."

The women both instantly said they wanted to go along, as did Rolf. In the coming week they had a lot of calling to do with the men and women they needed to screen, but they thought they'd have time for some joy rides in the mini-subs. They also needed to talk with Dave back in Washington D.C. They needed more information about how things had gone while they'd been at sea. They hadn't heard from him for a while, and they were anxious about how China and Iran were squaring off right now.

The girls excitedly gave them a detailed description of the submarine base in Jamaica. They had taken hundreds of digital photos and had even used a fishing boat rental to take pictures of the island from the perspective and GPS location that Dave had given them for entering the base from underwater. From the outside there was nothing viewable, and the pictures indicated only a faint glow of light from the inside of the pens when it was daylight outside and the outer door was open. The men were definitely excited to see the pictures. During the trip under the ice, the men had found that by using the same radio/phone feature available to them while deep under the sea, they were able to get onto the Internet once they had a facility set up to do so through a connected site. That's when Rolf interjected that they had just such a set up available in the house on the ground just above them. Everything seemed to be coming together.

The next morning the five of them began studying the pre-sorted pile of resumés that Dave had forwarded to them two weeks prior. They were able to get enough satisfactory looking people that they thought they could hire a complete crew with these and the others they'd already spoken with. By the end of the day they had a total of thirty day-long interviews set up for the twenty positions. They had a total of ten professionals to interview and twenty that were multi-talented, but with a real strength showing in the weapons and infiltration/abduction areas. They had thirty men and women to fill seven remaining professional positions— Marisa was filling one—and twelve multi-purpose positions. They'd be running the ship with twenty-two people onboard, including JD and Isaiah. They had decided to run on two twelve-hour shifts of eleven crewmembers each. In reality, there were only five positions that had to be manned all the time, and so of the eleven men on duty, they'd be serving only half of the twelve hours and relieving their own shift in between full-shift changes. Thus no one would serve more than six hours at a day unless emergencies arose. After further discussion, it was decided that there would be a need for full-time people such as Rolf at the different sub bases. The thought of all these people, all needing to be paid, worried JD and Isaiah. They knew it was a need, but they weren't sure how they'd be able to meet such a payroll. After Rolf went back to his duties in the house above, the four primary members sat at the conference table and discussed the concerns they had about money. Naomi had a great deal of money coming in, and would have for at least four or five years, but it couldn't really be expected to fund everyone's pay for the long term. They needed to find a way to fund their enterprise. They talked for a while and decided that since they had warehouse space available to them, not to mention the other special things they had that might be of use, they had to apply some of those things. They needed to go into a business that would gain them money. Naomi took that as a personal responsibility, and she had some ideas that might make use of the controlled environment warehouse space they had.

The next day JD and Isaiah took Marisa and Rolf for an undersea adventure around the eight fjords that made up the corner of the island closest to them. They used just one of the deep diving vessels to explore the bottom of the fjords. They could see some minimal activity above them in one of the fjords, but the others were very quiet and easily explored. In the third one they explored, they came across the remains of what looked like the keel of a Viking longboat. Sinking to the bottom beside the boat they waited a few minutes for the silt to quit swirling around them. Soon the powerful lights mounted all around the top of the sub cut through the remaining silt to show the deck of a longboat. The keel curved upward at the front, showing a tall dragon carved out of the keel timber. Whoever had made the ship had done intricate work on the breast of the dragon, with what looked to be a shield with crossed swords, and a Templar cross in the top quadrant made by the crossed swords, a very unusual design for Vikings. The Vikings were not Christians when they invaded England and France in the 9th and 10th centuries. What the Templar cross on the keel post said was that this boat was either built after the 11th century or had been reworked and sailed by Templars during the Crusades in the 13th or 14th centuries. Very unusual indeed. Seeing the templar cross had piqued JD's curiosity. He decided to get lots of pictures of the wreckage site. It was in deep water, nearly 1600 feet. The glow from the bright lights illuminated the wreckage site and the soft muddy silt that the ship sat in. It was buried almost up to the top deck in the soft mud, and only the ribbing and remaining deck planks showed above the mud, as well as the keel post. It was sitting upright, as if it had sunk on an even keel. Perhaps a storm had swamped her as she tried to make it into safe harbor. JD fantasized about the men on board her, pulling at their oars, trying desperately to pull the loaded ship into the fjord. As the ship seemed to be nearing the shore, a sudden wave swamped the back of the ship. She foundered, trying desperately to stay above the waves, but as another wave struck her stern, the ship stopped moving forward and started a death plunge beneath the waves. The men threw the oars over, hoping to grab them and hang on long enough to make it to the shore. Within seconds the hearty craft was gone and only the few men who could swim remain alive. They struggled to the shore only half a mile ahead. The crushing blow for many of the men was that they were only a scant hundred yards from the island, but its fjord walls extended straight up for hundreds of feet above the waves, giving them nothing to hold on to.

JD shook his head, clearing it of the vision of the death of this boat. It could have been that, or any of a hundred different deaths that he hadn't imagined, but he just couldn't get the picture of the men fighting against the cold winds and water to survive the loss of their sturdy ship. Now 1600 feet below, he and his compatriots took hundreds of pictures with the high resolution cameras mounted outside and in the submarine.

While they were out exploring the depths, Naomi made some calls to many of the companies that she had done business with over the years. She realized that underground controlled storage for computer data, whether on disk, tape, CD, or DVD, was hard to come by and expensive to rent. She checked with the heads of IT departments all across the US. Recent events in New York had made the places in the US less appealing to companies wanting to make sure their data was safe. By the time the four adventurers had returned from their six-hour exploration, Naomi had secured the beginnings of a new business. She had four companies signed up to place their data in the underground storage vaults they had at their disposal in Iceland, at the rate of $1000/month per shelf—an 8' by 2' by 2' area. She had secured ten shelves each for the four companies to start with. In a day's work she had secured $40,000/month in income for the group and had only used ten locking shelf units in one room of one floor of their facility. She also had ten other companies interested in doing business with them. Hopefully, they'd have at least that much more business before the week was out. If they were lucky enough to sell out one floor of the two that were known about and available to them, they would be raking in millions of dollars a year. They had approximately 20 of the shelving units in each of the 120 rooms the warehouse floor was broken into. At $80,000 per room per month, that made a total of $9.6 million a month, or $115.2 million per year. JD shook his head and couldn't believe his ears. In six hours she'd secured enough money to pay the salaries of at least 8 of his crew. The more they sold their new business, the more they'd be able to pay the crew, and he wanted to pay them well.

✠

With a little help from Rolf, JD and Isaiah had new Icelandic passports. They all left for Las Vegas at the end of July. It was there that they were to meet Olaf Jakees for the first time as well. They had suites waiting for them and the process of putting together a crew for their submarine awaited them. The group had sat down and agreed on certain criteria for the crew. The crew would have to be between the ages of twenty-five and forty, and would have to be single—no attachments, and none on the ship would be allowed. They would have to be a cohesive unit and they would have to live, eat, work, sleep and be together for months at a time without getting on each other's nerves. Trying to get a group together that would be able to do this was a difficult proposition, but one that they all realized would be necessary for a successful team. Olaf was waiting for them at McCarron Airport when the group arrived from Iceland. To say that Olaf Jakees was flamboyant was akin to saying that the SR-71 was a little bit fast. He met them at the gate, wearing gold chains around his neck, a purple velvet suit, a matching velvet fedora hat with a green feather band around it, and carried a black walking stick with a silver knob handle. Olaf was a young black man who was lean and tall. Only twenty-four years old, he had soft black skin that was light in tone, but with the typical broad nose and lips of the African race. He also had at his side two beautiful women. According to Dave, Olaf had a mind that was amazing, but with the temperament that kept him in hot water with his current employers. He was to be released from his contract with NASA because of his stormy outbursts and his inability to work well with others. Despite these things, Olaf was searching for someone to look up to, according to his psych profiles. That was exactly the fit that Dave was hoping for when he pushed the two together, and that was exactly what happened. Upon meeting and throughout the opening discussions, Olaf, JD, and Isaiah found within each other kindred spirits. While JD and Isaiah deferred to Olaf when it came to scientific exploration and real world ideas, Olaf found in JD and Isaiah men to believe in, and in the plans, an idea that he felt was worth pursuing. The group was growing and becoming cohesive. Very soon they would have a team that would turn out to be historic in nature.

While in Las Vegas, Naomi and Marisa took time to work further on their support business ventures. Within the next month they had recruited another forty-five businesses, all were ready to rent space in their underground storage facility. It was time to begin hiring for that business as well. Since Naomi's new job was to start the first of September, the running of the new storage business was turned over to Marisa and Rolf. Marisa had to be back at school for her final semester, but she had the freedom to help manage the systems, and JD had written software on the side to manage the burgeoning new businesses storage requirements. Rolf was the hands-on management, and he left the group early to return to Iceland to receive the documents and media that was stored in the facility.

By the end of August, the group had two complete rooms leased out and had the assets available to them to get down to their real business. Also, by the end of August they had interviewed the thirty individuals they had narrowed the search down to. Of the thirty they interviewed in person, they felt very strongly that all of them would meet the criteria they had set down, but only twenty had passed the "personality" portion of the interview. The team agreed to pitch the idea of an "unattached" group of mercenaries that were beholding to no government to the whole group of twenty at the same time. While video taping the meeting, they used the combined suites to set the twenty men and women down together and gave them the idea, leaving out any mention of the submarine. While there was a general consensus that a team like this was necessary, they also felt that without a command-and-control team to watch their backs, it would be somewhat naïve to think it could succeed. After some further discussion, JD and Isaiah revealed that the command and control would be there; it would just never be revealed at their level. After a promise that the command and control would be there and that they would each be very well paid and that their sense of adventure would be met, and lastly that they would all have an equal say in the missions that they went on, the group agreed. Each signed an agreement for total secrecy and for an equal share in the dividends realized by the group. They were given new identities, passports, spending money, and rooms within the Venetian Hotel. They were told to enjoy themselves, but not to draw attention to themselves and to be ready to leave by September fifteenth.

On the thirteenth of September the group, which had already started becoming a team, was called together into JD and Isaiah's suite and told to make sure that their other lives were wrapped up and put away because they were going to be leaving the country in two days. JD informed them that they would be going to Iceland, but would soon disappear from existence, and they needed to be sure not to have anyone looking for them. The group was given a list of reasons for their disappearance, and a P.O. Box that would be checked weekly and sent to their base in Iceland. They were told that they wouldn't be able to get back to the base on a regular basis, so to be sure and give parents or anyone else the idea that they would be completely out of touch for months, if not a year at a time. The group was getting excited about their future, and anxious to be a vital part of helping shape the future of the world. These were men and women who wanted to make a difference and felt rather like the men who volunteered before WWII for the AVG in China. They were looking for adventure as well as looking to make a difference.

September fifteenth arrived and with it, the men and women who knew each other only as "the team" came together in the Suite. Their hotel bills were paid by online checkout through a special American Express Black Card. JD, Isaiah, Olaf, Naomi, and Marisa were there together to give the group their instructions and to give the group their name. After much planning and thinking, the group had made sure that their plans were put into place. They also established a name, hoping that the entire group would accept it and feel a part of something much bigger than any one of them, but more as a team. The name they chose was "The Knights of Truth and Honor." Using the shield that both JD and Isaiah wore around their necks as a design, rings for each were made and presented to the group.

Isaiah spoke first. "Men and Women of our esteemed group," he began, "we are leaving today on the first leg of a trip that will be historic in nature. However, before we leave, we have decided that 'the group' just doesn't do our team justice. With that in mind, we have come up with a name that will be our name into the future. Henceforth and forevermore, you will be known as the Knights of Truth and Honor. May you always live up to this title."

JD continued speaking. "Our forefathers came to this country looking for freedom, whether it was freedom of religion, or thought, or just freedom from slavery. Today we seek to spread those freedoms to others through our actions. We are all tired of freedom being subverted by political maneuvering or by calling the powerful fear of others by the name of freedom, as in the communist regimes. We are all tired of having to play by the rules put in place by politicians that have subverted truth and honor for political correctness or for their own personal gain. Each of you, as well as each of us here before you, have reached the end of our patience with political systems meant to serve the common man across the world. Too often, men are left in the grip of tyrants and men without morals because a politician is afraid to upset the status quo. We hope to be free of those political decisions that keep good men in bondage, and to be brave enough to act on the tenets of Truth and Honor without worrying about the ramifications of doing so."

There was a cheer from the group.

"We have been secretive about our destinations, not because of a lack of faith in you, but knowing that you cannot be questioned about that which you don't know. Today, you will find out. We are going to Iceland for the first leg of our trip. We will be taking a small fleet of privately owned cars from the airport on an hour and a half long trip around the coast to our private base. There each of you will be given a room to put your supplies and gear into, but it is not where you'll be living. Once we arrive at the base, we'll finish the briefing as to where we'll be permanently stationed."

The group began talking amongst themselves, but they were silenced once again, this time by Olaf. "Ladies and Gentlemen, I also would like to say just one more thing to all of you. We have been gathered together by these four visionaries who have provided for us a chance to be what God has put the will within us to be. We all know that the way the world is currently is not the way we think it should be. We'd like to fix it, but alone we've never had the ability. Today, we have been given the ability to fix a little bit of it at a time, and I pledge myself to the credo of Truth and Honor and in service to these men and women who are leading us by those tenets." Raising his glass in his hand, he spoke the words that would be the toast from that moment on: "Truth and Honor."

"Truth and Honor," the group cried out as one. Each man and woman was called forward individually, and with those same words, presented with the ring. It was a moment of bonding for the team.

✠

Upon reaching the Iceland base, the group was called together into one of the two secret floors of the underground warehouse. Waiting for them were individual copies of the basic layout of the submarine and specific information regarding their individual duties. There would be ranks within the running of the submarine, but each would be given a chance to voice his or her individual concerns about the mission at hand if time allowed the convenience of such conversation. There would be no saluting or hierarchical nonsense, but when a superior gave an order, it was to be carried out without discussion until such time that it was appropriate. These were men and women who understood chain-of- command, and also who understood the bond of life and death, where men depended upon each other for strength that cannot come from a single person, but instead from a finely tuned team. Much like the men who trained from birth to be in the Army of Troy, these were professional soldiers who were unafraid of death and who were bent on the aim of making the world a better place for all mankind. Being the professionals they were, they each began studying their individual assignments. There were questions, but as an honor to each of them, there was no petty disagreeing about who was ranked higher or who had the better job. Each understood they had been given a chance to be on this sub, and they all realized theirs was an honor given to very few.

There was no discussion of pay. Each would have a base pay of $60,000 a year in US currency. The tax situation hadn't been worked out yet, but the initial feeling was that each would show up on the payroll of Icelandic Imports and their taxes would be paid by the company, so the base pay would be what they took home. Each would be covered by a medical policy, completely paid for by the company as well. The pay would be put directly into an account of their choosing, but it was recommended that they combine their incomes into an investment account administered by an outside investment firm. They all agreed to do so. While on board the sub or in one of their bases, the men and women would be provided with room and board. At present, they had only enough people to run the sub, but they were actively looking for others with their particular strengths so as to allow some liberty time during the year. The hope was to put together two complete crews so as to give each a three month on - three month off rotation schedule. Of course on their three months off they would be expected to work at the Iceland home office in order to continue to pay for the expeditions they went on. The other part of their charter was to make money by any means possible. If they were successful, for example, in capturing another submarine or naval ship or even private ship that was involved in evil practices, they would split the rewards or salvage rights. The men and women were looking forward to that aspect of their jobs. They moved like they were strongly motivated. There was no lackadaisical disinterest, or day-to-day routine. The team was anxious to get started. Also in the package was a brief overview of the political situations around the world, as well as a special briefing of the situation in Iran, with particular emphasis in the Chinese connection. It was clear that there was going to be trouble there. JD and Isaiah didn't tell the team the initial plan, but instead asked for input from the group after they'd had time to read up on the political situations. What came back was amazing.

The team had picked up on the possibility of a Chinese blockade, but most of the team had said they believed that the Chinese were likely to invade, not to blockade the Middle Eastern countries. The team believed that the Chinese would rather go for an all-out attack and invasion rather than try a blockade that they felt would have little chance of being successful due to the natural barricades between the Chinese and Iranian countries. JD and Isaiah looked at each other across the table, each thinking that an amazing thing had just occurred. This completely new team of individuals had tuned into the same facts and feelings that they and Naomi and Marisa had sensed a few weeks earlier. They knew that they would have to be faithful to these men and women who were now an important part of their lives. They knew that faith had to be repaid by faithfulness, and they were anxious to do that. In the next week, they had a whole lot of planning to get done.

It was at about that moment that Olaf entered the meeting room with his typical flair, proclaiming himself to be a genius above and beyond all other geniuses of the world. The men and women who were present, most of whom were beginning to get used to the ravings of the flamboyant young man, turned their attention to him as he set a small model car down on the table, carefully laying a very very thin sheet of metal on the table as well. Pressing a switch on the bottom of the car, he placed the car on the metal sheet, but instead of staying on the sheet, it rose several millimeters above the sheet and hovered there. Giving it a slight push, it glided effortlessly across the sheet silently until it reached the end of the metal, whereupon it fell down to the wooden tabletop and came to a stop.

"Okay, Olaf, what have we just witnessed?" asked Isaiah, knowing that an explanation would be forthcoming.

"What you have witnessed, my dear young engineer, is simply magnetic opposition between the car and the steel sheet. Nothing unusual about it at all, except that I have done so by using the power of a hearing aid battery to power the electro-magnets set in the base of the car. To do this normally would take a battery roughly the size of two 9-volt batteries, making it clearly impractical. Also, the power consumption would be such that it would be useful for about 10 minutes. You see, the problem of electromagnetic levitation such as you've just witnessed, is the power-to-weight ratio."

"So you've created a more powerful battery?" said JD.

"No, JD," said Isaiah, "he's made the battery more efficient."

"Right on the money, Isaiah," said Olaf. "I stumbled on a combination of metals, along with a ceramic shield that will give us the abilities of low temperature super conductivity. This is going to revolutionize the world!"

"Before you run out and announce it, I want you to think about how it'll be put to use and who'll take ownership of it," said JD.

Olaf blinked, sat down and began to think. "You're right, JD. They'd steal it from me, hide it from other countries, and use it to create an advantage for themselves while they make me sit waiting for patents and the like. Then they'd call it a national secret and forbid me to put it to the good uses it should be going into, just like the guy who invented flubber."

Both JD and Isaiah blinked at the reference to flubber. "You know, Fred McMurray in that old movie. You know, "The Absent Minded Professor," said Olaf.

"Oh yeah, I remember," said Isaiah. "One of my pop's favorite movies."

"Okay, so what can you do for us with the technology?" asked JD.

"You name it," said Olaf. "With this, I can make floating cars, computers that run at the speed of light, submarines that will run on electric batteries for a year with a single charge... You won't need nukes to charge them up; just charge it once a year and repeat as necessary. The same for anything else that runs on electric power. Imagine a car that runs continuously off of a single 12-volt car battery for a week without having to be recharged."

"How soon?" asked JD.

"It'll take a while to get people to use my alloys and ceramics as insulators, but as soon as they can tool up to do that, they'll create superconducting parts. Just add a battery, and away we go."

"How long?" repeated JD.

"At least a year from the time I give someone the specs if they don't go to the government and get stuck in the red tape. If they do that, it'll be ten years or more."

"Okay," said JD, "let's get Naomi in the loop and see if we can short circuit the red tape and get some of your better ideas into production first."

"Great," said Olaf. "I think I can build some of the easier ones here to take advantage of what we've got."

By the end of the week, Olaf had floating carts operating on all the hidden layers of the sub base, moving everything from food and stores to weapons and ammunition for the submarine. Simply turning a rheostat on the side of the pushcart would adjust the height of the cart from the floor or determine how much weight the cart would lift. Then moving the weight was as simple as pushing it to the desired location, where it could be lowered by turning down the battery power. Similar hand lifters were also available. By wrapping them around a torpedo and connecting them together, a person could grab the handles, initiating the power transfer, and lift one end of a two-ton torpedo as if it were weightless. Another person at the opposite end could do the same thing, and using the grips, the heavy torpedo could be moved on board the ship as if it were a weightless twenty-five foot long piece of pipe. Olaf brought enough supplies on board the Sea Wolf to start work on replacing the miles of existing wiring with his new super conductive wiring. He also requested two helpers to begin the process of outfitting the ship with his wiring while he continued working on new inventions aboard the ship. JD promised he'd add them to the compliment on the next run, but not on this one. Olaf was going to keep them busy with new things; that was obvious.

✠

Naomi was bored. She'd put together a team of people in the San Diego office, as she'd been requested to do. Building off of her original team, she put in place a support group for her database software that she felt would be able to handle any problems that might arise. Her next stop was San Francisco and her new apartment and office there. She felt like it would take another month or so to get her office set up there as well. She was anxious to see her software continue to grow into the best database software in the world. Martin was already touting it as if it were. She knew that the new capabilities of real world language in dealing with a database made it a great creation, but the capabilities of other databases, in terms of their data handling, were actually a little better than hers. She needed to see those capabilities ported into her database before she could really claim, within her own mind, the title of the best database in the world, but she also knew that Martin didn't have the compunction about such things like she did.

She wasn't being asked to do much of anything by Martin. That worried her a bit, but she was a self-motivated young lady and she knew that there was much for her to do, so she just got to it. Her third day at the San Francisco head office, a thought began scratching at the back of her mind like a mosquito bite on the back of her brain. It started with, "Why hasn't Martin been to see me since I got back from San Diego?" and it continued to grow from there. Soon she was openly thinking about Martin and what he was up to. She surveyed her surroundings with the eye of a private investigator. What she saw added more itch to the mosquito bite. There was a huge number of people that she recognized as the world's brightest people. They were semi-busy, but for the most part they seemed to be spinning their wheels on problems that any middle management techie type, as long as they were good, could do. After sitting through the first end-of-the-month meeting of the team, she was even more convinced that she was missing something.

Going first to one peer, then another, and then another, she started asking questions. Benign questions, of course, but she began asking the questions that were leading her to the real question in her mind: What was Martin Stanton doing and what was he really up to with these brilliant minds? What she got in return was double talk. Her peers seemed to be hiding what they were really working on behind a wall of double talk. She knew that the papers had picked up a little bit on the story of what had taken place in Iceland, but they had left out information about her relationship to the new company that JD and Isaiah owned in Iceland. When questioned about it by Martin when she had first come to work, she simply said she was there helping him get started when all the nonsense with the Sven and Jenn had taken place, but since that time Martin had been somewhat standoffish toward her. On top of that, she had a feeling that someone was watching her. What she didn't know was that Martin was definitely watching.

Although he had been very helpful in setting her up in new digs and in setting up her finances, he had a very deep look into those finances and her personal life as well. The apartment in San Francisco was bugged and he had people checking into her past and into her every move. So far she had been fortunate; her conversations with JD and Isaiah were conducted on the secret phone, away from her office and apartment, but sooner or later she'd make a mistake if she didn't learn the truth. The one thing she had going for her was the sense that her father had taught her to listen to. He'd always told her that when something felt wrong, it probably was wrong, and she needed to be extremely careful until she found out what it was that was wrong.

Chapter 9

China

Chaing Xau was not happy. For the last month the little pipsqueak of a president had been threatening to cut off the oil. It looked like the Iraqis and the Kuwaitis were ready to join in as well, but the Afghans knew not to climb on board with him. They knew that the Chinese would threaten an invasion through the small corridor that connected Afghanistan with China, and they were in no shape to have another invading army at their doorstep. Chaing didn't know how it would all shake down, but he did know that he wasn't going to wait and let some third-world nobody try to force his country to its knees. He called in Li Ming. After a short discussion with the premier, she took the information back to her computer and began typing a letter to the other 22 members of the politburo. The general secretary was obviously hopping mad and wanted the politburo to take decisive action before the Iranian government could convince the other members of the oil cartel to block the sale of oil to the Chinese people. Chaing wanted action, and decisive action. He did not want to be a reactionary leader. It was his opinion that the entire Middle East had held the people of the East hostage long enough. He wanted to hold them hostage for a while. Those were the words that he had used in Li Ming's presence, and she was careful to put the exact words down. She would draft the letter, and then take it back to him for final inspection before sending it out to the secretariat, with a special note from the general secretary, asking for the use of the Chinese Navy to carry out his plans. Within twenty-four hours, both the British Secret Service and the American CIA had full versions of the proposed letter, along with special interpretation by Chinese language experts into the full meaning of every nuance and inflection used in the memo. Even though the memo had not yet been sent to the rest of the politburo, the Americans and English were jumping with anticipation of what the reaction of the politburo might be. There was a faction that believed that the politburo would reject Chaing's proposed threat, then there was a faction that thought the politburo would do whatever Chaing proposed, and then there was a faction who didn't believe the document was real, but was instead a ploy by the Chinese to play the Americans and the Brits into making threats of their own. All in all, it was a real mess. Dave Benson read the memo, took all the special interpretations, and then placed a call to the president.

"Madam President," began her national security advisor.

"I hate it when you begin by calling me that instead of my name," said Debra. "It means I'm going to have to deal with something big and ugly."

"You are correct as always, Madam President," Dave continued. "The Iranians, as you know, have been making subtle threats about cutting off the supply of oil to China. Well, the Chinese have finally had enough, I believe. The Premier, Chaing Xau, is drafting a letter to the other members of the Secretariat, asking for action. He wants them to release the Navy, and possibly the Army, at his discretion. He hasn't sent the letter yet; in fact, it is still in his secretary's PC, but if he follows previous form, it'll be on their desks by Monday of next week."

"What exactly does he want the Navy to do, Dave?" was Debra's response.

"My guess, and the guess of most of the people I trust, is that he'll try and blockade the Gulf, not just blocking the Iranian tankers, but all of them."

"All of them? Why all of them? Do you really think he'd do such a thing? We'd all be up the creek then," she said as her eyes widened.

"You catch on very quickly Madam President," said Dave.

"If the Chinese are going to hurt, then everyone's going to hurt. Is that it, Dave?"

"That's about the size of it, Ma'am. I believe they'll do it, too."

"What would the Chinese want from us?" she asked.

"I believe they'd want us to pressure the Middle East to stand against Iran and force them back into shipping oil, maybe even into overthrowing the current government for another one that would be more amiable toward the Chinese."

"And what about the Iranians?" she asked.

"It's terrorism against them, pure and simple. The Chinese want us to accept this act as if it's a legitimate political move when in fact it's terrorism, plain and simple, with the threat being—play along or we'll unleash nuclear hostilities on the world," Dave replied.

"Hard to argue with someone who's got their thumb on a nuclear button," Debra said. "Okay," she continued, "what's the perfect outcome for this one, besides hoping that it just goes away on its own without us having to do anything?" she asked.

"Good question, Madam President. I think we can probably move some assets into the Arabian Sea, and possibly into the Persian Gulf, with the idea of dissuading the Chinese from attacking any shipping that might be heading our way or belonging to Kuwait or the Kingdom, but to be perfectly honest, it could get real dicey in a hurry if we get in between a Chinese warship and its target with one of our warships. We have to remember that we don't know about this officially yet, so now is the time to move our ships so they don't get the idea we're doing it after they announce it to prepare for a fight. We need to do it before they announce it so that maybe, just maybe, they'll think twice about starting down this path to begin with."

"Good. Make it happen, Dave. How much firepower should we move? One or two carriers and their task forces?"

"I'm thinking just one task force, Madam President. If we move two, they may get the idea that we're reading their mail," said Dave.

"What about the Brits, Dave?"

"I've already spoken with Sir Dalton at MI6. He informed me that he was going to recommend similar action to the PM."

"Let's see then, two new carrier groups in the Arabian Sea. It might make our friends in New Delhi a bit nervous. Do we tell them what we know or not?" she asked.

"No, I don't think so, but this is more a question for your Secretary of State. I'm just a lowly spook who doesn't want to burn our source," said Dave.

"Aren't you afraid that when both the Brits and us come barreling into the Gulf with another task group that they'll get suspicious?" she asked.

"Not really. We can cover it with another war game exercise," he speculated.

"Okay, Dave, make it so."

On the way back to his office, he stopped to take a walk around the mall. Stopping at the Lincoln Memorial, he placed a call to his daughter on his special phone. Within five minutes they had a four-way conference call underway with Dave, Isaiah, JD, and Naomi all in on the conversation.

"Who'll be sent, from where and when?" asked Isaiah.

"The Ronald Reagan is already in the Gulf and she'll be joined by the John C Stennis by mid-October. There's a compliment of two heavy cruisers, eight destroyers, and at least six other tenders and support ships to go with each of them. If I know Admiral Richardson, the Secretary of the Navy, he'll send in at least two more of the Tiger Shark class fast attack subs as well," said Dave.

"That's some real fire power," said JD.

"All in the Persian Gulf?" Isaiah asked incredulously.

"Probably not all at the same time, but you can bet that a submarine in the Gulf wouldn't stand a chance of getting out alive with the Americans, the Brits and the Chinese all pinging away, trying to make sure no one sneaks up on them, not to mention the rather puny Navies of Iran, Iraq, and the Kingdom. Being outside in the Arabian Sea won't be a picnic either. At least one American and one British task force, as well as one or two from India—who by the way are no slouches, and more Chinese and British and American subs than you can shake a stick at." You could almost visualize Dave's head shaking as he spoke.

"What are your experts telling you is the probable move on China's part?" JD asked.

"They're telling us to expect a Chinese blockade of the Gulf. No oil tankers going in or out," he said.

"We've been doing some analyzing of our own, Dave," JD said.

"We think Chaing's got something else in mind," said Isaiah.

"What do you mean?" asked Dave.

"We think he's not thinking blockade; we think he's going to invade," said JD. Dave got quiet.

"Daddy, we've been through the scenarios over and over—the way the Chinese and Chaing in particular think, it'll be his only recourse in his mind," Naomi said.

"I have to admit I've been thinking he might do that," said Dave. "I just can't get myself to say the words out loud. Do you really believe he'll make that jump, guys? I mean, that's an act of war."

"What's to stop him?" asked JD. And it really was as simple as that. What was going to stop him? No nation on earth was willing to push back and deal with the threat of nuclear retaliation. "Dave, we think we might be in the right position to do something about it. We can push back without China having anyone to retaliate against. They'll scream and shout, but in the end they won't have anyone to point a finger at, and they know that when the west says they didn't have anything to do with it, they always tell the truth. They won't have any choice but to back off...we hope."

"I don't want to hear any more. I've given you some information. I really don't want to know what you're going to do with it. Plausible deniability, you know?" Dave said.

With that the conversation ended, and Dave walked slowly back to his waiting car. In his mind he played over the conversation and the more he did, the more he liked the idea of putting the Chinese on the defensive. If they didn't know who was interrupting their plans, then they wouldn't know who to retaliate against and in turn they would be tentative about retaliating for fear of starting a war themselves. The threat of retaliation worked both ways. It was the same reason that they wouldn't try and invade through Russia, or go through the no-fly zones of Afghanistan or Pakistan, which were under American protection. On the other hand, he thought, these are my daughter's closest friends, even the young man he hoped might one day be his son-in-law. What they were proposing was extremely dangerous. It was so dangerous that he wouldn't even think about sending one of his own country's submarines, with all their capabilities, into such a mission. He fingered the phone in his pocket, wondering if he should call them all back and warn them to turn around and run the other direction. His heart said "yes" but his mind said "no." He arrived at his office and started making calls to the joint chief of staff, making sure that they would be prepared for whatever China had in mind. The world around him was making the decision for him. There wasn't time for him to deal with their plan, but in the back of his mind, he worried for the group.

✠

Back in Iceland, the sub was ready, and so were the men and women of the Sea Wolf. That night they would leave the safe confines of their Icelandic hideaway. The bustling warehouse would once again become the quiet home of Rolf, but now he had a purpose and was a part of something bigger. In China, the memo was sent out, virtually unchanged. Chaing called for each of the politburo individually. The discussions were held privately. Li Ming was not invited into the chamber as she was normally. To Li Ming, that meant only one thing: the premier did not want his discussion with the individuals recorded. She also noted that none of the other members brought with them recording devices or memo pads with which to write down their thoughts. Obviously, Chaing didn't want his discussions to get out. It was something that he had been worried about more and more lately. Li Ming noted that as they left, each seemed to be pale, unlike when they arrived. She also noted that they left without making any small talk. Usually the randy old goats would stop and make small talk with her, trying their best to talk her into their beds, but this time they each left without speaking, as if she weren't there at all. She was surprised, to say the least, and a little put out that none had wanted her enough to come to her. A meeting of the politburo was scheduled for the end of the week. She figured that she'd hear by then what the big deal was. In the mean time, she decided that she liked not being chased by the old geezers. She noted that even Chaing had been distracted. She hadn't been called into his parlor in nearly three days now. That was a record for the general secretary.

Battle Stations! Battle Stations! This is no drill.

Word was sent that afternoon to the John C Stennis and her escort group. The task force was being sent from their current assignment in the Mediterranean Sea through the Suez Canal and into the Arabian Sea for joint war games with the British. Proper notification had been given to the

Egyptians and the Saudis, as well as to the Indian Navy. In response to the buildup of Naval assets in the area, the Indian Navy was sending out a task group of her own. It would soon be very crowded in the Arabian Sea, as well as in the Persian Gulf. At the moment, the Ronald Reagan was cruising with her task force in the Persian Gulf, and she was joined there by several frigates of Her Majesty's Navy. With the addition of three new battle groups in the vicinity, there would be more firepower per square mile than at any time since the height of the cold war. In addition to the Stennis battle group, Dave had been correct about Admiral Richardson sending subs as well. The admiral had sent two additional attack subs to the Sea of Arabia. These two—the Tiger Shark and the Dolphin—were to join the Stingray, which was already on patrol in the Persian Gulf. Orders had been sent to the Stingray to get out of the Gulf before things heated up during the exercises. The subs were to deploy in a line, patrolling roughly from Somalia to the tip of India.

The Stennis Carrier group was to patrol inside the picket line that the subs had set up and were to hunt for any submarines inside the Arabian Sea. The Reagan and her support ships were to do the same inside the Persian Gulf. The Stennis would work in conjunction with the British Navy and her carrier group, the HMS Prince Albert.

The Indian Navy currently had a three-missile cruiser in the Arabian Sea, but with the news that both the British and Americans were sending additional carrier groups into the area, they had ordered a carrier group of their own to be sent into the vicinity. The Indian carrier group consisted of a carrier, formerly an American carrier that had been renamed the Delhi, and ten other ships. The ten other ships included five destroyers, two cruisers, and three oilers that rotated back and forth to bases in order to keep the ships' fuel supplies topped off. Their orders would be quite simple: shadow the American and British task groups and make sure that they came nowhere close to the international boundaries they were sworn to keep.

With the four carrier groups, submarines, and normal warships patrolling the area between the Persian Gulf and the Arabian Sea, there would very soon be forty-eight warships, representing five nations in the area. Those were the ships that the United States Navy was aware of; it was the ones they were not aware of that tended to worry them the most. The Chinese would most certainly add several submarines and at least another carrier task force into the mix. That would be another ten to twelve ships.

Admiral Richardson looked at a map of the area and imagined sixty warships in such an over-crowded area. It was a recipe for disaster. On top of sixty warships, there would be over two hundred jets flying around, watching and threatening each other. Very quickly it could get out of hand, and he was worried about what the consequences might be. He had checked the satellite maps this morning and had several notes from analysts, telling him what he already feared. Preparations were underway in Qingdao and in Hangzhou for Chinese naval ships. The thing that bothered him the most was the number of ships they seemed to be getting ready. He understood the ships at Qingdao that would be a carrier group getting underway, but the ships at Hangzhou were primarily transports. It didn't bode well for the Chinese to be getting things ready there unless they were planning an invasion. He studied the maps again and decided that it was China's way of confusing the issue. In the morning they'd probably see the ships leaving Qingdao and everything else would be quiet. Back in '91 they'd gone so far as to send a group of unmanned troop carriers into the Sea of Arabia to try and keep the US and its coalition of troops from invading Iraq during Operation Desert Storm.

On board the Sea Wolf, the throttle had been opened up to see just how fast and how quiet the sub really was. At 90 percent throttle, the Sea Wolf was making 60 knots, or approximately 70 MPH, at a depth of 800 feet. She had been registered as an anomaly as they had crossed the Mid-Atlantic ridge and the group of sonobouys that lined it. The anomaly warning had lasted for less than a minute and was dismissed by the operators watching it, and word was never passed to the submarines watching the ridge. The Tiger Shark was moving from her spot in the Caribbean Sea at 40 knots, or roughly 46 MPH, across the Atlantic as well. She was heading with all her speed, not waiting and listening as were normal tactics, toward her new station off the coast of Somalia. At the current speeds, the two ships would cross paths somewhere around the tip of Africa. The Sea Wolf was currently at longitude 30 by latitude 23.27, while the Tiger Shark was just off the coast of Ascension Island at longitude 15, latitude -7.5.

Olaf had been busy. He had converted the systems inside one of the mini subs to his new superconducting wiring. The result was what he believed to be an almost limitless amount of power on board the sub. He claimed it would be able to stay submerged for months at a time if need be, and that he had improved the power of the anti-matter ray on the mini sub by 1,000 percent. He promised that with a little work he could increase the speed of the mini sub so that it would be able to travel at up to 30 knots if need be. His only concern was that the propellers were too small and would reach a point where they would spin so fast that they would vaporize the water instead of pulling it through the blades. He had some new ideas for ramjet-type drive systems, using water instead of air that would be more efficient than the propeller drive.

JD and Isaiah were amazed at what he was coming up with. They had begun to think about the changes that superconductivity would bring, but they hadn't considered how much it would be able to change the whole world. Olaf was also working on turning one of the ship's drones into a superconductive version as well. His thought was that with the current battery and fuel combination, it would be capable of staying aloft for a year at a time, if need be. Both JD's and Isaiah's mouths fell open. A year aloft using only ten gallons of fuel and a battery the size of a motorcycle battery! They were pleased that they had been able to keep it aloft for a week before. Olaf explained that it was all about loss.

In a typical electric system, up to 90 percent of the power generated is lost due to the connections and transfer through copper wire. Even the best systems out there, using highly insulated wire and solid gold connectors, had 70 percent loss. With the superconducting alloy and the ceramic insulators, he had reduced the loss down to under .1 percent. He was drawing up plans for a hovercraft that would be able to not just hover over terrain, but fly as well. He had modified several of the torpedoes to use the "SC wiring," as he now called it. He figured that with it, the torpedo could run for days, if necessary, to chase its intended prey instead of the thirty or so minutes that it was good for until now.

He was planning also to copy the anti-matter ray and put a smaller version on board his modified drone. Such a weapon on board the drone would literally be able to destroy any missile or rocket fired that it could see. A flock of such drones flying over an area could reasonably keep airplanes on the deck of their aircraft carriers and knock out all weapons fired in anger at each other from ships at sea or on land. JD and Isaiah had a vision for the future that would keep those deadly systems at bay from one another.

The ship was getting a good shakedown cruise. With testing out the capabilities of the new drone in mind, JD ordered the crew to put the modified drone together and to prepare for an evening launch. They would program the drone to fly above them for a few days until power consumption could be monitored and verified, and if all was okay, the drone would be sent to overfly the Arabian Sea area until such time that they wanted to recover it. That evening, as the last rays of the sun glowed golden on the horizon, the Sea Wolf glided to a stop atop the waves of a gentle Atlantic Ocean. Turning its stern into the wind, the hump behind the sail opened up, the track raised, and the drone lifted itself silently into the night sky. In less than one minute, the Sea Wolf was once again below the surface and underway on her previous path around the African tip.

Each minute under the surface she came closer and closer to the submerged USS Tiger Shark. While there was no way that the listening devices on board the Sea Wolf were very good at the speed she was traveling, she was able to keep up with the surface traffic and submerged traffic through her connection to the SOSUS line. The software JD had written was the perfect interface between the military's sonic listening posts, their individual sonobouys, and the satellite information that was constantly being sent to the secret bases where they tried to interpret the vast amount of info being sent to them. With the processing power on board the Sea Wolf, making sense of it all was child's play, and presenting it was even easier.

The three-dimensional viewports showing the activity in the Gulf and the Arabian Sea were lit up like a Christmas tree. The Tiger Shark and the Dolphin were steaming at their best speeds respectively, and the Sea Wolf was in between them, but it would soon overtake the Tiger Shark. The Chinese had sent their submarine fleet first. The US knew about it, but probably no one else did; the Chinese had two subs already in the area and six more that would be there by the end of the week. Of all the ships and activity in the Persian Gulf area, only the Iranians seemed to be unaware of what was going on around them. They had continued to send their tankers in and out of the Gulf, with minimal guards. They had gun ships in the Gulf that escorted the tankers through the straits and into the Arabian Sea, but then turned back. Even her noisy subs had all been brought back to their sub pens just across from Oman. The only thing not quiet as far as Iran was concerned was their president. He continued to accuse the Chinese of causing his problems of the previous six months, and he was still calling for a boycott of sales to China. While the rest of the cartel put little stock in the little president's blustering and mouthing off, it would not do to have him completely lose face. The next meeting was at the end of the month of September, less than two weeks away.

As JD and Isaiah entered the library, just below the control room, they turned on the view screens, giving themselves a glimpse of the world on three sides, and a view from the drone in infrared mode on the fourth wall. They could see all the ships gathering, as well as the movements and satellite data of China that showed the activity going on there. Very soon, the Chinese fleet looked as if it intended to sail. Tomorrow would be Friday, and they knew that the Chinese politburo would meet then. Dave was supposed to call if he had any further information coming out of China as to what the politburo had decided to do. The drone had flown for three days, and it still had three-quarter charge showing on the battery. At this rate, Olaf was right; it could stay aloft for a long, long time. They decided to send it across the African Continent to meet them over the Sea of Arabia in a week or so, when they would arrive there. They called Olaf to the library, as well as three of their best officers—Jean Rene Black, Harold (Thump) Higgins, and Marty (Dinger) Boston.

Jean was a mathematical genius who had joined the Army in search of adventure as a 17-year-old female. Her mathematical prowess quickly came to light in her classes that dealt with the Patriot missile systems, and she quickly became known for being able to out-think the computers when reaching firing solutions. She wasn't satisfied with her work in missile defense and gradually drifted away from it, still desiring the adventure she'd joined for. She became known for her dissatisfaction and soon was marked as "damaged goods." Within the Sea Wolf, she had come alive, and she was the sub's finest navigator and missile commander.

Thump Higgins had received the DSC as a seal in action in Kosovo. During his time there, his ability to move so silently you could only hear his heart beat earned him the name "Thump," even though he said it was because of his love of using the repeating grenade launcher. Either way, he was highly respected by the crew and was the ship's light-arms officer.

Dinger Boston got his nickname from his love of baseball and his ability to hit homeruns. It was said that he'd been recruited by the Yankee organization in both high school and college, and had turned down a million dollar signing bonus to sign with Uncle Sam instead. He'd also wanted to help after 9/11, and after graduating from Stanford, he'd joined the Navy to become a Seal. While he'd loved the esprit de corps, he found the analysis paralysis too much for him. His commander had watched Dinger grow in dissatisfaction until he'd heard about Dave's request for people with that growing problem, and had sent his name in. Dinger also had come to life within the ship's crew. He was physically large, and with his extreme personality, the team had found him to be a natural leader. He was placed in charge of search/rescue, and interdiction.

The six of them sat in the library, going over everything that they knew, and everything that they could surmise from it. For nearly two hours they pressed back and forth, pointing out data on the screens, pulling up new data sources, checking their facts, and rechecking positions of ships and calculating the possibilities. The fact was, they still were uncertain. They had no other choice but to plan for two different scenarios. The first was a Chinese blockade, and the second, a Chinese invasion. As they began their planning exercise, a whistle interrupted the session and the voice of the first officer announced a new contact and bearing that had just appeared on sonar. The quiet ship had to be a missile ship of some kind, but the computer had not identified it yet. JD left the library while Isaiah continued running the planning meeting. JD would deal with the new contact.

The new contact had come out of nowhere and had been picked up by the extremely sensitive triple-towed array trailing almost a mile behind the submarine. They had been just south of St. Helena Island and just north of the Tropic of Capricorn, headed south-southeast toward the southern tip of the African continent when they heard the cavitation sound of a propeller in the water less than ten miles to their southwest. JD ordered for twenty knots, then turned into the sound. They would be on top of the sound in less than ten minutes at their current speed. Ten minutes later, JD ordered "all stop." He had just minutes to wait. The sound of the sub they had heard was heard again, this time less than two miles to their south, but now they had a heading and a speed. The contact was traveling at only 10 knots and was moving almost due south. Picking a line behind the sub, JD moved in behind it at 12 knots. When he was less than 2,000 meters from the sub in front of him, his computer was finally able to pick up the nuclear generator's signature. The sub in front of him was a U.S. Boomer, the Blue Fin.

While she was an older missile submarine, it was amazing how quiet she was. JD was impressed by her quietness, but he also felt good about having acquired her signature, and he decided to keep track of each submarine they were able to track and identify. Bringing up a world map, he plotted the point at which she was identified, the date and time, and put a mark at that location. This would be their private trophy case. Turning slowly away and from behind the boomer, the ultra quiet Sea Wolf slowly turned back to her path, taking her around Africa and slowly returned to her cruising speed. The boomer she had trailed never turned from her path nor noticed the ship that had snuck up on her tail. Ahead of her was the USS Tiger Shark. JD decided that he would follow the Tiger Shark around the tip of Africa and would wait and see which direction she headed after that, then split away from her.

On Sunday evening the two ships were less than a mile apart. JD marked her identification and point of acquisition at approximately -38 degrees latitude and -15 degrees longitude. As she pulled in behind the Tiger Shark, she slowed down to match her speed. Slowing slightly, JD let the Tiger Shark stretch out ahead of the Sea Wolf to a distance of about five miles and then matched her speed.

Inside the Tiger Shark, Captain Blake was unaware of the massive ship moving in her baffles.

That evening they received a call from Dave. Dave, Isaiah, JD, and Naomi were connected on a conference call and were soon talking about China's most recent movements and activities. JD and Isaiah were sitting in the library for their teleconference once again. They had the Chinese coastline on the screen in front of them, and were viewing the movement of a group of ships out of the port city of Qingdao. There were also the markings of two Chinese submarines in the Sea of Arabia, and six more that had made the turn through Indonesia and were nearly to the southern most of the Maldives Islands and north of Diego Garcia. All six were moving at around 10 knots. Garcia had clear plots of the sonobouys that were monitored by the station at Diego, and even when they had gone shallow in order to get instructions from Beijing.

Dave began the discussion. "We've got the Chinese sending a carrier fleet out of Qingdao, as well as six more of their best submarines that are almost to the Arabian Sea as we speak."

"We're aware of the movements, as well as the movement of your own carrier group making its way there. We've also noticed that the Russians are staying clear of the situation entirely. They seem to have pulled all of their naval assets clear of the area," said JD.

"JD, my best analysts are telling me that the Chinese are going to go for a blockade and not for an invasion," said Dave, obviously pleading for JD to leave the area.

"Mr. Benson, do you have any idea where we are right now?" came JD's reply.

"No, we've had no reports of anything unusual, but my guess would be somewhere headed south of the equator, maybe as far south as Ascension Island," said Dave.

"Dave, we've been playing hide-and-seek with one of your boomers—The Blue Fin, to be exact. That was a day ago; right now, we're behind your newest and most quiet attack sub, the Tiger Shark. Neither of them had any idea we were there, nor that we could hear them. The Chinese subs are no match for yours, and yours are no match for this one. As long as we keep our wits about us and don't get overconfident, we'll be able to carry out our plan and not be seen or heard by anyone," said Isaiah.

Dave was quiet for a moment, then spoke. "I don't want to know your plan or any more about where you are. As difficult as it is for me to not know, I want to be able to be truthful with my president if she asks questions. I just want to know that you'll be safe."

"We'll be as safe as we can be," said JD. "Dave, we've made some advances even you are unaware of, and we're not sharing with anyone for a while yet. We'll be fine. You need to just sit back and watch the show."

"Okay, well, here's what I do know, JD and Isaiah. The Chinese are making noises with their troop ships in Hangzhou. They've done that before, trying to make it appear that they're contemplating invasion. Our best strategists are telling me it's a feint and not to waste time with it."

"Dave, when the time comes, you just need to react in an outraged fashion when they accuse you of interrupting their plans," said Isaiah.

"Understood," said Dave.

Dave said his goodbyes and left the conference call. After he was gone, Naomi, who was taking the call at 4:30 AM, her time, rubbed her eyes and added her comments.

"Guys, how sure are you that you can get in without being spotted, or interrupt their plans without giving away your position to one of the Chinese, or for that matter the American subs?" she asked.

"Don't worry, Naomi, you wouldn't even recognize the crew any more. They are working as a team in every aspect. What we don't think of, they do, and everyone is freely giving ideas and information. We're working like a Swiss watch. And you wouldn't believe the things Olaf is coming up with. We'll be safe, I promise," said JD.

They also said their goodbyes and the conference call was ended. JD and Isaiah sat, looking at the wall.

"Do you think Dave's guys are right? Do you think the Chinese are just faking an invasion?" asked JD.

"Nope," said Isaiah. "They're going to invade, all right. They almost have to. By blockading, they don't win anything except status quo. Why take the chance of a nuclear war for status quo? You'll want to gain something if you are going to risk everything."

"You're right. It's the only thing that makes any sense. And the Chinese will always do what makes the most sense. They are a very logical people," said JD.

Staring at the picture on the wall in front of them, they watched as the Chinese carrier group passed the port city of Hangzhou. As they watched, new red specs began appearing at their trailing edge. More ships had appeared on the map. JD and Isaiah looked at each other knowingly.

"How many of the torpedoes have you converted to the new SC wiring now?" asked JD.

"Twelve are done, and thanks to the three guys working with me, we'll have twenty done by the end of the day," said Olaf.

"Olaf, you're a genius," said Isaiah.

"I've been telling people that for years, but you guys are the first to ever agree with me," he said laughing. "Really, though, the guys that are helping me really know their stuff. I showed them one time, and they've been on their own ever since, knocking out about one an hour each."

"How about the mini sub you converted? Is it ready and working with the disrupter ray?" asked JD.

"It's been converted, and it has a range that should exceed 100 miles, but I don't know how to test it," said Olaf. "I do know that the size of the beam will be about an inch in diameter and will go as far as you need it to go."

"Great," said JD. "Now, what about the disrupter beam to be mounted on the drone?" JD asked.

"Don't ask much, do you?" groused the scientist. "No, it's not done yet. I figured the torpedoes were top priority."

"They are, Olaf. I was just hoping for the impossible. You keep on your priority list. I'd say twenty torpedoes will be enough to convert for now. The drone-mounted disruptor can be your next priority after you get a little rest," said JD, patting the young scientist on the back. "Just want you to know that you're doing an amazing job for all of us."

Olaf just smiled and ducked his head. It was a rare moment when Olaf was left speechless, and the whole crew on the bridge laughed at Olaf's obvious red-cheeked happy embarrassment. JD touched the screen on the captain's chair that gave him the ability to speak to the whole crew.

"Knights of Truth and Honor, I salute you. We are very soon going to be entering into the Arabian Sea. We will be hunted by every nation on the face of the earth, but they won't be able to find us. We will stop the Chinese government from their plan. Their plan, we believe, is to invade the entire Middle East and overthrow the current systems of government and to take them as satellite nations, much as Russia did to the Soviet nations following World War II. Our plan is to keep them from doing this. At the same time, we hope to impose a little of our own will upon the nation of Iran. You are all aware of what Iran attempted to do to the United States back in July. We plan on sending a little surprise back to the men involved in making those decisions."

There was a general whoop of excitement upon hearing those words.

"I know that all of you will give your best in the coming weeks. I also know that we'll be in some very tense situations. I pray that all of us will come out of the coming weeks safe and without casualty. At the same time, I know that all of you will face the dangers without fear and with the tenacity and strength I have come to recognize in each of you. We want you all to know that we respect you already, and we are looking forward to going into battle beside you."

With that he closed the channel. Moments later he was impressed to hear the words "Truth and Honor" echoing between crewmembers throughout the sub as they clasped each other's hands or slapped each other on the back. He knew they were ready.

Passing Port Elizabeth on the Tip of South Africa, the Sea Wolf took a wide berth around the USS Tiger Shark and increased her speed to 60 knots. Leaving the Tiger Shark quickly behind her, they watched carefully for any notice that the Tiger Shark might take of their rapid push to the north. The Tiger Shark, however, didn't hear a thing and had no hopes of hearing the quiet Sea Wolf, even if she had been loud enough to hear. At her current speed of 40 knots, the Tiger Shark was for all intents and purposes, deaf. She had no array on the bow like the Sea Wolf, and with her current listening arrays all in the baffles of her wake, the Tiger Shark couldn't hear because of the turbulence caused by her own propulsion.

The Sea Wolf was not like that. She had arrays that strung out behind her, but they were far enough apart that the disturbance caused by her propulsion didn't affect the side-mounted arrays, nor the two outlying arrays that strung out behind her wide tail. This allowed the Sea Wolf to be almost as good at listening at 60 knots as she was at 10. As the Sea Wolf passed the eastern side of Madagascar, she picked up the signal from her orbiting drone, flying high above the Arabian Sea.

Upon picking up the signal, JD, Isaiah, Olaf, Thump, Dinger, and Jean met in the library to download the information the drone had gathered and to see what was going on. From 30,000 feet, the plane had quite a view of the sea below. With its wide-angle lens and its wide-angle infrared lens, the drone could look at an area of sea below that encompassed better than twenty square miles. The drone had picked up on the entrance of the British and American carrier groups through the Mediterranean, the Suez Canal, then the Red Sea, into the Gulf of Aden, and finally into the Arabian Sea. The drone had stayed fairly close to the British carrier group as they were headed east, across the sea toward the Indian coast.

The Stennis carrier group headed south after leaving the Gulf of Aden and was lost to the sight of the drone soon after. Watching the real time movements on board the Prince

Albert and her escort ships was amazing. They checked the fuel consumption and current charge. The drone had been in the air for nearly two weeks now, and it still had a nearly full fuel tank and a full charge of power in its batteries. The group decided to send it out to look for the other carrier groups. They set it on a course to cross the Arabian Sea like mowing a lawn, hoping to catch a glimpse of the Indian and American carrier groups as well. They had a good idea of where the American carrier groups—both the Stennis and the Reagan—were located because of the string of sonobouys they were leaving behind them.

Before twenty-four hours had passed, the drone had plotted successfully almost the whole of the Sea of Arabia. Thirty-four surface warships, eight massive oil tankers and six freighters had been spotted inside the Arabian Sea. Another sixteen warships were in the Persian Gulf, and at least ten submarines were lying in wait in the Arabian Sea. The submarines had gone quiet upon entering the Arabian Sea, so all the Sea Wolf had was an approximate last track for all of the Chinese subs. There had to be at least two other American subs waiting there as well. They had been very quiet, but they had to be at the far edges in order to not be seen by the active pinging of the American sonobouys. All in all, it was a mess. Along the eastern side of the of the Malay and Indonesian Islands, the Chinese task force was making its way toward the Indian Ocean. They were moving slowly, only about 15 knots.

The cartel had debated the issue of the Chinese and Iranian problem. Not really believing President Ahmadinejad, the cartel was in a difficult situation. The Iranian president had made the argument that to not stand together would send a message to the world that the cartel was fractured and they would lose their strength. The argument was a good one, and one that the cartel had succumbed to before, and Ahmadinejad knew it, so they had voted five to four to back the Iranians in their Chinese oil embargo. The embargo would only be lifted after a public apology from the Chinese and the repayment of losses to the Iranian government of 1.5 billion dollars.

The Chinese, in turn, had replied to the ultimatum by calling Iran's charges completely false and without merit, and any attempt to stop the shipment of oil to the Peoples Republic of China would result in appropriate action by the Chinese government. There had been several counters by the Iranians and by the cartel, but there was no further word from China. The situation was becoming very dangerous. The US and British governments had gone to bat for the cartel, asking for the Chinese to meet with them in a neutral location and using the US or the British as arbitration judges. Both the cartel and the Chinese had flatly rejected the offer.

Captain Sven Jorgensen of the triple-hulled oil tanker, Chairman Mao, watched as the three massive tugs pushed his nearly 900 ft. long ship slowly against the floating dock off the Kuwaiti coast. The ship had been given clearance to dock, but there was obviously something going on aboard the floating pumping station. There was chatter in their Farsi language. Sven was at a loss. He had enough problems with most of his crew speaking nothing but Chinese. He'd picked up enough to communicate with the crew, but throwing Farsi into the mix made it worse. His only English/Farsi speaker was out this trip and now he was being hailed by the dock master.

As soon as the ship was tied up, Sven and his second-in-command disembarked the ship and headed for the dock-master's hut. Upon entering, he found three men all talking rapidly and pointing at his ship. He spoke in English, asking for an interpreter. After a few moments, a man entered the building and began to interpret the ballyhoo that was taking place in front of him. After listening, it became clear that even though he had the proper clearance and the proper docking authorization, he was being denied the oil he picked up on a regular basis. He had been making this run from Kuwait to Guangzhou and back for the last ten years.

Suddenly, he was told to push off and wait for further instructions. He was to get no oil. Sven couldn't believe his ears.

"What are you going to do with it? Drink it?" he yelled at the little Arabs. "I need that oil to take back to China, and I'm not leaving without it," he said, placing his hands on his hips.

At that point, the Kuwaiti dock-master spoke into a microphone on the desk. His eyes never left the tall Norwegian captain, but there was no interpretation from the small interpreter. A moment later, another Arab stepped into the room, carrying an AK-47 rifle. He had it leveled at the captain. The dock-master spoke again, this time in English.

"Leave the dock now!" he ordered.

Sven took a long look at the harbor-master, then turned and left. Reaching his ship, he made ready, and without using the tugboat's assistance, pushed away from the dock and made his way into the neutral waters of the twelve-mile limit. Reaching it, he radioed back to Guangzhou and relayed the information of what had happened. It was oddly quiet on the other end—no yelling, as he had expected. He was told to make his way out to the Indian Ocean and await further word.

"Now that really seems odd," he said to his second-in-command, but he was a good captain and knew how to take orders. He headed out to sea.

There were three other tankers, all full and all heading out to various points of the world. On any given day, a dozen such tankers would enter, and a dozen more would leave the Persian Gulf. It was a dance that had to be well orchestrated in order to keep the flow of oil, the world's lifeblood, flowing to the world. Now that flow was being threatened, as was the dance. By sending the Chinese tanker away empty, they had enough oil to fill an extra tanker, but no tanker to fill it with. The three tankers that were exiting the Persian Gulf were all registered in the island country of Cyprus, but they were each headed in different directions.

The Athena was headed for Japan; the Cyprus Star, the newest of the three and triple hulled, was headed for Canada; and the Orion was headed for Argentina. The Cyprus Star made the turn around Oman and set a course for the Red Sea. Her intended path was to head for Canada by way of the Suez Canal, through the Med, and straight to Canada. The Athena was headed south; her plan was to set course around the Indian peninsula and around Indonesia, then north to Japan. The final ship, the Orion, was to head due south around the tip of Africa and then West to Argentina.

Eight hours later, the Orion disappeared in a huge explosion as she rounded the corner of Oman. The ship was within range of seeing the Oman coast if using a good pair of binoculars. Thirty minutes later, the Athena radioed an S.O.S. to all ships that she was going down. She had taken a torpedo to the bow of the ship. She'd lost all steerage, but the captain was trying desperately to run the ship aground along the Pakistani coastline. After hearing about the other two ships, the captain of the Cyprus Star turned into the shallow waters along the Yemen coastline and slowed the huge tanker to a crawl.

It took thirty hours from the time the Sea Wolf left the southern tip of Madagascar to reach the Sea of Arabia. Just as they entered the outermost portion of the Sea, they heard the explosion of the Orion. Slowing to thirty knots, the Sea Wolf set a course for the general area of the explosion. When they heard the next explosion thirty minutes later, it was obvious to them that two different submarines were responsible for the explosions.

Up on the surface, the US Navy was running in all directions, looking for survivors, and the Brits were trying desperately to get the Athena shored up enough to make it to the coast. There were a dozen ships between the British and American fleets now dumping sonobouys into the water outside the exit of the Persian Gulf.

Both Japan and Argentina were screaming bloody murder to the Kuwaiti government, and to the Cypriots. Cyprus was yelling at China, and everyone was yelling at Iran. It was quickly getting out of hand. China, in turn, was being strangely silent. Kuwait's response had been that the ownership of the oil was upon transfer to the ship. Once on board the Cyprus-registered ship, it belonged to Argentina and Japan. Both Argentina and Japan, on the other hand, were not happy with their response and were ready to sue, using the World Court system.

Even Lloyd's of London was in on the action, saying that they were refusing to cover the loss since it was due to what they were calling terrorism, and not because of an accident. The US had literally surrounded the remaining ship, the Cyprus Star, and they were using helicopters from the Stennis to drop sonobouys in the vicinity, watching intently for any subs in the area.

Three more tankers had been loaded at one of the two loading facilities inside the Persian Gulf; the Reagan task force was escorting the three tankers as they were heading out of the Gulf. At the same time, two more empty tankers were waiting outside the Gulf, ready to head in.

Captain Jorgensen was parked right where he had been told to park and wait. He'd seen a lot in the ten years he'd been captaining oil tankers in this part of the world, but nothing like this. Six hours later, things hadn't changed. The three ships waiting to leave were ready to head out, but they were afraid to go out alone. The US offered to escort the ships, using a destroyer for each ship leaving the Persian Gulf.

The Chinese task force was still moving slowly, taking the slow route between New Guinea and Australia. At their current rate of speed it would be another week before the ships crossed the Maldives and made it into the Arabian Sea.

The Sea Wolf had a good view of all the surface vessels. She also had a bead on four of the Chinese subs, as well as three American submarines and a British submarine. It was very crowded, but the knights had a plan of their own that they hoped would stop the violence.

Two hours later, they found the spot they were looking for. It was almost dead, as far as homing devices were concerned. Opening the outer doors, JD gave the order he had been thinking about for several days.

"Fire tubes one, two, three and four."

The submarine shuddered just a bit as each two-thousand-pound Mark 48 torpedo left the sub.

"Reload, using the SC modified Mark 48s."

"Already done, Captain."

"Fire tubes one, two, three, and four. Reload all tubes with two standard Mark 48s and two SC modified Mark 48s."

"Aye aye, Captain."

Again, the ship shuddered during the exchange of commands as the second four torpedoes left the tubes.

"Close outer doors."

"Aye aye, Captain." The team had responded without hesitation.

"Track the first four torpedoes."

"All four are heading to their designated locations at slow speed."

"Will they be heard, Jean?" asked Isaiah.

"No sir, they're moving low and slow, with no signature that anyone but us could read."

"Let me know when each one reaches their station," said JD.

"Aye aye, Captain," said Thump.

"Jean, get us out of here," said Isaiah.

"Aye aye, sir," came the instant reply.

Eight torpedoes slowly swam to their designated target locations. Within thirty minutes, all four had taken up position behind the known locations of the Chinese submarines. The other four had taken positions in the most likely locations of the other four Chinese submarines. Twenty minutes later Thump called out, "Number five has acquired a positive signal. Repeat, it has acquired a Chinese submarine signature right where we thought it would be and has set up in her baffles."

"Very good, Mr. Higgins. Keep me informed," said Isaiah.

"Aye aye, sir," came the reply again.

After an hour more, two of the remaining three torpedoes had acquired their targets and were behind them. Just about that time, one of the two tankers waiting outside the Gulf decided it was time to cross into the Gulf, thinking that doing so when the US escorted the first of the loaded ships out was a good idea. As the two ships headed out and the empty ship headed in, all hell broke loose. The sound of a submarine opening its outer doors sounded.

The escort destroyer, the USS Tuscany, radioed the tanker it was escorting to go full back; at the same time it attempted to radio the tanker going into the Gulf to push forward at full speed. Asking either to do what was asked was next to impossible. Both were about as maneuverable as elephants in an outhouse, and about as fast as a snail.

The Tuscany, however, did move quickly. She shot forward, ahead of the exiting tanker, and dropped a series of decoys to hide the mass of ships from any torpedo that might enter the water. At the same time that the Tuscany was dropping decoys, the Chinese officer aboard the Lotus Blossom was just about to order two torpedoes fired at the lumbering behemoth above.

Just as he opened his mouth to speak, the sound of a torpedo in the water behind them came over the sonar. The sonar man cried out, "Torpedo!" at the same time the sonar man aboard the Tuscany was yelling out the same thing, but in English.

The Lotus Blossom jumped forward and to the right. As they passed through the noise and bubbles created by the decoys, the Tuscany's first officer ordered evasive maneuvers. Turning starboard and pushing the throttle to full, the Tuscany nearly leaped out of the water.

Suddenly, the torpedo exploded just below the Lotus Blossom, and just behind her sail at a depth of four feet beneath her keel. The force of the torpedo caused almost all of it to push up. The keel of the submarine was literally broken into two pieces.

Aboard the Tuscany, Captain Jakees was counting his blessings because he'd turned to the starboard. The wave created by the blast pushed his puny tin can almost completely out of the water. Upon checking, it was found that the hull, while not breached, was buckled along a twenty-five-foot section. The tanker he'd been escorting had been lucky as well. While it hadn't gotten completely stopped, the "all back" command had saved the ship from being right on top of the explosion. As it was, the bulbous nose on the bow of the ship took most of the blast.

The Chinese aboard the Lotus Blossom hadn't been nearly so lucky. Almost all of them died instantly from the force of the blast. It was strong enough to blow the ship to pieces. The shock wave through the hull of the ship forced the air out of their lungs and had knocked them all instantly unconscious. It was over quickly.

Aboard the Tuscany, the sonar operator was practically deaf from the explosion. He'd been so absorbed in listening to the sonar, he'd forgotten to pull off the headphones. If it weren't for the built-in dampening of the headphones, he would have ended up deaf. The captain was yelling, the sonar operator was holding his ears, and the crew was excitedly running about the deck. The captain was trying to get the sonar operator to explain what had happened. A second man was shoved into the sonar operator's console, while the original operator came back to his senses.

Outside, the two oil tankers nearly ran together; only the expert experience of the two captains kept the two behemoths from colliding. The Tuscany was still moving at flank speed and heading for the coastline of Oman. After regaining his composure, the captain of the destroyer ordered a turn back to the main channel, and reduced speed to cruising speed, and went to active pinging. All around the ship was silence except for the sound of the last remnants of the submarine sinking to the bottom.

"Now what happened, Chief?" he asked as he turned facing the chief sonar operator.

"I can't be sure, sir, but I think the torpedo that was fired by the submarine turned on itself and blew itself to kingdom come," he replied still holding his ears.

"That doesn't make sense. Are you sure?" the captain asked.

"I can't be sure of anything until I listen to the tapes again, but I'm not sure I ever heard the torpedo launch. I heard the doors open, and then it was like the torpedo was in the water without ever hearing the torpedo getting pushed out of the tube." He stared into space as he relived the moment. "Sir," he said continuing, "I'm sure of it. I think there may be another sub out there that fired that torpedo. I don't think this one ever got a chance to fire."

"Very well, Chief. Get some rest. You won't do us any good until you get your ears back."

"Thank you, sir," replied the chief, saluting as he stood then turned to leave.

The captain ordered "all slow," and had the radio operator contact the oil tanker. Soon both ships had been checked for damage, and it was decided to continue the cruise out of the Arabian Sea.

Some 250 miles away, the Sea Wolf listened to the explosion and subsequent thrashing about of the remaining surface ships. Her torpedoes had been programmed to follow and monitor the Chinese submarines. When the message was sent that the Chinese sub was opening her outer doors, a short single transmission was sent back to the torpedo: "Fire." Six of the seven remaining torpedoes were still glued on their targets. The seventh torpedo still had not found its target.

Somewhere, probably within the confines of the Gulf of Aden, was the seventh Chinese submarine. It was only a matter of time before she was acquired. Inside the Red Sea, the seventh submarine waited for shipping that made it that far and was headed for the Suez Canal. With a little luck, Captain Li thought, our ship, "The Peoples Victory," will fire a torpedo of her own.

The position they were in was not conducive to receiving an accurate picture, but he was sure that only the Chinese were firing torpedoes, and he'd heard three explode so far. He'd been given clearance to fire hours ago, but he did not have a target as of yet. He'd lined up an empty tanker going through the straits at Djibouti an hour ago, but he knew he should wait until a tanker riding low in the water passed his sights. He could wait. He was to report his own firings within fifteen minutes of firing unless he was trapped or in danger of giving up his position.

Li decided to go to periscope depth and check for messages. He had restrained himself for hours, but with this last explosion he hoped to find out exactly what was going on. He took his time, making sure that fifteen minutes from the last explosion had elapsed before checking in himself. What he learned was that two ships had been sunk. Li reported the third explosion that he'd heard and was told that no one had reported in. That meant that whoever had fired the third shot had not had time to report as of yet.

On board the Tuscany, the captain had corralled his wayward oil tanker and was escorting her once again into the Arabian Sea. He'd radioed back to the Ronald Reagan and reported the incident. As a result, the small two-boat convoy would have a fighter and ASW helicopter escort all along the Indian coastline where she was headed. The tanker was headed for the west coast of the United States.

As they continued south along the coast, one of the ASW helicopters picked up the faint echo of a submarine. Relaying the information to the Ronald Reagan, the information went from there to the Stennis then on to the Prince Albert. The word echoed throughout the halls of government, and within minutes word came back to the chopper: it's not a friendly, so it must be a Chinese. The helicopter took off in pursuit, dropping a sonobouy where it had heard the echo. To their surprise, it disappeared. No further sound was heard.

Ten minutes later, another faint noise was heard further south. This time the Tuscany scooted out ahead of the tanker to chase down the sound. Keeping the last sound centered in her bearings, the ship charged southwest, listening for more sounds. Again, she picked up a faint sound and continued heading southwest toward it. She was getting closer. The helicopters were now out in front of the Tuscany, dropping sonobouys in an umbrella pattern out ahead of her. To her left, a stronger hit was received. The Tuscany jumped ahead, using two-thirds power. As she did, she turned onto a heading that would take her right over the latest hit.

Within two minutes she was on top of the last position. Listening again, the sub was clearly heading south-southeast at 20 knots. The Tuscany would be on top of her in no time. Radioing back to the Ronald Reagan, the captain of the Tuscany asked for instructions. She had left the tanker she was escorting to chase this bogey. Now she'd caught it, and he needed to know what his orders were for dealing with it. As he discussed the matter with the admiral, there was another explosion.

Onboard the tanker, headed for the US city of Portland, there was a huge explosion just off of her starboard stern for the second time in as many hours. The captain called for all stop and again asked for a detailed examination of her triple hull. The Chinese sub that had been trailing the ship had opened her outer doors, and like her sister ship had found itself being chased by an active torpedo.

No warning, no opening of another subs, doors, not even the sound of the torpedo being launched, it was as if it was just suddenly there. The Chinese sub had dodged the torpedo and gone to flank speed as soon as the sound of the propellers was heard, but the chase had lasted only 45 seconds. Like her sister ship, this Chinese marauder went down with no one close enough to know exactly what had happened.

Onboard the tanker, the captain once again received word that his ship, though dented along its stern, was not damaged enough to turn back. He wiped his brow and called for full speed ahead.

Onboard the Sea Wolf, the blinking Chinese submarine that was there a moment ago disappeared from the screen. The Sea Wolf had set herself on the bottom of the Arabian Sea, about 100 miles south- southwest of Bombay, India. From her position, 600 feet below the surface and some twenty-five miles out to sea, she was relatively alone. The closest ship to her was the Chinese tanker Chairman Mao, who was parked and waiting for word from her Chinese masters. While the Sea Wolf waited patiently, she had a communications buoy raised from a compartment within her sail.

She listened intently to the traffic being broadcast all across the sea. As she sat listening, the communications officer aboard the Sea Wolf, Lieutenant Sara Andersen, was paying particular attention to the information being sent back and forth by the Chinese. She had the recorder going and was homed in on the signals they were using. Feeding the recorded signals into the communications computer and its peripheral equipment yielded unexpected success. It seemed that the Chinese had failed to change their codes since their last known war games and those codes had been broken and documented within a week of their last activity.

Onboard the Tuscany, Captain Jakees called for flank speed and turned back toward the tanker that was several miles behind her. The helicopters continued dropping sonobouys all around the other submarine. He was thoroughly confused now. Two explosions, and two submarines down, another less than a mile away, and he hadn't even fired a shot in anger as of yet. It was all so confusing. As he turned back toward the tanker, the admiral aboard the USS Ronald Reagan was shouting at him, asking what was going on. He knew he couldn't explain it.

Captain Li listened intently, inside the confines of the Peoples Victory. He was at periscope depth and had his communications buoy floating above the ship. He was in communication. He contacted Admiral Yu once again with

word that he had heard another explosion. Admiral Yu had
problems of his own. He had lost communication with two
of his subs, and a third was surrounded by American
helicopters. It was time to contact Beijing and let them know
what he thought was happening.

Premier Chaing Xau picked up the phone that connected
him with the White House. It was answered immediately.

"Madam President," he said without the aid of a
translator.

"Chairman Xau," was the reply. "What is it that you are
up to?" she asked.

"I actually called to ask you the same thing, Madam
President. It seems that you are acting in an unprovoked
manner and sinking my submarines in the Sea of Arabia."

"Mr. Chairman, that is quite a charge that you are
leveling against the United States, and I must first tell you
that I am outraged by your charges, and second, I
categorically deny them."

"You deny that your Navy is involved in sinking my
submarines?"

"I thought I made that undeniably clear to you. Even so,
I will do you the kindness of answering your question again.
Yes, I deny it, and no, the United States had nothing to do
with the sinking of your submarines. According to our
captain on board the Tuscany, your torpedoes seem to be
exploding upon being fired."

"What are you saying, Madam President?"

"Premier Chaing Xau, are you deaf? I have twice now
told you that we have been monitoring your aggression on
the shipping coming out of the Persian Gulf, and have twice
been standing by listening as your torpedoes destroyed your
own ships. Do you understand now?"

The Premier was quiet. "Madam President, I don't know
what to say," he began.

"You can begin by telling me why you are sinking ships
of all nationalities in the Persian Gulf. Furthermore, you
can take my warning that if you should sink one of my

ships or one of the tankers heading for my country, I will consider it an act of premeditated war. Are we clear, Mr. Xau?" she said succinctly.

"Madam President, you have no right to..." she cut in on his blustering.

"Chairman Xau, I have said the way it is. Do not think I will fail to act. Is that perfectly clear? Any attack on any ship under our protection will instantly be regarded as an act of war and I will sink any and all Chinese warships in the area."

"If you do that, then a state of war will exist between us and attack would be imminent," said the chairman, blustering.

"Then you had better hope that none of your captains get antsy and shoot at one of our ships or one that is under our protection," said the president.

Without further word, the chairman hung up the phone. He knew how to read people, and he was confused. He had expected the Americans to admit to the attack on his submarines. He knew that this president couldn't lie convincingly, and she had convinced him that she was telling the truth. More so, she was not idly threatening to go to war. He had to be careful. What had happened, he wondered. Suddenly he knew he had to react instead of forcing the west to react. Who was playing in this field, if not the Americans? The British? They would be his next call. He reached for the phone to the prime minister. Before he could pick it up, it rang.

Now he was definitely a bit startled. Did they have his very office wired? He finished reaching for the phone.

"Yes, Prime Minister?" he said, his voice a bit shaky.

"Premier Xau, I need to understand what it is that you are up to in the Arabian Sea," he said.

"I was just about to call you, Mr. Prime Minister," said the heavy set Chinese premier. "We refuse to let the cartel force their will upon our people, sir, and we will not allow them to hold us hostage."

"That is all well and good, my good man, but what I want to know is why are you blowing things up down there, including your own submarines?"

"Mr. Prime Minister, I assure you we have nothing to do with the destruction of our submarines. In fact, I was going to ask you if you had anything to do with their destruction."

"Mr. Chairman, I assure you the British Navy has been watching the whole affair with quite a bemused stance. My admiralty assures me that it is your torpedoes that are blowing up your own submarines. I do want you to know that if you fire one of those things in our direction, we will blow the offending sub out of the water. Do you understand that, Mr. Chairman?"

"You will not threaten the Peoples Republic of China, sir," said the premier.

"I can, I have, and I will. Do you understand, sir? Any attack on English Shipping will constitute an Act of War with England."

"I will not accept this..." Again, he was cut off, this time by the English head of state.

"I don't care if you accept it or not, sir; it is the way it is. Don't attack us or our shipping and all will be okay. To do otherwise would be unwise on your account." And with those words the line went dead.

The premier was beyond insulted. He picked up the phone and threw it across the room. It smashed into a priceless vase from the Ming Dynasty, which made him all the more outraged. He literally screamed for his secretary and the Admiral of the Navy. Within moments both were standing in his presence.

"Admiral, recall your submarines and find out what is going on with them. I want to know what happened. I wanted deniability and instead I have two heads of state calling me to tell me what I don't know, telling me that my subs are shooting each other. What is going on?" He screamed.

"You!" he shouted at his male secretary. "Get me the general staff, now!" They both went scurrying out the door.

While the discussions were going on, a third explosion was heard in the Sea of Arabia. A third Chinese submarine had opened her outer doors to fire a torpedo at another ship. Word came down almost immediately to back off. Only five Chinese subs remained in the Arabian Sea area. By now they all knew that someone or something was hunting them. They had been told to back off, but they were in fear for their own lives.

Onboard the Tuscany, Captain Jakees was getting a better picture. The sonobouys that had been dropped ahead and behind the Chinese sub that he had chased down an hour before had painted a very clear picture. Not only was there a submarine in the picture, in its baffles was a picture of what had to be a torpedo. Upon further use of the sonobouys, it was clear that the torpedo was following the sub. Captain Jakees called the admiral and informed him. It was decided to keep it quiet until it could be found out whose torpedo was following the sub. After all, the torpedo was only good for an hour at most. Soon it would drop to the bottom of the sea floor, dead from lack of energy.

✠

In Tehran, President Ahmadinejad was hopping mad once again. He didn't know what was going on, but for nearly 12 hours now there had been no oil shipments out of the Persian Gulf. The schedule was shot, and his fellow members of the cartel were calling and complaining to him.

"Jimji, what is going on?" he screamed at his advisor.

"Oh Benevolent One, I have an idea that perhaps China is trying to interrupt shipments because of the embargo, sir," he said, keeping his voice low and steady.

"You are of course right, but what shall I do, Jimji? What shall I do?"

"Perhaps if you were to call another meeting of the cartel and see what it is that the other members want to do," suggested Jimji.

"I don't care what those fools want. I want to hurt those Chinese thieves. I want my money back."

"Of course, My President, but it might be a good idea to at least listen to what the cartel has to say. It is, after all, important to our future to remain in their graces, if only for appearances," said the doting Jimji.

"Of course you are right," the president said, "but above all we must get even with those Chinese bastards."

"What do you have in mind, My President?" asked Jimji.

"Perhaps another try at dumping some of our magic dust into the Beijing water supply," the ugly little man sneered. "Call the cartel and set up a meeting."

"Yes sir," said Jimji.

Aboard the Sea Wolf, discussions about the next slate of operations were under way.

"I'll need four volunteers," said Isaiah, "for the next two missions. It will be dangerous and time consuming. Quiet will have to be maintained for long periods of time on one and daring and the ability to speak Farsi for the other."

"We have several people onboard who speak Farsi," said Jean.

"As far as the others, I know the perfect two for you," said Thump.

"Who?" asked JD.

"Thump and me," said Dinger.

"I don't know if I can let you two..." JD started.

"JD, you can't say no to us. You know that there are a dozen others just as capable as us to run things here," said Thump.

"Okay, Thump" Isaiah said. "Point taken. You two will do for the first assignment, but what about the second?"

"What exactly are you looking for, Isaiah?" asked Dinger.

"I need someone who can infiltrate the staff of President Ahmadinejad," said Isaiah. "I think a woman would be best."

"I can think of two off the top of my head that would be perfect," said Thump.

"Are you thinking of Anna and Josie?" asked Dinger.

"Exactly," said Thump.

"Can they pass for Iranian?" asked Isaiah.

"Either one, with a little makeup to darken their skin, could pass," Thump replied.

"How about their Farsi?" asked JD.

"Perfect," said Thump.

"Okay, get them up here and let's see what they think," said Isaiah.

Two minutes later the two ladies were seated in the library with the rest of the group around the central table. Without question the two women volunteered without even asking about the mission. After it was described to them, they were even more enthusiastic to be a part of it. They asked for more information about the plan. Isaiah told them the whole plan. They were ecstatic.

Four hours later, the upgraded mini-sub was fully loaded with water, food, and everything necessary for a two-week stay at the bottom of the Arabian Sea. Thump and Dinger entered the mini-sub and the chamber was slowly flooded. After flooding, the outer door on the starboard side folded down onto the sea floor and the mini-sub swam out into the darkness. The two men were given one of the ULF phones with which to communicate, and as they headed out, they did an inspection of the Sea Wolf, sending back word that everything looked good.

As it swam off, JD and Isaiah also checked the video feed. As they did so, the phone rang. It was Dave, reporting back that the Chinese were backing off. He was sure that it was because of the work they'd done. Even though he wasn't sure what all had gone on, he wanted to thank JD and Isaiah for pushing the Chinese into the position of negotiating.

JD and Isaiah listened politely and thanked Dave for the information. They knew the time had come to quit giving any more information. The connection ended, and Dave realized that even though he had thought things were through, JD and Isaiah had other plans. He wasn't sure what they were, but he prayed that he hadn't created a monster. Slowly, he mulled over the situation and put the phone back into his pocket. That's when the president called.

"Dave, the Iranians haven't learned a thing from this. That little twit Ahmadinejad is still threatening the Chinese," President Beechum ranted as she paced back and forth in the Oval Office.

"Debra, we've been lucky so far with those exploding torpedoes, I don't think we have any more luck coming our way. What do you want us to do?" he asked.

"Speaking of lucky…Dave, just what did occur with those torpedoes?" she honed in on the "facts" he'd just mentioned.

"Madam President, I assure you that our military or CIA had nothing to do with those accidents," said her national security advisor.

"Dave, that sounds a bit rehearsed to me, but I'm willing to live with it for now, as long as you assure me that what you just said is completely true."

"I can, Debra. I promise," said Dave.

"Okay. Well, as for your question, I don't know. I was hoping you had a rabbit or two up your sleeve," she said quietly.

"You could try sending in the Secretary of State to the next cartel meeting. The prince owes us, and so do the Kuwaitis," said Dave. "We could try forcing their hand a little, especially since all the problems seem to have erupted. We could show them that the Chinese are still moving their direction with an attack force that will be there inside a week."

"All good ideas and we'll do that, Dave, but we need a backup plan. The last vote was 5 to 4 with Syria, Iraq, Iran, Afghanistan, and Pakistan voting as a block, following Iran's lead. There is nothing that tells me that would change on another vote," said the president.

"So we have to change at least one of their minds then," said Dave. "I'll work on a plan and get back to you as soon as I have one, Madam President."

The phone went dead on both ends and Dave's first instinct was to call JD and ask for another favor. It would be so easy for him to just blow up one little oil tanker that belonged to Syria or Iraq and everything would change. At the same time, he was restrained. He needed deniability. The conversation he'd just had with Debra proved it. He removed his hand from the phone he'd been fumbling with absently in his pocket. Instead, he picked up his desk phone and pushed the button connecting him with the CIA and then connected the STU scrambler to assure privacy.

Chapter 10

How to Disable the Enemy

Thump and Dinger swam to "the bottom of the pool," as they called it. Hovering just a few feet above the bottom of the sea and traveling at 25 knots was dangerous, so they had a very high-powered light on that showed the sea floor in front of them for a distance of more than 50 yards. Besides the light, a short-range radar swept the distance in front of the swift mini-sub and painted a bright red and black image of the sea floor in front of them on a screen directly below the window in front of the steering column.

The sub could run without a pilot and without fear of crashing, but Thump loved to guide the mini-sub by himself. Sitting in the command seat, he loved the view of the ocean in front of him. It made him feel like a modern day Jakeah, sitting in the mouth of a whale, but with the ability to guide it in any direction he desired. As they went over a wide chasm that stretched down out of sight, he took the opportunity to spin the sub in what an airplane pilot would call a "barrel roll." Dinger had been in his cot behind the front seat and was dumped unceremoniously out of the bunk and onto the ceiling as Thump shouted a rebel yell.

"Do that again, you ape, and I'll test out my home run swing on your skull," he said with a surly grin on his face.

"Sorry, man, but I just had to. This little sub is so cool. It's better than flying a jet fighter," said Thump.

"Yeah, I know, but just remember, you got passengers back here...okay?" Dinger said, picking the cot up off its side and placing it back on its feet.

The two were the closest of friends, despite the mild-mannered jabs back and forth at each other. They had a friendship that went back to their times together in Junior High, and nothing could ever separate them.

From the location of the Sea Wolf, just south of the parked location of the Lotus Blossom, was a distance of about 150 Kilometers. At their current speed they had calculated that they would arrive under the keel of the Lotus Blossom in six hours and fifteen minutes. With a slight current against them, it took six hours and twenty-six minutes. This would be the first real trial of the upgraded anti-matter ray, and everyone on both the Sea Wolf and the mini-sub were anxious to see it work.

Olaf had predicted that it would take just a one-second burst on each leaf of the four-bladed props to cut the blades away from the shaft. He also believed that it would take a four-second burst of the ray to cut through the shaft itself. "Six of one, half dozen of the other," he had said quaintly when asked which would be the best way to disable the ship. JD followed up the first question with another.

"Just in case we need to some time, how long to drill a hole through each of the three hulls of one of these ships? How long to put a hole in her all the way to the interior?"

"Well, basing my calculations on each hull being one inch steel and at least six inches of empty space in between, I'd say no more than two and a half seconds. If you went longer, you'd probably punch a hole right through the hull and up through the top hatch cover. If you were unlucky enough to go through into the superstructure, there's no telling what you'd hit—or who," replied the scientist. "That is if you don't get unlucky and hit a brace in between the hulls. If you do that…"

"I've got it, Olaf. Thanks. About an inch and a half a second through solid steel," said JD.

"Right," said Olaf.

"Okay, guys, it's your call. Just make sure you're far enough away that when the blade or the props fall you're not underneath them, okay?" said JD to the two men in the mini-sub.

"Got it, Captain," said Dinger, who was operating the directional ray.

"It's pretty dark outside," said Isaiah. "You aren't using the light, are you?" he asked.

"Thanks, sir," said Thump, switching off the white light and going to the IR light. The camera on the view screen switched to IR and the blades became clear from over 500 feet away. Slowly, the mini-sub crept up on the unmoving giant. When they reached a distance of 75 feet behind the ship and at a depth of 100 feet, the mini-sub stopped.

"Permission to disable the tanker," said Dinger into the openness of the cabin.

"Permission granted. Proceed, Lieutenant," came the reply from JD.

Dinger put the crosshair on the first blade of the first of the two giant bronze propellers. Interestingly enough, the IR display showed very little heat being created in the cut, no steam from water being vaporized, nor even a bright glowing edge where the blade was cut. If the IR display was to be believed, the temperature of the blade had barely changed. The molecules had become agitated to the point of releasing their bond with the adjacent molecule, and the result was a fine bronze powder that fell, along with the first blade.

In the water between the scope from which the beam had been fired and the blade was a stream of bubbles where the hydrogen and oxygen atoms had separated themselves. Olaf took note that this would be an excellent way to create oxygen and hydrogen from sea water. He scratched the idea on a note pad.

Inside the mini-sub, Dinger smiled at the ease of cutting through the bronze blade.

"Exactly four seconds," he said, smiling into the camera.

"Any kind of push back or recoil from the firing of the weapon?" Isaiah asked.

"None, sir," the two sailors said in unison.

"Very good. Continue with the mission," Isaiah said.

A minute and a half later, the last of the blades fell to the sea floor three hundred feet below. The mini-sub continued on its mission. It would take another two hours to reach the entrance to the Persian Gulf, and another six or seven to make it to the Iranian pumping station. They had been warned about the mines in the Persian Gulf that had been laid by both Iran and Iraq. Those mines were about to become useless to everyone.

Olaf was very pleased with the results of the "experiments," as he called them. He had been exact on his prediction of the beams' power, and now he had a few more ideas to try out. He had so many from the power at his fingertips... He was living a dream.

"By the way, JD, Isaiah, I have two new toys for you guys." He puffed up his chest as he spoke.

"Olaf, I can't imagine what more you could give us," said JD. "You've done so much already, I'm almost afraid to ask what else you've thought of."

"Well, JD, it was actually Isaiah's idea. I just finally got the time to work on it a little." Olaf whipped a small fist-sized object from behind his back as he spoke. "I give you—the airborne disruptor ray. It will fit into the same space and harness as the fuselage-mounted camera in the nose section of the drone. I've already taken the liberty of making it follow the other camera that is mounted further back in the wing section of the fuselage. The center point of where the second camera points will be where the beam is aimed, so basically, you can use the second camera as a targeting system for the beam."

Olaf was grinning from ear to ear at his own ingenuity.

"At what range is it centered?" asked Isaiah,

"No particular range. It adapts for distance changes automatically. Just don't try and target it inside of two feet," he said. "I can't get the front mounting to come into focus at any distance closer than that."

"Olaf, that's wonderful!" said Isaiah.

"You just don't know how much this is going to help us," said JD.

"That's not all, Ladies and Gentlemen," said Olaf, bending at the waist like a side show barker. "Thump, Dinger, are you still with us out there?" Olaf continued.

"You bet, Olaf," said Thump.

"You two will be especially happy for my next invention." Reaching behind him, he withdrew from his belt a futuristic looking device that resembled a flip phone. Slowly, he opened it up and pressed a button and then closed it.

"Ladies and Gentlemen, I give to you the phaser gun," he said, extending it in the palm of his hand.

"Like on Star Trek? That kind of phaser gun?" said Isaiah.

"Aye, Cap'n," said Olaf, imitating Scotty. "I actually used my old cell phone key pad and camera optics for the aiming device the power settings. There are two settings you change at the same time. The power settings are one through nine and the beam width, also one through nine. A power setting of one with a width of nine would be lowest power at the widest possible dispersal. With that setting, at ten feet the shooter would hit a nine foot circle with enough power to disorient any one in the circle. The other end of the spectrum would be nine-one. At that setting, at ten feet, the shooter would drill a hole through the person it hit about six inches in diameter. In fact, it would drill a hole six inches in diameter through solid steel in about five seconds. As you can see, it's not nearly as powerful as the mounted units, but I have to use NiCad batteries that are six volts and only ten milli-amps," the scientist explained.

The group was stunned to silence. For nearly thirty seconds no one said anything.

"Well," said Olaf, "what do you think?"

"Olaf, this is amazing!" said JD.

"It's more than amazing," said Isaiah. "It's stupendous, it's fantastic, it's marvelous. it's, it's, it's...I can't think of a word that it is... It is the greatest thing I've ever seen."

"It's yours," said Olaf. "I wanted to thank you guys for letting me be a part of this and, well, I knew you'd want something like this, so this is my way of saying thanks." Blushing slightly, he turned and headed back toward his lab.

"Olaf," JD said, stopping him, "thank you."

Olaf nodded and turned back to his path to the lab. He had more ideas and he didn't want to let them get away from him.

Isaiah was gingerly holding the small phone in his hand.

"I assume it's on," he said, looking it over.

On the top under the screen was a button that was normally used to take a picture.

"I assume that's the fire button." He continued looking at the device. Opening it up, he found that Olaf had instructions taped to the screen.

To change a setting you must change both power and width. Press the "power" setting first, then the "width" setting, followed by "enter."

To turn on, press "pwr" button and hold until the light turns green.

To turn off, press "pwr" button and hold until the light goes out.

To fire, close the unit cover, aim, using the lens at the top of the phone, and press the "ENT" button next to the outside screen.

"Well, that is very clear," he said, pressing the "pwr" button until the green light went out. "JD, I think Anna and Josie will need this more than anyone else in the foreseeable future. What do you think?" asked Isaiah.

"Agreed, Isaiah. When do we put them ashore?" he asked.

"It's been nearly twenty-four hours since the last attack; I think it's time to move now. What do you think?" Isaiah replied.

"Okay, but let's be very very careful. I don't want anything to happen to any of our people."

"Me either, JD," said Isaiah.

The Sea Wolf gently lifted off the floor of the sea a few minutes later in response to JD's orders. While JD took the con, Isaiah called for Anna and Josie. He asked them to meet him in the science lab with Olaf and his two assistants. Five minutes later they were all there.

Olaf had a room set up with varying widths and thicknesses of steel plates. The two women looked at Isaiah like he'd been watching Star Trek too much when he pulled the cell phone out of his back pocket and opened it up.

"About to beam up?" asked Anna.

It was part of her playful personality that had gotten her into trouble with the Army. She'd been a successful candidate for the Rangers, but had been labeled a troublemaker because she just couldn't keep the comments that popped into her mind inside her mind; they just kind of popped out of her mind and out of her mouth automatically. As soon as she'd said it, she closed her eyes and began to mentally kick herself.

Instead of being upset, Isaiah looked at her and laughed.

"Now how silly would you feel if I said, 'Party of three to beam up, Scotty'?" said Isaiah, laughing. The tension was instantly gone.

"I'm sorry, sir. I don't know why I said that," she began her apology.

"Don't apologize, Anna. It's the first thing I thought of when Olaf here gave it to me as well," he said. "But for the record, it's not a communicator, it's a phaser."

Anna laughed again, as did Josie. This time Isaiah didn't laugh. "You mean it really is a phaser?" Josie asked.

"Yep," said Isaiah, "but phaser is really not the right word, I guess. It's just the first thing that came to mind. It is really a hand-held disruptor ray. HHDR," he said, using the initials. "I guess we could call it a 'header' or maybe 'heater' for short," said Isaiah.

"A heater. I like it," said Olaf. "Yes, from now on we'll call them 'heaters.'" He burst out into another grin. "Have I told you what a genius I am, ladies?" Olaf said, smiling broadly.

"Not in the last five minutes," Anna quipped back at him, "but if you tell me again right now, I'll believe you," she said, causing Olaf to grin again.

"Ladies, you are going into action very soon. I believe that you'll need this more than anyone else in the foreseeable future, so I'm giving it to you with these instructions. Familiarize yourself with how it works and at what range you need to be to make it work safely. Olaf should be able to help there, and secondly, get yourselves ready to use it to kill if necessary, but also, use your best judgment. It can be used to disorient your victim. Make sure that is what you want if you're going to use that setting. If unsure, set it to kill," said Isaiah seriously.

"Aye, sir," they said together.

"Olaf," said Isaiah, "any chance you can get another of these ready in the next four hours?"

"Have you got another cell phone I can cannibalize?" Olaf asked.

"I do, sir," said Anna, "just like this one."

"Great," said Isaiah. "I assume they use the regular charger for the batteries?"

"Yep, but it only takes about ten minutes for a full charge and then the charge should be good for a full hour of discharge at full strength, and nearly ten hours at low strength," said Olaf.

"Simply amazing," said Isaiah.

"Simply super conductors," said Olaf.

"Ladies," said Isaiah, "get to testing the weapon. You

may need it on your mission. I hope not, but I wouldn't bet against it."

"Aye, sir," they said again in unison.

The Sea Wolf was well underway by the time Isaiah made it back to the control room. Looking at the 3-D display, he could see four of the remaining Chinese submarines, four US submarines, a British sub and the regular host of warships plying the waters of the Arabian Sea, Persian Gulf and Red Sea.

"I see we still haven't got a lock on that last Chinese sub," he said to JD.

"Nope," came the reply. "What do you think we should do next?" asked JD.

"Well, I think we need to bring the drone in for the refit, then probably pick her up about the same time we put Anna and Josie ashore. We also need to put out our messages to both the Chinese and the Iranians. I don't think we should do that until we've got the drone back up in the sky. I'd say four hours from now we drop off the ladies, take another hour to refit the drone, refill its tanks and an hour to get back into position. So I guess we should send the message in about six hours."

"That's what I was thinking too, Isaiah," said JD.

"Great. That gives me a little time to rest," said Isaiah.

"Go ahead, Isaiah. I get to sleep when you get the con," he said laughing.

"I'm your man," said Isaiah. Isaiah headed for his bed.

He still couldn't believe the comfort on board the submarine. He had a full size bed, bolted to the floor, but with a nice mattress and bedclothes. A 37-inch monitor was on the wall at the foot of his bed. A wireless keyboard with a built-in track ball was on the edge of his desk beside the bed. A soft reclining swivel chair was pushed into the leg hole of his desk, waiting for him to sit down. The wall in front of the desk also had a 37-inch monitor on it. With the switch of a button on the keyboard, the active monitor swapped from one to the other. On the side of the keyboard was a disk player. It accepted either CDs or DVDs. The data was transferred wirelessly. There was also a USB port on the other side of the keyboard. The CPU was under the desk inside a padded case that bolted to the floor. A cooling fan pulled hot air out of the plexiglass case with its strips of soft foam rubber that held the CPU in place when the case was shut.

Isaiah was amazed. He lay down on the bed and pulled up the overall view of the Arabian Sea. He pulled up another window and began composing a letter to Marisa. It is funny, he thought. He'd lost all track of time in this windowless environment. With that thought he pulled up the view from the drone. It was pitch black outside. Nighttime, he thought. At least eight hours ahead of the east coast and another four hours to the west coast. It would be light there.

Thinking of Marisa at school gave him peace of mind. He wrote to her as if he were talking to her. He laughed and told jokes and let her know that he missed her. Without realizing it, an hour had passed and he had written a letter several pages long. Without doing a spell check, he pressed the "send" button, and went back to jumping from view to view. He particularly liked the view from the mini-sub. Those guys were having a great ride. He envied them. All they had to do was listen and do what they were told. He and JD weren't having that kind of fun.

They were both a little stressed, and it showed on both their faces. They were responsible for the lives of all those on board the ship, and their deaths would be on JD and Isaiah's heads if any were lost. It was a heavy responsibility. As if reading his mind, there was a note from JD.

"Come to my stateroom when you get this."

Isaiah sat up on the edge of the bed, contemplating not going until after he got some real sleep, but the urgency was undeniable. Isaiah opened his door and went across the hall to JD's cabin, much like Isaiah's but with room for a table and six chairs, JD sat with his feet propped on the table, his eyes fixed on the display at the end of the room against the wall.

"Why are you still up, Isaiah?" he asked as Isaiah ambled over and sat in the chair opposite him.

"Couldn't sleep. What about you?" Isaiah asked.

"Me either," said JD. "You as worried about all these people as I am?" JD continued on.

"I guess so. It's got me where all I do is see what could go wrong. I'm worried all the time that I'm going to make a decision that's going to get someone killed," said Isaiah.

"Remember the advice you gave me when we first started this thing a couple of months back?" asked JD.

"I'm not sure. It seems like I've been giving a lot of advice and all I do is worry about whether it's right or not," said Isaiah.

"Take your time; think about your decision, and then don't worry about it. If you take the time to make the decision right, you'll make the right decision, or something like that," said JD.

"Yeah, I remember," said Isaiah. "Seems like it was you who was worried about making right decisions back then."

"Yeah, and what you said was right on, Isaiah. You're doing fine. We wouldn't be here and we wouldn't be making a difference if it weren't for you and the decisions you are making right," said JD. "I can't say it any clearer, man. You are doing everything right and making good decisions. Even so, it doesn't mean that some of our people might not die in the execution of their duties. But they all know that; and they all are ready, willing, and able to go on with their assignments. I can see the worry on your face, Isaiah, and I want you to know that it's okay. It may all crash around us tomorrow, big guy, but we all know the score, and we all have faith in you and your plans. So keep up the good work, okay?" said JD, slapping his friend on the back.

Isaiah's head drooped a bit and he let out a heavy sigh. "Okay, brother, I understand. It's not easy, but for what it's worth, thanks for the vote of confidence," said Isaiah.

"It's not just me, brother. It's everyone on the boat. We all believe in you," said JD.

Isaiah's head came up. "Everyone?"

"Yes, everyone, brother. They all believe in you and are all worried about you. I've had four people come to me asking if you've had any rest since all this started a day and a half ago. They've noticed that you've been on duty the whole time and they're worried for you. They know that they need you," JD said.

"Thanks, JD. Tell them thank you as well. They're right; it's time for me to turn out the lights for a while and get some rest. Just one more thing—what about you, partner?"

"I got six hours sleep just about twelve hours ago so I'm doing all right. You just worry about you for now," said JD. "When you get up I'll be ready to get some rest."

"Okay, JD, but promise me you'll call if there is an emergency" said Isaiah, getting up and heading back across the hall.

"I promise," said JD.

Isaiah entered his cabin and said, "Computer, set alarm for eight hours."

The computer responded by displaying an alarm clock on the screen, showing an alarm setting for 10:22 Zulu time, and by replying out loud "Ten Twenty Two, Alarm Set" in a slightly Japanese-tinged feminine English voice. "Lights out" said Isaiah next and the lights faded to a point where they were completely out. "Computer sleep" was his final command, and after saying it, the screen went blank, and all was completely quiet. Within two minutes Isaiah was in a deep sleep.

Across the hall, JD received a note from the computer in the same Japanese-tinged English voice. "Commander Diego is resting normally. Will there be any other monitoring necessary?"

"No, computer," said JD. He smiled, knowing that if Isaiah knew about this feature he'd have been monitoring JD as well. JD was tired too, but his chance to sleep would come soon enough. Leaving his cabin, he walked slowly to the library.

The message came at 0400 Zulu time. "Prepare the ship to be boarded by the Army of the Peoples Republic at 10:00."

Captain Jorgensen, aboard the Mao, tried to reply but got no answer. After keying the mike for the third time, he gave up. He knew his superiors didn't really care what he thought about his orders, but inside he was seething. His boat was meant for the carrying of oil, not soldiers. Still, he knew he had to follow orders.

6:30 arrived without any further explosions in the Arabian Sea. The Chinese task force had pushed around the horn of India at a faster rate than had been expected. Moving now at a pace better than thirty knots, the slower oilers and several troop ships were lagging behind. Still, it was an intimidating display of force. The Chinese aircraft carrier began its air flight operations as soon as they rounded the tip of India.

The Chinese Hongzhaji Dian, a Tuepelov 16 version HD61 bomber that had been modified for electronic surveillance flew in lazy circles above the outer edges of the task group. While it continued on its circular pattern, four Jianjiji MiG 17PFs made by Shenyang, continued their pattern of reconnaissance as well. While the four fighters swept by the main task group, on the deck of the Chinese aircraft carrier four Chengdu Jianjiji MiG 29Ls warmed up their engines in preparation for takeoff.

On board the John C Stennis, an E3C Hawkeye took to the skies. Preceding it in the air were two F-15 Strike Eagle's which circled the Hawkeye until it reached its cruising altitude of 36,000 feet. The sky above the Arabian Sea was quickly becoming crowded.

The British Royal Navy continued operations above the Chinese submarine that the helicopters of the Ronald Reagan had been chasing all over the eastern Arabian Sea. Now, two Linx Mk 8 ASW Helicopters from the Prince Albert were dropping sonobouys on either side of the first of the Chinese submarines while two Merlin HM-MK1 helicopters were chasing a second Chinese submarine flushed out by the chasing of the first sub. A wing of Harriers GR-7s from the HMS Illustrious were circling in the sky as well.

The Chinese MiGs and the Harriers were passing close to each other, getting closer with each pass. They soon would be joined by a group of four F-15s as well. While the E3C was watching and doing its best to keep the high-strung fighter jocks away from each other, there was the continuous threat that someone would make a mistake and the sky would rain fire across the Arabian Gulf.

The Chinese premier had sent messages to both the prime minister and the President of the United States to not interfere with their rightful actions and to keep away from Chinese military assets lest they be mis-identified as attacking aircraft and shot down.

The Americans and British both sent replies to the Peoples Republic of China, demanding that they stand down from military operations in the area. Since there were nations in the area that were under the protection of both the American and British Military, any aircraft or naval asset approaching the nations under said protection would be fired upon as enemy combatants. Any attack on either British or American military assets would be considered an Act of War. The chess game had begun in earnest.

While the war of words was beginning across the airwaves of the Atlantic, a young Chinese warrior, Lieutenant Yau Yung Te, was taking off in his MiG 29L from the deck of his home ship, the Aircraft Carrier Varyag, a Soviet cruiser that had been rebuilt in the Ukraine. Now under Chinese control, the Nikolayev shipyard had spent nearly ten years refitting the ship and turning her into the PLA's only operating aircraft carrier.

Along with his wingman, Lieutenant Wo Shan, Lieutenant Yau was looking forward to dueling with the heathen British and their Harriers. The British were fond of talking about the invincibility of their famous jump jets, but Yau Te was equally fond of his MiG29L. It too was capable of vertical takeoff and landing, and had better fighting specs than the aging British fighter. Yau Te was barely five feet tall. Smaller than most of his comrades, Yau had been given the nickname of " 矮子 " or "Shorty."

While he hated the nickname, he let it motivate him to the top of his class. In training, he had beaten each and every one of his peers, the last three in record time. It was a recorded fact that upon starting the exercise he had shot down each of the last three of his adversaries in less than 90 seconds. He had learned that upon passing his adversary in a head-on move by going vertical and using his landing thrusters to help push him over, he could rotate back to a horizontal but upside down position that put him on his opponents' tail if his opponent tried the normal turn move to position himself to chase the MiG. By using this move he had confused the pursuing classmates and ultimately turned inside them as they searched forward for his MiG29. Ninety seconds to victory was all it had taken each time, and for his reward he had been given the opportunity of flying the number 1 spot on board his country's only aircraft carrier.

British. He and Wo Shan were naturally exhilarated by the power of the moment, but on top of that, they were riding an unnatural high. The Chinese government had a practice of keeping their fighter pilots on a steady diet of anabolic steroids and gene therapy to keep their fighters at peak physical strength, as well as designer drugs given before each mission to enhance the pilot's reflexes and agility in flying the jet.

Unfortunately, all of these drugs tended to enhance the pilots aggressive behavior as well as enhancing their physical reflexes. After a few months of the steroids and gene therapy the pilots became violent and confrontational. The speed pills that were given before each mission tended to make them feel invulnerable to any attack. The combination added up to a pilot on the edge, begging for a fight.

As the two pilots made a pass by the aircraft carrier, they signaled the Tuepelov HD61 that they were available and ready for vectoring. Instantly, a young ensign operating one of the sensitive radar systems answered the call sign from the two lieutenants. He replied that there were two

British Harriers two hundred miles out, but approaching from the northwest on a heading of 160. The ensign pointed the two MiG29s in their direction with instructions to intercept on that heading before the two Harriers came within the 100-mile limit.

Onboard the Tuepelov, another young ensign sitting next to the one controlling the two MiG's asked who the two pilots were.

"Lieutenants Yau Te and Wo Shan," said the first.

"Yau Te," said the second. "They call him the 'Shorty,' or 'The Short Devil.'"

"Really!" said the first. "For what reason?"

"Because he is such a short man," said the second, "but a real killer, supposedly."

"Oh," replied the first.

Then, as a gesture of good will, he keyed his mike to speak once more with the team of fighters and said, "Good hunting, Shorty."

He had no idea the effect it would have on the young lieutenant. In the cockpit, Yau Te turned nearly purple with rage over the use of the name by a lowly ensign. Without clicking on the radio to respond, he shouted every curse he knew into the cockpit.

"Damn them!" he said into the early afternoon sunshine. "Damn them all!"

Sixty feet away, his wingman saw his lead pounding the canopy with his fists and yelling into the early afternoon sunshine and he smiled at the frustration he knew Yau Te was feeling. He knew the young ensign had meant well, but looking at Yau, he was afraid for the young ensign's life when Yau caught up with him.

Onboard the Sea Wolf, a beautiful picture of the four Chinese subs, the three American subs, and a British sub was painted by the continual pinging going on by the sonobouys being dropped by the ASW helicopters chasing about. The surface ships were running about, feinting and thrusting like huge swords wielded by nautical giants playing in the ocean.

Forty-eight warships were now in the vicinity, with eight others lagging behind the Chinese task force. There was getting to be no room to maneuver the ships. One of the Chinese warships, a missile cruiser, broke away from the main taskforce and headed for the Chairman Mao.

Just after 0800 Zulu time, the cruiser arrived at the location of the anchored Mao. Several small boats were sent from the cruiser to the Mao. Onboard each were thirty of the PLA's most highly trained army fighters. They, along with the weapons they brought aboard, twenty SAM missiles and the equipment to launch them, were to be taken to the Iranian oil platform in Iranian waters and they were to take control of it.

Captain Jorgensen was furious. He had his orders, but he was completely furious at having been ordered to use his ship as a landing craft for some elite attack force. He jumped on board the first returning boat headed for the cruiser. After twenty minutes of heated conversation with the captain of the cruiser, it was made abundantly clear to him that another word of complaint would ensure his removal as captain and immediate replacement by the cruiser's second in command.

Turning around, Captain Jorgensen stormed back to his own ship. When he arrived back on board, he found one hundred and fifty black- clad army soldiers crowding the area below decks. His foredeck, usually clear of all debris and clean as the proverbial whistle, was littered with boxes of munitions and equipment. The entire operation had taken just under an hour. The cruiser captain gave him orders to raise anchor and make way for the Iranian oil platform. Captain Jorgensen gave the commands.

Just as the ballet of movement was going on above, the Sea Wolf parked herself on the bottom of the sea floor just inside the Persian Gulf. Using the second of the mini-subs, this one not yet modified, a pilot and co-pilot took the two ladies, Anna and Josie, to a very slightly used port area along the Iranian coastline. They'd have to let them off in the shallows close to the shore, but it would be a little way from any inhabited area.

JD contacted Dave, and in turn Dave talked with his CIA chief Tom Putnam. After some mis-information about whom the two women worked for, Dave told Tom they were Mosad, Dave set up a meeting. The two women were met just a half mile inland by two of Tom's deepest cover assets.

They were armed with their new "heaters" and make up kits. Even in Iran, it was not entirely unheard of for women to carry purses, and in their purses to carry makeup— powder, but no rouge or lipstick. Armed in such manner and dressed so as to blend in with the local population, the two women headed into Tehran with their new escorts whom they learned were Ahmed and Achmed. As they hopped into the old truck with Ahmed and Achmed, the mini-sub turned and swam slowly back toward the Sea Wolf. That's when things went wrong.

After sending a message back to the Sea Wolf that the drop-off and reception had gone according to plan, the little submarine turned and went as deep as the bay allowed. The two pilots had an idea they passed back to Olaf. They thought it would be a nice touch for a sub to drive itself up onto the beach.

While they were describing their idea to Olaf, an Iranian scout plane was flying along the coastline. The shadow of the small submarine was visible from its height of 5,000 feet. Although the plane was un-armed it did have a radio, which the pilot used to send a message to a harbor patrol boat that was close enough to give chase. The patrol boat was in a state of readiness. They were anxiously looking for Chinese submarines in their waters, but they had never expected one this close to shore. While the mini-sub was somewhat stealthy, it was not meant to be invisible like the Sea Wolf. The scout plane continued to circle the little sub while the patrol boat sped to the destination the plane had excitedly radioed to the waiting boat.

In less than ten minutes the patrol boat was over the last location where the submarine had been seen. Inside the Sea Wolf, the quickly moving patrol boat had been spotted by Jean's counterpart, Milt. Milt quickly radioed the two pilots in the mini-sub. They in turn went to the deepest part of the little bay and then went silent. The patrol boat had some decent sonar gear on board, but nothing as new as what was on the mini-sub. Every time the patrol boat moved in their direction, the mini-sub quietly headed in the opposite direction, keeping two steps ahead of their every move. It would only be luck for the patrol boat to ever catch them.

Turning back toward the Sea Wolf, the mini-sub moved quietly across the Gulf toward the island nation of Qatar. As it crept across the gulf, a US destroyer, the Beatty, had been watching the patrol boat chasing about along the coastline with interest. After watching for a while, the Beatty started moving along a parallel path to the patrol boat.

Milt pointed out the array of ships blocking the return path of the mini-sub, but after a little discussion it was decided to try and run through the blockade and sneak back to their home. The Beatty was running at about 10 knots, just fast enough to maintain steerage and still keep the sonar array behind the ship taut and manageable.

Just as they started into a 180 degree port turn meant to enable them to get another sweep down the middle of the Gulf, the destroyer caught just the slightest bounce of a return from the mini-sub. Hurriedly, the captain ordered another 180 degree port turn. That was the captain's first mistake. By turning to port once again he turned into his trailing sonar array and managed to catch the last quarter of the array and sever it. His sonar operator was rewarded with an instant problem with the remaining 3/4 of the array.

Noise generated by the tangled wires and the length of the array caused the operator to throw his headset in disgust. Inside the mini-sub they heard the swishing of the wire tangled around the propeller shaft and were intrigued by the sound. They weren't sure what the sound was, and they had lost the sound they had identified as the Beatty.

At this point, even the Sea Wolf was confused as to what had happened and where exactly the Beatty had gone.

On board the Inchon, the sonar operator began making adjustments to filter out the constant noise and to get back to the sound that had caught their attention. Working quickly, the sonar operator had it back up and running within ten minutes. The mini-sub had decided to go quiet and sit on the bottom until it figured out what the new sound was. Instead of going on when they were safe, they had made the mistake of playing dead until they were free to find the time they needed. After deciding that the sound was indeed the Beatty and redefining its new sound signature, they continued on their way just about the same time that Beatty's sonar engineer had their sonar equipment back online and working.

The mini-sub began once again to head for Qatar, and the Beatty once again picked up the noise and headed for it and began calling for ASW help from the cruiser Goshawk. On the Goshawk, a SH-60B SeaHawk helicopter took off from the deck without delay. Within moments it was dropping sonobouys all around the little sub. Inside the mini-sub, warning lights were sounding all around them.

On board the Sea Wolf, alarms were sounding as well. That's when JD sent word to Isaiah that his time of rest was over. Jumping to his feet and heading for the control room, Isaiah was briefed on his way there by an excited young ensign who gave him a blow-by-blow of the last twenty minutes in a few quick comments. As he entered the control room, JD was making ready to get under way.

"I'm afraid we may have to sink one of our own in a few minutes if they keep it up," said JD.

"I've got an idea, if what the good ensign here told me is correct," said Isaiah. "He actually gave me the idea when he described how they were dropping sonobouys from several hundred feet up."

"What do you mean?" asked JD.

"My first thought was, I wonder how those things can take that much punishment and keep working, so let's stop them from working. My guess is they'll blame it on the height they were dropped from. Quick now, tell them to blast the sonobouys with the disrupter ray."

Without wasting time on commenting, the order was relayed to the mini-sub, and within seconds all four sonobouys that had been dropped from the SeaHawk helicopter were out of commission. Since the mini-sub they were in had not been upgraded yet to the SD package, the beam was only strong enough to shake the buoys into a broken state. That was actually better, because they were still there, seeable, but they didn't work. It was a very frustrating state for the Navy.

Four more soon hit the water and just as quickly were put out of commission. The operators aboard the Beatty were really getting frustrated. They had lost the signal of the little sub and were anxiously moving about, looking for it, just as the patrol boat had done. As they had done with the patrol boat, the mini-sub kept just out of range of the Beatty and was trying desperately to get back to the Sea Wolf.

For a third time, the SeaHawk helicopter dropped another series of four sonobouys, and the mini-sub put the buoys out of commission as quickly as they hit the water. Inside the mini-sub, the co-pilot, who was operating the beam, was enjoying the game, but he knew that they were in real trouble should he miss one of the buoys and leave themselves visible to the rest of the ships.

Aboard the SeaHawk, the pilot was as frustrated as the rest of the sonar operators. After the first drop, he'd been blamed for coming in too fast and dropping from too high. After the second drop, they said he was still moving too fast. The third group had been dropped from thirty feet, while hovering stationary. It was clear that something was killing the buoys, and that it was not a problem with the technology.

He called back to the CIC aboard the Goshawk and asked for support. He had dropped twelve sonobouys and only had two left. He wanted to try something different. Ten minutes later, two more SeaHawk ASW helicopters were flying in formation along with the first one. They were following a path headed toward Qatar and the last known heading of the momentary contact. As they flew, the two new helicopters dropped ten sonobouys each and the original SeaHawk dropped his remaining two, for a total of twenty-two sonobouys hitting the water in two parallel lines about half a mile apart.

As they began their first pinging, the outer door of the Sea Wolf closed and they began pumping water out through the small holes in the bottom side of the hull. Inside the compartment, the mini-sub was safe from the prying ears of the sonobouys' technology. As they began their active pinging, the Sea Wolf was resting quietly on the bottom of the Gulf. All around them, the helicopters buzzed like giant mosquitoes looking for something to bite with their 1000-lb. torpedo-shaped snouts.

Try as they would, the ASW helicopters, the patrol boats, the destroyers, nor the cruisers could find the Sea Wolf as she slowly lifted from the floor of the Persian Gulf and swam as if invisible out the Straits and into the Arabian Sea. As they left the Gulf, they also left behind them a small floating device that began broadcasting messages meant to go to completely different parties.

As the messages were broadcast, the huge oil tanker, Chairman Mao, had raised anchors and had its steam back up to operating levels. At 0900 Zulu, Captain Jorgensen gave the order to make way. Instead of feeling the ship shudder from the push of the giant propellers against the sea, there was no shudder; instead, there was only a whine as the huge shafts spun in their bearings without any resistance. The twin shafts spun so fast that the computer controls on the motor control unit shut down the engines for fear of overheating.

On the bridge, the captain heard the noise, felt the turning of the shafts, but didn't feel the movement he expected. He called down to the engine room. Ten minutes later the motor control units were back online and ready for a restart. As they checked everything and made sure the gears were aligned and the transmission was working and in order they pushed the button and allowed the motor to push the transmission again. The transmission pushed the gears, and the gears began turning the shaft. The shaft again turned and spun without resistance. Suddenly it was apparent to the captain and the chief engineer that they had lost their props.

They looked at each other in disbelief. What happened? They'd been parked here for just about 24 hours and there hadn't been anyone around them during that time except for the Chinese cruiser. Captain Jorgensen was at a loss as to what he would say to the Chinese cruiser captain, but he knew he had to face him.

Calling on an open channel, he got the Chinese captain and began to explain his predicament. To his surprise, the captain simply replied, "I see," and ended the conversation. It was almost as if he had expected the explanation that his propellers had been removed.

"What is going on?" Captain Jorgensen almost yelled into the microphone. "Tell me, please," he pleaded.

"I don't really know, Captain," came the subdued voice of the Cruiser captain, "but we began receiving a message in our own code about ten minutes ago. It told us not to expect to use your ship. It also gave us other instructions we will not discuss here. I'm not sure what happened to your ship, Captain, but with this latest disaster I cannot say that I'm surprised that you can't move. Now, get off the line and wait where you are. We have other things to get done. Oh, tell the major to set up his SAM missiles on your deck. Are we clear, Captain?"

"What? No, sir"

"Captain, this is not up for discussion. Do it or I'll have you shot," the Cruiser captain said calmly.

That was the end of the discussion. Jorgensen did as he was told and just shook his head as he smiled at the thought of someone stealing his propellers without him knowing it, unheard by anyone, while he was there, sleeping, on board the ship.

Aboard the Chinese carrier Varyag, the Chinese Admiral Fu Yang Yu was furious. He wanted answers, and he wanted them soon. Who was sending this message, and who knew how to send it on their private channels with their private code? It was embarrassing. He was almost afraid to forward the information on to Chairman Chiang Yao.

The message was to-the-point and had been sent to every ship in the Chinese fleet, even though it had been addressed to him and Chairman Yao personally. On top of that, there were other codes. For all he knew, they were copies of the message sent to the Americans, the British, and the Iranians. He was beyond mad at this point. He didn't know who was on whose side, and this threat sent directly to him and the chairman was personal.

The message said that any more aggression on the part of the Chinese would result in the destruction of all of the Chinese submarines in the Arabian Sea, and shortly afterward the sinking of all the Chinese warships as well. It said that "they" were responsible for the sinking of three Chinese submarines so far, and had done so when those submarines had attempted to fire their torpedoes on innocent oil tankers. "They" also said they had disabled the tanker Chairman Mao in order to keep her from being used in the upcoming fracas. The note also said that messages of a similar nature were being sent to the British, US, and Iranian Navies. A special message was also supposed to have been sent to the President of Iran, threatening him personally if he continued his unprovoked belligerence toward the Peoples Republic of China. "They" also said that they were aware that the premier had blood on his hands, as well as the President of Iran, and would be made an example of in good time. The question was who they were. The note did not give a name, was coded in their own language, and according to language experts was probably composed by either a Chinese or a Japanese person. Someone fluent with the nuances of the language.

Aboard the USS Ronald Reagan and the John C Stennis, a similar meeting was being held with similar head-scratching. The message was simple: don't get involved in the problems going on in the Persian Gulf, and stay out of the way. "They" claimed responsibility for the destruction of the three Chinese subs that had been sunk, and that any attempt to fire on a warship of another nationality would be taken as an Act of War and would be met with the destruction of the offending ship or ships. The threat was simple: stay out of it or be destroyed.

As you can imagine, the admirals aboard the two carrier task forces were not used to having this kind of threat leveled at them. They were angry about the threat, even angrier that their codes had been compromised, and at the same time, basically under orders to follow those instructions anyway. It was literally the same rules of engagement that they were already working under. They had located the device that was pumping out the repeating message, but again they were told by the coded message to leave it alone because it was booby-trapped and would soon self-destruct.

They were frustrated and angry, but unable to do anything about it. They had the president, chief of staff, and the national security advisor on the line with them, and the consensus was the same from all of them. While they didn't like terms being dictated to them, they really didn't have a problem with the terms and so didn't feel that anything needed to be done as long as they were happy. If things changed, they'd disregard the "advice," as it was now being termed, and deal with the situation as it became necessary. The two admirals hung up from the meeting, unhappy, but not really sure why.

Onboard the Prince Albert, a similar discussion was going on between the prime minister and the admiralty, as well as the commander of the air wing aboard the carrier. The same basic message had been sent to the British, and like the Americans, they weren't happy with being dictated to, but they were willing to treat these dictates as "suggestions" that they were willing to follow as long as no one started slinging missiles or torpedoes at anyone else.

The message to the Indian navy was the same: stay out of the fracas or have your ships sunk. Because the Indian Navy had recently changed its code, the Sea Wolf didn't have the latest code and had to use an older code for its coded message. The effect on the Indian admiralty was still pure amazement that anyone could know the codes they used so recently. They feared that the codes they used now were compromised as well. They reacted much the same way as the Americans and British, but they were in fear that it was a ploy by one or the other to threaten the Chinese. They decided to bring their ships into harbor and let this game play out without them.

For the Iranians, the message was more direct. It was directed at one man, President Ahmadinejad. He had been directed to make a public apology for his attempted terrorism and to offer restitution to everyone's family that had been destroyed by his desire to hurt others. The message was not coded, but on an open signal with no covert attempts to hide it. The message also had within it instructions to send the message to all news media willing to play the message on the open air. It went on to detail the entire attempt on the American continent, but left out the details about the submarine. It detailed the names of the people involved, including the Chinese premier and Osama Bin Laden. The request was simple: turn over a new leaf, make a public apology, and pay for the sins of their past— or else!

In the skies above the Sea of Arabia, events that could explode the situation into a full blown war were about to take place. The young MiG pilots, Yau Te and Wo Shan, were headed at mach 1.6 straight at the approaching British Harriers from the Prince Albert who were hurtling toward the MiGs at mach 1.0.

At the same time that the admiralty of the world's Navies were sitting down to discuss the messages they had just received, Lieutenant "Shorty" Yau Te was flashing by Lieutenant Hyman Reese of the 800th Squadron, flying off of the Prince Albert in his Harrier FA2. As they passed each other at a combined speed of 1690 MPH and a distance of less than 4 feet between wing tips, Yau Te pulled up into his move to turn and get on the Harrier's tail. As he did so, he had failed to understand that the older and slower Harrier had the advantage in turning because of its slower speed. Hyman Reese had made exactly the same move that Yau Te was making—to Yau's great dismay—along with the slower speed of the Harrier. This put Hyman Reese less than 2 kilometers away and directly on the MiG's 6.

Hyman called into the carrier's CIC and at the same time flipped on the high-intensity targeting radar, which set off a warning in the cockpit of Yau Te. He screamed into his radio that he was being fired upon and that they had missile lock on him. As Hyman nervously fingered the firing control of his joystick, he heard his warning system telling him that his own fighter had been acquired by another jet. While Yau Te was screaming into his mic, Wo Shan had turned and gotten on Hyman's 6.

The problem was one of speed. While Yau Te hadn't realized that he would soon be out of missile range by using the superior speed of his MiG, Wo Shan found that he was barreling in much too fast and would soon pass by his intended target because of that same speed issue. He had good tone and missile lock, but all his ears could hear were the cries of his wingman, screaming that he was being fired upon. And so, fearing that he would fly by and miss the shot, he decided to fire his missile.

The total engagement lasted no more than 30 seconds, a new record even for Yau Te. A flyby, a turn, and the flight of a missile. As the missile was released from the MiG29, Lt. Hyman Reese never had a chance. As soon as his threat indicator showed a missile being fired, he did exactly what he'd been trained to do—he fired his own missile at the target on his own screen and began a series of moves designed to throw off the missile trailing him, while simultaneously dropping every flare and bit of chaff that his Harrier carried.

It was of no avail; the missile fired by Wo Shan flew right into the tailpipe of the Harrier and it disintegrated into a cloud of fragments traveling at mach 1. Hyman's last act was to call for assistance, making sure that everyone knew that he'd been fired upon.

The American-made sidewinder missile that Hyman had fired had a good lock on the MiG29 it had been aimed at. Although the distance was at the maximum range for a sidewinder, Hyman had followed his instructions perfectly, and he believed the missile would find its target. Within 30 seconds, two American F15s had joined the remaining British Harrier in the pursuit of the MiGs. Just as they arrived on the scene there was a flash in the distance as Lt. Hyman Reese's sidewinder avenged his own death.

Lt. Yau Te had realized too late that he had not been fired upon. After hearing Wo Shan say "missile away," he discovered that he had not been fired upon as yet. He screamed to Wo to abort the missile, but it was too late. Two seconds later, he heard the sound of the "missile fired" warning on his own threat radar. He dodged and put the MiG into full afterburners reaching mach 2.1, but he was unable to shake the American-made sidewinder missile. In the end, he waited for the explosion to come.

Funny, he thought as the small missile exploded on his right side tail pipe, it is not as loud as he expected. No shrapnel, no fire, just a slowly failing aircraft. The MiG was a great aircraft, he thought. It was his own failings that had caused the loss of the plane. As he lost more and more of the plane's control functions, he calmly punched out of the cockpit. As he did so, he began to think how much happier he'd have been if only he'd been killed by the missile. "Why did I lose my composure?" he asked himself. Why did he reacted like that? As the chute drifted down to the sea below, he calmly removed his sidearm from inside his vest and took his own life.

From the British CIC aboard the Carrier Prince Albert and aboard the Carrier John C Stennis, the Americans and Brits were both screaming for their aircraft to return to the carrier and to cease hostilities. Aboard the Chinese aircraft carrier Varyag, the same thing was being shouted to Wo Shan. Inside the Tuepelov, two young Chinese ensigns turned and looked at each other, neither believing what had just occurred. One turned to the other and said, "Make a copy of the tape right away."

Aboard all the ships, the prayer for cooler heads to prevail was being issued by all of the admirals. Before any of the planes had returned to their own ships, all three of the nations' leaders were being contacted with the details of the event. The tapes from the E3C Hawkeye had been sent to the British government, detailing the death of Lt. Reese.

In Tehran, the president was an unhappy man. Too much information was being put out about this. Even in the Al Jazeera news he was being called "a traitor to Islam." Because of his collaboration with the Chinese, who were non-believers just as the Americans were, he was being publicly criticized. The information was too detailed to be false, and it had quotes that he had said, including his public predictions and the information he had gotten from the DNC and exactly who had leaked it. There was so much of it. This was going to bring down the senator from New York who had leaked it, the DNC for having had a hand in it, and the Chinese premier for making deals with the Iranian government that would make a profit for him personally, and the Japanese shipbuilder for having been involved in the plot. They were all going down, and there didn't seem to be anywhere to hide.

There was simply too much information and it fit together too well to be false. The only one who didn't seem to get any mud on him was Osama, who had publicly denied any involvement. An hour after the public denial was released to Al Jazeera, the president was sitting alone in his office. Picking up the phone, he dialed a number—a very secret number he had only used once before. It was the number that would get him in touch with Osama, who had patted him on the back and called him a hero of Islam. Osama, who now denied him and called him a traitor to Islam.

Ahmadinejad was a broken man. Even his trusted advisor Jimji had left him. He didn't show up when he called an hour ago. It was as if his entire staff had disappeared. He had to know directly from Osama what to do, whether this was just a ploy to bring out the Americans who had to be behind this or whether Osama had truly left him out to dry. As he picked up the phone and dialed the number, the number was being recorded by the two women from the sub—Anna and Josie.

Working around the building as cleaning women for Achmed, Josie had managed to find the junction box on the outside of the office complex and had managed to isolate the president's private line. Hooking a black box to the line, every number called and what was said was recorded for posterity. Every hour Anna would stop by the box and check its contents. After the events of the day, they both expected to hear the voice of Osama on the other end of one of those conversations. Thanks to the president, they were not disappointed.

The news spread fast around the world. President Beechum was as happy as a duck in a rainstorm. She had been proven correct; her adversaries had been shown for what they were—traitors to their own government, and that pompous Senator from New York was about to be eaten alive by the press. Even CNN couldn't find a way to spin his actions as anything but treasonous. World opinion was completely against the Iranians and the Chinese, and there was talk about trade embargoes with both countries. Without having to fight Congress or the liberals, it appeared to President Beechum that she might get an embargo passed. They were too afraid to look like they were involved in the scandal to put up any resistance.

Just a day before, the senator from New York had been the darling of the media. Everyone wanted to share the platform with him. Today, he couldn't get elected dog catcher. Funny how politics worked. Just like after 9/11. Everyone jumped on the band wagon, yelling for a war on terror, and then six years later, with a free Iraq and Afghanistan, everyone was yelling that we should never have been involved in it because a few soldiers had been killed. The press had a funny way of measuring success. The death of any soldiers at all made the war a complete loss. The Democrats were playing it up as a loss—a loss, that was, until this latest stumble by the senator from New York. Suddenly, the press was fully behind the "president's" war on terror. President Beechum wondered when it had become her war. She had always thought that this was her nation's war against terror, but all she heard on the news anymore was that it was the "president's" war on terror. Amazing, she thought. This information, from whoever it was, was a blessing from God Himself. It had shed the light of truth on all the countries of the world. She was happy.

In the skies above the Arabian Sea, no planes were currently flying. The Chinese had issued a statement saying that the British had attacked their MiG29 in an unprovoked attempt to keep the Chinese people from protecting their property. They said that the British had sabotaged their oil tanker, the Chairman Mao, and had then attacked the Chinese fighter when it was sent to protect the damaged ship.

The British, in response to the allegations, had released the tapes from the Hawkeye. The proof was irrefutable. The Chinese had fired on the British officer first and he had fired his missile in response.

The Chinese were even saying that the Americans had shot the Chinese pilot as he fell from the sky in his parachute. Again, the Americans had released all information proving that they had not attacked anyone. They even allowed the media to examine the planes returning to the carrier to show that no rounds had been fired and no missiles had been shot from their racks.

It was the same old way out of trouble for them: lies and falsehoods. When caught, lie about the facts, and deny,

deny, deny. It had worked for years and would probably work here as well, the premier decided. He laughed at the predicament of the Iranian president, but he was still angered at the loss of his own subs. He was determined. That determination would be the death of him.

The Chinese cruiser had lost two hours now, and would lose a third retrieving his men from the oil tanker. The task force was still moving steadily north along the Indian coastline and was even with the port city of Mumbai or Bombay. The Chinese admiral had been given his orders by the premier himself, and he was afraid to ignore them. He opened a channel to his flanking submarines and told them to begin operations again. He ordered the sub in the Red Sea to join them in the Arabian Sea and to prepare to defend the fleet from attacks by American subs.

The Chinese premier sent a message directly to the President of the United States, telling her to desist from the trickery. He accused her of being behind the messages and the attacks on his subs. Chairman Xau threatened retaliation if any of his ships were attacked. All the while, the captain of the Chinese cruiser was anchoring next to the stranded oil tanker and beginning his process of transferring the people and equipment back to his cruiser.

While he hustled his troops to their efforts, Thump and Dinger parked a short distance behind the cruiser and began the process of removing her propeller blades as they had done to the oil tanker. They finished much quicker than did the troops. After finishing this, they moved on to their next target—the main Chinese battle group, now miles ahead of them.

In the area of the Persian Gulf just outside the Straits, the Iranians had laid a minefield. The mines they laid were controllable electronically and were magnetically discharged. The mines themselves didn't have to be hit to be exploded; they only had to get within a few feet of the hull of a large enough ship to go off. The mines were laid so that they covered the bottom of the sea floor in zones. When a ship was allowed to enter the Gulf, the mines of a certain zone were turned off while the ship passed over the top of them. Once the ship had passed, the mines were turned back on.

This was the way Iran controlled who could and who couldn't pass into the Gulf. What they didn't know was that during the last twelve hours the mines had been swapped around by the first mini-sub. Now only Thump and Dinger knew which mines were where. No one would be entering the minefield safely any time soon.

After reporting completion, the Sea Wolf sent out another message to everyone in the area that the mines had been changed and were no longer being controlled by the Iranians. Instead, they were controlled by "them." No one would be allowed in or out without permission of the Sea Wolf. The Sea Wolf had also intercepted the message from the Chinese admiral to his subs. After an hour's computer time, the new code had been broken and a message was sent to the Chinese warships, in particular the subs, not to listen to the admiral for fear of their own lives. The threat was sent not only to the admiral, but to each ship in the convoy as well. JD and Isaiah didn't want any smart Chinese to die unnecessarily. Unfortunately, the Chinese didn't rise through the ranks by thinking on their own. They were determined to follow orders.

Isaiah ordered a decoy torpedo to be readied. It would be launched at dusk. An hour before dusk, the Chinese were still steadily moving toward the Straits of Hormuz, the entrance into the Persian Gulf. They were still six hours from entering into Iranian national waters, and the battle group had stopped and was waiting for stragglers to catch up to them.

At the same time, the cruiser was using its thrusters to push away from the stranded oil tanker. The cruiser captain's reaction to his own predicament was as easily flammable as was the oil that remained in the bottom of the tanker's hold. The captain notified the Chinese admiral that he had been sabotaged by unknown assailants and warned the admiral to be wary of any ships nearing the convoy. He sent divers down to investigate, but at first appearance it seemed that the propellers had been removed somehow. Five minutes later, the word was returned that each blade of the propeller had been severed by something that cut it like a blowtorch might. When asked how this was possible within the period of less than one hour, there was no answer. No one had any idea how such a thing were possible without the noise that a torch of that size would make. They were at a complete loss.

These were answers that were not acceptable to the Chinese admiral, nor to the premier. They decided to keep the propellers in motion, even if they needed to make circles to do so. Even though he did not believe his cruiser captain, he was smart enough not to allow the same trickery that befell the captain and his ship to befall him. The admiral felt that he was too smart for that to happen.

Starting his engines again, the admiral had the captain of the carrier engage the propellers and begin to make circles while they waited for the troop carriers. To everyone's surprise, only one propeller was left intact. Three other propellers had all four of their blades removed. At first the captain was at a loss, then he decided that with the single prop he could continue his mission, even though at only 1/4 speed.

Under the sea, about a mile away, the mini-sub was cursing their planning at not having disabled all four props by making them lopsided first instead of taking each propeller one at a time. They contemplated taking a shot at the one remaining propeller and removing the blades while it was moving, but they feared taking the shot in case the blades might fly away from the quickly rotating shaft and hurt others nearby. So, backing away from the task force, the mini-sub slowly swam away from the group of ships, hoping to spot any other warships that might be sitting still in the water and thereby be targetable.

At dusk, the Sea Wolf opened her outer doors and sent two torpedoes into the dark waters of the Arabian Sea. At the same time, the fifth and final Chinese submarine entered the Arabian Sea from its position inside the Red Sea and was acquired by the eighth torpedo that had been slowly circling outside the Red Sea for the past two days. Without making a sound, the eighth torpedo made its calculations and set its slow-turning propellers onto the path that would intersect with the Chinese sub in forty-five minutes.

The two new torpedoes released by the Sea Wolf had a different task in mind than sinking ships. The two torpedoes swam slowly away from the Sea Wolf on paths nearly opposite in direction. The first was sent to a point just southwest of the Chinese convoy. The second was set to head for a point just northwest of the British convoy.

In the sky above, the drone from the Sea Wolf watched the Chinese ships circling in the sea 150 miles west-southwest of Karachi, Pakistan. The British task force was 75 miles south of the Bay of Oman. Less than 500 miles of water separated the two battle groups. Further south and west was the Stennis battle group. It was slowly circling the Omani island of Socotra.

Chapter 11

Confusion

The Sea Wolf had been sitting on the floor of the Arabian Sea, right in the center. As night was falling, the two torpedo decoys reached their objectives. As the Sea Wolf surfaced and turned on her sail's invisibility screen, the two torpedoes began making first faint sounds and then louder as they supposedly approached the two convoys. The torpedo in the midst of the Chinese task force made the sound signature of a US attack sub, and the torpedo in the midst of the British task force had the signature of an older Russian attack sub.

As predicted, the Brits believed it to be a surplus Russian sub that was piloted by the Chinese. They called for help from the Americans as they began throwing sonobouys from every ship in the fleet. In the Chinese task force, the ships began moving away from the sound of the subs and a Chinese Merlin MK1 helicopter lifted off from the carrier.

The American task force headed in the general direction of the British convoy, while they sent two SeaHawk ASW helicopters; the British already had 8 Linx ASW helicopters up and searching. The Merlin MK1 came down almost on top of the submarine, or so it thought. Asking Admiral Yu for permission to go to weapons-free status, the admiral thought for just a moment before nodding to his XO and without a second thought, a torpedo fell free from the rack of the Merlin helicopter.

Onboard the British destroyer Man-O-War, the sonar operator listened with interest to the goings on inside the Chinese fleet's area. Hearing the torpedo splash and making high-speed turns, he shouted to his lieutenant, informing him that the Chinese were attacking a sub, and even though he knew it wasn't a British sub—none were in the area, it might be an American sub.

He pointed out that "Those Yanks are always thinking their equipment is better than it is, and thereby putting themselves into dangerous situations when they don't have to."

"Thanks for the info sparks," said the officer to the sonar operator, using the slang that had been used for a radio, radar, or sonar tech's since the beginning of the twentieth century. "Let me know if the sub gets it or if they fire back."

At the same time the Brits were chasing their own phantom sub and listening to the Chinese attack nothing, the trailing destroyer in the Stennis convoy had momentarily caught a flash on his trailing radar at a distance of nearly three hundred miles. Being a good operator, he pointed his array in the direction of the contact and put out a higher beam that "would bounce off of a rubber ball," as he was fond of saying. The initial contact had been just a small pip at about 10,000 feet. Focusing the beam and sweeping it, hoping to see a missile if it were there, but more so hoping not to see anything, he watched his screen closely.

"Nothing there," he said to himself, and, wiping his brow, he flipped the switch back to wide range, and…"there it is again, just for a moment. Sir, I think I might have a contact," he sang out.

The XO was not a man to screw around with, and the operator, Tom Hollingwood—known as "Hollywood" by the crew, was not fond of having to deal with crap like this on-and-off contact that would make him look bad in front of his XO. Still, Hollywood was not the kind to take the easy route just because his XO was a bit of an ass, and so he snapped to attention as the short XO with his almost drunken swagger strode to his console.

"What'cha got, Hollywood?" Jake Helms, the XO of the ChiChi Jima asked.

Helms seemed to always be trying to compensate for his diminutive size. He drank harder, swore louder, and used fouler language than anyone else around. He constantly threatened to "beat the hell" out of just about everyone that reported to him, and was too friendly, and too outgoing when the boss was around. In general, the crew hated him for his wisecracks and typically pissy attitude, but on the other hand, he rarely made mistakes, and when the crap hit the fan, his crew wanted someone who was never wrong on their side, so they put up with his nonsense and did their best not to get in front of the bellicose little man when he was on a rant.

"Sir, I have twice seen a return at around 10,000 feet out at a distance of 300 miles," Hollywood stated matter-of-factly.

"Well, where is it now, Hollywood?" Helms smiled wickedly as he asked.

"I don't know, sir," were the words Hollywood said, and hated having to say them.

"I don't know, sir? Is that what you said, Hollywood? We got all hell breaking loose in the Limey's ranks; the Chinks are running around apeshit, shooting at what may be an American sub, and you don't know? Did I hear you correctly, Hollywood? You don't know?"

Helms was in his element now. He had someone to take his frustrations out on and he was enjoying the sound of his own words. A small part of him was listening and letting his mind mull over the situation. What most people didn't know about him was that all his bluster was really just a way of making time for him to think through the problem at hand. The rest of his cranky attitude was just BS to maintain control of the situation and make others react to him while he made time to think. It worked every time.

"Yessss, sirr... I mean... No, Sir... I mean, I just saw it and thought it might be important, sir..." came the frightened reply of SFC Hollingwood.

"Okay, Hollywood, you've told me. Now turn that radar back to where you saw it and keep it there until I tell you different. And sing out if you see another hit. Got it?" yelled Helms.

Jake was sure he'd have Hollywood's undivided attention on that spot now. He was afraid there might be a missile out there, and he didn't want to get caught with his pants down.

Jake slapped Hollywood on the back and said, "Good Job, Hollywood. You'll make it to JG before you know it if you keep spotting the hard ones."

Hollywood was a bit confused. One minute he was afraid he was about to be put on report, and now he was being patted on the back.

Oh well, he thought, shaking his head as he replied, "Thank you, Sir." Sitting back down, he once again focused the powerful array toward the spot to his south where he'd seen the flash twice before.

Three hundred miles to the south, the drone was bobbing on the sea beside the closed doors of the Sea Wolf. The crew had been warned to remove belt buckles and jewelry and to open and close the outer doors quickly when putting the drone into the hold. As the drone taxied to the rear of the ship, it pulled up onto the rear portion of the aft deck. The engines shut down and two sailors grabbed the wingtips of the drone and pulled it onto the waiting deck. They had decided to open the doors, pull the drone inside, and do the necessary work inside the hatch before re-opening the doors and releasing it into the sky again.

The plan was a good one, but as soon as the doors of the hatch were opened, a return was sent back to Hollywood, who was watching the screen with real interest. Instead of a return the size of a marble at 10,000 feet, he got a return the size of a Volkswagen, floating on the sea. The echo continued for all of ten seconds before it disappeared again. On board the ChiChi Jima, Hollywood scratched his head, lifted his hand, and then slowly lowered it. He decided that whatever it was, it wasn't a missile, and it wasn't coming toward them, and he didn't need to cross the little Napoleon again. He just didn't know how he'd react. Better to just pretend he'd not seen it at all since it didn't appear to be a danger to them. He lowered his arm as if he'd been stretching and forced a fake yawn.

Onboard the Sea Wolf, the update to the drone was almost done. The fuel that had been used, less than 1/4 gallon, was replaced, and the diagnostics were run to make sure everything was working as planned. Less than thirty minutes had passed and no contact had been shouted across any radio frequencies. It appeared that no one had noticed them.

On board the ChiChi Jima, Tom Hollingwood was watching very closely indeed. As soon as the outer doors to the Sea Wolf were swung open and the launch rails raised, Hollywood sang out and pointed, shifting his screen to the main screen in CIC for Napoleon to see. Watching the changing shape on the screen, Jake Helms cried out for a flyover.

"Now!" he screamed.

The excited shouts drew the attention of Jean in the control room as she monitored the communications activity.

Almost instantly, two F-15 Strike Eagles were vectored in their directions at a speed of nearly six hundred knots. The drone took to the air as slowly and gracefully as ever. It seemed to be in no hurry to run from the approaching aircraft. Instead, it slowly skimmed along the surface of the ocean, headed westward toward the coast of Yemen.

The Sea Wolf's hatch doors had closed quickly and quietly behind the drone's take off, and had closed completely almost before the drone had lifted above the height of the ship's tail. As the hatch doors closed, the Sea Wolf began to sink out of sight.

It had taken just nine minutes for the first of the two F-15s to close to within visible range of the contact. When they arrived, they found nothing at all. Searching with their highest power radar in all directions, they found nothing. All the same, word was sent to head for these coordinates in the search for a probable hostile submerged contact.

As they buzzed back and forth above the Sea, the small drone slowly climbed, taking its time returning to its cruising altitude of thirty thousand feet. Below the surface of the sea, the Sea Wolf swam undetected, watching as two American submarines, one being the USS Tiger Shark, headed in the general direction of their contact above the sea. The ChiChi Jima also had turned and was steaming in the direction of where the Sea Wolf had surfaced. Under the waves, both JD and Isaiah, who was at the helm, watched the three ships converged on where they had been.

"Wow! They were quick getting here," said Isaiah.

"Yes they were. I'd say they got a whiff of us when the drone landed. Maybe even got a return from it, and then were watching closer when we opened the doors to launch it again," said JD.

"I'll bet you're right. They were puzzled by the first one and then ready to react when they saw the bounce the second time. I'll have to give that some thought. Maybe in the future we should launch and retrieve in one stroke," said Isaiah.

"Good thought, but it wouldn't have helped us this time, since we needed the upgraded drone for the addition of the disrupter beam," said JD.

"You're right, of course, but like I said, next time we'll do it a little different."

Turning to watch the activity from their eye-in-the-sky, they could see the whirl of activity above them. Now three jets were steadily flying tracks back and forth as if mowing the lawn. At their speed, they had little chance of finding anything worth reporting. Still, Isaiah ordered the Sea Wolf's direction changed to move even further away from the swaths the three planes were mowing in the field of ocean above them. In the sky above them, theirs was not the only drone in the air. The US had two drones with extremely good lenses, both IR and optical, just like theirs, up and flying.

The drones were not quite as good as those of the Sea Wolf, however, and could only stay up in the air for 48 hours. One of the drones had been within a hundred miles when the call came from the ChiChi Jima and it was instantly tasked to look for the surface submarine. Taking infrared pictures as it headed to the location, it managed to capture the odd-shaped conning tower just before it disappeared under the waves. Under the water, a distorted shape was partially visible to the IR camera, but only one frame was captured before the ship completely disappeared. Onboard the John C Stennis, there was a general wonder as to what it was that was on the photograph and how large it was. They had very little, but they knew that it did have a heat signature, albeit a very small one, comparatively speaking. Their first impression was that this was a submarine, but a small one. In all probability, less than a hundred feet in length but with a wide base. Still, it was something new to worry about. In all likelihood, these were the ones responsible for the threats and the oddities going on in the Arabian Sea. The small size was probably the reason no one had caught up to them yet. It was probably pretty fast because of its small size, allowing it to seem to be in multiple places at one time. Yes, they thought they had it figured out. Next, they needed to know with whom and how much of this new information to share.

In the thirty minutes since the two decoy torpedoes had gone active, a lot had happened. The British and American helicopters continued to chase the torpedo, thinking they had a Chinese submarine in their sites. The Chinese had shot a torpedo at their decoy torpedo, thinking it was an American submarine. The first decoy, the one the Chinese were chasing, had sped up to unthinkable speeds to avoid the Chinese torpedo, and upon dropping a second and a third torpedo into the water, the Chinese now had three torpedoes actively chasing the "American sub." To their chagrin, the American sub kept just ahead of them and kept doubling back on the three Chinese torpedoes as if it were playing games with them.

Inside the CIC of the crippled Chinese aircraft carrier, Admiral Yu was furious. The first of the torpedoes was slowing down and about to sink into oblivion. In frustration, he ordered the first torpedo self- destructed. The noise got the attention of every ship in the Arabian Sea. Everywhere, blind ships assumed that either another Chinese submarine had been sunk, or that the Chinese had finally hit something with one of their torpedoes. Aboard the Prince Albert, it was unclear as to who or what had been killed, but it was clear that a Chinese torpedo had struck something.

The communications officer on board the Prince Albert was given instructions to pass the information on to the Illustrious in the Persian Gulf, as well as to both American carriers. Within moments, the belief was that whoever had been playing games with the Chinese was now history. Shaking their heads, they continued to look out for their own issues. On board the Varyag, Admiral Yu was still furious, and now he was blind as well. The captain had tried to countermand the order, but he was too late. The noise and agitation of the water caused by the explosion of the torpedo had destroyed any chance that the other two torpedoes would find the American sub now. To his surprise, the sub seemed to be taunting them and had actually swum below the keel of his best missile cruiser and was reacquired by them, and very quickly the two remaining torpedoes were back on the trail of the American sub.

The British were getting nervous as well. The "Chinese sub" they had been watching seemed to be uncaring about the noise it was making. It seemed to be just enough to make sure that the British could hear them. While the Americans had run off to the south, chasing shadows, the Brits continued to chase the sub they were watching. For thirty minutes the Brits and Chinese, as well as the Americans, believed that they may have been chasing a decoy torpedo in disguise, but the longer the chase went on, the more convinced all three nations were that they were indeed chasing submarines. After two hours of chasing the shadow in the middle of the Arabian Sea, the surface ships of the American fleet gave up and headed back toward the area where two known subs were being pursued.

Just about that time, the sub the Brits had been chasing fell in behind a second Chinese submarine. Upon hearing what it believed to be another Chinese submarine, the real Chinese sub began a series of maneuvers designed to shake the helicopters above. Meanwhile, the first Chinese sub (the decoy) backtracked and headed in another direction. While this was going on, the decoy the Chinese were chasing began moving into the waters of the Straits of Hormuz. As the helicopter following it dropped down to dip its sonobouys into the water, the decoy switched its tone and began making the noise of a British submarine. This really confused the Chinese. As they listened, the submarine changed from British, to Soviet, to American and then to Chinese, and then just as suddenly, it went silent, disappearing from the sonar completely.

As Admiral Yu listened to the words of his best sonar operators and his captains, he became even more infuriated. To make matters worse, the final two torpedoes he'd launched at what he thought was an American submarine, ran out of power and sank to the bottom of the Straits of Hormuz. He stood, listening and waiting, while an awkward silence filled the CIC.

"Well?" he said questioningly.

"My Admiral," the captain said, "I think we are facing an enemy that is beyond our capability to track. I fear that he has the superior technology, and we will be unable to beat them."

"You have given up, Captain?" shouted the Admiral. "But to whom have you surrendered?"

"My Admiral, it must be to the Americans. They are the only ones that have this kind of technology," said the captain, his eyes downcast and his head bowed.

"The Americans!" spat the Admiral. "The Americans are running around chasing shadows at sea just as we are," Chiang said. "No, I am convinced it is not the Americans—or the British. I think that the Iranians are behind this. I intend to do the job I was tasked to do, and you, Captain, would be better served by doing your job instead of fearing someone or something you don't even know."

"Yes sir." The captain was devastated by the words of his admiral, and he slunk back to the rear of the CIC, hoping not to draw his master's ire any further.

Onboard the Prince Albert, two escort ships for each of the targets were made available. Four destroyers in total were making their way toward the two separate targets. Onboard the real Chinese submarine, the one spotted by the torpedo decoy, the captain began to panic. He had been told that his orders to destroy attacking vessels or any oil tanker coming out of the Gulf were back in effect. He was worried. There had been no oil tankers out of the Gulf for the last eight hours, and now the British had located him, thanks to that fat-head in the other sub. He was sure it was that idiot Huang Lu.

Huang always panicked when he was pursued. Now he'd given up his position by running around the middle of the Arabian Sea. Damn him! thought Chu Ling Juan, captain of the Hu Ying. Chu went deep, hoping to find a thermal cline to hide under. Unfortunately, in the Arabian Sea, there were few thermal clines anywhere. As he headed south, away from the two pursuing destroyers, he released noisemakers to mask his turn south and then tried drifting to a dead stop, calling for all quiet aboard the ship. At first it appeared to have worked, with the British missing the turn south, but then just as Chu thought that he'd escaped, there came the splash overhead of sonobouys. Then came the pings that he feared. In just seconds, the active pinging showed his boat clearly in the sonar picture, but even more startling was the picture of something that looked like a torpedo in baffles behind him.

Turning sharply, the Chinese sub began actively pinging. Chu had decided that he needed to know exactly what it was that was following behind him. To his utter surprise, the outline of a two-thousand-pound torpedo, a Mark 48 by the looks of it, was clearly visible. He was afraid, for the first time. He gave the order for maximum speed, and began a series of sharp turns, dives and sharp surfacing techniques. At each turn or juke, he would drop noisemakers and try to throw off the following torpedo. After ten minutes of juking and running, he dove straight down and leveled off at his maximum depth of 800 ft. Holding still and remaining quiet, he waited.

Time seemed to crawl by. Chu began counting back. Somehow the British had launched the torpedo at him without him hearing it, but that had to have occurred during the time that idiot Huang had stumbled on him. Perhaps the torpedo had been fired at Huang. Yes, that had to be it. It had been fired at Huang and then Huang had scraped it off onto his tail. Thanks a lot, Huang! Okay, if Huang had just had it shot at him; that would mean ten, fifteen, twenty—at least twenty minutes had expired. The torpedo had to die soon. While he listened, the time continued to crawl by and told Chu that they had obviously lost the torpedo. After two minutes of silence, Chu let out his breath. Just as he did, the sonar man called out "Splashes in the water! Sonobouys, I think." Chu called for an all-ahead flank, hoping to outrun the echo. It was to no avail. Just as he called for flank speed, the first of the sonobouys let out its woeful "ping," painting a picture of Chu's sub, and to his shock, the torpedo behind him. Then it started all over again.

As the British were playing games with Chu about one hundred kilometers south of the main British battle group, they had completely lost the original contact. In fact, they thought that they had heard an American sub, and then a British sub in the vicinity, and then everything had gone quiet. They were confused, and they felt that perhaps someone was playing with them.

In Tehran, Iranian President Ahmadinejad was afraid. He was losing the support of the populous. Even Jimji had quit coming when he called. He had asked to meet with Osama; if anyone could help him turn this around it was him. Osama had demanded that no one could know. The little puppet ruler knew that he would do anything to have Osama's advice. He had agreed to a meeting on the terms that only the two of them would know about it, and only the two of them would be there.

And so, here he was the President of Iran, the keeper of the faith, praised by Osama publicly, putting on a disguise and hiding from his own people. As he put on a shabby robe and covered his head with the red and white plaid wrap, he wanted to shout and to kill whoever was responsible for his rapid downfall, he who had come up through the ranks of the poor and had proven himself. He who had risen to the top of Iranian politics in a time when politics were a truly dangerous pastime, and to have fallen so quickly, It made him furious to the point of near insanity. He yelled into the darkness, cursing God and men, and then he finished putting on the disguise and left the building, using a passage put there by his predecessor. The passage was dark and narrow, and he was sure no one knew of its existence.

He was wrong. The CIA had known about the hidden exit for the past ten years. Many times they had watched as first Khomeini used it for meeting his many mistresses, and then Mohammad Khatami, who had used it for secret meetings with the west. And now, finally, Mahmoud Ahmadinejad was using it tonight. As he made his way through the tunnel, word had been passed to the two "Israeli" agents that he was on the move. Outside, at the end of the tunnel, an opening led to the inside of a small shop.

The other shopkeepers around him wondered how the old beggar kept his shop open. It seemed that he never sold anything, yet the valuable space he was squatting on inside the market center never became available. They didn't know how or why; it just seemed that the old man always had enough to keep the shop open. Waiting just outside the shop were Anna and Josie, dressed in chadors and overcoats; they were politically correct. Ahmadinejad being self absorb in his thoughts discarded his disguise and exited the shop before observing to ensure all was quite in the market place not knowing there were many who were waiting and watching his moves. A mistake he would never realize.

As "the man" exited the door of the shop, he was startled to see the two women still in their booth next to the other deserted shops. "Cool water, Sahib," said the first with the voice of an angel.

"Please, Sahib, for our poor father who can no longer work," said the second, bowing in front of the stranger.

"At what price?" said Ahmadinejad, dressed as a successful Iranian.

"For you, kind sir," said Josie, "A mere pittance."

"Just 150 rials," said Anna. "For a rich businessman such as yourself, we will make you a deal—two bottles of cold water for only 200 rials." Pulling out two bills, the president handed it to the taller of the two lovely women.

"Tell me, lovely ladies, I see by the chadors you wear that you are not married, and obviously you are law abiding and strong in your faith. Why is it that you are not taken already as wives?" the "businessman" asked.

"Our father has no money to make a dowry for the poor women you see before you, kind sir. And without it, we fear that no man will ever have us," said Anna, lowering her head.

Giving the two women the two 100 rial bills, he accepted the two cold bottles of water, with the label which read, "From the Wells of Abraham." He walked away from the two women, thinking, Such a pity, two lovely women with no hope of a husband. I wonder what their father did to be punished in such a way. It was, he believed, the will of Allah that these women should be punished because of their father's sins.

As he walked toward the meeting ground, he thought that he might be able to take advantage of the situation on the way back and perhaps help these two women monetarily at the same time. He actually felt that he'd be doing them a favor. But for now, he had a more important issue to deal with. Reaching the corner, he found the car that was supposed to be there waiting. Getting in behind the wheel, he drove to the other side of town. As he drove, he circled the blocks several times, making sure no one was behind him. As he made his way to the western edge of Tehran, he slowed the car, and finally stopped. He headed for a small motel on the outskirts of town, walking slowly, looking in all directions for anyone who might be watching him.

Outside the motel, he noticed several men standing by the entrance, all holding the Soviet-made AK-47 rifles that were prevalent in his country. He walked by the men, not bothering to look up or to face them. They, however, were closely watching him as he walked by, and two broke away from the group and followed closely behind as he walked toward a room at the end of the open walkway. As he stopped in front of Room 17, he wrapped his knuckles on the door four times as he'd been instructed to do. Immediately, a man opened the door, looked past the president standing in front of him, and then pulled the president into the room and stepped out to guard the door.

Standing in front of the door, with his arms crossed in front of him, the guard was sure that no one could get past him. As Achmed stood there, the two men who had followed the president to the doorway turned and went back to finish their conversation with the other guard at the front of the motel. A flash of light appeared to blink close to the doorway that was being guarded, and then nothing. As the three men at the front turned and looked toward the room, they noticed nothing unusual. They turned back to their conversation, then one pointed out the guard was missing.

Turning around again, they ran to the doorway. There, in the doorway, was a perfectly round hole about three feet in diameter and about an inch deep. There were no burn marks, nor did the ground feel hot, just an inch deep hole where there had been nothing before. They looked around for Achmed. It was not like him to leave his post, but then again, they didn't know where the light had come from either. Perhaps Achmed had left to chase the one who had pulsed the light. The three knocked on the door and were relieved to hear the voice of their master from the inside, asking what the problem was. After telling the story to the master, it was decided that it was time to leave.

Osama and the president strolled slowly, not hurriedly as one would have expected of a man with a 10-million-dollar price on his head. It was not as the press would have you believe, that Osama could walk around his country freely. He would be turned in for the money by nine out of ten men in the country he claimed as his home, and to tell the truth, they would have turned him in for a thousand American dollars, not the millions being offered. Most of the country hated him for the pain that he had brought to their country. When he had courted the Americans and helped to get the Russians out of Afghanistan, he had been a hero, but now, he'd turned on the hand that had helped them to find freedom, and had instead usurped that freedom by turning the mujahadeen from a group of freedom fighters to a band of thieves and bandits who made the countryside afraid to go out at night. They hated him in Afghanistan, and they hated him even more in Iraq. Still, the President of Iran knew that he could get himself out of the hole he had dug for himself with this man's help. Thus he had begged for his assistance. As they walked to the car, Ahmadinejad continued to plead his case. He needed—no begged the thieving cutthroat for a kind word. Osama had the press, and Ahmadinejad needed it badly, more than he needed anything else.

Osama hardly listened to the little man. He looked for Achmed. It was unusual for Achmed to leave his post, and then there was that funny round circle. It was something to ponder. Perhaps Allah was telling him something. Something important, he felt sure, and this stupid little man was talking non-stop about his own woes. He turned to Ahmadinejad and tried to focus on his words.

"Just a kind word on the radio, please, Master. If you were to tell the people that I am a good leader, they would listen to you. I know they would."

Osama finally spoke. "Dear President Ahmadinejad, you are in a particularly delicate position right now. If you want my assistance you will have to do exactly as I say. What I need from you right now is the assistance of your treasury. I am in need of money to fund more of my surprises for the west. Shall we say, 100 million euros?"

President Ahmadinejad was taken aback by the request for money. His eyes opened wide and he opened his mouth to speak, but no words came out. He blinked twice at the man sitting next to him in the car, but the only words he could think to say were "Where should we go?"

"Turn left at the corner, Mahmoud," replied the older man. "I want you to circle this block until I say differently. Don't be surprised by my request, Mahmoud. All wars need money. Ours needs much to fight the infidel Americans and British."

"If you say so, Master," said the little president. He continued to act as chauffeur to the older and more experienced Bin Laden. He came back to his senses. "But so much, sir? How come so much?" he asked.

"It takes much good, president," he said, stressing the word president to make his point understood. "But if you cannot find the money to pay for the service, well then..." Osama turned and shrugged as if to say no pay, no play.

"I understand," said Mahmoud. "It will be as you wish."

"Good," said Osama, cracking the top on one of the water bottles lying on the seat next to him. Looking at the label, he smiled in the darkness and took a long draw from the contents of the bottle. "Take me back to the motel and let me ride with my trusted men," he said. "Tomorrow I will release a statement of backing for you and your administration. It will make all the faithful publications before the end of the week."

"Thank you, Master. I will have the money converted to British pounds and sent to you through the normal channels. Will that be sufficient?" asked Ahmadinejad through gritted teeth.

"Very good, my friend. It is well that you have learned how our world really works. You are running a very important country and it is best that you know the facts of what is most important in doing so. You must always remember that it is your skin first and your country second. The people you represent would climb upon your back and sink you into the mire that surrounds them if you let them. You must always think of yourself first," the older Holy Man said into the night while taking another drink of the cold water in the bottle.

"Here, take a drink of this cold water. It feels good in the heat of the night," he said, offering the other bottle to the president.

"No thank you, Master. I am not thirsty at the moment," said the younger man. "I will drop you off and continue my duties." Suddenly, he felt the urge to wash himself in the river and be done with his part in the plans of this man, but he knew that he was too far in. He was a major player in this man's movement, and for the first time his eyes had been opened to what this man was really about. He wanted to cry.

He stopped the car and immediately a detail of men surrounded their potentate. Without hesitation, he stepped on the gas as soon as the aging Holy Man was away from the car and the door had been shut. Inside the car, he felt very alone indeed. He had much to think about. He turned the car around and found his way back to the shop where he had come out of the tunnel. He looked around for the two women. A shame, he thought, that they were not there to solace him. He felt a need for their solace right now, and he knew that they would have the need for his money.

Money, he thought. Perhaps Osama was right. The world seems to rotate around the need of it, and he who has it is the one in charge, and today it was I who has it. He puffed up his chest and walked back through the tunnel. In his right hand he carried a bottle of quickly warming water.

Onboard the Hu Ying, Captain Chu Ling Juan was at his wit's end. He'd had a hard time when he had taken on the assignment as captain of this submarine with the crew. They all knew the fate of the ship whose name this one had been taken from. On October 8th, 1937, the namesake of the Hu Ying had met an untimely death, along with most of her crew, when the Japanese attacked. She had barely entered the fight when a bomb from a Japanese Kate bomber had pierced the thin deck armor of the destroyer's hull and exploded two decks below, igniting the store of munitions below and literally blowing the rivets loose all over the stern half of the ship. It sank in less than a minute. Captain Chu had fought the reputation from the day he took command of the sub. Now, as he fought to maintain his own composure, he began to think that maybe his crew had been right about the fate of this ship.

As he looked at the scope again, he saw the reflection of his tormentor still following on his six. The torpedo is the devil, he thought. "How can it still be there?" he shouted at the sonar operator. The shaken crewman stared at his captain in fear. "Do not answer, fool," he said to the crewman. "I don't expect you to know, since I don't know." In his mind, he was furious. It wasn't possible for the torpedo to stay on his tail for this length of time. It should have sunk to the bottom by now. On top of that, why was it not attacking him? It just stayed on his tail, tormenting him, pointing the way for others to find him. As if in response to his thoughts, the splash of two more sonobouys sounded. He gritted his teeth as the sound of the inevitable ping reached his ears. He turned to the dive officer and ordered his tanks blown dry. It was time for his dive officer to look at his captain as if he had gone mad.

"Do it, dive officer," Captain Chu shouted.

Without hesitation, the dive officer pushed the four handles upward, forcing air into the four main ballast tanks. The air forced seawater out of the ballast tanks, reducing the weight of the small ship. The weight difference made the ship buoyant and it began an unstoppable push upward through the waters of the Arabian Sea. As it rose to the surface, it became more and more buoyant, gaining more and more speed as it raced upward. Upon crossing the 100-foot depth line, it was beyond anyone's ability to change the process. The Hu Ying was about to become airborne.

On the surface, the British sonar operator aboard the Man-O'-War was tracking the small ship as it made its way to the surface. The operator yelled out that the sub was surfacing. To his surprise, it was surfacing right below them. He called to the captain, warning him that the sub was surfacing. The pitch of the young sonar operator's voice drew the attention of the captain. He turned to check the plot; he suddenly understood why the sonarman's voice had gone up two octaves. It only took a quick glance to recognize that the ships were going to collide, and there was nothing he could do about it. He called for flank speed, knowing that it wouldn't help, but giving the order anyway.

On board the ChiChi Jima, Jake Helms was on top of the spot the Sea Wolf had last been seen. In the water, five hundred feet below, the Tiger Shark and Captain Blake were also sniffing the water for any scent of the submarine that had been spotted here only forty-five minutes ago. Bud Williams was carefully monitoring the waves for any sound. Under his breath, he cursed the noisy destroyer above him. Captain Blake had turned over control of the helm to Bud, letting him have free reign to track the phantom sub. Something at the back of his neck told Bud that this was the same ship they had come across a month ago. He couldn't tell anyone else because he had nothing but the itch at back of his neck to go on, but he would have bet money. This ship could disappear, and no other ship had been able to do that. Up above, the ChiChi Jima drove in circles, waiting for something to show up.

Bud pointed the ship to the east, following a hunch. As the sub drove its way through the murky waters, the quiet attack submarine slowly broke away from the surface ship above it. Sooner or later the phantom submarine would slip up and he would be there. Up above, Helms ranted and raved in his typical manner, making himself obnoxious, as inside he fretted over the mysterious ship he knew was watching him. Thirty miles to the east, the Sea Wolf listened to the racket of the surface ship. Even though they had caught a scent of the two subs nearly an hour and a half ago, they had lost track of both of them.

Three hundred miles away, in the Gulf of Aden, an escort destroyer, the USS Ipswich of the U.S. fleet, was on the outermost ring, surrounding the aircraft carrier John C Stennis. It was less than one hundred miles from the African nation of Somalia. At its location, it could use its older sweep radar to see the entire Gulf. A small ship had passed through the Strait just an hour ago, leaving the Red Sea and entering into the Gulf of Aden. This small ship was carrying supplies for the operators of the oil-pumping stations in the Persian Gulf from the foreign supply depots in the Mediterranean Sea. The trip past Somalia was always worrisome for the supply ships, but they believed it would be easier this week because of the number of warships in the vicinity. As they watched, a small boat—no more than thirty feet in length—became evident, leaving the Somali coast on a somewhat straight course toward the supply boat.

The captain of the African Queen, Johann Sebastian, had taken the name of his ship from the name of Humphrey Bogart's movie supply boat in the Oscar-winning movie of the same name. At the time, Johann had thought it a good omen to name his supply boat after the boat of movie fame; now he worried that it would not be the Kaiser's gunship that sank his source of income, but Somali or Yemeni pirates instead. When word got out earlier in the week about the tensions in the Arabian Sea, Johann had thought it would be a good idea to take advantage of the abundance of military might to safeguard his passage through the Red Sea and the Gulf of Aden right into his destination of the Persian Gulf; so far he had been correct. He pushed his 100-foot-long supply boat to its best speed of 14 knots and watched the radar for problems.

Onboard the thirty-five-foot modified fishing boat, the radar painted a beautiful picture of the African Queen for her captain. There were forty-five men crowded on the small fishing boat, and all were heavily armed. Besides the normal RPGs and AK47s that were prevalent amongst the warlords of Somalia, these particular pirates had managed to get their hands on a two-thousand-pound Mark-48 torpedo and launcher. They had mounted the launcher tube on the bow of their boat with the intention of aiming the ship at their target and letting the torpedo run straight and true. No complicated computer guidance or wires to help the torpedo find its target—just point and shoot. Pietro, the captain, kept his eye on the prize, with the hope that just the fear of seeing the torpedo launcher would entice the larger supply boat to stop and allow them to board.

Captain Sebastian eyed his own radar screen carefully, watching the position of the new contact he had just picked up moments ago. Even an amateur could see that the captain of the new contact intended to cut across the bow of the African Queen. Coming from Somalia, he could only assume that this would mean trouble for him and his crew. There were international laws that forbade having guns on board a cargo vessel, but like most of the captains in these waters, he had a .45 caliber pistol under the pillow in his cabin, as did most of the other sailors aboard. It was time to alert them. Reaching for the claxon, he pulled the cord, allowing it to warble its alarm to the crew members. Following the short alarm bell, he spoke into the microphone, letting the crew members know of the impending trouble.

"All crew members, get to your 1st level alert positions. I want two men on each of the water hoses in the bow section and two each on the hoses in the stern section. I hope there will be no trouble, but I want you to protect yourselves as you see fit." The last part of his message was a clear invitation to the crew to arm themselves with whatever weapons they had smuggled aboard. "I hope that we will be able to frighten them away by not stopping and by hitting them with the high-power water cannons, but if they do manage to stop us, it will be each man for himself."

There were only twelve crew members on the African Queen, including the captain and the navigator. Johann knew that these power boats could outrun the slow diesel engines that drove his boat on the long journeys across the sea to his still distant destination. He also knew that these pirates had been emboldened lately because of the lack of aid from US warships. With the pressure from liberal representatives in the House, the President had withdrawn support of American warships in the area. The liberals in the House had decided that it was not in the interest of the American people to protect innocent shipping in the area and they had pushed the president into turning a blind eye to piracy in the area. As if on cue from the DNC, the news media had also dropped the subject from their nightly news broadcasts, thereby freeing the pirates of the area to do as they pleased. At that moment, Johann Sebastian didn't like the new policy very much. He felt very alone.

Less than forty miles east-northeast of the African Queen, the USS Ipswich radar operator, Toby (Rat) Ratcliffe, watched the courses of the two ships with some interest. He called the captain to the radar console and plotted the courses of the two ships, showing how in twenty minutes the two would intersect at a point just twenty miles to the west-southwest. Captain Melinda Gregg knew she couldn't go after pirates, but she also knew a way around it. She smiled as she ordered flank speed and turned the ship 150 degrees. Calling the fleet, she reported that radar had picked up a "point of interest" that the Ipswich was going to "check out." She knew that piracy was out of her venue, but like most captains, she recognized the situation and hoped that just the presence of her ship within view of the cargo vessel would make the pirates nervous enough to avoid a confrontation. Besides, she thought, if they fire at a US naval ship they would be in violation of my guns-free status and I could send them to hell.

Captain Sebastian adjusted his course slightly and headed straight toward the American tin can. He prayed that they would arrive sooner than the speedy fishing boat that was quickly headed his way. Aboard the fishing boat Amaliea, Pietro pushed the throttle to wide open. He could see the change in the American ship's position and realized they were coming to investigate. Pietro was not stupid, and he knew that the Americans were not allowed to get involved in the problems of non-American boats. He intended to make sure that he stayed in between the cargo boat and the American warship. He would make sure that no one crossed the Americans or let them become involved. Yes, Pietro knew the rules the Americans played by, and, even though he frequently couldn't understand why they played such games, he was thankful that they did.

Just over 15 minutes later, Pietro spotted the shape of the African Queen just off the port bow. Calling to the men aboard the Amaliea, he yelled out the position of their conquest. Moments later the men crowded the deck, some firing their AK47s into the air and others shouting their glee at catching the first glimpse of their conquest.

Aboard the African Queen, Captain Sebastian pointed his Nikon 20x binoculars to the starboard side of his vessel and was rewarded with the view of the Amaliea jumping the small three-foot waves, her decks crowded with gun-toting pirates. He knew that pirates typically ran in two types of packs—either three or four in a small boat using RPGs to frighten people into stopping, or organized bands of thirty to fifty men who would most likely force the target to stop, kill the men on board, and take the boat and cargo just as the pirates of the Caribbean did hundreds of years ago. Just my luck to run into the latter, he thought. He checked the radar scope and saw that the American destroyer was still five miles to the west. It was time to yell for help. Taking the microphone, he turned the radio to the emergency band and began a series of short messages asking for help.

"This is the cargo ship African Queen, at latitude 13.11 N, longitude 51.4 E. We are being pursued by Somali pirates and need assistance. Repeat, we need assistance from any friendly ship in the area. Please help us. We are an unarmed cargo vessel and need the assistance of any armed ship that can help us." Captain Sebastian sighed heavily, knowing that the Americans could not come to his aid, but hoping above hope that they would anyway. To his surprise, he received a response.

"This is the USS Ipswich. We are en route to your position and will render any aid that we are able. Please continue your current speed and bearing and we will intersect you in ten minutes."

"USS Ipswich, this is Captain Pietro of the Somali Republic Navy and the ship Amaliea. Your assistance is not needed. The Somali Republic is boarding this ship as is our right and we will not need your assistance," replied the Somali pirate captain. "Is that clear USS Ipswich?" Captain Pietro asked and pushed back.

"I'm sorry, sir," replied Melinda Gregg aboard the Ipswich. "I do not have verification of your status as lawful representatives of the Somali government and do not recognize your right to board the vessel calling for help and will therefore remain on course to meet them."

"Thank you, Captain," the delighted captain of the African Queen almost shouted into the radio. His delight was short lived.

"Captain of the Ipswich, you will stand down and stay out of our business or you will be in violation of the treaties signed with the Somali government. To fire upon us or keep us from dealing with this vessel as is our right will constitute an Act of War. Stand down, Captain," said Pietro across the airwaves.

All three ships continued in silence. Two minutes later, Pietro ordered the first shot to be fired. In the distance he could just make out the smoke from the funnel of the

American destroyer. As he turned to look back at the African Queen, the twenty millimeter shell fired from the cannon mounted on the bow of the boat landed just ahead of the cargo ship. The splash from the shell threw spray across the low bow of the African Queen. Aboard her, the crew was nervous. They knew they would be hard pressed to keep running if the ship started hitting her with twenty mm cannon fire.

"Hard to port, half speed," cried out Captain Sebastian.

As if on cue, the water in front of the African Queen began splashing with the falling 20 mm shells. The shells walked their way backwards toward the Queen.

"Hard a starboard, full speed," cried out Sebastian to the helmsman.

The falling shells crossed behind the Queen, falling short now. As the elevation was adjusted, the shells were getting closer and closer to finding their mark. Aboard the Amaliea, Captain Pietro was shouting violently at the gun crew.

"How can you miss them? We are less than a mile away now," he shouted at the older man aiming the gun. "Those shells cost me fifty American dollars apiece, you great ape. See if you can make one of them actually hit the boat," he raged at the giant of a man who was shooting.

"One more word from you, Pietro, and I'll aim it at you. Do you understand?" the man shouted back

Without hesitation, Pietro pulled the .44 caliber Smith and Wesson revolver from his belt, raised it and pointed it at the giant black man holding the cannon's controls. Without hesitating, Pietro fired his magnum pistol, killing the old man. "You! Yes, you holding the next round, you are promoted to gunner," he said to the young man standing next to the dead man who was lying on the deck.

Without hesitating, the young man replied, "Yes, Captain," and pushed the older black man over the side of the deck into the sea.

"You'd better be a good shot or you'll end up like him," Pietro yelled at the young man.

On the African Queen, Sebastian didn't know what had happened, but he was thankful for the respite. No shots had been fired for the past minute and he actually had the hope that the pirates had run out of ammunition. He looked through his glasses again as the faster boat continued toward him. What was the contraption on the front of the boat? he wondered. Then he recognized it. It was a torpedo launcher. "Oh no!" he said out loud. Then to his dismay, the cannon fire resumed.

Thump!   Boom!
Thump!   Boom!
Thump!   Boom!

"Ninety degree port turn, full speed," cried out Sebastian.

Thump!   Boom!

Thump! Then everything seemed to jump around him as the 20 mm shell found its mark. The captain was knocked off of his feet as the shell came down just ahead of the bridge. Two men had been standing on the walkway just in front of the bridge when the shell hit. Now they were both gone. Sebastian had no idea where they had disappeared to; his only hope was that they hadn't been killed.

"Ninety degree starboard turn, half speed," he yelled to the helmsman.

Smoke began drifting up from below as the ship sluggishly turned to starboard.

"Captain of the cargo ship, this is Captain Pietro. You are instructed to stop your engines at once and prepare to be boarded."

As if to punctuate his demand, another shell hit the cargo vessel in the bow, just above the water line, ripping a small hole in the bow of the boat but causing an explosion inside that Sebastian had no way of knowing the effects of.

"All hands report damage," he called on the ship's internal radio. Without hesitating, he also called to the helmsman, "All engines stop."

"We took a hit in the forward cargo area, Captain, but it appears we are still water tight," said a young crewman in the forward area.

"Morten and Jansen were both knocked off the bridge catwalk. Morten has a broken leg and Jansen is dead, but the ship is unhurt," said another crewman.

From the radio came another message from the pirate ship. "You recognize our superior firepower I see, Captain," said Pietro. "You will lower a ladder so that we may board you."

Sebastian made no reply but nodded to the first officer to drop a ladder over the starboard side. Silently, he made sure that the crew was ready at their positions. "When they get alongside us, hit them with everything we have. Make sure that you knock the man on that twenty millimeter off the side of the boat with the water cannons."

"Aye, Captain," the first mate replied through clenched teeth. "We'll do it, sir."

Slowly, the Amaliea turned to approach the African Queen. While the small boat turned, Captain Pietro centered his attention on the swiftly approaching American destroyer. "Captain of the Ipswich, I see you are still approaching. Halt now or we will sink this vessel," the tight lipped captain said into the radio microphone.

"Sink that boat and I will consider it an act of aggression against the United States," Captain Gregg bluffed.

While the two were speaking, Captain Sebastian ordered full speed on the African Queen. She began moving forward again, catching the gunnery crew on the Amaliea off guard.

Seeing smoke pour from the small stack at the back of the boat, the young black man manning the 20 mm gun squeezed the trigger. The closeness of the two ships worked to the advantage of the small cargo vessel. The shot flew bridge-high across the foredeck of the boat, missing the main cargo boom by scant inches. The young gunner couldn't lower the gun mount any lower so he pointed the next round toward the bridge.

Just as he pulled the trigger, a burst of water from the ship's water cannons sprayed across the cannon emplacement. Unfortunately for the bridge crew of the African Queen, the blast of water came after he had pulled the trigger. The shell from the cannon burst through the window of the bridge, shattering glass and slamming into the back wall of the bridge and exploding, sending glass and shrapnel in all directions and punching a hole in the back wall of the bridge two feet wide. On the bridge, the captain was severely cut by the flying glass as the shell entered the cabin, and then he was almost deafened by the concussion of the explosion. The ship's engineer was not so lucky. He was standing just in front of where the shell exploded. Unfortunately for him, his body absorbed most of the energy and shrapnel from the exploding shell. In the cabin behind the bridge, the two-foot section of back wall sent a shower of fragments throughout the room. Fortunately, no one was there.

As the water hit the young gunner, he held on to the grips of the gun, involuntarily pulling the triggers on the grip. The gun swung up and to the right as he was swept off of his feet, while the gun continued to sound its thump, thump, thump, thump, thump of shells being fired. The remainder of the six-round clip was sent on its way as the gunner struggled to get back to his feet. Half a mile away, the first round splashed harmlessly over the bow of the Ipswich. Onboard the Ipswich, the crew was already moving.

"Return Fire," cried Captain Gregg on the intercom, but it was already too late. The second of the five accidental rounds flew into the side of the upper bridge. It bounced off the thick plating, leaving a dent the size of a dinner plate before falling to the deck and exploding. The third round also found the bridge deck, this time slicing into the plate glass window and exploding. The blast killed the XO and sent safety glass flying in all directions, causing two other young sailors to be cut to ribbons. The last two rounds flew well over the top of the ship.

At exactly the same time, the submarine Hu Ying plowed headlong into the British cruiser Man-O-War. Captain Chu Ling Juan never saw the British cruiser and never understood what had happened. He had become so fixated on the torpedo following him and so exasperated by the chasing by the Royal Navy that he hadn't bothered to check for surface ships when he ordered all tanks blown dry. It had been sheer frustration.

Aboard Man-O-War, the captain couldn't have suspected that the Chinese sub would do an emergency surface right into him. He had just arrived on the scene painted by the two Royal Navy Helicopters and their sonobouys. The two helicopters had front row seats to a crash to remember. As they stood off from the cruiser by only a hundred yards or so, suddenly the cruiser seemed to jump out of the water by nearly twenty feet, first coming up by the stern and then by the bow. As soon as it jumped, it seemed to sink back into the wake, settling a little askew of its position from before. Aboard the cruiser, all hell broke loose. The captain shouted for information. In CIC, the sonar operator and the entire crew had been knocked out of their chairs. The captain shouted for a damage report, and as quickly as he could, the commander in CIC radioed to the captain that they had been rammed by the Chinese submarine.

It took just moments for the captain to radio the fleet, notifying them that he had just been attacked by a Chinese submarine. At the same time, the Americans were radioing that they were under attack.

Aboard the British Carrier Prince Albert, Admiral Lord Hampton was in the midst of his own crisis. Three Chinese MiGs were approaching the battle group at mach 1.6 and were not responding to warnings to turn off. As they continued to approach, the admiral cursed himself and the admiralty for having grounded his planes after the previous problem. Now they were under attack and he had no planes in the air. Turning to his chief of staff, he ordered guns free aboard the carrier.

In the time it took for all five shells to land, the Ipswich had thrown a wall of lead and explosives at the small launch. Three seconds after the first shell hit the Ipswich, the first of nearly one hundred twenty mm shells and ten 50 mm shells hit the small launch. Forty-five men ceased to exist in the blink of an eye. No remains of the launch larger than a five foot section was left.

Aboard the African Queen, the crew was too shocked to cheer. They had been within water cannon range of the ship when it literally disappeared in front of their eyes. One second it was there, the next it was kindling, floating on the sea. After the fact, many of the crew ducked, thinking they would be next, but for all of the noise moments ago, it was now deathly quiet.

Captain Gregg was immensely impressed. She had been at the helm during target practice on many occasions and had been duly impressed by the capabilities of the small destroyer, but this was beyond anything she could have hoped for. "Cease Fire!" She didn't need to say it, but she did so anyway. A small cloud of smoke drifted away from the guns of the tin can. "Damage Report, all stations report," she said into the microphone, still slightly dazed by the action. "I want emergency crews to the bridge immediately. Get me information on what happened up there, and I want confirmation that those Somali's are DOA."

"Captain, we have casualties from the bridge," said the doctor, reporting from the bridge.

"How's it look up there, Doc?" she asked

"Really not bad. It looks like the bullet proof glass took most of the blast but managed to get turned into a quissenart by the exploding round," he replied.

"How many hurt?" the captain asked.

"One dead and two wounded. I'm afraid Simmons may loose his sight. I can't be sure until I get a good look, but right now it doesn't look good. As for Astor, I think he'll be fine, just cut up by the flying glass," the doctor pronounced.

"Who was killed, Doc?" Gregg finally asked.

"It was Lieutenant Watkins, Ma'am," he replied.

"Damn!" she said.

"I concur," said Doc.

Turning to the radio operator she said, "Phillips, get a message to the battle group right now that we've sunk a small Somali gun boat that fired on us. Relay the information about two men injured and one killed and give them the pertinent location information."

"Yes, Captain," the young radio operator said.

Up on deck, those who had been manning the guns were whooping and hollering and patting each other on the back. None had ever witnessed the destruction and power of a US warship when she was angry before. At the same time, they were upset that they had been hit first. It was unbelievable that they had taken casualties. Still, they felt inspired by their response and were anxious to flex their muscles again.

The three MiGs continued their faux attack run on the carrier. They were completely unaware of the events that had transpired just moments ago across the Arabian Sea, and without worry, they continued their mock strafing run at the massive British carrier. As the first plane moved into attack position on the starboard side of the ship, the Phalanx chain gun opened up on the MiG. In less than three seconds, the radar- controlled gun cut the plane into thousands of small pieces. The second jet never had time to react to the burst of fire. Following close behind his leader, it seemed that a ribbon of fire had burst forward from the side of the large craft and had touched his leader's MiG and had shaken it like a dog might shake a rag doll, continuing to shake it until it had broken into a thousand pieces right before his eyes. As he pulled up on the joystick, the ribbon of fire reached out for him as well. Saying only "Oh no," the pilot of the second MiG also disappeared in the hail of .50 caliber bullets. On the port side of the ship, the third MiG was desperately trying to pull up and away from the death spray that had destroyed the first two of his fellow pilots.

The third pilot began gibbering almost incoherently. He had never seen a chain gun operate before. He had never seen a gun fired directly at him before. He had never seen anything as devastatingly powerful, and now he realized that it was coming for him. "Under attack, red snake," was all he managed to get out before the port side Phalanx gun opened up and reached out for his fighter. At first it shook the tail a little, and then more, and more until he thought his body would be shaken apart, then his craft began to tumble through the air. He reached for his ejection handle, but to his amazement as he looked down he saw the water, and not the floor of his compartment. It happened in slow motion. First his sense of up and down seemed to go away; then he watched out the window as both wings folded up around him, and then broke away and flew off. The jet engine continued to push the angry missile through the air until a sudden "poof" signaled the end of the engine. Just as suddenly, the fuselage rolled in the air, sideways. The pilot was close to blacking out from the whipping and swirling of the remains of the cockpit. At that point the remains of the cockpit hit the water, skipping like a stone over the choppy surface for nearly a half mile. Each skip tore more and more pieces of the skin from the fuselage, leaving the pilot strapped to a chair like he was in the midst of a torture device. After slowing down enough to reach a speed slow enough to begin sinking, the cockpit, now sans canopy, fired its ejection seat, throwing the now unconscious pilot a hundred feet into the air. The seat parachute opened, but being designed to simply slow the chair enough to allow the pilot to pull the second chute, it simply fell less quickly back into the blue waters of the Arabian Sea. Watching from the bridge, the captain ordered a rescue helicopter to recover the Chinese pilot.

It took nearly ten minutes for a chopper to get in the air, find the now floating chair, and for a frogman to go into the water and connect a cable to the floating pilot's chair. To everyone's surprise, the pilot had survived.

During the ten minutes that it took to rescue the downed pilot, a world of confusion was taking place aboard the American, British and Chinese task forces. The Chinese were yelling that they had been attacked, the British Cruiser Man-O-War was taking on water and saying that they were abandoning ship, and the Americans were trying to decide who had fired the shots into their destroyer. The Chinese submarine Hu Ying never had a chance. The bow of the submarine had been destroyed when it crashed with enough energy to lift the 60,000 ton vessel completely out of the water into the bottom of the 80,000 ton cruiser. The result had been devastating to both ships. The bow of the Hu Ying had been completely crushed, splitting the hull backward from the front panels all the way back to the conning tower. The Man-O-War had fared no better. Its hull had been breached by the blunt-shaped nose of the Hu Ying, causing a hole the entire width of the vessel and with a length of at least seventy-five feet. Beyond the crush zone there was a zone around the hole that was wrinkled like it had been made of aluminum foil. The Hu Ying had hit the cruiser at mid ship and slightly from the port side. The result was the hole in the center of the bottom, as described, and a wrinkled area extending all the way to the back end of the ship along the port side. It looked like every steel plate had buckled down the port side, leaving gaps between them anywhere from an inch to five inches in width.

Water was pouring into both ships. Being at battle stations had saved many of both crews from an instant death. The water-tight doors of both ships had been closed when the collision occurred, keeping a semblance of buoyancy on both ships. The submarine began to sink from the bow, but because of the integrity of the doors, it hung in the water bow down, slowly losing its buoyancy, but remaining with its propellers pointed toward the sky in an odd, partially afloat configuration just a hundred or so feet from the cruiser.

The Man-O-War had water pouring into the bottom of the vessel all over. Without hesitation the captain called "abandon ship." Going up to the bridge, the captain could scarcely believe his eyes. The propellers of the Chinese submarine were extending out of the water, still turning, as if to push the ship back down into the water. His own ship was a cacophony of noise. He heard one of the boilers blow and felt his feet vibrate with the explosion while the deck took on a port side slope. He knew the Man-O-War was dead and his only hope now was to save as many of his crew as possible. He heard the shouts of his crew. It all seemed to happen in slow motion. All around him, men were running and yelling; and yet he couldn't seem to move. He stood on the bridge, looking at the scene below. The first officer seemed excited and was trying to get his attention, but his mind couldn't focus on one man. He had a ship full of men to worry about, and they were dying.

"Captain... Captain... Can you hear me, sir?" yelled the first officer. "Sir, we have to get out of here. We have to abandon ship. Do you hear me, sir?" he yelled again. He reached out and slapped the captain across the face hard.

"What is it, Barrett?" asked the captain when he came out of his reverie.

"Sorry, sir," replied the first officer, "but we need to leave now, sir."

"Right, Barrett. You go ahead and I'll be right behind you. Now go on, Barrett, and take care that all the men get off that you come across. Right?"

"Right, sir," said the young first officer. "Sir, you are coming, aren't you, sir?"

"Yes, yes. I'll be right behind you. Now go, Barrett! Now!"

The first officer left the captain on the bridge and headed down the stairs to the main deck. It was the last time he would see the captain.

Onboard the Hu Ying, Captain Chu had been killed instantly by the initial concussion, as had the entire crew in the control room. Everyone in the front half of the submarine had been either killed or incapacitated by the collision. In the back half of the submarine, the crew had been knocked off of their feet and were now standing on the walls as the submarine, which was suspended by its tail like a giant fish hung up as a trophy. The people inside were frantic. There was a rear escape hatch in the engine room, but at present no one could reach it. There were twenty-two men still alive and trying to reach the rear escape hatch, but they had been unable to get to it. It had been a scant ten minutes since the collision, but it seemed like forever. Finally, a young engine room tech managed to climb up to the escape hatch. He looked down at the small group of men below him and let out a shout of victory. He reached up and grabbed the handle and pulled. There was a "whoosh" of air escaping, and then quiet. The young man spun the wheel and pushed. Suddenly the door gave way and instead of air as he expected, the door swung open to reveal a torrent of water. It knocked him backwards off of his precarious perch and down onto the throng of men below. The loss of air was just enough for the sub to lose its buoyancy.

From the bridge of the Man-O-War, which was now listing eighteen degrees to port, the captain watched a bubble emerge from around the tail of the Chinese submarine, and then it began to slide beneath the waves.

The captain smiled. "Damn them and their ship too," he muttered. Picking up the microphone, he pushed the transmit button with his thumb and said, "God save the Queen, for her good ship Man-O-War has died."

Just ten seconds passed from the time of the opening of the hatch until the last remnants of the Chinese sub had disappeared from the face of the earth, never to be seen again. Suddenly, one man bobbed to the surface like a cork on a fishing string. One man of a crew of one hundred and twenty-two had survived. The captain locked the door to the bridge and watched. It was his turn now. Slowly, the water came up to meet him. It lapped at the door frame and then the window until it completely covered him up. It was happening faster now. What had taken ten minutes to climb to the bridge now covered it and submerged it to a hundred feet in less than a minute. Ten more seconds and he lost sight of the sunlight filtering in from above. The ship was two hundred feet down when the glass imploded around him and crushed the air from his body.

Chapter 12

Revenge

Onboard the Prince Albert and every ship of Her Majesty's Navy, the last broadcast was heard. Anger seethed in the mouth and in the nostrils of every man who heard the broadcast.

On the Varyag, Admiral Fu Yang Yu was also listening to the broadcast. He called to his missile cruiser Yang Tze.

"Captain Loa, fire your missiles and sink that British aircraft carrier—now." Next he spoke to the radio operator. "Get me all the remaining submarines and ships. We are now at war with the British. Sink any and all British ships and aircraft at your discretion."

The radio operator sent out the message. Unbeknownst to him, the message was intercepted by the Sea Wolf, as was the message sent from the British admiralty giving all British ships and aircraft permission to defend themselves from any attacking craft. The Chinese and British were now at war.

Captain Loa didn't hesitate. He'd been targeting the

British task force since the first aircraft incident. Now four of his brothers in the air wing had paid the price, as well as the destruction of at least four of his nation's submarines which had been sunk. It was time for payback. It mattered not at all to him that the British were responsible for none of the submarine problems; he was ready for retaliation and the British would make fine targets.

"Fire one, two, three, and four of the Hai Ying missiles!" he shouted in CIC. Without hesitation, the young lieutenant pressed the buttons on the console, letting the first four of the twelve Hai Ying missiles stored below the deck of his missile cruiser fly toward their preprogrammed target position. In this case, the target position was the aircraft carrier Prince Albert, now located at 17.82 degrees north by 63.75 degrees east in the Arabian Sea. The missiles were ejected one at a time from below the decks by compressed air. After being thrown fifty feet in the air, the rocket engine came to life, pushing the missile upward to the northeast at an increasing speed until it reached mach 6.2. The missile was capable of mach 8.4, but the first of the four disappeared in a blinding flash as it passed mach 6.2. The second missile met a similar fate as it passed mach 6.9.

Onboard the Prince Albert, the radar operator in CIC yelled out that he had multiple missile launches from a Chinese missile cruiser. That brought everyone to their feet. Suddenly, one of the missiles disappeared from the radar.

"The first missile has disappeared, sir," cried out the radar operator.

"How?" asked the CIC commander.

"Unknown, sir. It just disappeared, sir," the young lieutenant replied. Then just as suddenly, he spoke again. "Sir, the second missile has disappeared also."

"What?" was all the young commander could manage.

"Yes, sir. It disappeared from the screen, just like the first one," the radar operator said.

"What the bloody hell is going on out there?" said the commander to no one in particular.

On the Yang Tze, Captain Loa was asking the same question. "Well, what about numbers three and four?" he yelled at the radar operator.

"They are both flying hot true and normal, sir," came the instant reply.

"You are sure?" asked Loa.

"Yes, Captain, they are... Wait,! Number three has disappeared as well," said the young radar operator, his voice trembling with fear.

"At what speed did it explode?" the captain asked, believing that they must have been shot down by some means.

"Mach 8, sir," said the radar operator. "The remaining missile is flying at maximum speed now and should be safe from anything except a PAC3 missile, sir."

"Did you see a PAC3 missile go up from any of the ships?" the captain asked.

"No, sir. None showed on the radar screen. They must have made them stealthy now, sir," the radar operator replied.

"Damn the Americans and their technology!" Loa said.

Aboard the Prince Albert, the commander in CIC called for anti-missile defense to fire two patriot missiles. They didn't have the newer PAC3 missiles yet and would have to make due with Patriot missiles. No sooner did he get the words to fire out of his mouth than two Patriot missiles flew from the deck of a missile cruiser ten miles to his east. The two patriot missiles arced high into the air, locking onto the radar contact to the northeast. Within sixty seconds, both of the Patriot missiles, as well as the remaining Hai Ying missile, blinked out of existence just as the previous three missiles had done.

"Damn the Chinese and their technology!" said the commander.

Lord Hampton had had enough of this. He had been sitting in CIC watching and listening to the exchange between the missile commander, the commander of CIC, the captain and the radar operator with a mixture of anxiety and fear. "Damn it all, Captain," he finally broke into their argument about the missing missiles with his own thoughts. "We are at a de facto state of war with the Chinese. I want our fighter wing over us now."

"What about the admiralty's uh…suggestion that we not launch our fighters, sir?" the captain replied hesitantly.

"That suggestion, as you call it, was made when things were different, Mallory. I'm telling you to get us some protection up there right now. I don't know who or how they took out those missiles, but I don't intend to let someone attack us without protection of some kind over us. Is that clear, Mallory?" Lord Hampton growled.

"Yes, sir. Hugh, get a defensive umbrella over us immediately," he said, turning to the air wing commander.

"Aye, sir," said air wing commander Hugh Laughlin. "Scramble Blue Flight now," he said, turning to a young lieutenant who in turn relayed the command to another, who in turn relayed the command to the intercom in the flight ready room where four young lions waited impatiently for their chance to defend the fleet.

Captain Loa on the missile cruiser Yang Tze was furious, but at the moment he didn't seem to have time to fire more missiles. After his first four had disappeared from the sky, his boat had suddenly become less seaworthy than it had been. He was getting reports of mysterious holes in his ship from all over. He ordered another missile launch after the last of his original missiles had gone down, but the next four had not responded, and then the reports started coming in. The first had been from the forward oil compartment. It had suddenly sprung a leak. It was followed closely by another report from below the missile compartment. It seemed that a hole five centimeters in diameter was visible from the deck all the way to the sea, allowing a jet of water to spray up from the bottom of the lower deck. The second occurrence was followed closely by a third and a fourth. Loa was at a loss as to what was going on, but he didn't feel like waiting for another problem.

"What missiles are showing ready now?" he bellowed at his missile control officer.

"All of our sparrow missiles are still functioning, sir, but all of the Hai Ying's are showing to be...gone, sir," he said lowering his head.

"Gone? How can they be gone? They were loaded and ready in the launch tubes thirty seconds ago. What could have happened to them?" he shouted. "Never mind. Just fire the damn sparrow's before they disappear too," he said to the young man. "And reload the damn Yings!" he bellowed.

"Yes, sir," replied the frightened young man. "Load the sparrows with the target data," he shouted to the missile team.

Moments later a young man spoke. "The coordinates are loaded into the sparrows, sir."

Pushing the button on the control panel, four sparrow surface-to- surface missiles fired off from their tube mounts just aft of the missile silos. The four sparrow missiles flew at mach 2 almost from the outset. They streaked across the sea at an elevation of just twenty feet. As they approached the outer ring of defense, the first two locked on a British destroyer named the Devonshire. Without the slightest difficulty, the Phalanx gun system on the Devonshire fired two bursts of radar- controlled .50 caliber rounds that destroyed both missiles before they reached 250 yards of the ship.

The second two missiles locked on a target closer in to the center. They found the missile cruiser Dauntless just a mile from the Prince Albert.

Aboard the Dauntless, a repeat of what had happened aboard the Devonshire was playing out. It took less than thirty seconds from the time the missiles were detected until they were destroyed by blasts of the Phalanx gun system. Two hundred thousand yen worth of missiles destroyed by less than twenty British pounds worth of lead, copper, and gun powder. The captain of the Dauntless responded with four silkworm anti-ship missiles of his own. These missiles were designed to be sea-skimming missiles that were radar controlled and flew at mach 4 or better, depending on the weather.

Just like the Hai Ying missiles fired from the Chinese missile cruiser, the four missiles from the Dauntless winked out of existence one at a time and in mid-flight.

From inside the CIC, a young lieutenant was trying desperately to explain what had happened to the missiles in flight when the ready lights blinked off of his remaining onboard missiles one at a time.

"Captain, crew members report a beam of light that seems to have targeted our ship. A young ensign said he saw a bluish colored light hit the missile deck and then there was a hole where it had been," said the communications officer.

"Sir, that must be why my missile ready lights have been going off," said the young missile officer.

"Undoubtedly," said the captain. "What can we do about it?" he asked.

"It must be a laser of some sort, sir," said the fire control officer. "I've heard that the Americans are working on something like that, but I had no idea they were close to making it work yet."

"I doubt that they have. The Americans wouldn't be using it against us," said the captain in response.

"But who is, sir?" asked the fire control officer.

"My guess is that it's the group that suggested we not get involved," said the captain to the young officer. "Now, let Admiral Hampton know exactly what we know, and make sure it goes over a scrambled line. Are you clear on that?"

"Aye aye, sir," said the lieutenant.

In the Sea Wolf, JD and Isaiah were both staying busy, trying to keep their eyes on what was going on with both the Chinese and British Navies. They had warned both, and now both were in violation of the warning. It would be difficult to rein them both in without killing anyone. So far, they had managed to destroy most of the missiles shot off by both sides, but at this pace they needed more drones in the sky to be able to get them all.

"What do you read in the skies above us?" asked Admiral Hampton, having learned about the laser holes appearing in his ships.

"Nothing, sir," said the radar operator in the CIC.

"Let the Americans know what is going on," he said, then added, "be sure to ask them for information about space as well. The Americans should be able to tell us what is circling above us in orbit."

"Aye, sir," said the young communications officer.

It took just moments for the Rear Admiral Willard Whyte aboard the USS Ronald Reagan to grasp what was going on and send the information back to Washington. He was sure now that if they had a grasp on how this mysterious weapon was being controlled they could stop whoever it was from ever threatening them again. He was sure the Air Force had a weapon that would knock any satellite out of orbit.

Admiral Whyte contacted the joint chiefs, who in turn contacted NASA. In the matter of an hour, a LaCrosse imaging radar satellite had been tasked to turn and monitor the space above the Middle East instead of its normal path of 500 to 1200 kilometers of earth. Turned on its side as it crossed 400 Km above the earth, it sent out a strong radar signal, analyzing the space above the earth looking at a swath roughly from 100 kilometers above the earth to a point roughly 700 kilometers directly above the Persian Gulf. Based on all the calculations done by NASA, a space laser would have to be located somewhere in that area to be effective on earth. To their surprise, the only satellites that were seen in the area were owned by the US government and none had the capability to shoot a laser beam down to the earth. They were back at square one.

Upon hearing the information from NASA, Admiral Whyte pulled together a conference between the four task groups representing the Western Powers. He believed it was time for total collaboration. What he didn't realize was that there was an uninvited guest watching and listening to the conference 800 feet below the surface of the Arabian Sea. In the conference room below the control room of the Sea Wolf, six members of the crew were listening and watching the stolen signals of the American and British warships.

"It has to be a jet or airplane of some sort," Admiral Whyte was saying as the Sea Wolf crew opened the stolen signal.

"I say, but how large a plane would it take to house a laser strong enough to burn holes through solid steel," asked Admiral Hampton aboard the Prince Albert.

From the Stennis, Admiral Scott Reynolds joined in the conversation. "My specialists claim that it would take a jet the size of a 727 to house a weapon big enough to do what they're doing. In fact, my man Johnson said that he worked with a military project to do just that last year and they used a retrofitted 747 to house the laser and power it. The laser came out of the nose of the craft and its purpose was to heat up missiles as they came into the atmosphere and make their controls cease functioning."

"You mean they couldn't destroy the missile outright?" asked Lord Hampton.

"No sir. At that range they were not strong enough to cut through the steel of the missile body, but they are strong enough to bake the components inside like they were in a microwave oven," replied Admiral Scott.

"Well, someone is doing it," cut in Admiral Whyte, "and they seem to be able to do what NASA can't with a laser. One of us has to have seen something on the radar large enough to house a laser."

Admiral Harker aboard the British carrier was at a loss as to why or how this destructive power was being delivered, or who was controlling it.

Captain Loa of the Chinese missile cruiser had forgotten all about the failure of the missiles due to more and more reports from below deck of the 5 cm holes that appeared from one end of the ship to the other. The sieve-like holes were letting in more of the sea than the bilge pumps could pump out. The main deck and the sea seemed to come closer to each other. The men below deck had already seen the light and were preparing to leave the ship before the captain reluctantly decided the same thing. Abandon ship! The remaining Chinese ships had finally taken to heart the warning from the unknown source and turned 180 degrees with no intent or desire to continue the aggression. They had more fear of an unknown force that could destroy missiles, airplanes and cause mysterious holes to penetrate the bottom of their ships than they had from their supreme order giver, Chaing Xau.

The American and British fleets were still trying to interpret the confusion and assess the cost of this fiasco, both in men and material. Both admirals were on the radio with their superiors in Washington and in the UK, trying to explain the unexplainable. This little "demonstration of war games" had taken on a whole new reality. Neither the Americans or the British or the Chinese could comprehend what power had been demonstrated before them, each attempt only generated more questions. The only concrete thought was that they—any of them—did not own the technology to defeat or defend against whatever it was that had somehow ended this deadly game.

Chaing Xau was trying to find out from his field of sea captains what had happened. His submarines had disappeared; the convoy had reversed its course because of a warning coming from its own secret code. What was going on? He would have someone's head, or possibly several heads, for this disrespect of his orders. The insubordination was eating on Chaing like a bed of ants. Chaing Xau had now turned his aggressive anger away from the world and toward his own military.

Chapter 13

Where Do We Go From Here?

President Beechum and Dave Benson were discussing the events that had just been reported to them from their fleet commanders. Debra was confused by the many reports and denials from the admiral that the fleet had committed any hostile action that had not first been initiated by the Chinese. Dave knew in the back of his mind that JD and Isaiah were probably in the middle of this whole thing, and he knew that he had given them information that could destroy him and those he associated with. Dave turned away so his facial expressions didn't show that he knew more than he was saying as he responded to Debra's many questions. Debra new him like a book, and Dave knew it. He implied—not lied—to Debra that they may never find out the real happenings. Debra was still puzzled, but confident that it would all clear up as more information was made available.

JD, Isaiah, and the crew of the Sea Wolf were still deep below the scattering ships, some going back to their country and some being deployed elsewhere, but away from each other and the threat of hostility.

Onboard the Sea Wolf, Anna and Josie had just been recovered from the little sub and had told about being sooo close to Ahmadinejad himself, and that they had sold him two bottles of tainted water, not really knowing that the second bottle had gone to Osama Bin Laden. Both miniature subs had been retrieved and secured in their places. The drone that had watched the whole situation from above and had also had a part in the action, reported the movement of ships and aircraft away from the area of conflict. JD said, "As soon as it's dark we need to surface and recover the drone, that is if no other ships or aircraft are in the vicinity." The plans to move back to one of their bases had not yet been considered. Things had happened so fast in the last few days that they needed to get back to Dave to find out what the situation in Washington was. They would wait until he would not be in his office or the Oval Office.

8:00 PM Washington time

It was after 8 PM Washington time when JD made contact on the encrypted circuit. Dave was just sitting down in a restaurant near his apartment when his secure phone began to vibrate. It gave him a chill, knowing that he might find out more than he wanted to when he answered. Dave scanned the area around him to see if any people or waiters were near enough to hear, then, "Dave here."

"Hello, Daddy Warbucks. Nemo here. We feel that the hostile activities in this section of the world have started to calm down to some degree. How do things look from your point of view?"

"Nemo, you scared the hell out of me! People here are still trying to figure out what happened over there and how it all happened. I am certain that I don't want to know anything—nothing—except...are all of you safe. Have there been any casualties?"

"No, we are fine. No problems, but we would like to know if there are any other immediate problems in this part of the world," said JD.

"None that I know of at the present. Why don't you and Rex take your crew out of the spotlight and give them some sort of a vacation so I won't worry myself to death?" requested Dave.

"Okay, Daddy Warbucks. Sorry that we have caused you so much worry. Really, we were very careful and worked not to cause you or the country any trouble," said JD.

"You did a commendable job, Nemo. Give my congratulations to your crew," said Dave.

"Thank you, Daddy Warbucks. I will. Over and out," stated JD as he signed off.

"Hey, Isaiah, lets move this party to the south."

"Okay, Cap," said Isaiah in his usual good mood as he moved to one of the plush navigating chairs and began tenderly pushing at the touch screen. The movement of the Sea Wolf was barely noticeable and there was hardly any sound as they got under way. It would be great if they could just surface and cut through the Suez Canal, but that was out of the question. Their trip around the horn of Africa would be a long one, but not rough like the surface ships had had. Years before, when the Templar Knights made this trip, it was made "when the ships were wood and the men were iron," as an old Navy saying that implied that the old "salts" were tougher than the new swab jocks. JD and Isaiah were familiar with this and knew how much better they had it than those who had gone on before them. JD had heard from Naomi and was calculating just how long it would be before they would see each other again. She had related to him how nice the "quarters," or sub pens, were in Jamaica and suggested that it may be a good place to see each other. Even talking over the secure communications gear, she didn't mention where either of them were or that there was a submarine involved. Even high tech gadgets could be compromised. As the conversation ended, JD was ready to set their course for

Jamaica, and he would do so as soon as they round the Horn.

The preceding events had taken only a few days, but they had been very exciting. The stealth of the Sea Wolf and its peripheral equipment had ended a potential war and had done so with minimal loss of life—not bad for a bunch of amateurs.

Ahmadinejad had paid for and received the blessing from Osama Bin Laden and had high hopes of gaining the loyalty of his people again. What he didn't know was that the bottles of water that he had purchased from the two unknown vendors was tainted with the very poison that he had sent to the sinful city of Las Vegas via his missing submarine. There was something else that was bothering him: the plague that he had predicted Allah would bring to Las Vegas had never materialized. One other little gnawing thing in the back of his mind was that his loyal advisor Jimji had called in sick and the hospital had recognized a familiar virus and had placed Jimji in isolation. How was that possible? The hospital had gone to Jimji's home and recovered several items that may have given him the virus. They found that there was a trace of the virus in the water bottle. How could it possibly have gotten into the bottle of water? Jimji had told them that he had picked up the water at Ahmadinejad's quarters. Could Ahmadinejad's life be in danger too? Who could possibly be upset with him? Was it in the bottle of water that was given to Osama? Ahmadinejad's little warped scientist Dr. Macmoud had disappeared with his expensive submarine and its crew. Were they behind this? Ahmadinejad was starting to have second thoughts about trusting anyone. Trust and Honor, any one?

As the Sea Wolf made its day-after-day journey toward Jamaica, the crew managed to stay active by learning each other's jobs, even taking turns at the cooking. The moral of the crew was really lifted as JD and Isaiah took their turn in the galley. They were equals aboard this boat; no one could stick their nose up in the air as if one were better than the other; however, they knew that JD and Isaiah would have the final say.

After all of the excitement and the days under water, all of them were ready for a little R and R. JD and Isaiah had already discussed how long they would be on leave. The crew could take 30 days off and go anywhere, but they would have to take a phone along in case of a national emergency. They were not to talk about where they had been and really couldn't talk about where they would go next. They were about Truth and Honor, and each crew member felt it in their bones.

As the inertial navigation data and the GPS coordinates confirmed that they were just outside the sub pen in Jamaica, JD called for Rolf or Naomi to open the submerged doors. Naomi had sent for Rolf to come down from Iceland to get the Jamaican sub base into full operation. The beauty of these installations was that with all the automation, electronics, and hydraulics, it would take very few people to operate them. As the doors slowly opened, the Sea Wolf ever so gently and silently moved into the under-mountain sub pen. Upon surfacing, they found Rolf standing by, ready to handle the lines that would secure them to the dock. Naomi was there, eagerly wanting to hold JD close.

JD noticed the pendant around his neck seemed to vibrate on his chest as he emerged from the sub into the cavern. Could it just be the getting out of the confines of the submarine, or was it the sight of Naomi on the dock, or was it something else? Isaiah had a similar experience as he came from below decks. Should he mention it? No, the vibrations could have just been his imagination.

The crew of the Sea Wolf was now at their temporary home. Their quarters had been assigned, their gear had been stowed, and they were ready to hit the beach. JD had called them all into one of the large rooms. JD said, "Ladies and Gentlemen, I want each of you to know how much Isaiah and I appreciate the skill and knowledge that each of you have shown during this part of the adventure. The success of this and other voyages depend on the skills you have demonstrated. Your courage during times of stress has been strength to Isaiah and me. Any future deployments and a continued place of employment depend on how well each of you can keep confidentiality. Any bragging about what we have accomplished could compromise this and future adventures. That's about it. In your pay envelopes you will find an additional bonus for this past deployment. Thanks again. Truth and Honor."

"Truth and Honor," was the loud reply of the crew.

Marisa had arrived at the sub base. She and Naomi had already planned a few days of rest and relaxation in Jamaica with JD and Isaiah. Kingston was just a hop, skip, and jump from the base and the tourist attractions were waiting to be explored. There was a cruise ship docked in Kingston and the town was overrun with tourists. The crew of the Sea Wolf mixed in and was unnoticed by any prying eyes. They booked into hotels, bought tickets to various places, and just disappeared from view.

JD, Isaiah and the girls would have time to explore their new surroundings. The sub base had an elevator that had brought everyone up from the sub pen, but the stairs that had been carved out by someone ages ago needed to be explored. JD and Isaiah had not had much exercise on the Sea Wolf, so making a trip up and down the stairs seemed to be a good idea to help get them back into shape. Marisa and Naomi had thought that a few trips up and down the beach would be a better idea, so they decided to stay topside. The steps down to the lower cave had been unused since the elevator had been installed so it was slow going as they descended toward the cavern below, moving debris left over from construction as they went.

JD said, "Isaiah, does this give you a funny feeling? A feeling that we have been here in the past?"

"Man, I thought it was just me. The pendant on my chest just seemed to vibrate."

"Mine too," JD said. "It must be the darkness of this cavern, or maybe there is some magnetic material in here that causes this feeling." As they returned from the sub pen, the same sensation overcame them as they passed the half-way point ascending the stairway.

"We are going to have to research this phenomenon when we get a break," said JD.

"You bet," said Isaiah, "but first let's find out what Marisa and Naomi would like to explore."

✠✠✠

The End—or the Beginning?

About the Author

This novel was written by my late husband and me. It was written during the last 6 months of his life and I have just recently completed it. It was a work of love between both of us during a difficult time in our lives. It was a way of continuing to live while we knew he was dying, something we could do together and share with our children and family for years to come and even after we were both gone. He was only 48 at the time of his death in 2008, too young to die from cancer, but his prayer and wish was for me to continue to live. This past New Years Eve I flew to Bermuda and spent the holiday bringing in the New Year, completing our work. Now that it is complete I feel it is a novel that can be shared with all who enjoy the read of a fiction action novel. My late husband's name was David and mine is Debra, hence the author being "D Benfer." We were soul mates, so it is only fitting that this novel be authored as such.